Drop Dead Demons

The Divincus Nex Chronicles: Book Two

by

A&E Kirk

Book layout by Cheryl Perez; www.yourepublished.com
ISBN-13:9781494224882

Visit us online at: **www.aekirk.com**

Dedication

Dedicated to you! Yeah, you. Wipe that bewildered look off your face. It was you, one of our fabulous, loyal, and exceedingly patient fans of DEMONS AT DEADNIGHT, who helped drive us to keep writing DROP DEAD DEMONS. When we felt down, stuck, inept, and lonely, it was your emails and comments on AEKIRK.COM, Goodreads, Facebook, Twitter, and more which kicked us back into high gear. So close your eyes, give yourself a nice pat on the back, and accept our heartfelt air hug!

CHAPTER ONE

I'd been hogtied, then shanghaied, and that led to my current state of whole-*lotta* petrified, trapped in a small, dark space, drenched in cold sweat, shivering, waiting for my way-too-short life to flash before my eyes. Trust me, when I'd fantasized about getting "jumped" on tonight's date, this was *so* not what I had in mind.

If I thought the dark cloth hood over my head had started me in panic mode, the fact that I was now trapped in the trunk of a car boosted the panic by exponential factors. I knew the kidnapping drill, and all the experts agreed that you never get in the car because once you're in the car you're dead.

Well, tortured first to the point you wished you were dead. Then dead. For real. That's me, Aurora Lahey, always the optimist.

I rubbed my cheek against the rough carpet lining the trunk until the hood slipped off. Didn't help much. Probably because a generous chunk of my long red curls had been shoved into my mouth along with a gritty rag that tasted like rotten fruit wrapped in a yummy layer of sweaty socks.

I tried to Zen it out, forcing deep, shaky breaths through my nose, the humid air thick with musty odors of metal and rubber.

Muted light came through the red glow of tail lights, but I couldn't see much.

Didn't matter. I knew where I was. Parking lot of *Sapori d'Italia,* the only Italian restaurant in the Southern California mountain town of Gossamer Falls, where I'd been stood-up by my ever-elusive, possibly-pretend boyfriend who was at least supposed to definitely be my bodyguard.

It was a classic, age-old story. Girl with sucky superpower of tracking demons through psychic visions needs protection from aforementioned demons and their ravenous attempts to flay her alive, but she doesn't want to arouse the suspicion of her thankfully clueless family.

Sooooo…what to do?

In my case, the answer came in the form of Ayden Ishida, an uber-delicious package of fiercely formidable demon hunter, *smokin'* hot because of both his swoon-worthy good looks *and* the fact that he controlled fire, who offered to pose as my enamored beau, and despite the fact that I knew it was all a ruse, I was falling hard and head-over-heels crazy about him, and frankly — deep breath, Aurora — I thought he was too, but lately he'd been more absent than attentive, canceling plans and disappearing without explanation, so when he'd insisted on an official date for tonight with just the two of us, I'd let my hopes soar heavenward.

So, naturally, I ended up hogtied in hell.

I realized this wasn't the optimum time to be contemplating my love life, because, let's face it, if the *life* part was soon to be snuffed out, the *love* aspect wouldn't matter much. But seriously, what guy makes a big hullabaloo about us finally having time alone then cancels last minute?

Granted, Ayden sent four other guys from his demon hunting team, known as the Hex Boys, in his stead, but lotta good they'd been, happily chowing down on garlic-infused delights while I was snatched during a trip to the restaurant bathroom.

Sure, I'd landed a few good licks, but ultimately, my attacker had gotten the better of me—gag, hood, arms zip-tied behind my back—and now I was trapped in the trunk of a car.

Lamb, meet slaughter.

CHAPTER TWO

The only plus to my present perilous situation was that, based on the feel of his body— hadn't gotten a look at his face— my abductor was human. Not normally one's definition of good in this kind of impending-doom situation, but for a gal usually in some sort of demon deathological situation, my bright sides tend to be warped at best.

As to the culprit's identity, I had plenty of options. Someone working for a demon, someone on Madame Cacciatori's Divinicus Nex extraction team, someone working for the Mandatum traitor trying to assassinate me, or even a good old-fashioned, random serial killer. I was hoping for the latter.

Focus, Aurora. You were trained for this. Kind of. Okay, not really.

I tucked my knees to my chest, then ignored the scream of my shoulders as I wriggled and twisted my restrained wrists past my butt, legs, and around my feet. Yay, me. Small victory but I'd take it. I ripped out the gag. Huge, deep, beautiful breaths sucked in.

A few of weeks of the Hex Boys' so-intense-it-should-have-killed-me training didn't much count when this is where I ended up. Matthias was *so* going to never let me live this down. He'd been constantly on my case about how well I *wasn't* doing. But I'd take the ragging.

Just had to survive first.

I was still cramped — it was a trunk after all — my long legs having zero chance of stretching out. The plastic ties were boa constrictor tight around my wrists, but I'd deal with that later. Getting out *before* the car started and headed for this psycho's Chamber of A-Million-and-One Tortures was top of my to-do list. My hands groped. Found a crowbar. And if it was a late model car it should have a—

Bingo.

I slipped shaking fingers into a death grip around the trunk's release latch and struggled to steady my breathing because my ragged inhalations made it a tad difficult to listen for movement outside. I needed to make sure the attacker wasn't waiting next to the car ready to snafu my big escape plan.

All seemed quiet.

Still cautious, I dragged my forearm across my sweat-ridden brow, took a deep breath —which almost ended in a cough — and pulled down the latch, easing slowly against the resistance until…

In the silence, even the soft *pop* of the latch releasing sounded like a rocket launch. I cringed and caught the trunk before it sprung fully open, keeping it lifted only a crack. Frigid air scuttled in, turning the already cold sweat on my skin to an ice rink and giving credence to the weatherman's forecast of a spring snowstorm. My breath fogged into the air as I peeked out, eyes darting across my limited field of vision.

It was quiet and dark in this distant end of the parking lot. Secluded from the road and the restaurant. Only a few quick steps from the edge of the eerie forest with all its creepy shadows and sounds.

In this isolated area, light was spotty at best. Casting deep shadows across the parking lot, a hulking yellow snowplow loomed to my left along with a tow truck a few aisles up. Not to mention the multitude of meaty, man-sized pickup trucks and SUVs that every mountain-loving family — except the Laheys — seemed to own, standing Paul Bunyan tall amongst the baby sedans.

I didn't like being this far from the restaurant and the Hex Boys, but I was fast, and once I was out of the trunk, I'd book it full-throttle to safety. I just had to make sure the coast was cl—

Someone stood a few yards away.

My throat garbled some terror-ridden noise. I panicked, twitched, and lost my precarious grip on the trunk lid.

It started to rise.

I groped, frantic to stay silent. In my peripheral vision, I couldn't see details, but the single dark figure had his back to me.

Lucky.

He started to turn around.

Not so lucky. If he saw me now, he'd just slam me back inside. Probably conk me over the head first.

I pressed my lips together to silence the whimpering, caught the edge of metal, and brought the lid back down, low enough so it seemed closed, but not so low that it re-latched. Oh, the subtleties of surviving a kidnapping were intricate indeed.

Then I held my breath. Waited. Ready to kick the trunk open if it sounded like he was coming, which I may not even be able to hear over the erratic pounding of my heart or the whitewater rapids of blood roaring through my ears. Sweat dripped into my eyes. I blinked to cut the sting.

After precious seconds passed without disaster striking, I cracked open the trunk again, raising it only high enough to see the back of his thighs. He wore dark pants, seemed sturdy and powerful — to my distress — but he hadn't moved — to my relief — and he was turned away from me — another plus.

I licked my salty lips. Squinted. He was about three or four strides away. I could do this. I was fast enough. I had to be.

I counted to three— Okay, maybe it was eight…or even twelve, but who's counting? Oh, right, that would be me. Well, at the count of *whatever* number it was when my guts finally overpowered my sheer terror, I sprung the lid and leapt out swinging.

The crowbar made contact with my attacker. There was a satisfying *thud.*

All the more satisfying when I realized who it was.

The evening mist gathered, snaking low to the ground and so thick cold droplets already clung to my hot cheeks and shimmered on the edge of my lashes. I blinked to focus through the blur as he crumpled to the ground, but there was no question.

I knew my kidnapper.

Stocky, just taller than Amazon me, his mahogany waves curling around the collar of his wool jacket, and dressed in all-black like the darkest pit he called home.

Matthias Payne, leader of the Hex Boys.

CHAPTER THREE

Satisfaction was short-lived as anguish and confusion quickly took center stage. Despite being on my list of top five people I'd like to smack silly — mission accomplished — Matthias was, first and foremost, *supposed* to be my ally.

Begrudgingly, perhaps, but still.

I prodded Matthias's face-down and unmoving form with the crowbar. He didn't so much as twitch. Even when I dug in with the pointy end. Ha. I had a mean swing, sure, but mean enough to kill him?

Crap.

I dropped beside him faster than the freefall of my stomach and jammed my fingers against his throat.

"Bummer. Alive." I sat back on my heels with a sigh of relief. "Kidnapping doesn't make sense, Matthias. You can't stand to be around me, so trying to carve out some alone time for us? No way. Unless…"

Something ugly and vile slithered through my gut.

Unless he planned to hand me over to the secret, worldwide demon hunting society the Hex Boys worked for, the Mandatum. The one I was desperate to hide from. The one hellbent on imprisoning me for the rest of my life to use as their personal demon radar system. Just like they'd done to every other Divinicus Nex century after century.

Yeah, no thanks. I'd decided to break with that charming tradition.

Besides, I'd done a bang-up job of keeping my Divinicus identity hidden from the Hex Boys. Sure, they knew about my explody power — a white hot light thing that wiped out anything in its path, demons included. A power that I'd yet to control or even replicate since I'd nearly brought down a massive convention center in Los Angeles a few weeks back. There was no way Matthias had found the other skeleton in my closet. And even if he did, he wouldn't turn me in.

Would he?

"Noooo. That...ahhh...can't be." I tittered a laugh. "Matthias, you big joker you."

Joker? The Aussie? I must have a concussion.

I grabbed the collar of his jacket, lifted his head up, and leaned over to get a close look at his face. I paused.

Dealing with the angry Aussie and his nasty temperament, it was easy to forget his hunkifiable good-looks. But at the moment, relaxed and devoid of his near-perpetual scowl, most often directed at me — *unjustifiably*, thank you very much — the handsome features of a classic Gothic romance hero were readily apparent. Even without the benefit of having those crystal grey-blue eyes open. And on those rare occasions when he flashed a smile wide enough to crater his dimples, he could light up a room.

But most of the time he blackened it. Literally. He controlled darkness and shadows. I sometimes wondered what had boiled the joy and good humor from his soul. But right now, I couldn't care less.

"Hey, jerk-face, what's going on?" With my hand gripping the thick wool of his jacket, I shook him hard.

No answer. He was out cold.

I heard a noise and tried to jump out of my skin — didn't work — while letting Matthias thump to the ground as I reeled back.

Muffled voices?

We knew someone in the Mandatum was sending demon assassins to murder me. This faceless traitor in an organization that was *supposed* to be fighting demons was instead working with them to remove me as a threat. A threat to what? No idea. But the Hex Boys, including the Aussie, had agreed that while we tracked the culprit they would keep me away from the society. Agreed to keep me safe. But maybe the traitor didn't get that memo.

The parking lot was still devoid of people. Or so it seemed. An entire army could be hidden behind the cars and trucks, or hunkered down in the beds of the pick-ups. I backed toward the woods, but—

I whirled, shifting my fearful look into the dense forest, searching for danger in the bank of trees melting into the darkness. I strained my eyes to catch movement, shadows, anything.

Voices again.

Crap, they were coming for me. But from which direction? And how many? Were they armed? Did they plan to kill or kidnap?

Light and sound caught my attention. On the ground. I breathed easier. It was just Matthias's phone which had fallen from his hand. I picked it up and held it to my ear.

"—are you done with your *vitally important* job? I can't get ahold of the guys. Did they take care of Aurora? Matthias? Matthias, are you there? What's—"

I clicked off and dropped the phone like it was a live grenade. But I'd already been blown to bits. Because I recognized the voice. The sound was deep and rich and most often brought goosebumps to my skin. Especially when it was whispering sweet *anythings* in my ear.

It was Ayden. On the phone. Collaborating with my kidnapper.

An anvil of dread dropped on my chest. Was he in on this? Could I be so utterly wrong about what I *thought* we were both feeling?

Fan-freakin'-tastic. I was falling hard, all right. Smack dab into a concrete slab of deception and betrayal. My bones chilled. And it wasn't the frosty night or the wet fog lacing out of the dark forest to creep around my ankles.

I looked back at the car from which I'd just escaped.

Panic renewed in icy streaks down my spine because even without Selena's car seat strapped in the back, I knew this sleek, black BMW.

It belonged to Matthias.

Nice pick, Aurora. You always find the most trustworthy souls. My gut wrenched threatening to discharge the breadsticks and antipasto salad. I leaned forward to put my head between my legs.

"Nice shot, dove." The voice came out of nowhere.

I jerked in surprise and, since I was already leaning over, it cost me my balance. My feet struggled for purchase, but no sale. I tumbled forward. My shoulder hit hard. Last second, I tucked my head. The awkward front-roll had to be painful to watch—goodness knows it was painful to do—then I scrambled to my feet like a newborn foal, all leg and zero grace.

"I knew we'd make quite the team." Strong hands picked up the limp Matthias off the ground like he weighed no more than a damp towel, and slung him onto impressive shoulders. "Where should I dispatch this betraying son of a jackal?"

I stared, stumbled backward. Shock quivered through every cell of my being.

"No way." I shook my head, slowly at first then with frantic, staccato jerks. I pinched myself to make sure I was awake — ow — then stood tall and waved my arms like I could erase what was in front of me. "Not happening. No dice. Nuh-uh."

Denial and I were old friends.

And good thing too, because if I were to believe what my eyes were seeing, it meant that my night had just gone from dire to disastrous.

Chapter Four

No question this guy was a fairytale-fantasy to look at. Eyes the color of dark jade and a shade of sultry just shy of indecent. Perfectly tanned, with an Adonis physique, his curls gleamed a rich, burnt gold. And to top it all off, luscious lips that offered my heart's desire.

"What say you to my heartfelt proposal?" he said.

Probably what few had ever told him. "No."

Weeks ago he'd shown up in an uncomfortably romantic psychic vision where I'd seen enough of his hunka-hunka body to blush, and wish I'd seen more — hey, never said I wasn't hormonal — and where he tried to suck me into some quid pro quo of giving me everything I wanted for some small favor in return.

But my visions tracked demons and my vision had tracked him so, ergo—loved when I could use that word—I'd pulled out of the vision as fast as possible.

Now he was here, dressed like some Indiana Jones wanna-be. Khaki shirt stretched over broad shoulders and tucked into the trim waist of tan cargo pants, a spool of weathered rope hanging off his belt. A battered, brown leather jacket, fedora, and even a leather satchel strapped across his chest. He looked mid-twenties but carried himself with a mature confidence of someone much older.

Unfortunately, this wasn't the kind of Prince Charming any seventeen-year-old girl needed. I may be confused by his lack of the usual fangs, claws, and oozing putrefied pustules, but, demon or not, he was trouble in every sense, especially supernatural. Dangerous as a swaying cobra, hypnotizing me just before he lashed out with the fatal strike.

I wanted to run, but even if I could on jellified legs, he still had Matthias in his grip. Not that I cared.

My wrists still zip-tied together, I lifted the crowbar with a white-knuckled grip, resting it on my shoulder so he couldn't see it shake.

"Go back to wherever you came from." I fought hard to keep horror from injecting every syllable, but I feared it was a losing battle. "Now."

He flashed the most disarming smile. Seriously. I almost dropped the crowbar.

"You naughty girl." He wagged a long, slender finger. "Last we met, you ran away before we could conclude our business."

"No, I left because I didn't want to *do* any business with you. Not then. Not now. Not ever. Go away. I've dubbed this a demon-free zone."

"Ah, I see the misunderstanding." Charming nodded and readjusted Matthias's dead weight — bad choice of words — on his shoulders. "This would have gone eminently better if this fool hadn't interfered with my plans."

"*Your* plans." I blinked. "Wait. Who kidnapped me? You?"

"No. The boy was kidnapping you," he said amiably, "I'm just here to kill you."

"Super." My lungs iced. "Gosh, I'd love to help you out with that, but the licenses for this year's Aurora Hunting Season just sold out yesterday. So sorry. Now shoo or I'll shoo it for you." Whatever that meant.

I twirled the crowbar with menace. Or would have if it didn't nearly fumble from my hands, because I forgot my wrists were still shackled by the stupid zip-ties.

"Although I can't blame him." Charming sighed and looked thoughtful as he purred on in his velvet voice. "You've put all the Hex Boys in the precarious position of risking their families to protect you. And this one most of all can't afford to lose anymore. But I digress." Charming let Matthias tumble backward off his shoulders. The Aussie hit the ground hard but showed no signs of waking.

Charming waved a hand around. "I'm aware this all looks bad."

"Ya think?" I barked a hearty laugh and swung the crowbar.

The curved end hooked his leg out from under him, laying him out on his back. Before he could move, I nailed him hard in the gut. Once, twice, three times. I was in a frenzy, sweat dripping, the iron slipping in my hand. I re-gripped. Not easy with manacled wrists, but I managed a fourth blow and—

"I surrender!" His palms jerked up.

I considered slamming him again, but he was curled halfway into a fetal position. And shaking.

He peeked past his upturned arms. "Please, little dove, if you only listen—"

"Shut up," I snapped. "Turn over."

He obliged. I grabbed the rope from his belt to tie his hands behind him.

Why didn't I just run from the guy intent on murdering me? Because stupid Matthias was lying here all useless and helpless. The only credible reason as to why was I protecting my kidnapper was that I wanted to kill him myself. Later. In a slow and painful manner.

But right now, if my hands would stop shaking, I could at least lasso this lunatic assassin.

"But I don't *have* to kill you," Charming said, his face kissing the dirt.

"Lucky me." I struggled to loop the rope around his wrists, glad he didn't resist, and noticed that despite his rugged attire, he exuded an enticing scent, something fresh and fragrant and full of life.

"Actually, yes. Hear me out. I'm no demon. I am a former Mandatum hunter. Gone rogue." He chuckled. "Call me Rose. And as much as I hate the society I do still love humanity and would rather not help demons kill the Divinicus Nex."

I froze. Glanced at Matthias. He was still out. Good. But my heart kept up its merciless pounding.

"Yes, Aurora. I know who you are, but I will let you live and keep your secret. All I need is a little help from you to ascertain a mutually beneficial bargain." As I yanked a final knot in place, he flinched and grimaced over his shoulder. "Ow! That's a little tight."

"It's supposed to be." I stood and backed off, wiping my arm across my forehead, confident the restraint would hold. For now.

Rose rolled onto his back and sat up. "As leverage against me, the demons put my sister in hell. When I kill you, I get her back. Win for me, lose for you."

My foot to his chest pushed him flat back on the ground. "I don't think you get the concept of *mutually beneficial*."

I wish I could afford pity, but in my experience it was better to find more rope to tie his feet. My gaze swept the parking lot. Most folk around here kept all sorts of junk lying around in the back of their pickup trucks. Chains, cables, even tools. Had to be something I could scavenge.

"However — and here's where I need you to stay with me, dove." Rose flashed dazzling white teeth. "The alternate scenario would be for you to help me get my sister out, after which I lead you to your enemies and assist you in dispatching them. Hence, the previously mentioned, win-win."

"What a giver."

"You have no idea." He gave me an inviting look. "But I'd love to show you."

"Riiight. Let's book that for the weekend between *never* and *not in your lifetime*." Maybe I could tie him to a bumper.

He continued in a smooth, confident rumble, "Rest assured I have high hopes for our relationship, and it is my sincerest desire that you choose the latter scenario because otherwise you put me in an awkward situation." He shrugged. "Nonetheless, family first. You understand."

I more than understood. Which meant I needed to ditch this psycho quickly.

"Oh my God!" came a woman's voice.

I whirled.

A middle-aged couple wearing matching flannel shirts stood a few cars away. Keys jangled as they slid out of the woman's hand. The man threw a protective arm across her and they both stared horrified at Rose beaten and bound.

A few steps more would offer them a delightful view of my other victim, as utterly unconscious as he was unhelpful.

I shoved the crowbar behind my back. "Uh. This isn't what it looks like."

"Of course it is." Rose smiled so bright he practically brought on the dawn. "So we like it rough. Nothing to be embarrassed about."

Mr. and Mrs. Flannel choked. So did I.

"What?!" My cheeks burned to the point I was sure my skin would blister.

"But fear not. We have a safe word. So if you wouldn't mind moving along." Rose winked. "I still have a fantasy I'd like her to fulfill."

I cringed and regripped the crowbar, ready to conk him out despite the audience.

Mr. Flannel's look changed from horrified to sly. He glanced at his wife. "Oh, it's like those books you enjoy."

Mrs. Flannel hissed, "I told you not to tell anyone," then she gave us an embarrassed smile. "I don't know what he's talking about. Goodnight." She picked up her keys and dragged Mr. Flannel off.

I slapped my hands over my face and tried to massage away the sting of humiliation. "I can't believe that worked."

Rose shrugged. "People tend to believe whatever I say."

"And that's what you went with? My reputation is shaky as it is."

I watched the couple duck into the restaurant and scanned the lot to ensure we didn't have any more surprise visitors on the way. Clear so far, but how long would that last?

"I'm trying to help, but we've run out of time." Deep sadness rippled through his words.

"Yes, we have." I motioned toward Matthias's car. "Get in the trunk."

A temporary solution, sure, but at least it got him out of my immediate hair. Who knows what tricks or powers he had up his sleeve? I started to shiver, watching my breath huff out into the cold night air in shaky spurts.

I was about to go from kidnapped to kidnapper. Better not put that on the college applications.

"This isn't a good idea," Rose said, but got up and strolled toward the BMW. With an apologetic look, he fell gracefully into the trunk. "You'll regret not accepting my help in," he smiled, "three, two…"

Then the trunk magically closed on its own, and I was about to make a sarcastic comment when—

The ground shuddered behind me and cracks crunched into the pavement. Before I turned I knew what it was — my Divinicus Nex senses were tingling. And by tingling, I meant trembling with terror.

Demon.

CHAPTER FIVE

The hellion hunched in a low squat. It was a hulking gorilla covered in cracked obsidian glowing from within because of the lava coursing just underneath the surface. Like a walking magma flow from an overactive volcano. Each breath exhaled embers.

I looked at my crowbar and still zip-tied wrists. Looked at Matthias's unmoving form. Looked at the eight foot tall hellifed flaming ape.

"Rose!" I dropped the crowbar and slammed my hands on the trunk. The Mandatum hunter gone-rogue didn't emerge, so I fumbled keys from Matthias's pocket and popped the trunk.

Empty. Not good. Very bad actually. My head swiveled. No sign of Rose, but the volcano demon had climbed onto a silver SUV several rows away.

"Matthias!"

I turned to my only dim light of hope and kicked his side like I was trying to make a fifty-yard field goal. The amber light in the parking lot couldn't hide the paleness of his skin.

"Wake up now and you can torture me later," I said.

Nothing. Well, if that didn't get a rise out of him…

The demon pounded his chest. Flecks of lava showered down.

I hunched over, and with muscles strained to the breaking point, dragged the Aussie toward the snowplow. I hunkered us both behind the blade of curved steel attached to the front of bright yellow truck, then used the sharp edge of the front bumper to saw the zip-tie binding my wrists.

Metal crunched. The demon landed on the roof of an SUV parked on the other side of Matthias's car.

I jerked. My hands slipped and the bumper's metal edge sliced shallow cuts into my arms. The demon gripped the edge of the car, fingers melting through the metal as it lowered its head to search below. For me. It roared in frustration. I sped up my frantic sawing.

A shadow and heat ghosted over me from above. The snow plow shuddered and shrieked as the demon crunched onto its roof. The windows exploded under the weight. Glass sliced down.

When the demon spotted me, a blast of hot, sulfur stinking air blew back my hair as the creature's roar broke the sound barrier. Its fists slammed the roof with a squeal of metal. Lava splattered and pooled. The demon hopped up and down, swung its arms from side to side, knuckles dragging sparks along the metal, and made several low-pitched snorts that sprayed an impressive amount of lava snot.

I wasn't nearly as thrilled to see it as it was to see me.

The zip-tie broke with a sharp *snap*. My hands flew apart. Freedom.

Blood oozed from small scrapes on my wrists. I ran out and grabbed the crowbar, then staggered away from the snowplow, hoping to keep its attention off Matthias. The demon huffed a few times, shook its head with fury. Crusty bits of black rock flew off. It closed its eyes and leaned back to pound its chest again, grunting and snorting and generally going all jungle-fever, making a big show of force and giving every impression it was about to attack.

So consumed with his big, bad display of gorilla power it didn't see me reel back my pitching arm, and hurl the crowbar, spiraling the rod of metal through the air. Just like a spear.

Hey, two could play the jungle-fever game.

I'd shown a natural propensity for throwing sharp objects and this time was no exception. The crowbar rocketed through space and buried dead-nuts into the center of the demon's belly. As if popping an enormous zit, liquid spurted and boiling magma poured from the wound.

Nice.

I nodded and gave myself a mental pat on the back, wishing there was someone around to appreciate my greatness and—

Aw, crap.

In seconds, the metal crowbar simply turned red hot, curled around itself, and melted, disappearing into the glowing guts of the gorilla, becoming a harmless part of the churning hot mass. A layer of hardened rock shored up any sign of the wound. The demon wasn't so much injured as just royally ticked off.

He raked a hand up his belly, gathering up a clump of himself, and threw what took me way too long to realize was a sizzling fireball of molten lava.

Headed right for my chest.

I spun backwards and leapt into the bed of the navy blue pickup truck behind me. A violent shudder rocked the vehicle as the lava ball hit the side. A thundering *boom* followed. The truck jumped then listed to one side, as hot lava melted and popped one of its tires.

I stayed low until Flaming Kong belted out a repeat of his blow-drying battle cry and flung another orb of lava. Illuminated against the backdrop of the night sky, it sailed a smooth arc directly at my hiding place. I shoved aside a bag of aluminum cans and latched a solid grip onto the handle of a snow shovel. I stood and swung, putting my whole back into it.

I'm sure it would've been a homerun, but hard to prove because instead of hitting it out of the park, the lava ball splattered into fiery orange bits, the intense heat warping the shovel's metal blade.

The demon kept throwing fast balls, and I kept swacking them until the shovel curled and warped into something resembling a twisted piece of abstract modern art.

And became utterly useless.

I leapt from the truck, scrambled across the tops of two sedans, slipped on their polished surfaces wet from the mist, fell, scrambled to my feet, leapt onto an SUV, stumbled to my knees, slid over its hood. When another lava ball whistled behind me, I lurched up, grabbed the hook hanging off the tow truck's tow bar, and swung Tarzan style — seemed appropriate — over a VW bug, and when I was clear, let go, and sailed through the air.

I thumped to the ground in a blurring spin. Which stopped when I tumbled into a high-gloss orange Harley Davidson motorcycle. Which crashed it into the Harley next to it. Which crashed into the next, and the next and...you get the idea. A colorful array of matching helmets also toppled into the clattering mess.

The Aurora Lahey Disaster Domino Affect brought down seven motorcycles in all. Maybe eight.

Great, I'd have hell's demons *and* Hell's Angels gunning for me now.

The molten monkey bounded from above, landed in front of me, and took a swing with his big hulking, lava infused arm.

I dropped low and dove under a fallen Harley. Metal screeched and sparks flew as the demon tossed aside the motorcycle like it was an annoying afterthought. He leaned his face in close, fangs dripping molten goo, heat so intense I thought my skin would melt off the bone. Between his glowing eyes, a series of tiny red lights blinked in a circle the size of a quarter.

Strange, but no time to contemplate the oddity.

I grabbed a helmet painted with, of all things, orange flames and rammed it across his dribbling jowls. The clever move was supposed to slow him down enough for me to run, but he snatched the helmet one-handed and lifted it up, me still clinging on — not sure why — sneakers dangling several feet above the ground. He flung me through the air.

I landed in a flatbed truck, on a pile of chains laid in a neat coil. That was gonna bruise. Wish I could ice it up, but the demon kept coming, throwing a lava ball for good measure.

I rolled to the side. The truck's rear window shattered. I smelled the odor of burning hair and squealed with panic. After swatting steaming, red-hot sludge from my curls, I gripped a length of chain from the pile, hefted it up, twirled it over my head, and flung it hard.

It unfurled in the air. The demon bellowed with rage as the links whipped around him several times with a loud *sizzle*, effectively wrapping him up, confining his arms and legs. He tried to walk, but fell to the ground in a thick, hot heap.

I fist pumped the air. "That's what I'm talking about!"

Except...as I watched him struggle, the chunky metal links were slowly melting, giving way. His tether wouldn't last long.

"Oh, *come* on!" I slammed my palms on top of the truck's cab.

If only my super-duper, demon-annihilating explody power would kick in, I could zap him back to hell in a blink. But no. It remained mercilessly MIA, which left me out of options.

So I leapt to the ground and ran for what I hoped didn't end up being a colossal mistake.

CHAPTER SIX

Through the restaurant window I saw Blake's massive bulk and flung my arms in frantic motions.

He was too busy flirting with the waitress to notice. I was too far away for him to hear my shouts. The ground trembled as the demon shook off the last of its chains like a wet dog. He roared and bounded after me.

I raced for the corner of the building, but my sight blurred and weightlessness swept over me as my Divinicus demon tracking power kicked in.

My vision tunneled and left my body, zooming forward and around the corner.

A wolfish creature the size of a rhino galloped in long, supple strides, head dropped, ears flat, its body laid low. Smoke flared from the end of its pointy muzzle. Round, deep set eyes glowed a pupil-less silver. The darkness seemed to lap against the monster, flattening the thick layer of wiry fur mottled with colors of dirty water, dead leaves, and weak tea. Curved, spiral horns spiked out along its spine and tail, ready to skewer me if the foot-long fangs happened to miss.

My vision snapped back to my body. The sudden return of weight to my limbs disoriented my equilibrium.

I didn't fight the fall. Instead, I turned it into a slide on my side just as I came to the corner. The wolf demon came up through the ground, not bursting from it in a hail of dirt, but more like it was liquid that simply poured up from beneath the earth. It leapt through the air, a gaping mouthful of serrated teeth ready to chomp me in half. With my body so low to the ground, its feet only clipped my head, but if the Nex vision hadn't warned me to duck, I'd be dead.

The feral creature landed in a crouch, shining eyes scanning the ground like a silver laser beam. It saw me. A low growl rumbled the ground under my feet. It lifted its snout and howled a lonely lament.

Calling the rest of its pack? Not good.

It dropped its head, licked its lips, and charged.

Even worse.

My feet scrambled to find traction on ground shaking from the pounding gallop. He was fast, and the fangs and claws would gouge through my guts before I had a chance to get my sprint on. An oily stench of rot seared my nostrils as he raced closer.

From the parking lot came a vicious scream. Spewing a fiery stream of lava spit, the molten monkey bounded from the shadows, bringing a wave of heat rolling over my body. I dived sideways. A blast of scorching air hit my back and launched me further, the punch and subsequent hard landing spitting the air from my lungs. I wondered if my intestines would be ripped from my belly before or *after* my flesh burned to a crisp.

The wolf demon blurred across my path and hit the fiery ape like a freight train, catapulting them both into the forest amid a snarling spray of red. Trees split and uprooted in their path, the sound of violent destruction continuing even after they disappeared into the night.

How sweet. They were fighting over me. Over who got to *kill* me, but a girl has to take her attention where she can.

I rolled to my feet and ran with a hearty limp back to the restaurant window. I slammed my body against it, arms splayed high.

The waitress screamed.

Blake grinned.

“Babe! The guys are trying to find you, but I knew you’d come back for me. You look so funny.” The rich tan of his skin paled as he squished his face up against the glass. “How about me? Still irresistible, right? Take my picture.”

Yep. I was dead.

Chapter Seven

Blake's eyes swirled from his normal hazel to bright copper, which meant his powers were working. Which also explained how he literally walked his pro-wrestler bulk through the window without breaking it. He controlled anything made from the earth — like glass. After I'd explained my eventful evening in breathy, shrill tones, and embarrassingly wild hand gestures, Blake's features darkened, and he slipped into serious demon hunter mode, calling Logan on his phone to have the rest of them meet where I'd left an unconscious Matthias.

As I fought to keep up with his jog through the parking lot, I pointed toward the fiery spurts and savage sounds of the demon battle raging out of sight in the forest.

"Did they come through the hell portal?" And if yes, did that mean there were more on the way?

"No." Blake pulled me along next to him, acting as a formidable barrier between me and the demons. "There wasn't an alert. Portal's been inactive since before you moved here."

"Shouldn't we deal with them first?"

"They'll probably kill each other," he shrugged and kept moving forward.

As we reached the far end of the parking lot, I said, "And if they don't?"

He didn't answer. Too busy crouching low to study the empty ground behind the snowplow blade. Where Matthias was *supposed* to be.

"Do you think this Rose guy took him?" I asked. Hmmm. Not sure I'd be too disappointed if that was the case. "Or maybe he just left." Humiliated by how I brilliantly thwarted his evil plan then saved his life.

"I can see where you dragged him here, but nothing else is disturbed around this spot. And no footprints but yours." Face in a rare expression of grim concentration, Blake scratched his mess of short cinnamon curls. "It's like he just vanished."

Dreams do come true.

Blake dipped his fingers in the dust and brought them to his nose. "Smells like…springtime."

"I know, right? That's Rose."

"The dude you say disappeared from—"

"The trunk." I still had the keys so I popped it open.

I stared into my former prison which wasn't as empty as I'd anticipated.

Emotion bubbled. Overflowed. Then, fists flailing, I launched my attack.

Chapter Eight

"Calm down, babe."

Blake pulled me off my frenzy of beating the crap out of Matthias who, at some point, had been magically transported into the trunk of his own car. Still unconscious. And, as far as I was concerned, he could stay that way. Forever.

Blake carried me a few cars away as Jayden ran up, flip-flops slapping a frantic rhythm, his tropical print shirt unbuttoned and flapping against the tank top underneath. Despite Jayden's surfer brah-look, his brain worked on a level five hundred IQ points past genius, so I was counting on him to figure out what the heck was going on.

He jerked to a stop in front of us, the shiny curtain of long ebony hair swinging across his shoulders as his hands patted vigorously over my body. "Have you accrued any anatomical irruption?!"

Only trouble was half the time — okay, more than half — I couldn't understand what the heck Jayden was saying without the *Dumb It Down Dictionary for Idiots*.

"I have no idea. Please stop." Still in Blake's grip, I pushed him away best I could.

Jayden looked perturbed. The usual relaxed state of his lean, lanky frame turned rigid, arms folded tight across his chest as he looked at me with expectation, thumbs popping furiously in and out of joint, a sure sign he was nervous.

"He wants to know if you're hurt," came a voice behind me.

I yelped.

A ghostly figure front-flipped over a pickup and floated down beside us.

Not some haunting ethereal being, thank goodness. Just a freakishly pale, neon-white haired Hex Boy who liked to use his control of air to drop from the sky. It always spooked me.

Blake held my squirming body with annoyingly little effort and shrugged. "I'm fine, thanks for asking. But babe's a tad upset."

"Not you. We were talking to Aurora." Logan tucked his tie back into his vest and re-adjusted his sport coat. Then, although half Blake's size, he whacked the big guy's shoulder. Not that the giant noticed.

"My car!" wailed a woman from somewhere in the lot.

Heels clicked furiously, then we saw her run back inside the restaurant.

I surveyed the damage. Cars were wrinkled like wadded paper. Smoldering and smoking holes in the metal dripped with lava. Windows shattered. Glass twinkled on the ground amongst the mists. A few trucks on their sides, their contents strewn on the ground.

Even this far from the restaurant, I could see figures inside starting to stand, crowding the window. Too many.

"Aw crap," I said.

"Tristan will contain the bedlam," Jayden said.

As he spoke, the windows cleared. People sat back down. Creepy.

The alabaster swirling in Logan's eyes finally returned to the usual dark emerald green, but his hesitant, faltering look had a hard time meeting my gaze. "Are you…alright?"

"I am *not* alright!" I fumed and saw Logan cringe. "Sorry, it's not you. It's *him.*" I pointed at Matthias. "That sleazy son of a jackal!"

"She's fine," Blake said.

Ayden's red sports car skidded into the parking lot. He fishtailed to avoid crashing into a pickup truck searching for a parking spot and squealed to a stop in front of us. Subtle. He jumped out without bothering to turn off the engine or lights. Or close the door.

They all groaned.

"He's gonna freak," Logan said under his breath.

"Aurora!" Ayden yelled. "Your mom's on the phone!"

Oh, super.

Blake dropped me on my feet and took off toward the BMW with the other two Hex Boys.

Cowards.

As I watched Ayden approach, cell phone pressed to his ear, I expected to feel cold suspicion radiate through me, but for the first time that night, I felt safe. Must've been the hormones.

Ayden's handsome features still struck me dumb as the first day I'd met him. I'd called him Mr. Exotic because of the stunning mix of ancestry that melded a mutt of Hawaiian and European blood into a purebred of gorgeous.

His cheekbones could cut glass. His skin looked airbrushed over a jawline worthy of Zeus. His short, spikey ebony hair mussed into a perfect, unintentional mess, and silk between my fingers. Those full lips ready to ease into a heart-stopping smile. Eyes of dark chocolate that made promises which brought a blush to my cheeks.

A weathered black leather jacket stretched over broad shoulders, and his T-shirt was just tight enough to be clear about the fine condition of his body. Solid chest, ripping abs, tight waist. And off those hips, his jeans always hung just right.

I caught myself before the sigh went too audible. Which was hard because as he came closer, I got a whiff of that heady mix of leather and sandalwood and...Ayden.

I really had to get a grip. This guy had me a twisted mess. Half merry, half miserable. And completely confused.

It'd been a different story when this started weeks ago. Talk about attentive.

Besides all the workouts and training, Ayden drove me to and from school every day, walked me to class, got my lunch, and carried my books. In the afternoons, he hung out with my family playing games and sports. He'd taken me to movies, dancing at the country club, kayaking on the lake. Horseback riding on Blake's ranch hadn't been the disaster I'd expected. And milking the cows was a blast, until evil Bessie let me know with a well-placed hoof that she had an issue with my technique. Still had the bruise.

It was a whirlwind of wonderful as we talked, laughed, and shared. Ayden oozed charm and wit, asked a lot of questions and listened to all my answers. So what was I complaining about?

Lack of...intimate moments.

Sure, in the beginning I was way more comfortable with the crowd. Ayden scared me. Still scared me. But now...

Now, I was smitten. Now I craved time alone with him — a lot of it — and I craved it in spite of being scared. I was willing to take the risk. Big move for me.

Unfortunately, our time together had the opposite effect on Ayden.

He no longer tried to ditch the rest of the Hex Boys. It seemed ages since he stole a quiet moment to hold my hand, nuzzle my neck, or murmur in my ear. I swear, just when the attraction had become too much for me to resist, he'd backed off.

Not the attention so much. Just the physical…stuff.

It was embarrassing. I must have read things terribly wrong. As I watched him now, I still wanted him. Wanted to both kiss him and kick his sorry butt. Although, his butt was anything but sorry. Which added to my problems.

He smiled into the phone. "No, everything's fine." He pressed the cell phone to his chest and whispered, "She thinks we've been out to dinner together this whole time." Then he held it out to me.

"Hi, Mom."

"What took you so long to answer?"

"I was, uh…"

Ayden whispered, "I told her you were in the bathroom."

Ha ha. No, that was earlier in my would-be kidnapping.

"Needed a few minutes in the bathroom," I said.

I backed away as Ayden started talking in a low voice with Jayden. It was always a bit odd seeing the two of them side by side. Although they were fraternal twins, not identical, the two shared a strong genetic resemblance. But only one of them sent my heart fluttering into overdrive.

Mom's rising voice broke through my musings, her words rushed. "Just checking in because there were calls to the police about cars vandalized at the restaurant you're at."

"Really?" I ruffled a few shards of glass and dirt out of my hair. "Wait, how do you know?"

"Your aunt's police scanner. A woman just saw people in ski-masks fleeing the scene!"

Hmmm. Tristan's creativity needed some work if clichéd criminals were the best new reality he was…*implanting* into the restaurant patrons' heads.

The society called Tristan a *Hallucinator*, which meant he did a type of mind control. He could create illusions, making people see or think what he wanted them to. And in some cases, erase their memory entirely.

Didn't work on me though. And if he tried…well, let's just say it sent me to suburb of a place that rhymed with swell, but definitely wasn't. Swell, that is. Long story.

"I'm good, Mom. No need to worry."

"What else does a mother do?" She tried to sound lighthearted but couldn't pull it off. "And if you were in the bathroom, why did I just hear a car?"

Ah, she was in mega-mom mode.

"Because I'm now in the parking lot."

Ayden got louder. Smoke even started to trail off his shoulders. Awesome. A few more minutes of rising temper and he could literally *whoosh* into a human torch. Sure, Ayden controlled fire, but at times, it seemed *fire* controlled *him*.

A pickup truck pulled in and parked a few spots over and a rowdy group of guys I recognized from school piled out. The Hex Boys were too busy to notice. I turned away and put finger in my free ear to hear Mom better.

"Aurora," Mom sharpened her tone, "I thought you were having dinner. Why are you in the parking lot?"

A new voice on the phone snorted, "*Parking*, obviously."

It was my Aunt M, wife of my dad's brother. She'd been staying with us for a few weeks.

"They are teenagers, after all," she said.

"M," Mom said with irritation, "why are you on my phone call?"

"Don't get snippy." Aunt M sounded snippy. "I was about to call Ken."

Mom sighed. "Call your husband on your own time with your own super secret undetectable *cell* phone."

"Satellite phone. Big difference. But…fine. Sorry." Aunt M didn't sound sorry. "This pregnancy is frying my motherboard. And speaking of babies—"

Here it comes.

"—that's what parking with your boyfriend leads to, Aurora. Save yourself the agony. My bladder will never be the same."

"I'm not parking with my boyfriend!" I screeched.

The group of guys from school stopped on their way into the restaurant and laughed.

One of them yelled, "You can park with me, hot stuff, and I'll show some good lovin'." He pumped his hips a few times just in case I didn't get his totally subtle sexual innuendo. "Like a real man can."

"Hey!" Ayden turned a furious glare and raised a hand.

Sparks flew off his fingertips lighting up the night. The bright embers fused into jagged, mini-bolts of orange lightning that torpedoed through the air, straight for the loudmouthed group.

My breath caught. On one hand, I was flattered at the intensity to protect my honor, but on the other…the sharp, glowing ember streaks would boil through anything in their path. Especially little things like flesh, bone, and vital organs.

"Ayden!" Jayden flicked his own hand in a harsh twist.

A flurry of snowflakes came out of nowhere and wrapped themselves around the flying shards of heat like antibodies on a virus. There was a liquid sizzle. Bursts of steam. Then the orange, glowing lightning disappeared into bubbling puddles on the ground. Jayden often used his control of water to counteract Ayden's fire, but this was something I hadn't seen before.

Ayden growled, and his arm tensed, started to rise again.

"Don't engage!" Jayden caught Ayden's wrist, fighting to lower his brother's arm, steam rising off the leather as water drenched Ayden's sleeve.

The guy who offered me the good-lovin' pointed our way. "Did you see that?"

"Didn't see a thing!" One of his buddies shoved him toward the restaurant. "Shut up and get inside, you idiot. That's the Hex Boys. Herman's still missing, and I don't want to join him."

"Herman's not missing," my would-be parking buddy said. "He's at some family counseling thing."

His friend grumbled, "So they say." Then with a stiff smile and awkward wave, he hustled the entire group into the restaurant.

Ayden jerked from Jayden's grip and, arms flying through the air, continued his heated discussion. I couldn't hear what they were saying because Mom wouldn't pipe down.

"Honey, I don't think you should stay if it's not safe."

"Mom, we're with the guys. Checking their cars for damage. So far it's good." I put the phone on speaker. "Everyone say hi!"

"Hey, Mom Lahey," Blake said. "When are you cooking me another delicious dinner?"

"Anytime you want, sweetheart." I heard the smile in Mom's voice, the tension gone. "Okay. Well, Ayden, you remember curfew's in…" Mom waited expectantly. "Ayden?"

I gestured, and Blake thumped Ayden to get his attention.

Ayden stumbled from the blow then recovered. "Thirty minutes. Yes, ma'am."

"Actually, thirty-two. I'm not *that* strict, but keep up the good work," Mom said in a cheery voice. "Because otherwise I'll have to retrieve Dr. Lahey's syringe of exotic poison that's untraceable in an autopsy."

"Mom!"

"Oh, he knows I'm just kidding."

Ayden shook his head and mouthed, "No, I don't," then he and Jayden were back at it.

Something crashed and thundered out of the forest. I whirled. The lava demon opened its cavernous mouth and let out an ear-shattering roar, pounding his chest with triumph.

I panicked, jumped one way then another. Ready to run for cover. But where? Find a weapon. But what? He'd proven invincible. What could—

Logan shouted, "Pull!"

The albino's bow and arrow, made of compressed air, materialized pale and glimmering in his hands. Feet planted, he pulled the weapon taut, knuckles brushing his cheek, alabaster eyes swirling bright and penetrating.

Without looking, and not even stopping the intense conversation with his brother, Ayden's hand lit up, and he casually tossed a fireball over his shoulder.

Logan released his arrow. It rocketed through the air and pierced Ayden's flaming orb just at it reached the demon. The explosion rocked the earth under my feet and the molten monkey shattered into fiery smithereens, raining through the air, scattered over a wide area.

The chunks of splattered demon jumped and quivered, and after several seconds, gathered together in a dark tornado that vortexed into the ground.

Just like that, the demon was gone. Easy peasy.

Logan's bow dissipated. He straightened and grinned like a five-year-old. "So cool."

I stared at him. "I hate you."

He blinked, smile fading. "What'd I do?"

"What was that?" Mom cried.

"Sounded like an explosion," said Aunt M.

"M, I told you to get off the phone." Mom's voice was rising. "But she's right, Aurora—"

"No," I laughed. "Just the Dumpster…dumping…stuff."

"Maybe you should come home now," Mom said with renewed tension.

A trembling hand reached out of the car trunk. Matthias had regained consciousness, and although a little shaky, was climbing out of the trunk. The fact that he could move was a problem I needed to rectify.

"Gotta go, Mom. See you in thirty. Love you."

"Love you too, but it's twenty-seven now. And I'm not kid—"

I clicked off and headed for the Aussie.

Blake moved to block me, hands palms out. "Easy babe."

"Ayden, wait!" Jayden grabbed at his brother's jacket.

Ayden shook off his twin and pushed past even Blake to get to Matthias. Ayden's eyes tracked him like he was prey.

He grabbed the Aussie and yanked him out.

"You set me up!" Sparks flew off Ayden's shoulders. "You had me take that meeting with Bancroft tonight. You knew I couldn't back out because I couldn't tell him I had a date. You wanted me out of the way. *This* was the vitally important thing you had to do?!"

Then he swung a solid right hook. When it connected with Matthias's jaw, a sharp *crack* resounded. The Aussie spun and went down.

CHAPTER NINE

"Yes! A training exercise!" Matthias was on the ground rubbing his jaw, sitting behind Blake who'd put himself between the Aussie and Ayden. "Just like the ones we all went through. If you were acting like a hunter instead of a lovesick dingo you'd be fine with it!"

Ayden railed, "She wasn't ready for this!"

"Obviously," the Aussie said dryly.

"It's usually done at the end of *extensive* training. This was too soon." Ayden's eyes had a predatory squint and a dangerous glow. "She still has nightmares from her attack in the alley by people she *trusted*. So your little stunt just made her worse."

Worse than what?

"Okay, we don't need to bring up my personal history." My insides were shaky enough as it was.

"She'd better get over it, mate. Fast." Matthias was equally heated in his fury, but unlike Ayden he didn't actually smoke and almost spontaneously combust. "We've got hunters and traitors and demons coming at us and we're flying blind. We don't have the luxury of time."

"He has a point," Jayden commented.

Ayden whirled, eyes dancing with bright embers. "No one asked you, Jayden!"

"Of course, I wasn't agreeing with the dingo reference." Jayden seemed unfazed at the outburst. "Just the fact that we've all been through it. And the Mandatum was far more abhorrent in its treatment of us. So Matthias must have been fairly easy on her because she has no dislocations, protruding or broken bones, lacerations, contusions, or fractures. Not even a shattered patella."

Logan flexed his knee. "That was painful."

Ayden turned his ire on his brother. "How in the *hell* could you let this happen?"

Now Jayden looked fazed. As in hurt.

I put a hand on Jayden's shoulder. "Ayden, it wasn't his fault."

Jayden tucked his long black hair behind his ear. "We went looking for her almost immediately. But Matthias happened to call and said he'd cover the parking lot, so the rest of us dispersed in other directions."

"Except me," Blake waved. "And I'm the one who found her."

"I found *you*," I said.

Blake pursed his lips. "Potato, Romano. Same difference."

Logan looked up at the big guy. "Do you ever hear yourself?"

Blake beamed. "I'm my biggest fan."

"Your *only* fan," Ayden said.

"Hurtful, dude."

"The good news," Matthias ranted on, "is that she actually got the drop on me, so if you guys would train her for real, she might have a shot at *not* being the weak link that gets us all killed."

Was there a compliment in there somewhere?

"Nice work, babe," Blake grinned. "Gave him a roundhouse kick, right? I told you a woman's real strength is in her lower body."

"Yeah, right." Tristan jogged up. His butterscotch blond hair stuck up like he'd been electrocuted, and his earnest sky blue eyes looked tired, but otherwise the freckle-faced, boy-next-door look was intact. "We all told her that. Now let's wrap this up because—"

"But I'm the strength training guy, so I'm the one she listens to."

"Are not," Tristan said. "She hardly tolerates you. But let's hit it before—"

"Nope." Blake wagged a finger. "She just has to make it look that way so Fireboy doesn't have a meltdown. We're trying to find a way to let him down easy. As always, babe, you're my hero. Nothing hotter than a gal that can kick some serious boo-tay." He ruffled my hair. "Wanna make out?"

Ayden slapped the big guy's hand away. "Back off. She's been through enough."

"Quit wasting time." Tristan glanced over his shoulder. "If we don't hurry the—"

"Exactly," Blake said. "And I'm her reward, Fireboy. You've really got to know when to fold 'em and let the lady fall into the arms of Team Blake."

"Team Moron, more like it," Ayden muttered.

"You're all morons," Matthias growled. "Quit babying her."

Then they started arguing, the volume rising, and my head started to pound where I *did* have a *contusion*, thank you very much. Stupid wolf.

"Shut up!" I waved my arms. "So this kidnapping wasn't you guys turning me into the Mandatum to save yourselves and your families."

It was dead quiet.

Then Ayden exploded. He raged on Matthias. "See! Now she thinks we're *all* in on your harebrained scheme!"

I flipped a thumb toward the jerk, a.k.a. Matthias. "Mostly him because he hates me, *and* he can't afford to lose any more family."

There was another creepily quiet moment, then Matthias erupted, turning swirling onyx eyes on his team, livid and roaring like a bullet train at warp speed.

"Who told her!" The lights in the parking lot flickered. One exploded into a shower of glass and sparks, then another. "Who bloody broke the code and *told her?*"

"Rose told me," I said before Matthias started splitting atoms. "Nobody broke any codes. Jeez. Who's the moron now?"

The Aussie's eyes cleared slowly, reaching a dull, dolphin gray before I could be sure he'd powered down from going nuclear. Self-preservation warned me not to wade into the toxic dump of Matthias's cold, dark past. At least for now. Instead, I needed clarification for something I didn't want to believe.

"Let me get this straight." I massaged my temples. "You're telling me you've all been kidnapped as part of your training?"

"More than once." Jayden's nod was crisp. "A surprise attack executed by an experienced team. It's a test to evaluate your readiness for real world scenarios."

"Which you failed," Matthias kindly pointed out.

"But very few people pass the first time," Logan said with a reassuring smile.

"*We* all did," Blake said happily, then looked confused when Logan slapped his shoulder. "Ow."

"Okay." I dug my thumb and forefinger into my eyes. My vision had sparklers of light around the edges. "I get it. So we'll up my training, and I'll be ready next time."

Matthias looked wary. "What kind of game is she playing?"

"No games." I blinked. "I don't like it, or *you*, but I get it."

Ayden spoke softly, "Aurora, you don't have to do this."

"Yeah, I do. Matthias is right." Wow. That tasted like battery acid, mixed with jalapeno cyanide and shoved down my throat with a spiked spoon. But I always griped that Matthias didn't treat me like a real team member and now that he was, I didn't get to complain. Be careful what you wish for, Aurora. And don't whine when you get it.

I took a deep breath. "If I'm part of the team—"

"I never said that."

"Shut up, Aussie." My voice was venom. I wouldn't complain. But I could still be ticked off. And I didn't have to like him. "I *am* part of this team, whether you like it or not. I'll do whatever it takes to be an asset, whether you like it or not." I stalked up close and looked him in the eye. "And *you,* like it or not, can either help or get out of my way."

Sirens wailed. In the distance, lights flashed a frantic red and blue.

Tristan glared at us. "Like I've been trying to tell you, police and rescue are on their way."

"No!" Matthias looked stricken. "You're always supposed to make sure no one calls the police!"

"A few people need medical attention for some minor injuries when the demon fighting rumbled the building and brought down a few shelves." Tristan narrowed a look at Ayden. "*And* I was distracted because I had to take care of more memory erasing on Herman's friends because *someone* used their powers in front of *civilians!"*

Ayden's jaw clicked shut. Teeth audibly ground. "But you didn't hear what they said."

"I *did* hear! And wanting to be the macho, jealous boyfriend isn't a good enough reason to break the rules."

"Shut up!" Matthias sliced a hand through the air. "My dad can*not* find her here."

Tension rippled through the group.

I cocked my head. "But your dad's the sheriff. He'll cover this up, right?"

Matthias turned to Ayden. "She can't talk to him."

"Why not?" I asked.

"Let's get you home." Ayden snatched my hand and dragged me along as we sprinted for his car. "I'd really like to avoid that syringe."

My smile was bleak. "She really is kidding."

"I'm not so sure."

"Hey, guys." Logan stood over by where the molten monkey was last seen.

He picked up something and held it high as he walked back. It was a round black metal disc, the size of a quarter. Around the edge a series of red lights blinked in a moving circle.

Logan looked grim. "We've got a serious problem."

Chapter Ten

As Ayden's car screeched to a halt at the far end of my block, I jumped out.

"Wait!" Ayden killed the engine, got out, and moved to the back of his car.

"We'll miss curfew!"

"I know but," he pulled something out of the trunk, "here." He handed me a bouquet of flowers. "I meant to give it to you earlier but— Oh." We both noticed the flowers were tattered and broken. His face fell. "Guess they got knocked around when I was driving…fast. Sorry. Where's Blake when you need him?" He snatched them back and rummaged in the trunk. "At least there were some chocolates here somewhere. Just give me — Found them! Oh, crap. That, uh, that's not good."

"It's okay. It's the thought that counts." I kissed his smooth cheek. It felt newly shaved and had a fresh, clean scent. "Thank you."

He looked like he wanted to say something, but then took my hand, and we raced along the fortress of fences lining the backs of houses on my block. Ayden had one hand fired up as our unsettling — at least for me — torch in this moonless night. It helped guide our way through the mist which poured out of the forest on our right and added to the already creepy vibe chattering my jaw.

"About this tracker," I said, referring to the metal disc with the red lights that Logan found on the ground. It had been embedded in the lava demon, and when the guys had zapped him into smoke the disc had been left behind.

"Don't worry."

"But you guys said that it's a tracking device exclusively used by the *Mandatum*. So if the demon was sent here after me, doesn't that mean the Mandatum could have hunted me down? And that they're ready to attack?" I glanced up half expecting black-ops helicopters overhead.

"Someone else could have gotten hold of one of those trackers and planted it on the demon," Ayden said over his shoulder. "Could be anyone. Even Rose."

I knew he was *trying* to make me feel better.

"Besides, Jayden disabled it." He cut the flames as he stopped and opened the back gate to my neighbor's yard. "If he and Tristan can track where it came from, might be a blessing. Give us a lead on whoever is after you."

The bright side to every assassination attempt.

"Okay then." I exhaled. "Last one in gets rotten egg status." I pushed off his chest and dashed through the backyard.

"Aurora, wait. You shouldn't..."

I raced across the yard, burst through my neighbor's back door, and headed for the stairs. Despite my less than stealthy entrance, I heard a distinctive *click-click*.

Hmmm. Nothing like the cocking of a deadly weapon to boost the old adrenaline.

And stop you in your tracks.

I stared down the dark, menacing cylinders of two double-barreled shotguns. Which made this double the fun. And I'd be double the dead.

CHAPTER ELEVEN

My hands flew heavenward, and after I made some odd chortling-squeak noise, I managed the tried and true, "Don't shoot!"

Because that always worked with deranged killers ready to blow your head off.

Ayden yelled some weird word as he raced in and threw himself between me and the double-death barrels of doom.

I breathed a *little* easier when I saw who had me in their sights.

The elderly, surprisingly fit, silver-haired couple holding the guns relaxed their stance but didn't lower their weapons.

"I'm so sorry," I gushed from behind Ayden's back, keeping my hands high because elderly or not, Tristan's grandparents were scary. "I should never have just come in your home like that. So late. Without announcing myself. Or asking permission from you lovely folk. I was rude and you have every right to threaten me with deadly weapons, but maybe you could find it in your generous hearts not to splatter my guts and brain matter around your lovely abode." I stuttered a weak smile into the tense silence.

Mrs. Grant glanced at her husband. "She's always so fidgety. Like a canary." She narrowed her eyes at me. "I hate canaries."

I squeaked again. But not like a canary. I hoped.

Their serious faces suddenly burst into laughter.

Mr. Grant said to his wife in his faint southern accent, "Sugar, you have got to quit scaring the child."

"She makes it too easy. But he's right." Mrs. Grant lowered her shotgun and smiled at me. "Did you miss curfew again?"

"By less than fifteen minutes this time," Ayden said.

"Pssh," Mr. Grant snorted. "That's nothing. Get going."

They headed back into the living room which was scattered with rope, backpacks, sleeping bags, and general heavy duty, cold weather camping equipment, if you didn't count the handguns. And rifles. And very lethal looking knives.

Tristan claimed his grandparents were a quiet couple puttering through retirement. So why were they armed to the teeth and dressed in camouflage?

Ayden pushed me upstairs.

"They aren't going to rat me out, are they?" I took the stairs two at a time.

"Not since your parents referred to base-jumping as suicide." Ayden laughed.

"Base-jumping *is* suicide."

I shouldered open the door to Tristan's bedroom. Otherwise known as nerd-vana.

Posters of spacey-looking weirdos covered the walls. Shelves overflowed with video games, action figures, and comic books—sorry, *graphic novels.* His closet doors were painted blue and decorated like an old-fashioned London police box.

That took effort.

On the floor, bits of electronic parts and tools were scattered everywhere as if a computer had exploded. Over a desk was a computer screen bigger than the enormous windows in his room.

I staggered to a stop because there was a new edition to the nerd's room.

Ayden thumped into my back. "Wha—? Whoa."

Pictures of a woman in her thirties were tacked on the wall next to the computer as well as displayed on the massive screen. While the scene behind her differed from photograph to photograph, she never did. Pale, ash blonde hair securely wound in a tight French twist, she wore a crisply ironed button-down shirt over a dark skirt. Sharp rectangular glasses framed calculating ice green eyes.

Oh, and she was seven months pregnant.

I walked to the wall. "Why is Tristan stalking my aunt?"

There were documents taped up between all the pictures, lines of yarn networking them all together. I started taking it down.

Tristan stumbled out of his closet pulling on a sweater. "Hey!" He tried blocking me from his stalker wall.

I swatted Tristan's head with a fan of pictures. "What is this?"

"You know her aunt is married, right?" Ayden said.

"Gross!" Tristan scrambled to pick up everything I was tearing down. "I'm just…"

"Obsessed?" Ayden smirked.

"Yes. No! Not like that." Tristan ran his hands through his hair. "I've been telling you, technically, she doesn't exist. On paper, the Internet. Anywhere. And it's not just her!" He started typing furiously on his keyboard. "Neither does her husband— your dad's brother. And your grandparents." He pointed at the very official looking documents that popped up across the screen, his eyes wilder than the ocean during a hurricane. "I even found some death certificates that say they died eighteen years ago!"

"Oh my God!" I gripped Tristan's shoulder in mock horror. "I must be able to see ghosts too! But they felt so real when I hugged them a few months ago."

Ayden chuckled. Tristan did not.

I ignored his grim expression and gestured at the computer. "I don't know about all this, but I've known my uncle all my life and my *mom's* parents died twenty-some years ago, so maybe you got things mixed up."

Tristan shook his head. "You don't think it's weird you don't know your aunt's first name?"

"Of course I think it's weird. Nothing about her is *not* weird." I shrugged. "But she runs some international security firm and thinks governments worldwide want to torture her for her super-important clients' secrets. She already told us that she went a little overboard making sure no one could trace her back to us."

Ayden raised a brow. "A *little?*"

Tristan punched at his keyboard. "But there's no website for *M-terprises International* — what kind of name is that? — or record of her company anywhere."

I spread my hands. "I think that's how clandestine operations work."

Tristan grabbed my shoulders and gave me a shake. "But we're *Mandatum.* No one can scrub their existence, digital or otherwise, so well that *we* can't find them. It's just not possible."

"Oookay." Ayden guided Tristan out of the bedroom. "New topic. *Your* grandparents, certifiably alive, are gearing up for a mission."

"What?!" the blond bolted downstairs. "You guys swore you retired!"

"Thanks a lot, Ayden!" Mr. Grant shouted.

"You saying we're too old?" Mrs. Grant snapped.

"You're *ancient!* And if you think I'm letting you go off and risk …" Tristan's screeching faded the farther away he got.

I sighed and kept ripping pictures off the wall.

"Deal with it later." Ayden put a hand on my arm. "Let's get you home."

"Not yet." I shrugged out of my jacket and used it like a basket to catch all the crazy coming off the wall. "I don't want my family involved in any of this. I know he's trying to help, but this is too creepy."

Ayden caught my chin with gentle fingers and lifted my face to his narrowed eyes. "What happened to your nose? Matthias swore he didn't hit you."

"He didn't." I dropped my jacket and gingerly touched my nose. "That was me. Headbutt gone wrong."

He smiled. "Yeah, not your strong suit. We'll have to work on that."

"How bad does it look?" I said, giving in to vanity.

"A little swollen, but not terrible. Just more of you to lo— Uh." He took a step back, cleared his throat. "Look. I'm, uh, sorry I wasn't there tonight."

"You already said that." A bajillion times. But I didn't mind hearing it again. "It's okay. I blame Matthias because he deserves it. Not you."

"Thanks." He turned my body to face his, hands caressing up my arms, his expression serious. "But I want you to know that I mean it. I know things have been," he breathed deep, tracing his knuckles down my cheek, "kind of strange and I wanted tonight to be...different. If I'd known what was going to happen I would've never," he leaned in closer, "*never* left you alone."

"I know." I rested my hands on his solid chest, feeling his heart start to beat faster against my palms.

When I looked up, his gaze trapped me. It was full of sincerity and a desperate, deep need to make me understand. The intensity of his look prickled my skin. My eyes dropped, running from the emotions building between us. I was so confused and unsure. About myself. About him.

I heard him sigh. His fingers tipped up my chin, and his tone lightened. "Not that you needed any help, Lady Croft."

I smirked. "Yeah, I might have overstated how that whole battle thing went down."

"Don't sell yourself short. Between the demons and Matthias you kicked some serious boo-tay." His grin was devilish. "Nothing hotter."

I laughed. "If you ruffle my hair, I'll seriously kick your boo-tay."

Being in his arms eliminated any ounce of cold. But I absolutely had chills.

His voice lowered to a husky purr. "No, tonight I definitely had something else in mind. We just got sidetracked. But maybe now…"

Ayden trailed his fingers over my cheek, watching me closely, studying my reaction. Waiting. His fingers slowly slipped back into my hair. His touch radiated through me, chasing away fears and lighting nerve endings to delicious attention. When my lips parted, his eyes were drawn to my mouth.

His body went very still. He licked his lips. Swallowed. Warm air swirled around us. My breathing hitched. My entire body seemed to hold its breath, waiting for the pleasure of his touch to bring it to life. Then the corner of his mouth twitched upward, and his head lowered.

His lips, full and sensuous, touched mine, playing a delightful rhythm. Fast then slow. A game of touch and go where he pulled away, then came back with renewed hunger. Hard and demanding, then soft, inviting, his mouth molding against mine, caressing with rising desire. A slow burn traveled across my skin, seeping into my muscles, and I relaxed against him, enjoying the languid sensation. One hand slipped around his neck, pulling his mouth harder onto mine.

His arm around my waist tightened, pressing me closer as my other hand moved over his shoulder. The muscles rippled beneath my fingers. He moved deeper, his mouth never letting go, tasting every inch. Coming up for air was not on his agenda.

Or mine.

The kiss was heady and hot, a delicious and welcome change from chaste pecks I'd been getting. This was more like that time when he'd nibbled my neck just before he'd shut that down to go off to another mysterious meeting, and it felt like…my body's own Fourth of July party. I wasn't complaining. I reveled. Like firecrackers bursting under my skin, nerves exploded, hot and tingling, awakening my body to glorious sensations.

His chest pressed against mine, I felt his heart jackhammer in a rhythm matching my own. His hand around my waist moved up, kneading my back, my shoulder, then cupping my neck and cradling the back of my head, to crush our lips closer and—

"Ow!" I jerked back.

He jumped away, his arms flying out to the side. He looked terrified. "I'm sorry! I didn't mean to!"

He reached for me, then caught himself and backed away, staring at his hands in horror. One of them was smeared with red.

"You're bleeding! How'd I do that?" He went to rake his fingers through his hair. Stopped. Stared at his hands again. Clenched them. Shook them in the air.

Was he having a seizure? It didn't look like he was breathing.

"Ayden." When I reached for him he spun away.

"How ba—?" He choked on the word. Turned back to me. Swallowed hard. Blood drained from his face. "How bad did I burn you?"

My forehead creased as I touched softly around the wound on my head.

"It's a gash. From the wolf demon. I'm okay. Are *you* okay?"

"Wolf?" He breathed. Finally. "Oh. The thing that's like a hellhound but isn't. I'm not sure what it was, because hellhounds don't have spikes. Or silver eyes."

"Whatever it is got a swipe at me. Like I said, I might have oversold my Lara Croftiness. It was more dumb luck." And a Divinicus vision, but he didn't need the details.

"So I didn't do anything to…hurt you?" Some color seeped back into his cheeks.

"No. Of course not. You just touched it by accident." I grinned. "Because I'm so boo-tay-licious."

He didn't laugh. Just blinked like he was coming off a concussion-level blow to the head. So much for my comedic career.

"Okay, what's going on?" I took his hand and wiped off the blood. "Since when do you get so freaked out over a little blood?"

"Nothing. Let me see."

Then his hands were all over me. And not in the kind of way you hope the super-hot guy puts his hands all over you. No, he was more like a mother ape picking through my hair for fleas and ticks.

I winced. "Ow."

"Sorry. But hold still. This doesn't look good."

"It's no big deal."

As I started to push him away, I caught a glimpse of Tristan's stalker wall and froze. There was something new. When I'd pulled off his piles of paranoid paperwork, I must have partially uncovered another picture which had been hiding underneath. I recognized this face too, but in a very different context.

Last time we met, this someone had tried to kill me.

Chapter Twelve

I reached past Ayden and snatched the photo, ripping the paper and sending the pushpin flying.

My hands shook. My stomach lurched, sloshing bile up my throat. I swallowed it down but couldn't stop the memory of that stupid college field trip, the party gone wrong, and me walking back to the dorm, alone, in the dark, where things had gone…fatal.

At least for parts of me. Like my appendix. Not that I needed it anyway.

But trust? Yeah, that one I'd like to have back.

"Where are they?" I seethed. "Where are the pictures of the rest of them?" In a wild burst of energy I clawed at the papers still pinned on the wall.

"Stop!" Ayden held me from behind, pinning my arms to my sides. He spoke close to my ear. "There's no more. Only Heather."

I fought hard, but his muscles overcame my desperation, and I finally stilled. My chest heaved rattling breaths through clenched teeth. I choked on the words a few times before I could create a sentence.

"Why does he have a picture of Heather? How do you know her?" My hair tangled in a red mess across my eyes. "I've never mentioned her. Or any of them. I don't ever talk about them, don't ever want to think about them. Ever."

My eyes burned. I ground my teeth and bullied back the tears that threatened, refusing to shed any more over the maniacal group of people who had delivered the most horrifying living nightmare of my life. And the way my life had been going, *that* was saying something.

Ayden turned me around and smoothed back my hair. He smiled, dark chocolate eyes shimmering with compassion.

"Listen." He held my face in his warm hands, thumbs gently wiping the tears from beneath my eyes as he gave my forehead a soft kiss. "Fiskick said that your friends attacked you because a Hallucinator controlled their minds and manipulated them into…" His voice trailed off.

I gave him a pained smile. "Beating the crap out of me?"

A muscle ticked in his jaw. "Yes. So we decided to track them down."

"And get all the gory details? Jayden has the police report for that."

"No." He smoothed his hands over my shoulders. "But we wanted to check a theory which…Tristan found was true."

I breathed deep. "What?"

"Tristan can get into a person's mind." Ayden ducked his head to catch my gaze. "He can tell if another Hallucinator has done something to mess with their brain. It leaves a sort of," he glanced sideways, thinking, "he calls it a signature. Anyway, the kids Tristan talked to who were involved can't remember the attack on you at all, but he confirmed that each of their minds had been manipulated. And by the same Hallucinator."

I let this sink in. It felt too heavy. My knees buckled. Ayden caught me in his arms and pulled me to his chest, holding me upright when I would've fallen into a pathetic heap.

This night…had just been too much. I felt drained and broken.

"Why didn't you tell me?" I put my arms around him, hands under his jacket, feeling the strong, solid body through his T-shirt, listening to the steady beat of his heart. The photo was still in my hand. I crumpled it up. "Why does he still have Heather's photo?"

Ayden tensed.

So did I.

"What's wrong?" I leaned my head back to look at him. "Ayden?"

His lips rolled in and out of his mouth. "She's missing."

"Missing?" I pulled away and this time he let me go, freeing me to pace around Tristan's room. "Missing like she escaped detention and is wandering around with a screwed up mind and going to find me and go all psycho again?"

"No." Ayden raised his palms at my freaked out look. "Missing like someone went to the trouble to forge documents to transfer her from the detention center, and then effectively hide her without a trace." He paused. "Or…"

"Or what?"

Ayden looked uncomfortable. "Maybe she knew something they wanted to keep quiet, and they…"

I felt cold. "*Killed* her? Would they do that? The Hallucinator? The Mandatum?"

"We don't know. We'll keep looking. She could still be alive. And if we can find her, we can get answers."

"*If* she's alive."

I scrubbed my face with my hands. It was a never-ending nightmare. Heather dead because of me. Some girl in hell because of me. Who was next?

My gut bubbled acid.

"Aurora."

Ayden reached for me. I rested my forehead on his shoulder, but only for a moment. This romantic evening had taken one too many fatal blows to be salvageable. I needed time alone.

"Don't worry. I'll be okay." I hoped it was the truth.

I opened the window and climbed out onto the gnarled branches of the old oak between Tristan's house and mine. Cold mountain air tackled the heat ravaging my skin.

Mother Nature's earthy scents filled the night, but either a chainsaw or power drill screamed from my garage. Joining the cacophony was a baby's wail, an angsty teenager's doom and gloom music cranked on high, and my mother screeching for silence.

Couldn't wait to wade into that.

I straddled the branch and started to make my way across to my bedroom window.

"Wait." Ayden picked up my jacket, his worried look hard to miss. "At least let me clean that wound before you go."

"I'll do it. Besides, I'm a fast healer, remember?" At least physically. One of the perks of my Divinicus powers. I reached back for my jacket. "Just don't tell my parents."

Ayden lost all color. His voice flooded with dread. "Your *parents*."

He pulled my coat out of reach, and bolted out of the room, door slamming behind him.

I stared at the closed door. I was alone, miserable, and dangling two stories above ground with my inner klutz ready to rear her ugly head and have me cracking my skull down below.

I nodded. "Yep, that's about right."

I grumbled all the way across the oak, slid open the window to my pitch-dark room and would've slipped quietly inside if my toe hadn't caught on the sill and sent me thudding to the floor.

"Oh, for the love of—" I hauled myself up to close the window, thankful for the household noise because with all that hoopla no one would notice my kaboomie entrance.

The lights flipped on.

"Gotcha!"

CHAPTER THIRTEEN

I whirled, catching my shoulder on the curtain which then wrapped across my face.

Blind! I'm blind!

I flailed, yanked it away, bringing the curtain, along with the rod, crashing down on my head. Real smooth.

Hysterical laughter ensued. Not mine.

"Thanks a lot, moron!" I rubbed my scalp. Like it didn't already hurt.

My sister Luna sat at my desk stroking my gray cat, Van Helsing, who sat on her lap. She finally contained her merriment. "Well, well, well. The golden—"

The cat made a break for it.

"Helsing!" Luna scrambled to control him, resumed stroking methodically, and cleared her throat to continue in a deep, dramatic voice. "The golden child breaks curfew. Again."

Helsing let out a low mewl.

"Shhh." She scrubbed his head and gave me a cunning look. "What could possibly keep me from telling dear mother and father?"

I smirked. "The fact that I know how you really spend third period."

"Stupid Blake!" Luna slapped her knee. "I knew he couldn't keep a secret."

I plucked Helsing from her lap and stroked him till he purred. "Now be a good little minion and scram."

Our front doorbell chimed. Luna and I shared a confused look.

"At this hour?" Luna hurried out of my room. "Must be drama."

"Super." I dumped Helsing and followed her.

From the top of the stairs, I saw Mom answer the front door adjusting my one-year-old brother Oron on her hip. She wasn't happy.

She glared at Ayden. "If you brought back my daughter's jacket and not her, the fact that you blew curfew is the least of your problems, mister."

I rushed down the stairs. "Mom, I've been home for ages. Chatting with Luna." I turned to my sister. "Right?"

Luna flicked me a cold look. "Yep."

Ayden laughed nervously and sidestepped in, flashing a way too charming smile. "I was halfway home when I realized she forgot this in my car." He held out my jacket.

"How thoughtful of you, honey," Mom said sweetly then stepped back to bang on the wall to the garage and screech, "M! It's after nine o'clock! If you don't stop, I'll make you change diapers!"

The sudden silencing of power tools left a ringing in my ears.

With a wary eye, I snatched my jacket from Ayden. "Thanks. See you tomorrow."

Ayden gasped and pointed. "Oh my gosh! Mrs. Lahey, look, she's bleeding!"

The way my night had been going, I really should've seen that coming.

CHAPTER FOURTEEN

My head smashes into the dumpster. I collapse. Pain sledgehammers across my shoulders. I claw the ground, try to find purchase to drag myself away. Another blow knocks my breath away. My lips are wet. I taste blood.

No escape. Too many of them. And only one me. Broken. I can't fight. Can't understand. I trusted them. My frien—

Nails rip through my arm as they wrench me onto my back. A rotting wooden two-by-four slams into my side so hard it splinters apart, and I'm not sure if the sharp "crack" *is the wood or my ribs as they shatter. Maniacal laughter shreds fresh pain. Hands slip on the blood on my throat. I feel hands choking the life from me.*

"Fight!" orders a voice which whispers harsh, like sandpaper across my brain, jolting through my paralyzing fear. Words fade in and out. "I'll find...you safe...forever...until then—"

A roar charges through my ears, cutting off the rest of the words. Pressure on my chest. Too much. Something over my mouth. Can't breathe.

"Fight!" the command echoes, faint but no less demanding.

I know I need to grab and shove and—

High pitched giggles pulled me to consciousness. Something fuzzy crushed over my mouth. Someone sitting on my chest.

"It worked!" The smiling five-year-old lifted her stuffed toy off my face and held it high in the air. "Prince Bubbles to the rescue!"

"Selena?" I gulped down air, blinked rapidly.

I'd been seconds away from strangling my sister, taking out Bubbles' only remaining eye, and chucking the lot of them across the room. I steadied myself and scooted her off my chest to sit beside me.

"Daddy said I got to wake you up, but I couldn't." She shoved her stuffed platypus in my face again. "So Bubbles pretended to be a prince and kiss you awake just like Sleeping Beauty, and it worked." She poked me in the face, just shy of stabbing out my eye. "Why are you crying?"

Dad, who'd been passing my door, immediately backtracked into my room. "Is it your head? I *knew* I should've put stitches in that. Stupid curtain rods!"

The story of the curtain rod causing my head injury wasn't a hard sell, given I'd waged a war with coordination since birth.

He kicked the clumped drapery fabric still lying on the floor. "When your aunt lets me back into my garage, I will cement this to the wall."

"I'm fine. And I'm not crying." I rubbed a hand over my face to find my skin dewy with sweat and tears.

Selena dropped her forehead against mine and squinted into my eyes. "It looks like you're crying." I pushed her away, but she just crawled up to lay on my chest and stare intently into my eyes. "Did you have a scary dream? I have scary dreams. They're scary. But

Bubbles can make them go away because her pirate patch gives her superpowers. Matty said so. Here." Selena tucked the platypus under the covers. "You can borrow her."

Dad scooped up Selena. "Let's get you and your gender-fluid platypus some breakfast." He studied my face, touching my nose with tender fingers. "Swelling's down, but ice it up before you go to school. I'll redress the head wound too." He tilted his head. "Sure you weren't crying?"

"Yes." I yanked the covers over my head to hide the contradictory evidence.

"Maybe a present would help," he said cheerfully. "You expecting a package today?"

"No," I mumbled through the blankets. "I just need a few more minutes. Alone. Please."

Selena pouted, "She's a Grumpy Gus."

"Yet we love her anyway. See you downstairs." Dad patted my arm before he left.

Grumpy? You bet. I didn't exactly sleep last night. And when I did, it wasn't delightful visions of wreaking a satisfying revenge on Matthias dancing in my head.

Nope, his little stunt last night — and the whole Heather fiasco — cracked the surface of the barrier where I kept nightmare memories safely buried beneath steel traps and mountains of denial. Memories of the night which seemed like both a lifetime ago, and yet fresh as yesterday.

My "friends" had used pretty much anything they could find in the back alley Dumpster. Fists and feet as well as wood, pipe, bottles, and —

I threw back the covers, rushed out of my room and downstairs, heart pounding blood into my head with a steady ache as if Thor himself was mercilessly wielding his mighty hammer inside my skull. I needed to *not* think about that night if I was going to make it through the day.

Denial was how I functioned.

At least The Voice was back. The one that shows up in my nightmares when I'm scared out of my mind. The one that promises to find me, protect me. It was male as far as I could tell, although it wasn't much more than a raspy whisper. The man of my dreams was the invisible hero my subconscious had conjured up lately to help me through those nights when the Terror Train ripped through the tunnel of my psyche.

Hadn't heard him in a while, but that was because I hadn't had nightmares for the past few weeks.

Thanks, Matthias.

At some point in between nightmares, I'd vowed to find a way to get the Aussie back, but my brain was on slow-mo. No brilliant diabolical plan. Yet.

I opened my door and tripped over Van Helsing as he sprinted into the room.

"Hey!"

He ignored me, raced to his royal purple cat bed, frantically dug under the cushion then sprinted out, a feather gripped between his teeth.

"You are so weird."

The feather was from the wings of my guardian angel, Gloria. Helsing was obsessed with them. I hadn't seen my perky, costume-loving angel in weeks. Guess that was a good thing. As long as she was in the background protecting my family, that was all I cared about.

At the bottom of the stairs, I white-knuckled the railing, determined to clear my head which felt heavy, filled with a sludge of dread and exhaustion. I needed something to lighten the load of my dark mood.

As if on cue, Dad darted out of the living room past the front windows then slowed to a hunched creep across the foyer. He scowled through the spyglass in the front door and chuckled darkly.

"Wanna dance mailman? Let's dance!" Then he ducked outside.

Yes, if there was one thing my family was good for, it was distraction.

"Breakfast!" In the kitchen, Aunt M pointed to a steaming pot on the stove. Under an apron, she wore her ritual skirt, blouse, and blazer, and the French twist was smoothed to perfection. I felt more like a zombie than ever.

"Burnt oatmeal, two weeks straight. Yay." Luna grimaced from her stool, actually looking like a zombie with all the pale makeup and dark, artfully ragged clothing.

My brother Lucian patted M's back. "Maybe I'll make scrambled eggs tomorrow."

Aunt M folded her arms on top of her swollen belly and narrowed a look. "You don't like my scramble."

"Because you burn it," Luna muttered.

Lucian said over our sister's complaints, "We just want to help out."

"And not be nauseous all through first period."

"Luna!" I smacked her.

M jabbed an oatmeal covered spoon Luna's way. "Your parents asked me here to help take care of you and that's what I'm doing."

"We don't need a babysitter," Luna protested.

M waved a hand over Luna's Gothic ensemble. "You're morgue make-up says you're not getting enough attention at home."

Mom came in from the backyard with Oron on her hip and fresh flowers in her hand. "I like her vampire look. Makes me feel tan. Leave her alone, M. And Luna, be nice."

"Ugh!" Luna stomped out. "Why can't we just lock her in the garage?"

M snorted. "If only."

Mom watched Luna go. "What's her problem?"

I chuckled. "M blocked her from the Internet last night."

"Just the social networking sites. She was *supposed* to be doing homework. Speaking of children misbehaving." M looked down at me. "Where's the nervous gervous from next door?"

"Tristan?" I shrugged. "Home, I guess. Why?"

"He didn't spend the night scouring the world for my identity."

I sighed. "You promised you wouldn't spy on my friends' computer activity."

"I haven't. Mostly because I can't. Yet. They have an impressive firewall." She dumped oatmeal into a bowl with a dull *plop* and handed it to me. "But I do get an alert when anyone attempts to investigate me. Been getting one a couple times a day from that jumpy brat since the day I showed up. Decent little hacker. Thought he'd try looking longer than a few weeks."

"I'll relay your disappoin—" I choked on a mouthful of breakfast, fatally forgetting the gag-worthy flavor of M's concoction. It stuck to the inside my mouth, thick as cement and just as tasty.

"I don't want you relaying anything." Porridge hung like dog drool off the wooden spoon M pointed in my direction. "Because I don't want you to talk, kibitz or socialize in any way with any of them. I've checked around. Those Hex Boys, as they're called, have a bad reputation. Danger follows them and it already caught you in its wake in Los Angeles. Almost got you and Luna killed at the concert hall."

Mom shook her head at my aunt. "The explosion wasn't the boys' fault."

She was right on that score. *I* had blown up the building. The boys had been the heroes that averted disaster.

"They saved my girls, so be nice, M," Mom said.

"What about her grades?" M asked. "I hacked into the school's system and ever since she's been here, *spending time with those boys*, her GPA has plummeted."

"That's got to be illegal!" And downright rude. But she wasn't wrong. At Mom's questioning, borderline *testy* look, I said. "It's not the boys. I started here in the middle of the year and was already behind because I missed so much at my old school because I was…recovering. Then I missed school here because of the coma and…" I shrugged. "I'll get them up. I promise. Please, give me a chance."

The explanation was partially true, and hopefully my pathetic history of horror would deflect her anger and suspicion and bring on the protective mom mode.

Her eyes softened.

Man, I'm good.

"Fine," she said. "But if your grades aren't improved by the mid-semester progress report, we're getting a tutor and you're grounded, with no social life, until they are."

M made an exasperated noise. "Okay, forget about the waste of her education. You're telling me you're not worried about your *daughter* hanging around with six *boys* with dubious reputations? *And* dating one of them who looks at your daughter with…*that* look?"

My brow creased. "What look?"

"Oh, please," Aunt M scoffed. "*That* look. And not to mention *that* smile. Hungry," she growled the word, "and hot enough to make a nun's panties spontaneously combust."

Lucian choked, laughter spewing juice out his nose. I glared at him as the blood rushed to my cheeks.

Aunt M gave me a meaningful look. "And you're no nun, sweetie. I'm just saying."

"Mom!" I was beginning to seriously sympathize with Luna.

"M, that's enough," Mom said in her And-That's-Final voice, then kissed the top of my head to cover the fact that she was fighting a smile. "We trust Aurora and so should you. Even if you don't approve of the boys. Now, I've got to open up shop. I don't know what is in the air, but people have been buying bouquets like it's Valentine's Day." She grabbed her purse and rummaged through the contents. "Remember, M, Clyde's giving you a ride to the church. Have you finished the baby's christening plans with Father Bancroft?"

"We're…still working on things," M grumbled, filling up the oatmeal pot with water to let it soak. Not that it ever helped much.

Speaking of stuff that makes me nauseous.

It wasn't that I begrudged my unborn cousin a christening, but it meant that—just my luck—my aunt, the most anti-social person in the world, had started hanging out with Father Bancroft, the Mandatum's go-to guy in charge of this portal location. The good Father's responsibilities included overseeing the activities of the hunters stationed here, a.k.a. the Hex Boys.

I wasn't sure what kind of disaster could come from the two of them spending time together. I just knew it would start with a capital letter and end with an exclamation point. Would I ever catch a break?

"You know," Aunt M said, "even Father Bancroft has reservations about Aurora spending time with those boys. Says he loves them, but they can be…rambunctious."

Nope. No breaks today.

"He hasn't said anything to me," Mom replied. "Besides, Aurora can handle herself. She has two rambunctious brothers. And sisters." Rummaging through her purse, she added under her breath, "And aunt, for that matter."

Lucian and I snickered.

"I heard that," my aunt said loudly.

The front door slammed and Dad said, "Aurora, sure you aren't expecting a package?"

I leaned back to find him army-crawling under the window in the living room. Like all dads do. "Already told you no, Rambo."

"The new mailman is back." Dad reached up and pulled the curtains closed before standing up and peeking out. "Won't come to the door."

"M shot a tranquillizer dart at the last guy." Mom gave a tired look at M who shrugged unapologetically. "The fact that there's a new one willing to be on our sidewalk is a miracle. Don't scare him off, Clyde."

Dad tried to block me when I went for the curtains. "He won't let me sign for your package. Demanded you come out in person."

"I'll get my tranq gun!" M made for her room.

"Don't you dare!" Mom chased her.

I swished back the curtains to get a look at the petrifying postman.

"I find his interest in my teenage daughter creepy," Dad grumbled.

Oh, he had no idea.

Chapter Fifteen

Fog snaked through my ankles, adding to the already formidable sense of doom as I stalked with what I hoped was an air of menace across my lawn.

Our new mailman smiled and tipped his postman hat at me. "Good morning, Aurora."

"It was until you showed up," I said.

Rose spread his hands. "I bequeathed you the night to think it over, alone, when we could have been together doing much more...*pleasurable* things." He winked. "What say you to my proposal?"

I grimaced. "Down boy."

I had thought it over. And talked it over with the Hex Boys who were supposed to keep watch so they could catch Rose next time he showed up and interrogate him. I glanced at Tristan's house, but no nervous gervous appeared. Glad that plan was working out so well.

"Oh, come now," Rose sounded bored. "Do you want me to kill you or not?"

I was really sick of his cocky attitude, but keeping him talking and buying time seemed my only option. I shoved my nest of curls off my face.

"Well, when you put it like that." I bowed slightly. "I'm at your service."

"Excellent." Rose snapped his fingers. "You won't regret our dalliance. No woman ever does. And once you find the treasure we'll both have everything we need to be safe. Our loved ones as well." He waved at my dad.

"Her aunt's loading the tranq gun!" Dad called from the front porch. "She doesn't miss."

"Dad, I got this!" I gave him a thumbs-up. "You can go inside."

Dad stayed put. Even grabbed the hose and started watering Mom's flowers while squinting at Rose with disapproval.

"There must be something wrong with your family. People usually find me irresisti— Ow!" Rose flinched and turned to grab the back of his leg.

He was wearing shorts, and we could see a thin, shallow gash dripping beads of blood across the back of his calf. We could also see Helsing, feather in his mouth, run off in a blur to disappear behind the garage.

"Did that feline just *bite* me?" Rose was thoroughly affronted.

I stifled a smile. Sometimes I thought my cat knew more about this supernatural stuff than I did.

"Can we focus?" I said. "What treasure?"

With a dark look at Helsing's last location, Rose frowned and started rifling through his mailbag.

I held up a hand. "Never mind. First, you have to meet with the Hex Boys."

Rose looked dubious. "The boys who kidnapped you last night?"

"Right before you threatened to kill me then left me for dead. What can I say? I keep a misshapen social circle. How'd you get out of the trunk?"

He waved a dismissive hand. "I'm a Joat."

"The outfit's definitely a joke. You rob the post office?" Although, if anyone could make the frumpy blue postal service shirt and shorts look good, it was Rose.

He gave me a sultry look. "I was told women love a man in uniform."

"Don't think they were talking about this one," I smirked.

"Pity," he sighed. "My intelligence must be faulty. And it's not *joke*, it's *Joat*. J-O-A-T. It stands for Jack-of-all-trades. You probably haven't heard of us. We tend to be considered the Mandatum's low man on the totem pole. Not much respect."

Then like Mary Poppins yanking a floor lamp from her way too small carpet bag, Rose pulled out a large cardboard box, the size of a file drawer, from his small blue mail satchel. I blocked Dad's view.

"Taking awfully long to deliver a package!" Dad said.

"Because you make him nervous!" I motioned for him to go inside.

"That should make him faster," Dad pointed out. "What is it anyway?"

"Uh."

Rose whispered, "Tell him it's the Kama Sutra book you ordered."

I yelled over my shoulder, "It's the Kama Su—" I turned to Rose. "Wait. Isn't that the—"

"Ancient text of sexual pleasure?" he nodded. "Yes. Quite riveting. I'd be happy demonstrate. My skills are legendary."

"Oh, thanks very much."

"I'll take that as a yes."

"No!" I glared at the impish Rose. "Dad, it's just some more mythology books!"

"Admittedly less hedonistically pleasurable, but still an excellent choice of literature." Rose rested the box in my arms. "Now, I'm not quite as trusting of those boys as you are, but since I know you're going to show the contents to them anyway, might I suggest not letting them find this."

He slapped a piece of parchment on top of the box just under my chin.

I struggled to get a good grip. Wouldn't have been surprised if he had stashed an anchor in this thing. "What is it?"

"Where you must begin your hunt. I'd advise you to get there first. Alone. Because the paper and circumstances could possibly, well, most likely…" he looked pained, "reveal to the Hex Boys that you are the Divinicus."

The box slipped through my fingers.

Rose caught the ridiculously heavy thing one-handed and set it at my feet. "Worry not. As long as you help, I promise to keep your secret. You and your boys get to work. The faster you get through the files, the faster my sister is out of hell, the sooner I don't have to kill you. Once you have the treasure, I'll explain our next move. So be quick. I do have a deadline to keep."

"What deadline?"

"Did I not mention it? Details are such a bore." At my look of irritation, he sighed. "In addition to the deadline I've been given for your death, there might be a few — maybe a horde — of demons on their way here for…various purposes."

"What purposes?"

"None good, that I can tell you," he chuckled then waved a dismissive hand. "But that's not for a week."

"A week!" I struggled to keep my voice low so Dad didn't come running.

"Give or take. More take than give. But I have taken precautionary measures."

"What pre—"

"Hide this quickly. They're coming." He shoved the parchment into my hand and pointed over my shoulder.

I stashed it in my pocket and turned, half-scared that the demon horde had already arrived. But Tristan's front door opened and out came a pack of Hex Boys. About time.

I whirled back to Rose.

He was nowhere in sight.

CHAPTER SIXTEEN

"I can't believe you said yes!" Ayden said.

"Death was my only other option since you guys weren't around." I bit my lip. "And if there really is some girl in hell because of me, we should help get her out." That thought had plagued me during my sleepless night. Sure, I'd always worried about my family being collateral damage from my Divinicus drama, but strangers?

"If there is a sister," Ayden growled. "And the killing-you part loses him some sympathy points."

"I know but…" I looked around. "None of you saw him?"

"Not a good look." Ayden grabbed my hand looking worried. "I woke up, saw you outside talking to a mailman and came running, but he was gone."

"I'll traverse through the security footage." Jayden jogged back inside the house.

"We spent the night at Tristan's to keep an eye on you," Logan said.

I frowned. "Where is Tristan?"

Ayden was scanning the street. "Left at three a.m. to take his grandparents to the airport. They're headed to Nepal."

"On a mission to shut down a mass demon escape." Blake yawned. "Mandatum got some anonymous tip, so could turn out to be nothing, but they love to volunteer for this kind of stuff. Thought Tristan would never stop yelling at them."

So they *were* hunters.

"What are their powers?" Guessing it wasn't being awesome at shuffleboard.

"Just don't make them mad." Blake patted my shoulder. "We wouldn't have had this problem with Rose if you guys had just let me sleep in babe's—"

"Shut up, Blake!"

The four of us stood around Rose's stupid box on my lawn. Van Helsing had come back featherless in the boys' wake. Currently, purring vigorously as he alternated between rubbing his face against my legs and the box. The grind and scream of power tools signaled my aunt was back to work on whatever in our garage. Dad had gone in to explain — yet again — why she couldn't start working until she'd given the chance for at least one rooster to crow.

Ayden rubbed his eyes. "I set the alarm. And we were all taking shifts but…none of us could keep awake."

Blake stretched. "I was having some awesome dreams. Taking hula lessons with a flock of half-naked beauties in grass skirts and coconut on their coconuts, if you know what I mean." He cupped both hands on his chest and wiggled his hips.

"Please stop." Ayden put up his arms to block Blake's gyrations. "Could Rose have drugged us?"

"No way," Logan said, but he looked concerned.

"He said he was a Joat," I said. "Can they do that?"

The guys shared a look, but Ayden shook his head.

"That would take someone powerful, and Joats aren't that good at anything," Ayden said.

Helsing sprung on top of the box and gnawed on a corner.

I shooed him off. "Go do normal cat things."

Which in feline vernacular must have meant *sit down and stare at the box*. I'd get him a non-supernatural related cardboard plaything later.

"Let's see what we can get out of this," I said.

Logan knelt and opened the box. Inside was an antique, weathered wooden trunk trimmed with straps of black metal and worn leather.

Blake grinned. "A treasure chest?"

Logan pointed to the stylistic letter M burned into the top. "The Mandatum symbol. This can't be good."

When was it ever?

With a nervous look around, he opened the squeaky, hinged lid.

No gems or gold, just a mess of files and paperwork.

Logan plucked out a folder and read, "Flint?"

"*Nathan* Flint?" Ayden snatched it and swore under his breath.

"The European duke who built our high school?" I flinched under their intense looks. "What? I *do* pay attention in History."

Ayden knocked Logan aside and dug into the contents. "This can't be them. No! Not *the* Flint files. Logan, call Matthias."

Logan walked toward the house and pulled out his phone.

Something banged in the garage then silence finally blessed the dawn. Until M started yelling at my dad.

Blake raised his brows. "What exactly is your aunt up to in there?"

"Some surprise present we can't see yet." I started to pick out a folder from the box, but Ayden pushed me away.

"Blake, get this out of here." Ayden slapped his folder back into the chest. "Now!"

"Why are we scared of a file?" I said.

Ayden hauled the box up with a grunt and dumped it in Blake's arms. "The less you know, the better. Trust me."

"I do." I put a hand on the box and gave Blake a warning look. "But since it's my life on the line, let's take this to my bedroom."

"That's exactly what you said in my dreams last night."

"Shut *up*, Blake." Ayden shoved him toward the street. "Put them in my car."

"Wait." I slammed a hand into Blake's abs — ow—and glared at Ayden. "When has you keeping secrets not ended in a huge miscommunication where I wind up chased and nearly killed by demons?"

Ayden clenched his jaw. "My meeting with Bancroft last night had to do with the Flint files, *these* files."

He slapped a hand on the box and flames erupted, scorching the cardboard and startling Blake into dropping the package which dumped out the trunk and spilled a mess of paperwork onto the lawn. Van Helsing immediately dived into action, pouncing on papers with kitten-like glee.

"Blake!" Ayden looked stricken and knelt on one knee, dumping aside Helsing, who let out a *meow* of protest, and gathering papers at a frantic pace.

Blake started to help. "That's your fault, dude. Lately you light up at any little thing. What is with you? "

"Nothing!" Ayden snapped, then paused and leaned a forearm on his knee. "Well, *right now* what's wrong is that these files were stolen from Sophina Cacciatori and by giving them to us, Rose just put us in her crosshairs."

Chapter Seventeen

I jumped back from the box like it was grenade and we'd just pulled the pin.

"Blake, get them out of here!" I ran around to pick up papers blown away by the wind. Wrestled a few from Helsing. They wilted, already damp and flimsy from the dew on the grass. "Why is Cacciatori interested in the long dead Flint?"

"Because he was Mandatum." Ayden flipped one file closed and shoved it in the trunk.

I handed him more papers, noticing some of the ink was smudging, causing words to run together. "A hunter?"

"Yes and no." Ayden's lips thinned. "He was a mechanic."

I gasped. "An assassin? Like the guy in the movie?"

Ayden sighed. "No, a Mandatum mechanic has the ability to invent and put together mechanical…contraptions. And in Flint's case he could create machines way beyond what was available in the late 1800s."

Blake squished more papers into the box. "His old house — the high school — is rigged with all sorts of hidden doors and secret passageways. And some weird gizmos that even the Mandatum can't figure out."

"Don't worry," Ayden said. "The Mandatum shut all that stuff down a long time ago."

Blake deepened his voice to an ominous tone. "But you should worry that Flint was an evil man who practiced the dark arts, did weird experiments, and was known to," he hissed the next words, "raise the dead."

"Blake, those were stupid rumors," Ayden said, then stood and gave my shoulders a comforting rub. "The truth is that when they found the hell portal here in Gossamer Falls, Flint was the guy they sent to watch over it and manage the hunters who came through to guard it. Basically, what Father Bancroft does now."

Blake said, "He built cool machines to clear the passageways to the portal and maintain security."

I put my hands on my hips. "The portal that's behind the waterfall? The portal that you won't let me see?"

Ayden gave me a tired look. "It's safer that way."

"True, babe. Portals are dangerous. Can suck you right into the bowels of hell if you're not careful."

Yeah. Not good.

"But Flint died over a hundred years ago," I said. "Why is the file important now?"

Ayden rubbed his jaw. "Remember I mentioned the school had a dark history?"

I raised my brows. "I believe you said 'insane asylum.'"

Ayden smoothed back his hair with both hands. "When Flint ran things, hunters from everywhere passed through his estate all the time. Everything ran perfectly until the Mandatum found out Flint was a serial killer."

"Told ya," Blake nodded. "Dead were raised. Zombies roamed."

"There were no zombies," Ayden said, giving Blake an irritated glance. "But at some point Flint started quietly killing off hunters and stealing their Mandatum artifacts. No record of exactly what, but probably jewelry, books, weapons, art. Whatever the psycho could get his hands on."

"Priceless and powerful stuff for sure, babe."

I hugged myself. "Anything that would help Rose get his sister?"

"Don't know." Ayden shrugged. "Mandatum couldn't find it. Flint went insane before they could get him to talk."

Blake was trying to stuff way too many pages into a thin file folder. "Then, so they could spend years looking for it, they turned the house into an insane asylum."

"It was a good cover," Ayden said. "Became a prestigious facility which made a healthy profit, and if anyone saw anything weird, they were crazy. Right?"

"Clever," I said. And creepy. "But they never found it?"

"The legend of Flint's lost treasure lives on," Blake grinned.

Ayden blew out air. "Every now and then someone living out their Indiana Jones fantasy comes looking for it. Like—"

"Rose," I murmured remembering Rose's attire from last night.

"With the files stolen," Ayden said, "the Mandatum assumes another treasure hunter is on the way, and we're supposed to stop that because if there is a treasure, the society wants it. If we admit we have the files they'll demand to know how we got them, probably send a team." Ayden punched the air and growled, wisps of smoke trailed from his fist making curly designs in the air. "Ugh! Rose. I hate this guy. Let's just kill him. He already threatened Aurora so we just lure him—"

The ground underneath Ayden bucked hard enough to almost knock him off his feet. He steadied himself and made a face at Blake.

The big guy shrugged. "Gotta chill, dude. We can't kill a fellow hunter in cold blood. We need a council directive termination order classified as extreme prejudice. Besides, babe is fine."

Sure. For now.

"Why is Cacciatori so interested?" I asked in what I hoped was a casual voice. "Is there a Divinicus connection?"

"Not that I know of." Ayden wiped a hand down his face.

Lucian poked his head out of the front door. "Aurora, you should get Ayden out of here. Remember Aunt M's breakfast conversation?"

"Lucian, don't *even!*" I warned, just as Aunt M pushed past Lucian onto the front porch.

She saw us and ordered, "You two hurry up. Your boyfriend is giving me a ride to the church."

Ayden raised a brow. "I am?"

"Since when?" I said.

"Since I told your father you were no nun." She ducked back inside.

"That would do it." My sigh came out a growl.

Ayden looked me up and down, then grinned and headed for my brother. "Hey, Lucian, I'm thinking I need more details about this breakfast conversation."

CHAPTER EIGHTEEN

Dad decided that Aunt M's big belly was too tight a squeeze to be safe in Ayden's small sport's car, so we'd dodged that bullet, and before he changed his mind, headed to school with a screech of rubber.

The Gothic wonderland that Flint built, and what we now called high school, was a monolith of carved stone, with lofty archways, spires that pierced the heavens, soaring turrets protected by grim gargoyles, towers awaiting their damsels, and miles of twisted hallways for a girl to get lost in. It belonged on the misty moors of medieval England with bustle-skirted beauties, waistcoated gentlemen, and Gothic romance lovers stealing secret kisses in dark alcoves.

Instead, I was in a dark alcove — alone — yanking on one of Luna's black hoodie jackets, stuffing my mass of red curls into one of Lucian's baseball caps, and peeking out into the hall to make sure the coast was clear.

A strong floral aroma wafted through the air as several girls and boys in shiny red capes carried a multitude of flowers through the halls. As part of a fundraiser for next month's Spring Fling students could buy their choice of a single bloom, which Mom's shop provided at a substantial discount, and have them delivered to those they wanted to ask to the dance, or at least request a reserved spot on their dance card. Business had been especially booming this week.

Staying hunched to keep from towering over the rest, I pulled the hood over my red curls and waded into the throng of students with their chattering hum of white noise and tried to remain inconspicuous. On the third floor hallway, I moved along the wall of windows, face averted toward the outdoors to help avoid eye contact and keep from being noticed.

Through the endless panes of glittering glass, fog lapped over the sprawling lawns of the extensive grounds. White swans glided across ponds, towering trees dotted the manicured landscape, blossoms sprouted through the earth, and forest rimmed the far edges.

Despite the serene beauty, my insides twitched because any moment now Rose could ride out of the woods on the blanket of mist, like some ethereal being coming to collect his bounty. Me. Although that might be preferable to the anxious anticipation of doom currently gurgling my gut.

I was double-jittery because I was in the process of ditching Physics and hiding from the Hex Boys. Third period was the one class I didn't share with any of them, and therefore, the one class I could ditch and not be followed, allowing me to do some Nancy Drewing on my own regarding the sweaty, crumpled paper in my pocket.

The yellowed-with-age parchment document Rose had given me, the one he claimed could blow my Divinicus cover with the boys, was a map. Faded ink sketched out a basic floor plan of a room which, using my mad deduction skills, I'd deduced was the library in this mansion that Flint built.

Well, mad deduction skills along with the fact that someone — probably Rose — had used fresh ink and a flowing curly script to write on top of the page, "Flint's Library."

Anyway, on the map, one of the walls was marked with a weird doodle. It was a single line which curved at either end into two distinct spirals. The spiral on one end was made of straight lines connected at sharp angles. Very geometric, it reminded me of the Greek key motif I remembered from art class. The other spiral was the typical curly, smooth flowing curve.

Didn't know what it meant, but Flint's old library was also the high school's current library and that's where I was headed for a bit of sleuthing. On my own.

"Blake!"

I froze at Ayden's voice.

"Hey!" Some kids directly behind me stumbled and bumped my shoulder ducking around to avoid a full collision. "Watch out," they grumbled.

"Sorry," I muttered.

I kept my head down, but watched Blake who was headed toward me. He paused and turned, waiting for Ayden to catch up. But suddenly Ayden stopped, a look of fury flashed, and he shoved his way across the hall, ignoring all protests, too focused on…

Uh-oh. It was the guy who had offered me his "parking" services last night.

Out of the flow of bodies, Ayden grabbed him two-fisted by the shirt, and after a violent swing around that knocked a couple of people aside, he slammed the guy's back up against the wall. The guy's feet dangled off the floor. His eyes bugged. Ayden dug a forearm into his throat, pinning him like a bug in a science project.

A collective gasp and a couple of squeals echoed through the hallway as the crowd backed away in a semi-circle. Then there was silence but for guy's choking noises.

Ayden got right in the guy's face and spoke in harsh, guttural tones. "You think last night was funny?"

The guy clawed at Ayden's arm. "What the hell are you talk—"

"Don't speak." Ayden shoved harder into the guy's throat. There were desperate gurgling noises and the guy's face looked red enough to burst. "Don't you *ever* say *anything* to my girlfriend *ever* again. Or so help me—"

"Dude!" Blake cut through the crowd like a bull through tall grass, smiling easily at everyone before placing a thick hand on Ayden's shoulder and moving so he could get in Ayden's line of sight. "You got the wrong guy. It was some *other* jerk that mouthed off at Aurora. I'm sure this fine gentleman doesn't remember a thing about the conversation last night. Just ask Tristan."

That subtle reminder that Tristan had altered the kid's memory of last night's incident, along with Blake's firm shoulder shake, broke Ayden from his ferocity. He released his forearm and stepped back. The guy dropped.

Blake caught him and smoothed his shirt along with the situation. "Just a case of mistaken identity. Ayden is very sorry. Right, Ayden?" Ayden nodded curtly. "And so am I. So no harm, no foul. We're good?"

The guy rubbed this throat and looked like he might say something harsh, but after a glance at Ayden who still seemed ready to blow, and then cranking his head back to take in the full size of Blake, he shrugged.

"Yeah, we're cool."

"Awesome." Blake slapped the guy's shoulder and led Ayden away.

The crowd, murmuring softly, parted for the guys to pass, then flowed again, drama over, and it took me a few moments to realize Ayden and Blake were heading toward me once more. I spun around and scurried in the other direction, but I was bucking the tide of students, and it hindered my speed. I heard Ayden's voice getting closer.

"Thanks but I don't have time to explain. I'm headed to her Physics class right now. Tristan got me assigned as the T.A. until this Rose thing is over, but make sure you're available."

Great. Even if I gave him the slip, once he got to my class he'd go on Red Alert to come and find me. Already seriously worked up, he'd be on a tear. My skin itched. Felt like cockroaches skittered up my spine. I didn't have much time.

Ayden was saying, "When you take Aurora home after school—"

Since when was Blake taking me home?

"—do *not* mention where I am."

"But I don't know where you are."

"Exactly."

"Hi Blake. Hi Ayden."

"Hello, ladies." I heard the smile in Blake's voice. "Gotcha on my dance card for the Spring Fling. Don't know how I'll survive until then." The girls giggled, and after they passed, Blake nearly did too. So macho. "Dude, I love our new reps. Luna and Danica really did us a solid when they talked us up after we saved them at the concert hall. People — *girls* — actually talk to me now. Don't ruin it by setting some dude on fire. So where did you say you were going after school?"

"I didn't."

"Come on, what could keep you from a hot girl except...I've got it. You're seeing another woman."

"What?!" Ayden did a lot of sputtering.

"Holy crap, look at your face. It *is* another woman! Aren't you the *play-ah*."

I tripped. Nearly fell on my face.

"Blake," Ayden hissed, "that isn't it."

"Then why do you look so guilty? It explains why you've been so on edge."

"I don't— Argh! You need to shut up. I'll tell you everything once I finish off with…my…"

"Other woman?"

"I will kill you."

"You can try. What's her name?"

"If you even mention this to Aurora, I will…"

Ayden's voice faded off as I slipped around a corner and fought the urge to run, but there was no way I could shove through this mob before the guys came into view.

It was hard to breathe. Other woman? Then why defend my honor? Could he really be seeing someone else?

Don't think about that now. I needed a way out.

Several utility closets were along this hall. I pushed through the crowd toward the nearest one, risked a glance behind me — no Ayden and Blake — grasped the long curved handle, shoved down and…

Thumped into the door, my cheek squished flat. It was locked. I jammed the handle up and down a few times — just because I wasn't frustrated enough — then headed to the next closet, then the next. But each was locked.

As sweat beaded on my forehead, my peripheral vision picked up Blake's huge form lumbering around the corner. I turned and barreled forward. The next door was an old, wooden original fixture adorned with wrought iron hinges and thick bands of black iron wrapped horizontally across. With little hope, I grabbed the handle.

It didn't budge. Of course.

I leaned my boiling forehead against one of the cold bands of metal, waiting for a brilliant next move to enter my brain.

The door shuddered with a low hum. The handle quivered in my palm. I heard the metallic *clicks* and *grinds* of gears turning, and just when I was ready to jump back, the handle gave way, the door opened, and I fell into a black pit.

Chapter Nineteen

Okay, not a pit. Just a small, circular windowless alcove in one of the many towers and turrets of the Flint mansion. I hit the stone floor with a painful blow to my elbow then tumbled sideways. Then the door swung shut, and I was left in pitch black.

I scrambled to my feet using my hands on the rough, uneven stone of the walls to steady my progress, then made my way to the door. I breathed with relief when the handle opened easily and I peeked out. No one in the hallway seemed to have noticed my exit. I eased the door shut and waited for the boys to pass.

The darkness was absolute. I blinked, eyes aching for a shred of light. A rushing sound whispered around the room. I cocked my head. Wind? But I didn't feel a breeze.

The sound grew louder, building into a mechanical *whirring*, as if a large machine was lumbering to life after a long hibernation. Gears clicked in a slow rhythm then picked up the pace. The floor rumbled beneath my feet. An oily scent drifted from above, wilting the floral aroma that had followed me in.

Lights of various colors flickered to my left. Just above the door handle, like new buds bursting through the earth, a series of blinking buttons, knobs, and switches appeared on a metal panel which all emerged from within the solid wood of the door.

I sucked in a breath and retreated, back pressed against the wall, heart jumping into double-time.

"Ohhh, no."

The glow from the controls lit up the room. The stone walls seemed to blur. I rubbed my eyes but instead of clearing my vision, I watched the stone shimmer out of existence, replaced by large rectangular sheets of metal. Dark bronze. Shiny. Heavy bolts rimmed the seams holding the pieces together.

I tensed. Someone in the wall stared at me. A black-hooded figure. Wide-eyed and slack-jawed and looking like they were ready to freak out and attack—

Oh. Right. My brain finally calculated the obvious. It was my own reflection in the glimmering walls.

"Please enter destination request." A woman's voice echoed against the metal-lined space.

I ducked, covering my head with my arms, looking for the threat.

Nothing happened. Other than I had the heartbeat of a canary, and my vital organs had turned to mush.

"Please enter destination request," she droned.

My gaze roamed the empty room. "How about the heck outta Dodge."

My head jerked back to the door where, just beyond the hinges, with a loud metallic *clankity-clank-clank*, a wall of one-inch wide metal lattice rolled out from the side and started covering the door.

Caging me in.

The lattice traveled smoothly. Was halfway across the door.

I launched my body up, came down with my full weight on the handle, felt it resist, thought I might break the whole thing off. The lattice rolled into my back, pressing hard.

I braced my foot on the slim edge of the door frame and used my full weight to push back, struggling against the metal threatening to shut me off from freedom.

The lattice kept coming, forcing me forward. I banged on the door.

"Help!"

There was less than eighteen inches before the moving wall would shut me off completely from the door. I was losing ground. And I'd be losing a hand if I didn't let go of the handle which in the next few sec—

The handle dropped, the door opened, and I spurted through.

Careening into another body and bringing us both down.

CHAPTER TWENTY

Light from the stained glass windows stretched a rainbow of colors throughout the elaborate acres of books in Flint's cavernous library. It was as impressive as the rest of his estate with high ceilings, ornately carved wood bookcases, polished and shiny, many built into the walls and reaching two stories. Spiral staircases led to narrow walkways along the higher level. Heavy carpets blanketed the hardwood floors, muffling students' footsteps and any attempt to break the reverent silence.

There were open areas with tables for studying, some casual seating arrangements with comfy chairs and sofas, and several cubicles that housed computers. The place smelled lemony. Surfaces gleamed.

The librarian, Mrs. Caviezel, took her job very seriously, running it like a military contingent, keeping it shipshape using her dogged determination and an army of student volunteers.

Of which my sister Luna was now one. A fact she wanted to keep from my parents — wouldn't tell me why — and the reason she'd agreed to help me find the wall marked with the spirals that was on the parchment.

She'd been looking for me when I fell out of the alcove and knocked her over. Couldn't explain what I'd been doing. Was it one of Flint's gizmos? So much for being turned off. But she was more interested in complaining that I damaged her dangly ear cuff.

Once at the library, she led me deep into the labyrinth of books to a remote room way in the back with no windows. The dark interior had a small rectangular table and desk lamp which provided little illumination.

"This is the section with local info," Luna told me. "All the books are about Gossamer Falls' history and stuff about Flint. Did you know this place was an insane asylum?" She gave a shiver and lowered her voice. "Rumor has it they never got rid of the patient wards in the basements and all the vile torture chamber treatment machines. That's why the lower levels are off limits and locked down tight." She spoke in a haunting, supernatural wail. "Ghosts of the crazies are still trapped down there, wandering secret passageways, fated to relive their torment over and over, and in the dead of night their screams of horror still reverberate through the very foundation."

"Yeah, right." She loves drama.

"You have no imagination." Luna rolled her eyes, then pulled a set of keys from her pocket. "I wonder if my library keys would open up the basements."

After she scurried away, I studied the wall marked on Rose's map. It was about fifteen feet long and ten feet high and had a solidly built-in bookcase.

The wall behind it was made of stone. I ran my hand over all the wooden shelves and then the spines of the thick volumes, many made of smooth leather and all very dusty. I was scanning for…not sure what…the double spiral? But I came up empty.

Something flashed bright white at the corner of my eye, to my right and high up. I jumped and whirled. But nothing was there.

"See," I said to no one, "my imagination's working just fine." I scratched my head and studied the shelves. "What am I supposed to find?"

The books didn't answer. And my spidey senses weren't tingling. So I squatted down, pushed up my sleeves, and started pulling out books from the bottom shelf, moving methodically up to the next shelf, hoping one of the texts turned out to be a lever that opened a secret passageway.

Hey, you never know.

I climbed the shelves to reach the higher levels which made the book pulling slow and awkward because I had to simultaneously hang on. But I kept at it and eventually, behind the books on one of the top shelves, something caught my eye. An etching in the stone wall itself.

A double spiral. Like the one drawn on the parchment.

I smiled. "Bingo."

I scooted closer, moved books aside, and reached out, hovering my hand over the spirals. Something tingled on my palm. I thought I saw the etching move. Weird. Then I felt some kind of heat which didn't make sense. Not that much did these days. I reached my index finger closer and—

"I just left the principal's office."

Matthias stormed in.

My toe slipped off the bottom shelf. I grabbed one edge and hooked my elbow on another to keep from falling. At best, it was precarious.

The Aussie had his back to me, pacing, a phone pressed against his ear.

I held my breath and tried to hold tight, hoping he'd disappear.

No such luck.

He inhaled deep and lowered his voice. "She's fine but…yes, the training worked but now it's a big spectacle and…I don't know, but…uh-huh…right…" His shoulders relaxed and his voice softened. "You're right. Thanks."

Layers of polish on the wood made it slick, which was why my elbow was slipping toward the edge. I tried to scoot it back, squirming as quietly as possible, muscles straining, but for every inch I gained I lost two, and finally, I lost altogether.

I fell with an utter lack of grace. Matthias, on the other hand, in one smooth motion grabbed a book, turned, and flung it. He couldn't have had time to aim, yet the thick hardcover jettisoned straight for my head, ready to conk me into oblivion. His only mistake was not anticipating my stealth maneuver of falling, so it sailed over my skull and crashed into the bookcase as my butt hit the carpet. Not as cushy as I would've liked.

"Bloody hell!" Matthias's eyes blazed. "Are you following me?"

"Of course not." I rubbed my behind and pushed to my feet. "Be quiet or Caviezel will have us both in detention."

Matthias glanced over his shoulder then seemed to remember the phone and ducked it behind his back. "Then what are you doing here?"

"Nothing. What are *you* doing here?"

"Nothing."

We stared at each other for a long moment.

Then I asked, "Who's on the phone?"

He paled. "My…uh…dad." He brought the phone around and spoke into it. "I'll have to call you back…*Dad*." He shot me a nasty look. "No, I'm with Aurora…What?... I'm not *with* Aurora…Don't be…"

I squinted. "Is that a new phone?"

"No." He looked offended. "Same phone. The only one I have. Why would I have a second phone?"

"I happened to get a good look at your phone when you were out cold last night and that's not it."

"You're wrong. Moron. It's the only phone I have."

A phone rang. And not the phone in his hand. Another phone. In his jacket pocket. His regular phone. I recognized the ringtone.

Matthias locked his gaze with mine. I smirked. He closed his eyes and sighed, chin dropping to his chest.

After a moment he spoke into the first phone. "Gotta go." Then he shoved that phone in one pocket and pulled out his regular phone from his other pocket. "What!"

I wasn't sure what was going on, but I sensed I had just gotten some leverage on the Aussie.

"Wait, Ayden." Matthias's irritated expression cleared, and he actually smiled. "What about Aurora? She *ditched* you and you don't know where she is? That's interesting because I think I might be able to help you out with that."

So much for leverage.

I waved my hands and shook my head whispering a frantic, "No, I'm not here!"

Matthias held the phone against his chest and whispered, "And I don't have another phone, right?"

"Fine." I gave him a look. "No second phone."

Matthias got back on with Ayden. "Yeah, I found her."

I stomped my foot. "Really?!"

He rolled his eyes. "She's in the library. She didn't ditch you. Luna needed her help. Everything's fine. Go to class. I'll make sure she gets to P.E." He ended the call and turned his attention back in my direction. "Do I need to know what you're doing here?"

"No." I brushed past him. "But you might want to check out a certain alcove on the second floor. I think something of Flint's still lives."

"Great. What did you do now?"

"It wasn't me."

"It never is."

I made my way out of the library and down the hall toward the gym, Matthias right on my tail.

"I can get there myself."

He didn't answer, didn't look at me, just made a dismissive "keep going" gesture.

If he didn't leave, I couldn't double-back and figure out what was up with the spiral. Usually wasn't hard to get the Aussie to keep his distance. There had to be something I could …

I flipped my hair back and smiled over my shoulder.

"Just can't get enough of me, huh? First the kidnapping then following me to the library and now the gym."

"I didn't…do any of that."

"Jeez, Matthias. I get it. You adore me."

He snorted. "You are a certifiable loon."

"But you keep following me which just proves how deeply you've fallen for—"

The lights went out. People screamed and raced around in the total darkness of the windowless hallway. The walls and floors shuddered and groaned, like the entire building was some stone giant waking from a deep slumber.

Something slammed me up against the wall.

"Get off!" I pounded my fists, fighting for freedom, but the monster was made of brute force and brawn, and rigid as rock.

And it wasn't letting go.

CHAPTER TWENTY-ONE

"Shut it!" Matthias hissed in my ear. "Stay still."

Oh. The Aussie had me pinned. His chest was rising and falling at a rapid rate, muscles flexed into granite. At first, he got jostled from the running crowd while protecting me from the fray, but then he used his power of seeing in the dark to shove off people before they even got close.

"Did you do this?" I tried to scratch my nose.

"No," he snapped. "I said *stay still.*"

"Then quit moving your head. Your hair is tickling my nose. It's getting really long."

"Well sor-*ry*, but I'm scanning for threats trying to save your worthless hide."

"If it's so worthless, why are you trying to save it?"

"Because I'm an idiot."

"Finally we agree." I sniffed. "Are you wearing cologne?" It was nice, but I wasn't about to tell him that.

"Shut—"

The school stilled. Lights came on. The crazed crowd froze, looked around with anticipation, then as the lights stayed on, they relaxed. Someone starting hooting, others clapped. Matthias kept me covered, his hair still wisping across my face. I thought I was going to sneeze.

Three girls in my P.E. class walked by and one of them, Katie, our local basketball star, who towered over even me, lightly backhanded Matthias's shoulder.

"Jeez, you two. Get a room."

Matthias looked as if he'd just drank sewage. He quickly shoved off the wall — and me — but kept monitoring the immediate area.

"What was that?" I asked.

"Don't know, but I don't like it. I'll get Blake or Jayden and check it out." He grabbed my bicep and gave me a forceful push. "Right after I drop you off."

We walked for a while then I said over my shoulder, "Why don't you go take care of it now? Could be serious. I can get myself to P.E."

"Just keep moving."

He dug his fingers into my back and shoved me forward.

"Ow!" I grabbed my calf, hopped a few steps to the side, and leaned on the wall. "Shoot. Must have pulled something when I fell in the library." I massaged my leg. "But, hey, don't let me slow you down. Get the guys and take care of things. I'll, uh, rest a minute then get to the gym. Unless," I reached out a hand and grasped his wrist, my look pleading and pathetic "you want to carry me the rest of the way?"

He looked at my hand on his arm, then back at me, his grey eyes cold and flat. "I don't think so." He shook off my grip. "You can manage."

"Yeah, sure. You go…save stuff."

I waited until he turned his back before I smiled. Such a sap. My phony damsel in distress routine got him every time. Brilliant. Now I just had to double-back and—

Matthias whirled around and scooped me up into his arms so fast my lungs *whooshed* out all air.

He caught the look on my face and smirked. "Not this time."

I glowered. "Think you're so smart."

"Smarter than you." He headed down the hallway.

I squirmed. "Let me down."

His grip became steel. "Oh, no. You wanted to play this game. Let's play." He picked up the pace and pushed through the crowd speaking very loud. "Excuse me! Watch out! Coming through."

We got a lot of looks and several wolf whistles as he carried me through the halls.

"I hate you," I muttered under my breath.

That made him smile.

"I said I'd get you to P.E. and now," he shouldered open the swinging door to the girls' locker room and literally threw me in, "you're at P.E. Whatever you do from here, don't make it my problem."

As my butt *thumped* to a stop on the cold linoleum, I ripped off my shoe and threw it at him, but it only hit the door which had already closed behind the annoying Aussie.

"Jerk." I got up and found the three girls that had seen us in the hallway staring all moony-eyed where Matthias was last seen.

"He is so cool," said Mika, a short brunette who seemed incredibly shy but worked diligently as the editor and photojournalist for the school paper, and all around Gossip Central. The other two girls nodded.

"You can have him," I muttered.

"Don't we wish," sighed Katie. She picked up my shoe, handed it to me, and gave me a hand up, smiling easily. "But when Mika asked for an interview about saving your sister in L.A., he shut her down cold. She did manage to get a few photos before he ditched her. Keeps them on her bedroom wall." She turned to Mika. "Aurora might not appreciate that."

Mika blushed.

"Don't worry about me." Jeez, did everyone in this town have a stalker wall?

The third girl, Natasha, was our head cheerleader who also happened to be captain of the debate team, founder and captain of the archery team, president of the chess club, *and* class president. Such an over-achieving configuration I figured she had to be some sort of supernatural being.

Or I was jealous.

Behind her thick black frame glasses that somehow managed to be cool instead of nerdy, she narrowed big, dark Indian-from-India eyes at me. "I thought you were dating Ayden."

"So did I." Although at this point, it may not be as exclusively as I thought.

The girls circled me.

Natasha pushed her not-nerdy glasses up on her nose. "Because he denied my request for a dance at the Spring Fling. Said they were all for you."

"That's what he told me too," said Mika.

Katie rolled her eyes. "That's what he told *everyone*."

I found myself smiling. "Oh, well, that's good."

"So if you're dating him, what's going on with Matthias?" Natasha asked.

Mika cooed, "And the other dreamy Hex Boys?"

Then just because she could — stupid taller-than-me girl — Katie gave me a playful tap on the head. "Yeah, when are you going to share? Give up at least one of them."

"Trust me," I laughed. "It's not like that."

Katie's blonde ponytail swung as she tilted her head. "That's what you keep saying, but you never tell us what it *is* like."

Natasha removed her glasses and began nibbling the end of one ear piece. "Come on, Aurora. Give us *something*."

Mika smiled slyly. "Or some*one*."

There was a collective gigglefest.

I folded my arms and smiled. Usually, I brushed off the questions I got from girls about the Hex Boys, but today a delightful thought slipped into my head.

"Okay. Actually," I looked over my shoulder and lowered my voice, "there is something you might be interested in."

The girls eagerly huddled around and minutes later as I finished giving my new BFFs *The Scoop*, the gym door opened and another girl poked her head in, face flushed, eyes bright.

"Oh, my God!" she squealed. "You have got to see our substitute teacher. He's so hot!" Then she disappeared.

The rest of the girls in the locker room dashed to the door and peeked out.

"She's right!" Katie confirmed.

"Ladies, please join us." The deep voice came from within the gym.

The girls shoved and fought each other for who would get out the door first.

I ran too, but stopped short when I looked out the door. "Oh, no."

CHAPTER TWENTY-TWO

Holding a clipboard and wearing a blue track suit, baseball cap, hightops, a pencil behind one ear, and an orange whistle hanging from a lanyard around his neck, Rose ushered students toward the door that led to the outdoor fields. He gave me a brief glance and winked before returning his attention to the class.

"Yes, I'll be there shortly, but now everyone, especially you lovely ladies, make sure young Logan gets that dance class started. I hear he's quite the Fred Astaire."

"Who's that?" someone asked.

"Oh, my," Rose breathed a weary sigh.

After the gym emptied, Rose strode over. I considered running but had a scary thought. I met him halfway and thumped his shoulder with my fist.

"What'd you do with Coach Slader? He better be okay or I will—"

Coach Slader burst out of the boys' locker room wearing street clothes and slapped Rose on the back as he rushed by.

"Thanks again! What luck you happened to be here visiting when they insisted I bring in the car right now or forfeit the claim. Idiots."

"Coach," I said, "you okay?"

"It's that stupid insurance company demanding another investigator see it for themselves. They never believe me. How would I know how some hoodlums covered my car in lava?" He backed out the door. "I was inside the restaurant enjoying a plate of spaghetti!"

"Oh, boy," I sighed. "I'm so sorry."

Coach disappeared without hearing me, but Rose raised a brow. "Something you want to tell me?"

"Get lost."

"Interesting." Rose plucked the pencil from his ear and scribbled something on the clipboard. "Now perhaps you'd like to take another crack at the library?"

"How did you know about that?"

"You should hurry. I'm not sure how long I can keep young Logan occupied."

"If I go, you promise no one gets hurt?"

"Not by my hand today." He bowed deeply and his expression turned serious. "I swear upon my solemn oath. And in my world, that means something."

I was halfway out the door when he said, "Although…"

"What now?"

"With all this," he swept a graceful hand from his head to his toes, "I cannot promise that hearts will not be broken."

CHAPTER TWENTY-THREE

I weaved through the library and toward the back room, taking Rose's map from my backpack, studying it like I could find answers. Didn't happen. I almost made it to the Flint section when the girls working the counter said, "Hi Ayden!"

Oh, come on! I skidded a sharp right and hunkered down, peeking through shelves.

Ayden strode past the front desk. "Ladies. Don't you all look especially radiant today."

They giggled like toddlers. Pushovers.

"Ayden, could you help us put some books away on the taller shelves?"

"Can't. Sorry." He faced them but walked backwards, arms spread wide. "I'm on a mission. Maybe you can help. Did you happen to see a stunning redhead? Tall, leggy. I call her my goddess of a girlfriend."

More giggles. From me. Pull it together, Aurora.

"She just headed back there," one of the traitors told him. "Is Matthias with you?"

"Not my day to watch him. Check with Blake."

They laughed. "We will."

I jammed the map into my back pocket and took off along the far wall of a remote back aisle at high speed. But not high enough. I felt Ayden's presence behind me.

"There's my—"

"Goddess," I snorted and kept moving. "Yeah, yeah. I heard."

"Where are you running off to? Although, thanks." I heard the smile in his voice. "The view is *pleasurable*."

"Oh, for—" I shoved my backpack over my behind.

"Ahhh, that's just cruel."

I whirled around and walked backwards. "Would you please—"

"Full frontal." His smile broadened. "That works too."

"Don't—! Oh, forget it." I grabbed a book off the shelf and ruffled the pages to hide my smile.

"You know you love it." He sauntered down the aisle, a mischievous grin on his face. "The chase. The bated breath of anticipation as you wait for me to track you down. It's the only explanation for why you ducked out of P.E. to hide in the most isolated part of the library *without* your smokin' hot boyfriend."

"You need to let that one go." But I laughed.

As he neared, the scent of sandalwood and leather came with him, the aroma slinking into my subconscious and acting like a drug to ease my tension and chase away doubt.

He stood close. I felt his gaze upon me. I tried to control my breathing but my out-of-control heartbeat wasn't helping. I stared at the pages of the book, words blurred and shaky. Kind of like my emotions.

His hand stroked my cheek. "Imagine the things we could do."

I closed my eyes as a few thoughts came to mind. More than a few. Between my lascivious imagination and his gentle touch, heat took no time infiltrating my cheeks.

Suddenly, his mouth was brushing my cheek, trailing kisses over my skin. Then his lips tickled my lobe as he spoke next to my ear, his voice low and smooth, a gentle caress.

"And what a pleasure it would be for us to do more than just imagine." He nuzzled my neck. "But to generate that kind of heat takes energy and to create energy you need sustenance." His teeth nipped softly, and I shivered. "So I thought it prudent to provide one of your favorites."

He leaned away and tossed something at me. After some spastic juggling, I held the yellowish-green pear in my hands.

"Got myself an apple." Ayden held up a shiny red fruit, his grin wicked. "Because I love a good temptation."

He took a generous bite and chewed slowly, leaning up against the bookcase. And looking himself to be quite edible. I shuddered my breathing back to normal and did my best to ignore the chill I felt since he backed away. The pear tasted juicy and sweet, although I was sure nowhere near as yummy as the Hex Boy staring me down.

"So," he said with an all-too-knowing look, "fess up."

I studied my fruit with great intent. "About what?"

"Oh, come on." Ayden's tone took on a frustrated edge as he rested both hands against the shelves just outside my shoulders, standing way too close for me to keep my wits about me. "Enough with the secrets. Give it up on whatever shady, secretive mission you've been up to."

"Don't know what you're talking about."

One hand dropped to my shoulder, slid down my arm, and snuck into the curve of my waist. He pulled me close. I felt his body, hard and unyielding. Once again, my heart tried to escape from beneath my ribs.

"Perhaps," he said, breath hot on my cheek, "I could find some way to lower your defenses. Some way to make you divulge your secrets from these very…luscious lips." His index finger slowly traced the outline of my mouth.

The touch jolted through me. My hand convulsed around the pear so tight that juice trickled between my fingers. "Ah, I don't have…any…"

His voice deepened. "Or perhaps I'll simply find that your covert operation has something…"

His knuckle slipped under my chin, tipped it up. Then his warm lips touched softly on mine. Once. Twice. Oh, the delicious taste of him. His breath still sweet from the forbidden fruit.

Sparks lit up my spine, tickled the back of my neck. As I waited for the charm of a third kiss, the hand on my waist slid down, over my hip. Then it dipped lower, slipping through the curve of my back…and lower still. I held my breath, wondering how far he planned to go with this current…exploration. How far I'd let it. Because so far, it was all-systems-go and if—

"Something to do…with this." Ayden snatched the map out of my back pocket and spun away.

Chapter Twenty-Four

"No!" I lunged, grabbing for it, but he moved easily out of my grasp.

He opened the map and held it high. I hopped vigorously, trying to snatch it, but he kept it just out of reach. He wrapped an arm around me, quelling my jack-rabbit routine, the iron grip holding our bodies together as one.

He said with amusement, "That's better."

Not really.

Because as he studied the paper, his expression disintegrated from amused to…seriously *less than* amused. By the time he glanced down at me, one could say it was downright hostile.

He spoke slowly, clearly attempting to control his emotions. "*Where* did you get this?"

Better than "Oh my god, you're the Divinicus," but not by much.

"Give it back."

Ayden grabbed my arms and pinned me up against the wall, the paper crackling as the map crushed in his hand. His gaze held me as much as any vise. Heat was rising, swirls of warm air ruffling my hair, heightening that enticing scent of sandalwood emanating off his skin.

"Where?" Jaw muscles jumbled in knots. His voice hardened. "It was Rose, wasn't it?" His eyes searched my face.

I cleared my throat. "Yes, but—"

He pushed away.

"You ditched me to do his bidding?" Both hands raked through his hair. "It could be a *trap*. Dangerous. How can you trust some stranger over…over *me*?"

"It's not like that."

"That's exactly what it's like." His eyes blazed. "How could you?"

"It's the kidnapping." Logan came around the corner. "She's still freaked. Doesn't trust us."

I shook my head. "That's not true." …exactly. Man, I wish I could tap dance. "It's just that you guys have your priorities and—"

"Yes!" Ayden whirled on me. "And *my* priority is *you!*" He paused. Looked away and gripped the back of his neck. "I mean, you're," his arm made a wild gesture toward Logan, "*our* priority. Keeping you safe and…"

"Don't worry," Logan picked up the book I'd dropped and replaced it on the shelf. "Nissa was on watch."

"Nissa?" I said.

"My guardian." Logan offered me his pocket handkerchief so I could clean up from the half-squished pear. "Looks like a firefly."

As I wiped my fingers, I remembered the flash of light, and wondered how much she'd seen.

Ayden scowled. "We agreed to keep our guardians away from Aurora."

"Why?" I asked.

"They're sworn to protect us," Ayden said reluctantly. "And if they deem you a threat, they could bypass our commands and turn you in to the Mandatum."

Peachy. Like I didn't have enough threats over my head.

"Relax," Logan said as he pulled out another handkerchief from inside his coat and arranged it neatly in the breast pocket of his sport coat. "She only reported Aurora's whereabouts, then I dismissed her. When the substitute disappeared and I couldn't find Aurora, I came here."

I winced in anticipation of my next revelation. "The substitute…that was Rose."

Ayden gave me a deadeye stare. "So now you're working with him?"

"No!" Jeez this was a mess.

"She had this." Ayden handed the map to Logan.

He nodded, and they both almost sprinted for the back of the library. In the Flint section they started checking through the books on the wall.

At the wrong end.

"Ah, screw it," I muttered. It wasn't like they weren't going to find it. I climbed up the shelves and pushed books aside, uncovering the etching. They were too busy to notice. "It's over here."

Logan turned.

Ayden kept searching through books. "What is?"

"The drawing." I looked closely at the spirals. As my fingers moved closer it definitely moved. Kind of pulsed darker and expanded *out* of wall. I waved my hand over it. Felt the heat again, and a pull, like a magnet. "It feels really weird."

"Aurora, don't." Logan stepped toward me, a hand up.

We all heard a click. My palm prickled.

A blast of heat exploded from the wall. Like a zombie bursting to life from a grave, a metal hand burst through the stone.

I screamed, reeled back, and lost my footing. But I didn't fall because the thin fingers of the skeletal robot hand grasped my wrist and forced my palm down over the spirals. My shoulder nearly pulled out of the socket as I dangled above the ground.

Suddenly there was no wall. Nothing made of stone, anyway, just a web of snaking metal that *click-clacked* and slithered and opened a gaping black hole in the center. My heart constricted. My free hand clawed at the monster fingers around my arm, but the metal held me trapped.

"Aurora!" Ayden sounded far away.

I turned my head. Wind blasted. The roar filled my ears. Ayden flew back. Books tumbled on top of him until he was completely buried.

I tried to go to him, but like the legs of some alien spider robot, shiny cords of metal burst from the black pit in the wall and snapped around me. The wind increased, howling and swirling into a ferocious tornado. My hair whipped across my face. The metal tentacles tightened their bonds and catapulted me into depths of darkness.

CHAPTER TWENTY-FIVE

An abrupt stop. I was dropped on my feet. But between my head spinning and being surrounded by pitch black — no matter how hard I blinked for focus — I gave up the fight for balance and let my knees buckle.

My palms flattened on a floor of cool earth. A loud *ca-chunking* sound was followed by light. Some old Victorian-looking lamps dripped along the walls and came to life, one by one, vibrating with a low hum, a muted amber light illuminating a few yards down either side of a tunnel. The walls were neatly bricked with stone of varying shades of gray and brown. Further down, the cold and musty passageway curved out of sight.

Great, I was trapped in Flint's tunnels with the ghosts of crazies reliving their torment. And screams of terror. How could I forget that?

Stupid Luna.

At least my arm was still attached.

I stood, slipping on small pieces of rock. Maybe broken off when I came through, but there was no more hole. I pressed my ear to the wall and slapped my hand upon it, yelling, "Ayden!"

Something grabbed my shoulder. I screamed and threw an elbow.

Logan ducked out of the way. "Easy. Just me."

"Jeez!" I slumped. Attempted to swallow my heart back down. "Where's Ayden?"

"Still in the library." Logan licked his lips. "I think."

"How did you get in here?"

"Joined the wind before the door closed."

"What?" I remembered the wind, but no door. I rubbed my forehead. Things were still fuzzy.

Logan studied the stone wall we'd just come through. Another double spiral was carved into the rock.

He pointed at it and said, "Touch it again."

I flinched back. "No thanks. Once was a way bad enough idea."

"Come on, Aurora." Logan rubbed his hand over it. Nothing happened. "I think it's our way back in."

"Warning." The woman's voice came out of nowhere. "Mandatum infiltration. Proceed to sanctuary."

I twirled a quick circle, but saw no one. Logan had his bow drawn, an arrow of compressed air ready to fly. His eyes glowed white in the dim yellow light.

"What is that?" I whispered. "I heard the same voice when I was stuck in the alcove."

"Don't know." His voice was low and tight. "Matthias said he couldn't find anything weird in the alcove. We'll figure it out later. Now, since you're not hurt," he indicated my hand, "touch it and try to get us out of here."

I blew air between my clenched teeth and moved a tentative hand over the spiral, ready to bolt, but…nothing. I wiggled my fingers, moved them closer. No response. I placed my palm over the etching. Slapped. Then pushed. A cool sensation breathed goosebumps up my arm.

"Warning," the voice repeated. "Mandatum infiltration. Proceed to sanctuary."

One of the lamps puffed smoke. A baseball-sized piece of gray metal popped out, hovering above the light. Rows of spikes *clicked* onto the ball's surface, each kicking out a flame.

Then, because it wasn't lethal enough, the orb's surface started rotating like a mini buzz saw, and then the thing flew directly at us.

Logan's arrow hit dead-on and shattered the orb into a burst of flame. Embers cascaded to the ground. Nice shot, except a dozen more fiery metal balls were clicking to life above the lamps along the hall and heading our way.

"Hurry, Aurora!" He kept shooting and exploding more spikey fireballs. "Before things get worse!"

"It's not working!" I tried rubbing. Hard. The rough stone, with plenty of sharp edges, scraped and sliced my hand raw. I was bleeding, but I kept rubbing until—

Heat bubbled under my hand. I pulled away. Swallowed.

Logan shouted something, but I couldn't hear him. I was too busy staring.

In horror.

My blood had seeped into the etching, and was flowing, in some bizarre, anti-gravity sort of way, back and forth from one end of the spiral to the other, a bright red, angry river. Oh, and that blood?

It was boiling.

A steam-rising-off, bubbling, full-blown *boil.*

"Warning," the female disembodied voice intoned. "Blood contract activated."

Logan backed into me with a sharp bump. "What happened?"

"Things just got worse."

Chapter Twenty-Six

The floor rumbled under our feet.

"What did you do?" Logan yelped.

"I don't know!" I ducked behind Logan as sparks flew.

The spike balls increased in number and speed. Logan kept up. Sparks, flames, flying embers. The hallway lit-up like a Fourth of July sky. The caustic smell burned my nostrils and when it hit my throat, brought a fit of coughing. I covered my mouth.

Logan's concentration was absolute, never missing a shot.

"If I keep this up, the whole place might explode," he said.

Contrary to popular belief, I did not like a good explosion.

I picked up the largest of the rocks that littered the ground and chucked them at the flaming metal balls.

"What are you doing?" Logan said.

"Going low-tech."

While the rocks didn't explode the metal fireballs, like Logan's cool trick, my Lahey star-pitcher moves knocked several to the ground where they rolled to a stop, flames sputtering out.

"Good work," Logan said.

"Thanks, but I'm running out of rocks and I can't get the wall to open! What do we do?"

"I'm thinking." Logan's eyes flicked constantly. "Okay. Run to the opposite side of the tunnel and get down. On the count of three, I'm going to blow the wall."

"But—"

"One."

I bolted across and thumped into the wall. "Maybe we should rethink—"

"Two."

Guess not. I hunched in the fetal position as Logan swung around so his back was to me.

"Three!"

He pulled the bow string taut. Not just one but *six* arrows appeared lined up in the bow. He let them fly all at once straight at the wall. As soon as they released, Logan's bow disappeared in a puff of smoke. He jerked an arm up and dove toward me. A gale force wind blew straight up, acting like a shield as he dropped his body over mine.

The arrows hit with a great, thundering noise and massive shake. But instead of blowing out the wall, the force ricocheted back at us in double-time.

Logan had anticipated a blast from the explosion, and created the counter force shield of air to protect us. However, he didn't bargain for the wall not blowing out, causing the full force of his attack coming back at us. The immense blowback slammed us so hard we literally rolled sideways up the tunnel wall, until we struck the ceiling, then flopped back down.

I fell on top of Logan who had wrapped himself around me. Sure he missed coverage by more than a few inches, but it was the thought that counted, and his body did cushion my roller-coaster ride up the wall and consequent fall. My hands over my ears had kept me from going deaf. Hopefully.

I pushed up. Dust thickened the air. Debris *clinked* or drifted down.

Logan wasn't moving. Eyes closed. Face smudged with dirt.

And blood.

"Logan?" I batted away the flameless scrap metal of the spikey balls glittering amid the rubble around us and shook him, coughing on the dust and dirt coating my throat. "Logan!"

I checked my panic, then his pulse, and breathed easier. Unconscious, yes, but breathing normally, and his heartbeat *th-thumped* strong and steady. I convinced myself that he wasn't any paler than usual. Seriously, how could I tell?

A low *whirr* ruffled my hair. Dots of flame glowed in the clouds of dusts. Another spikey ball was tearing right at us. Fast.

I scrambled in front of Logan, pinning his prone form against the wall behind us. I raised my palm, hoping my explody power would make a grand entrance, but just in case grabbed a rock to club the flying orb out of the air. It raced closer. I could see the fire glint orange-red off the spikes, waited for it to get closer so I could strike.

I swung. And missed.

Crap!

I braced for a fiery, skin-shredding impact.

Through the fog of my broken eardrums, I heard a weird hissing, but I didn't *seem* to be on fire. Or getting flayed alive.

I opened one eye.

Three spikeballs hovered just out of arms reach. They had stopped inches from my hands, still flaming. I opened the other eye. I could see a patchwork of rivets beneath the spikes.

"Warning. Mandatum—"

"There is no intruder!" I shouted to the faceless wonder wench.

The spikeballs rose high, like a rearing horse ready to stomp me down. The flames went out. The spikes *clicked* back into the balls and they all somehow folded in on themselves until they were smooth spheres about an inch in diameter. They dropped from the air.

I caught one, of course. Stupid! Stupid!

I chucked it across the tunnel. Something *thumped* onto my chest.

"Ack!" I slapped the glittering globes to the ground and kicked them away. They scattered off harmlessly then all three changed course and rolled back. I got to my feet, stepped away. They followed like I was some sort of mama duck.

"Flattering, but I've already got an entourage," I muttered.

I spit the grit from my mouth, kneeled, and pulled the linen handkerchief from Logan's suit pocket to clean off the trickle of blood along his temple. Just a scratch above his brow. I felt a bump on his head, but no other visible injuries.

As I stuffed his handkerchief back in, I felt a lump inside his coat pocket. I pulled out his cell phone, but…no service.

Shocker.

The woman droned on in an annoyingly calm voice. "Breach neutralized. Sentinel in transit. Proceed to sanctuary. Await assistance."

As the dust cleared I saw the tunnel wall was intact. Logan's blast hadn't made a dent in the stone. There was no escape.

A rumble. A rising hum. I braced for another attack, covered Logan. But all that followed was a series of *ca-chunk, ca-chunks* as the Victorian lamps turned on down one end of the tunnel, lighting as far as I could see. As if beckoning me to follow.

Then the blood from my hand, which had been boiling in the spiral, crawled up the wall like some thin red wormy serpent, and trailed down the tunnel via the ceiling. It slithered a few yards, then stopped, shimmering and swirling from side to side, but going no further.

Options? Well, the arrows hadn't worked. At least the spikeballs had stopped. Did I just sit here and wait?

The lights along the wall flickered.

"Proceed to sanctuary."

Obeying the bossy, disembodied voice wasn't my first choice, But sanctuary sounded good. So did assistance. Especially for Logan.

I stood, hauling Logan onto my shoulder and shifting him to a somewhat comfortable position, hoping this *sanctuary* wasn't far.

"Proceed to—"

"Yeah, I heard you," I snapped loudly to drown out her annoying voice then picked up a rock. "And you'd better be right."

Chapter Twenty-Seven

Despite Logan's small frame, my shoulders were on fire. Despite the cold, my clothes clung with sweat. And despite my dry throat, I didn't risk drinking the water that trickled down the walls of the tunnel as I delved deeper into the pit.

Of despair.

Okay, I was being dramatic, but there was no sign of sanctuary, and the air just kept getting heavier, mustier, and wetter. At times the tunnel opened up and a rushing stream babbled alongside the path before disappearing into the rock.

I'd been trudging for what seemed like hours, following the trail of light. And blood. Once I started moving, my blood on the ceiling had kept a steady pace in front of me. Little creepy. I also wasn't too thrilled by my faithful golden ducklings rolling behind me. I flinched every time the deactivated spikeballs *clinked* and *dinged.* I was still worried they were going to attack.

The lights seemed to be leading me in a straight shot, no turns or corners, but it was hard to tell. If they went out and I had to double-back, Logan and I could be lost forever. I'd just passed through a dark intersection when I heard the shouts.

"No bloody way!"

I stopped. "Matthias?"

I retraced my steps. The intersection was a round chamber with six tunnels shooting off in different directions. Four of them were dark.

"Try that again, you crazy bugger!"

It *was* the Aussie. As much as I hated him, I was glad to hear his voice.

"Oh, no you don't. I'm— Ow! Bollocks! Now you asked for it!"

Thrashing sounds. A whip *cracked.* An angry, glass shattering squeal followed. Along with sounds of a battle.

That Matthias wasn't winning.

I couldn't run with Logan on my shoulder, but I tried. Following the tunnel that echoed the Aussie's cries the loudest.

Of course the tunnel dead-ended. Must've taken the wrong one. I started to turn.

"You bloody son of a—Ugh!"

I whirled. Nope, Matthias was definitely on the other side of this wall. I set Logan down and lightly tapped his face.

"Hey, wake up."

Nothing.

I tapped — okay, slapped — harder. "Logan!"

The fighting sounds were getting worse. Matthias's grunts increased. So did his colorful language. And my anxiety. My body started to prickle. I was tired and scared, and he needed to wake *up*!

"*Logan!*"

I grabbed his shoulders. The contact came with a flash of light from my hands. His body jolted, eyes flew open.

I jumped back, let go. "What did I do?!"

He flopped to the ground, coughing. Alive. I breathed easier.

Logan pushed back his hair, streaking blood into the neon white, and looked around.

"What happened?" He touched his chest. "Ow."

"Matthias is in trouble."

I helped him up, and he cocked his head as the battle sounds echoed.

Logan put his ear up against the wall, slid his hands over the stone, eyes roaming the space. "I've never seen these tunnels before. I don't know where we are."

Oh, great. Why did I expect good news? We'd be lost forever.

The ground trembled. Logan jumped back as rock crumbled and trickled down the cave wall. Keeping his eyes forward, he gestured me to retreat. The ground shook harder. More and more stone fell from above.

I covered my head with my arms. "What's happening?"

"Not sure."

His translucent bow and arrow materialized in his hands. His eyes swirled pale like they were whipping cream. He aimed at the wall.

We heard a muffled screech and the wall shook as if a wrecking ball crashed into the other side. Fissures cracked in the stone, spidered out.

Something was coming through.

"Get out!" Logan yelled.

I wanted to comply, but my muscles revolted. I was too tired to run.

A small tornado whirled around Logan and levitated him a foot off the ground. As the tornado carried him backwards toward me, four more arrows appeared in his bow. Cool.

Another mighty blow hit, and the wall gave up, shattered like a pane of glass, as a deranged demon with eyes the blistering yellow of a sun flare burst through.

Suddenly, I wasn't too tired to run. But the blast threw me off my feet. I landed on my stomach, lungs collapsing, and rolled sideways, ducking behind a pile of fallen rock, fighting to suck in precious air.

Pulverized stone along with pieces of sharp, twisted metal rained down, *clanging* against the rock around me.

I stayed low as the creature with the head the size of a minivan and the body of a giant centipede barreled toward Logan. The valiant Hex Boy remained levitating, arrows poised, and held his ground, letting the demon get closer…and closer…waiting to shoot the arrows because—

Who the heck knew? It was stupid!

"Logan, shoot!"

He did. Five arrows flew. But three pinged harmlessly off the demon's side, and the two that buried in its flesh didn't seem to stop it at all.

Logan reloaded and—

"No!" came the guttural command.

Four black ropes shot through the opening, whipped around the demon's body, and stopped it in its tracks.

Matthias stepped through the broken wall.

Scowling, scraped, scratched, bloody, dark hair caked with dirt and stringy with sweat, T-shirt ripped, and eyes filled with fathomless black, the Aussie strained at the end of the black ropes. Or as I called them, his shadow whips.

"Shove off! This nasty bugger is mine!" The demon lurched and nearly jerked Matthias off his feet. He grunted a crazed smile at Logan. "On second thought, mate, maybe you could give me a hand getting him back to the portal."

Logan dropped to his feet and said, "Stay back."

The white-haired wonder studied the demon, rolled his shoulders, then brought his bow and arrow up, holding steady. At the last second he shifted his aim to the left.

The arrow pinged off the wall and ricocheted back toward the demon. Instead of piercing flesh, the arrow arced around the demon in a spiraling rotation down the body. It created a whirlwind, encapsulating the demon and lifting if off the ground, swaddled like a babe in the eye of Logan's tornado.

The arrow made one final pass to swirl once around Matthias, ruffling his sweaty hair, before evaporating in wisps of pearly smoke.

"That's new." Matthias commented, grunting a pull on the shadow whips and dragging the centimole with relative ease along on a cushion of air. "Something you been working on?"

Logan blushed. "Well, you know, just trying to, uh, change things up."

The bow disappeared as Logan followed Matthias, readjusting his suit coat.

"I like it," Matthias said. "So where did you and the nitwit come from?"

I came out of hiding and lifted one side of my lip in a sneer. He sneered back. So mature.

Logan shook his head. "Craziest thing…"

He got Matthias up to speed as they dragged the monster, kicking and screaming but held tight by the wind, back through the hole and down the corridor. I started to follow, but the golden spheres were hot on my heels. Would they go after the Aussie? It wouldn't pain me, but I scooped them up and dropped them in my pocket. I hurried to catch up with the guys at what I hoped was a safe distance, trying to keep out of the demon's line of sight because it seriously creeped me out.

I hated bugs.

Even when they weren't ten feet tall, had a segmented body longer than a bus, and looked like a supernaturally overgrown, demonic centipede. Why couldn't demons ever be pretty?

Undulating from each body section were dozens of thin, pointy yellow legs, layered with sharp spikes. The body was covered, in part, by scales — more like armor plates — and the rest sprouted thick, chestnut fur lined with jagged black stripes.

The head, other than the six glowing yellow eyes, resembled a mole's. Long and conical with a pointy nose and long whiskers. The ears stuck out like rolled-up pieces of pink leather, and next to them protruded two very long...horns, I guess, but they acted more like arms and ended in some nasty looking pinchers. One of the pinchers was tied shut with a black whip, but the repeated *click-click* of the other was an ominous sound.

When its yellow eyes tracked me, a low growl rumbled in its throat. I felt a serious need to itch. Everywhere. I did my best to angle myself out of the beady eyes' reach.

We lumbered along for a while and eventually entered a massive cave. My neck craned to take it all in.

Over his shoulder, Logan smiled at my awe. "Welcome to the portal."

Chapter Twenty-Eight

It was an oblong, basketball stadium kind of space. Maybe bigger. The domed ceiling, some thirty feet high, gave it an illusion of greater grandeur.

Stalactites hung from above looking like the gnarled fingers of an ancient giant. They pulsed with inner light that bathed the room in an eerie glow reflected in the pool of clear aqua blue water below. Liquid dripped off their tips, and small ripples fanned out on the pool's steaming, lightly bubbling surface. The entire space was warm and humid with a faint aroma of sulfur.

Matthias wiped sweat off his brow. "The pool started bubbling and the place has been a sauna ever since this bloody runt broke through."

He gestured across the cave at a massive metal, net-like structure that fed out from the ceiling to the floor, some twenty feet in front of the portal. Made of wide latticed-metal strips, it weaved together in a variety of colors from bright silver to dull steel, shiny bronze and glittering copper. Part medieval castle drawbridge, part net. Only instead of butterflies, it caught monsters.

"Ripped through it like it was friggin' paper." Matthias pointed at a huge gaping hole in the center. "Never seen that before. And tough to kill. Kept breaking my lines, making a run for it. But may have something to do with Rose, so we keep it alive for now. Maybe we can use it against him."

The metal structure looked like it could hold back a tank, but the hole said otherwise. Through it, I had an uninterrupted view of the far stone wall.

At least I think it was stone. Currently, it shimmered in and out of focus, blurring periodically like it was trying to transform into something else. Or it was trying to dissolve.

When Logan cut off the wind around the demon, the creature dropped onto its side. Matthias immediately pounced on one of the mid-sections. Muscles bulging and straining through the barely-there remains of his tattered shirt, he quickly had the squirming demon hogtied with dozens of shadow whips.

Matthias smiled a grin that dimpled his red cheeks.

"This one was almost a challenge," he said to Logan, then turned to me. The dimples disappeared. "Quit touching things you shouldn't."

I rolled my eyes. "Shut up. I'm the one who found you so you owe me."

From atop the demon, the Aussie cracked a whip at my feet. I jumped back with a yelp and glared at him.

"Stop it!"

He did it again.

"Ow! You got my toe!"

"I was aiming for your face." His dimples were back. "This time I won't miss."

As Matthias lifted his arm for another "crack" at me — jerk — the beast squealed and struggled beneath him, forcing the Aussie to bend his knees surfer style to ride it out. The demon flung its head side to side. Thick webs of drool slung across the cave and stuck to the walls like just-cooked spaghetti.

Logan stepped in front of me and into a shooting stance, slowly readying his bow with six arrows. "Aurora, get to safe ground."

Like I knew where that was in this labyrinth of Crazytown.

The creature's low growl amplified to frenzied-screech levels in zero point scare-me-silly seconds. Rock cracked and pebbles crumbled off the walls. In a colossal burst of power and rage, the pinchers broke through the shadow whips and snapped open.

Click, click, click.

Matthias yanked back to tighten the whips around the legs, but in a blind fury the demon twisted and bucked, nearly folding its body in half and flinging the Aussie up and across the room. He bounced off the hanging stalactites with a hideous *crunch*, cartwheeled through the air, and landed with a dull *thud*, kicking up a cloud of dirt.

He didn't move.

The whips around the monster's legs unfurled and the ground shuddered as the hellion heaved to its feet with a ferocious roar.

"Stay back!" Logan told me and started shooting arrows, but before he could get a decent hit, the demon swung its tail around and smacked him into the air. He ricocheted off a side wall like a rag doll and thumped to a stop near the Aussie.

Logan didn't rise, either.

Just when I thought my stomach couldn't plunge any lower, the beast turned on the boys' prone bodies, letting out another sonic-boomified, spittle-splattering screech. I fought the instinct to cover my ears against the ear-piercing pain, and instead waved my hands above my head, jumping up and down, shouting.

"Hey! Over here!"

The hellion swung its massive head. The quivering nose dropped to the ground and shoveled back and forth, advancing on me, a bloodhound on the scent.

I spun and bolted.

A claw slammed down in front of me. The thing was seven feet wide and dug its pointy ends into the dirt, blocking my path. I spun, changed direction.

Another claw slammed down, blocking. I ran from side to side, forward and back, but at every escape, a giant claw dropped like a prison door. When the cat played with its food, being the mouse sucked.

The jaw opened so far it practically unhinged. I saw fangs. Long ones. A burst of air brought steaming layers of air scented with the putrid stench of rotted meat. A skeletal arm, still dripping with shredded, decaying flesh, wedged between two of the monster's back teeth.

My stomach lurched.

The mouth *snapped* shut, nose scooted along the ground and slimed onto my toes. The head lifted then cocked to one side as it studied me closely. Long whiskers tickled my neck. Its tongue flicked out. I cringed. Tried to squeeze through the claws. Felt heat and pressure around my body. If my explody power would just get the heck in gear it could save my sorry—

Too late. The demon made contact.

CHAPTER TWENTY-NINE

"You can't kill it."

"Oh, I can kill it."

I squinted at Matthias and stepped in front of the demon which had rolled onto its back, feet waving aimlessly in the air. It even wiggled back and forth, like it was giving itself a good back scratch.

It had been doing this lap-dog routine ever since its tongue slurped up my side with a disgusting amount of vomit-o-licious saliva. I'd screamed, batted the monster away, waiting for the beast to wedge *my* severed arm between its serrated snappers, but instead, a cold, wet nose had butted under my armpit, flopping my arm up and down until I finally figured out it wanted me to pet the short, wiry hair on its snout.

It had growled when I tended to Logan and Matthias who woke up quickly. Water dumped in his face helped Matthias come alive.

Now, upside-down, the multitude of glowing eyes watched me while the…green and purple tongue — ew — unfurled onto the ground, dirt sticking to it like fly paper. A happy chittering tickled from her throat. She nuzzled my hand.

How did I know the centimole was a female? I didn't. But since I was already surrounded by way too much testosterone, it made me feel better.

I nudged her off and pointed a warning finger. "Lick me again, Fido, and I won't stop him from killing you."

Matthias snorted. "Like you can stop me." Then he looked at me with disgust. "Fido?"

I shrugged. Clueless as a puppy, the panting demon flumped back onto her belly and playfully batted at the ground before she trapped something black under some of her front legs and used her teeth to tear it apart.

"Matthias!" Ayden's frantic voice echoed through the cave before he rushed in. "Forget the portal! We still can't find Aurora and Lo—" He stumbled when he saw us. "Oh, thank God."

"We're fine," I said.

He gathered me into a rib-breaking hug and slapped Logan on the shoulder.

"What happened? I would've been here sooner but Caviezel found me and had a fit about the books. I had to clean up or get detention so I called Blake and Jayden to—" His eyes focused over my shoulder. "Why is there a demon here? And why is it using Matthias's coat as a chew-toy?"

"What?" The Aussie jerked toward the pile of slobbered black fabric then shoved a fist through the air. "Come on! I should get to kill it for that alone."

"No!"

Matthias pointed an angry finger at me. "Yes!"

"No." Ayden stood next to the creature. "You can't."

Matthias gave him an ugly look. "I should've known you'd take her side."

"Oh, grow up." Ayden his ran his hand under the demon's neck. He fished around, then pulled out a circular piece of metal, a tag of sorts hanging off a chain that none of us had noticed. Within the metal something swirled.

Ayden gave Matthias a tired look. "You can't kill it, because a blood contract has been activated."

Matthias's head flopped back. "No. Bloody. Way." He heaved a dramatic sigh then turned on me, furious. "I can't believe you ran off and made a blood contract with a demon!"

"Yes, Matthias," I smiled sweetly. "In between Tristan's jogging with me at four a.m. to the Ishida's where Ayden and Jayden take over my weapons and hand-to-hand combat training right before Ayden drives me to school where I'm stuck with you all day until everyone but you heads over to Blake's for weight training, homework, and stealth tactics with Logan after which Ayden drives me home where my clandestine-operation-running aunt locks me in the house, I ran off and made a blood contract with a demon!" I huffed a breath. "By the way, what the heck *is* a blood contract?"

"Don't worry about it," Ayden led me toward the cave opening.

I resisted his pull on my arm. "But a blood contract sounds serious. I'd really like to know what kind of danger I'm in."

"School's almost out," Ayden said. "You've been gone too long. Luna covered with your other classes. I'll be *so* glad when Tristan's back. But now I need to get you back so Blake can take you home, because the real danger is your parents if they find out you've been missing."

Or see that D on my last homework assignment. Hopefully, Jayden could tutor me tonight.

"But we need Blake down here so he can map those new tunnels," Logan said.

"He's right, mate. We had no idea about those. They could lead to the treasure."

Ayden's jaw ground shut. "Then Matthias, you can take her."

"Too busy." Matthias slicked clumps of hair off his forehead. "Besides, she's your *girlfriend*. You've got to play the part even when it's not fun anymore."

Ouch. I think he nicked an artery.

Ayden slammed an elbow into the Aussie's shoulder. "Shut up!"

"Forget it. I can get myself home." I turned to walk away.

"Not a chance." Ayden grabbed my wrist and pulled me around. "Don't listen to him. It's not that I don't want to—"

The floor rumbled. Ayden shoved me behind him and turned to face the portal, arms alighting with flames.

The wall still shimmered, but now, as if made of a thin, rubbery membrane, it was stretching toward us in three places. As if some *things* were determined to break through.

It stretched farther and farther until, with a wet *thwap*, two demons burst into the cave.

The size and shape of chubby ponies, they flew on leathery wings and dripped pus-green goo off flayed, hairless skin. They had manes and tails of blazing fire which reflected in the shiny orbs of their bulging black eyes.

Logan's arrow took out one in a hail of splatter just as Fido flipped her head up and snapped massive jaws around the second, easy as catching flies. She crunched a few times, swallowed, then flumped back down to rip on Matthias's jacket, drool now tinged with pus-green soaking into the wool.

A third demon, finally *thwapped* through, but the wall suddenly re-solidified and cut the creature in two. Its head tumbled down the wall, streaking the sticky green slime from its severed neck. Before the still-flaming body part hit the cave floor, one of Fido's antennae claws flicked out, snapped it up, and brought it back to stuff into her mouth. It was gone in one gulp. She didn't even chew.

Ayden's arms snuffed out. "What is going on?"

"Hell if I know." Matthias let his whips disappear. "I came down here because the warning sensors activated. Then that thing," he scowled at the centimole, "crashed through and ever since the portal's been unstable. I think it broke it."

I peeked over Ayden's shoulder. "Broke the portal to *hell*?"

"To the Waiting World," Ayden said. "It's like the transfer station to hell."

"Whoa." I backed up. The Waiting World was my least favorite neighborhood. "Should we be standing so close? What if it sucks us in?"

"Good thinking," Matthias said. "You should get closer."

I backed up further. "So it's not supposed to be doing…that?"

I pointed to the wall which kept changing form, blinking in and out from solid stone to a shimmering swirl of liquid, as if a giant blender was trying to make a sedentary-rock smoothie.

"No," Ayden said as we all stared through the hole. "It's supposed to be solid rock ninety-nine percent of the time. But then, without warning it can open, the rock disappears for a few seconds, and a demon, or two, can get in." He eyed the centimole chomping on Matthias's jacket. "Usually, the net contains it until we get here to send it back."

I stared at the hypnotic blur of the wall. "How do you open the portal to send the demon back?"

"You twit," Matthias scoffed. "Nobody can open a portal. We kill the demon as usual and it disappears back to hell. As usual." He rolled his eyes. "Open a friggin' portal. You're such a moron."

"Well, how am I supposed to know, Captain McSmarty pants? It's not like you guys tell me anything."

Logan shrugged, "Truth is, Aurora doesn't even need a portal to travel to and from the Waiting World."

He said that like it was a good thing.

"Good point." Ayden paled and moved me back. "But since it puts her body into a coma in *this* world, while she runs for her life in the Waiting World, let's keep her far, far away."

"Sounds good to me." I backed up even further. "Can it really suck us in like Blake said?"

"There have been stories," Ayden said. "Portals are unpredictable and uncontrollable. Once the Mandatum finds them, we mostly just monitor activity and contain what comes through."

I kept backpedaling because if the Waiting World was just on the other side of some *unstable* supernatural doorway, far, far away was even too close for me. My tension ebbed when, in a few moments, the wall became solid with only a few spots of liquid blur.

"Looks like it's stabilizing." Ayden sounded relieved.

"The net is going up for repairs." Logan pointed to the large metal net that was rising and feeding into the ceiling. The broken pieces in the middle sparked and sizzled, already starting to reattach. "It fixes itself up there," He told me. "Comes down when it's done. I'll stay to make sure it rolls all the way up. I'll keep this demon too." Logan nodded at the centimole. "Don't want it running around school."

"Fine." Ayden led me out of the cave. "We'll send Blake to help."

The centimole started to follow us, the jacket hanging from her slobbery mouth.

Ayden said, "Aurora, tell it to stay."

"Why?" I glanced back nervously.

Ayden sounded grim. "Because if you don't give it an order to obey, it will follow you and potentially eat anyone in its path."

Chapter Thirty

Ayden had been rushed and on edge ever since he'd hustled me out of the caves and into his car, which we had to ourselves since Luna and Lucian were at their afterschool clubs. He was talking about as fast as he was driving.

"I canceled our golf game at the country club today, but kept next week's tennis reservation. For now. And I already signed us up for a hot air balloon ride. They start next month so shouldn't be a problem." He laughed nervously. "We hope, right?"

I'd thought we could squeeze in a mini-date, kind of make up for last night's fiasco, maybe even find out what he wanted to talk about. I was trying to find a bit of personal life in the midst of this demon crap taking over my existence, but he'd shut me down on all counts.

"Sure you don't want to stop for coffee?" I tried again, talking in a rush to get in an entire sentence. "My treat."

He looked uncomfortable. "I would, but I've got this...meeting thing. Rain check?"

"Sure."

Why not? I might be dead by morning, the whole assassin thing going on and all, but what the heck, rain check sounded peachy. I white-knuckled the door as Ayden fishtailed around another corner.

When the car was back on four wheels, I said, "I could've taken the bus."

"Don't be ridiculous." Ayden shook his head, eyes straight ahead. "If you're not in a shielded building then you need to be with a hunter. And if you remember, the last time you ditched me for the bus, things turned disastrous."

"Sure." I thumped into the seat. "Bring that up. Like I was supposed to know a Kalifera would hunt me down."

"Sorry. I'm just…" He sighed. "Please. Stay home so I know you're safe while we figure some things out. Now, what was I saying before?" He worked the clutch of his Audi, shifting hard as he weaved in and out of what little traffic Gossamer Falls could muster on a weekday afternoon. Someone honked. Again. "Right. Explaining blood contracts."

Because that was so romantic.

"I get the gist." I gripped my seat to help steady. "Someone, somewhere, sometime made a contract with the demon to protect me if certain conditions were met. We don't know what conditions or who set it up, but my hand bled. It activated. And now I've got a slobbering demon guard dog. See, I was listening." I chewed my lip. "Will she go after Rose?"

"If he was attacking you directly, yes," Ayden said. "But he's too smart for that. And since she's more brawn than brains, it's your family I'm worried about. Best she stays in the tunnels."

"Meaning?"

"For instance, if she saw Lucian fighting with you for the remote or Oron throwing oatmeal at your head, she'd take them out as fast as if Rose was coming at you with a chainsaw. She can't differentiate between threats."

My eyes bugged. "Oh, God. What if she shows up at my house?" I leaned toward him and put a hand on his thigh.

He jumped, the car jerked left, we swerved into oncoming traffic, horns blared, Ayden swung the wheel right. The seatbelt checked my sideways freefall as we skidded briefly onto the gravel of the shoulder, clipped the metal guardrail with a high-pitched ping then steadied into the correct lane.

"You alright?" he almost shouted, his head swiveling back and forth from the road to me.

"I'm fine." Once I'd swallowed down the multitude of internal organs that had jettisoned up my throat.

He swore under his breath and thumped the steering wheel. "We don't have to worry about Rose killing you. I'll do it for him! I am such an idiot."

I nearly choked on the pungent smell of burnt rubber. "What's wrong? Are you worried about this afternoon's meeting?"

"What?" Ayden barked another nervous laugh then cleared his throat and wiped a hand across his mouth. "Why would you say that?"

"I don't know. Maybe..." Juggling two women can make you jumpy. Literally. "What's the meeting about?"

He regripped the steering wheel. "Boring stuff. You wouldn't be interested."

"Sure I am." I struggled to keep the frustration from my voice. "Is it Mandatum stuff?"

"Uhhh, yes." He nodded. "Stuff I'm required, as part of my training, to analyze with...someone my dad knows regarding recent incidents and how best to," he pulled one hand off the wheel to wave it in the air, "handle the fallout of some unexpected supernatural reactions that could have disastrous long-term effects on...various scenarios that hunters have to deal with and — Trust me. Boring stuff. Oh look, we're here."

We actually weren't there. We were still a few blocks from my house, but Ayden cut off his babbling and used the time to grab my backpack from the rear seat and plop it on my lap. As we pulled up to the curb outside my house, he leaned across me for what I thought was an amorous move at a kiss, so I started to pucker up. Even closed my eyes.

"That son of a—" Ayden glared out my window.

Then he was out of the car. Halfway up my driveway he doubled back and opened my door.

"Sorry." He took my backpack and hauled me out of the car, nudging me and my shredded ego along faster.

CHAPTER THIRTY-ONE

Our kitchen smelled heavenly, but I made a face because it was infected with Australian scum. Ayden hadn't been happy when he'd seen Matthias's BMW in the driveway. I was less so.

Mom plopped a slice of banana bread onto Matthias's plate.

"Not another one." The Aussie sat at our kitchen table playing thumb war with Selena who was perched on his lap. "I'm stuffed."

Mom pointed the knife at him. "It's still warm. Eat."

"What is the royal Payne doing here?" Sometimes I cracked myself up. What didn't make me laugh was mom treating him like a king and serving him yummilicious baked goods that he didn't deserve.

The glass on the French doors to the backyard squealed as Helsing pawed frantically to get in.

"Ugh." Mom groaned. "Ayden, could you get the door? What a spaz! He was doing this a few hours ago to get out. Make up your mind, cat."

Ayden opened the door and did a quick glance over the backyard. Helsing darted in, flung a hiss at Matthias and laced through my ankles with a motorboat purr. At least one family member was on my anti-Aussie side.

"I thought you were busy?" Ayden flicked the back of Matthias's head, then stole the banana bread Mom had put on the Aussie's plate and made a big show of taking a huge bite.

"Ayden!" Mom admonished.

"Sorry," Ayden said through guilty mouthfuls. "Too delicious to resist."

"There's plenty." Mom smiled and pulled on her bright red lobster claw pot holders to pull out a fresh loaf from the oven. "But Matty gets the most because he saved my baby."

Matthias blushed. "I didn't do anything."

Selena trapped his thumb. "I won!"

"Saved her from what?" A centimole demon? My heart stuttered. No. That didn't make sense.

"Some boy tried to kiss her on the playground." Mom turned to Selena. "Show them what you did, honey."

My pint-sized blonde sister scooted off Matthias's lap, handed him Bubbles, and got into a fighting stance, feet planted, fists raised like Popeye after he'd downed a can of spinach. She scrunched her face into a scowl and yelled in a faint Australian accent, "Get the bloody hell away from me!" then she jabbed a tiny fist into the air.

"Yeah," Ayden smirked. "Kind of has your name written all over it."

Selena climbed back onto Matthias's lap. "Then he cried. There was blood."

"A little bloody nose. Nothing he didn't deserve. Principal threatened to suspend her. Unbelievable." Mom made a disgusted noise. "I gave them a piece *and a half* of my mind on that. Then Aunt M threatened a sexual harassment lawsuit with her corporation's team of 'best lawyers money can buy,' and Sheriff Payne showed up to smooth things over. It's all good now."

Great. The big jerk was a hero. Man, I hated when they treated my nemesis like the golden boy. If they only knew. Kidnapping, anyone?

Matthias caught my sneer, and smiled ever so sweetly. "Mrs. Lahey, I'm just glad *someone* was able to protect her."

What was that supposed to mean?

I wanted to strangle the obnoxious creep, but had to refrain because Mom smiled and kissed the top of his head as she went by. He flinched. Mom didn't notice.

But I did.

I strode over from behind and wrapped an arm around Matthias's neck in a loving chokehold then put on my most perky voice, infused with cheerleader-level enthusiasm.

"Oh my gosh, Selena, isn't Matty like the best big brother ever!"

Then I started kissing his cheek over and over with loud smooch noises.

"What the bloody—"

He stiffened and was about to shove me off, but Selena squealed, "Ever, kever, tever!" and started kissing his other cheek — like I knew she would — and Mom uttered a sentimental, "Ahhh," and he had to freeze and suck it up. It was a beautiful thing.

Until Ayden pulled me off.

"Can't have my girlfriend kissing other guys," he said with a laugh. "Selena, I think Bubbles' eye patch is coming off."

"No!" Selena took the toy to better light and studied it closely.

A strange look passed between Ayden and Matthias. I didn't understand it, but the high color in the Aussie's cheeks started to dissipate.

Peachy. Along with keeping secrets and his distance, Ayden was ruining what little fun I had torturing Matthias. I couldn't win.

"I've got homework." I glared at Ayden and grabbed for my backpack, but he slid it out of reach with his foot and caught my elbow.

"Sure, right after you show me that thing outside that you promised to show me." When I tried to pull away, he whispered, "I think the demon followed you home."

Chapter Thirty-Two

As Ayden led me through the sliding French door and headed toward the rear of the backyard, I frantically scanned the area.

"Where did you see her?"

"I didn't," he said. "You were angry and I needed you alone to say sorry, but I had to shut down that down. Matthias couldn't take anymore."

"What? You scared me to death!" I hissed as my adrenalin pumps switched from fear-based to fury-driven. "Besides, I thought it was because you didn't want your girlfriend kissing other guys."

He pulled me behind some hedges then let go, facing me.

"Not that I'm worried about Matthias, but come to think of it, no, I don't want my girlfriend kissing other guys."

"Why not?" I grumbled. "Not like you're doing much of it."

Disbelief contorted his face. "Wh-what?"

"Nothing." I folded my arms and kicked my toe into the grass.

"Oh, no. Let's...*explore* this." He flicked his jacket back and rested his hands on his hips. "I take you places. We do things together. Share interests. I enjoy your company because I enjoy spending time getting to know you. We talk. But...and let me get this straight, I am a bad boyfriend because I'm not trying to jump you twenty-four seven. Did I," he cleared his throat, "did I get that about right?"

I didn't know where to look. Just knew I didn't want to look at him. "I didn't say, 'bad.'"

"Not in so many words but…" He tried to catch my eye. "You do know how that sounds, right?"

"Sure, now that you said it like that." This was embarrassing. The guy practically wrote the Perfect Boyfriend Manual, and I was complaining.

"Said it…*like that?*" He spread his arms and leaned back. "How else am I supposed to say it?"

"Maybe a better term would be…neglectful?"

"Neglectful."

"Not as far as…doing stuff." Explaining this was a little tougher than I thought.

His lips curved into a suggestive smile. "No. Just as far as *doing stuff.*"

I blushed. "You know, maybe I meant more that you seemed...uninterested. In, ah, in ahhh," I moved my palm in circles in the air in front of me.

He lifted one brow. "Uninterested in your…*chest?*"

"What?" I realized my hand had been circling right over my boobs. Nice move, Aurora. I rolled my eyes. Was he playing with me? Didn't matter. "No! Not…that!"

"Good." His dark eyes glittered with amusement. "Because I can assure you I find your chest *very* interesting. At times, downright mesmerizing."

I folded my arms over my chest. "Me! Uninterested in *me*."

"Uninterested." He looked to the heavens for a brief moment then sighed. "You mean sexually. Uninterested. In you."

Why did he keep repeating everything I said? Certainly didn't sound better a second time around.

He shook his head. "This just gets better and better."

Really? Because that wasn't how I was seeing it.

Then he started laughing. It built from a chuckle to full-on shoulder-shaking, near knee-slapping guffaws.

I squinted. "This is funny to you?"

"Oh," he wiped his eyes, "you have no idea."

Humiliation stung. "Glad I could be such a joke."

"That's not what I meant."

"You should go." I made a shooing motion. "Don't want to keep you from your important meeting thing."

"Won't do me much good if you think—" He laughed again. "Never mind. Sorry. Everything can wait. Let's stay on topic. You feel I've neglected you. Physically in general. Kissing specifically. Fair enough. Challenge accepted."

"Challenge? I didn't issue any challenge." Did I?

"Let's do this."

"Do what?"

"I'm going to kiss you."

"Whoa!" My hands flew into the air and I moved to escape. "This is stupid."

He blocked my path. "Hold on. Not stupid at all. You have a valid point, just give me a minute." He rolled his shoulders, shook out his arms, rocked on the balls of his feet a few times, took a deep breath, and exhaled slowly. "Okay. I'm ready."

I frowned. "You have to *gear-up* to kiss me?"

"Aurora." Ayden's voice was low and deep and seemed to reach across to stroke my skin. He walked toward me with slow measured steps. Under heavy lids, his eyes stalked me, the faintest amber simmering in the dark brown depths. "You have no idea what I go through when I'm near you."

And he was near me now. So close the heat from his body snaked around and enveloped mine, holding us in a cocoon, isolating us from the cold outside world. Even without touching me I felt like his captive, wrapped within some aura of daring emotions that weaved around us, waiting for a chance to strike. Waiting for a chance to hook under my skin and never let go.

He murmured, "Close your eyes."

"What?" I started to step back, but he caught my arms, fingers tight around my biceps, keeping our bodies close.

"Aurora." His voice took on a commanding edge that made it clear he expected no argument. "You've made your concerns clear. Now give me the chance to…address them."

"By kissing me?"

"By kissing you."

He really liked to repeat stuff.

One side of his mouth quirked up. "At least, that's where we'll start."

Ohhh, boy.

He sighed. "Don't panic."

"I'm not panicking." I was so panicking.

"I can see you panicking."

"How can you see me panicking?"

"I see a lot more than you give me credit for. So for now, just a kiss, I promise. Better for both of us, anyway." Before I could ask what that meant, he slid the fingers of both hands into my hair and held my face in his hands. His look filled with intensity. "Close your eyes. No, I didn't say roll your eyes. You know what, just hold still."

"Wow. You really know how to sweet talk a gir—"

He kissed me. Quick and fast. Like he was tasting a medicine to judge the level of horrible flavor.

Odd. Borderline insulting.

He raised his head and let his gaze meander over my features. He appeared pleased, seemed to relax. A faint smile touched his lips.

He breathed deep, gave an almost imperceptible nod then his head lowered.

This time the kiss was slower. Softer. And short. His lips barely brushed mine before he pulled away. But his mouth hovered, his breath coasting across my lips and cheeks, tickling down my neck. I smelled the sweet aroma of baked banana bread. And licked my lips.

My hands came up, grazing across his stomach. My fingers skimmed over the firm contours of his abdomen, and through his thin T-shirt, I felt the muscles tense harder at my touch. His breath paused. His eyes flicked down, but otherwise he seemed to freeze. When I laid my palms lightly on his chest, his heart *th-thumped* several quick beats, then steadied. He inhaled slowly, regripped my face in his hands, and moved in again.

Lips against mine. Tender. Lingering longer between the moments when he took his mouth away. Tingles zinged across my skin. I was *zingled.* Great new word. I raised on tip-toe, trying to follow his lips each time they backed off, because the zingling was oh-so delightful, but his hands firmly held my face and kept me at bay.

Was he teasing? Playing with my emotions. But his expression was so serious, as if he was concentrating hard to…

What? I didn't know. But I had his full attention now and didn't want to break his avid focus. My skin prickled with goosebumps, awakening new sensations, feelings of desire bubbling up from deep within.

His hand slipped behind my neck, and his head dipped, and I readied for a real kiss, a hard kiss, something to help alleviate the mounting pressure of my cravings. But his lips merely brushed mine, so soft it almost wasn't a touch, yet my body reacted as if electrified.

Nerves ignited. Anticipation fluttered in my stomach as his lips dropped faint kisses along the line of my mouth, taking great care to cover every inch, and taking way too much time about it.

My hands clenched. He was kissing me, but he wasn't *kissing* me, and he wouldn't let me kiss *him* and…I wanted to.

When his tongue flicked the corner of my mouth, my breath hitched and my lips parted with a sigh. Although why I could still breathe was beyond me. My knees were trembling. They'd probably give out any second. Not that I cared. I'd closed my eyes ages ago because these overwhelming sensations sapped my strength, leaving me on just this side of limp, and it was way too much work to keep eyelids open.

Ayden's tongue traced along the delicate skin on the inside of my lips. It was as if every nerve ending gathered to each spot he touched, making the flesh so terribly sensitive the contact was almost painful. Almost.

When I shivered, he paused, and I took the opening to capture his lips with mine. Finally.

He jumped at the contact. His hands tightened on my face, became warmer, and just when I thought he would back off, his shoulders relaxed, and he returned the kiss. A huge relief, because stopping now should be against the law. Maybe it was.

Cruel and unusual punishment.

His touch was sensuous and unhurried and settled all of my anxious energy into something languid. I leaned into him, my fingers spreading over the solid feel of his chest. The rhythm and pressure of his kisses increased, and he seemed more and more reluctant to pull his lips from mine.

His hands slipped down to cup my neck, thumbs stroking slowly up and down my throat. My pulse quickened. I reached one hand up to slip it around his neck, to pull us closer, to have his mouth stop teasing mine, to crush him into me.

But he pulled away, and took a step back.

I wanted to tell him to stay close, to keep touching me, but with my breath coming in such halting bursts, I couldn't speak.

Staring at the ground, he licked his lips — luscious lips that should be on mine. Then he swallowed. Blinked slowly, lids heavy. I knew that feeling. But in his case he was probably having trouble holding up those ridiculously thick lashes that cast mysteriously sexy shadows on his cheeks. Mysteriously sexy shadows? Yeah, I was in trouble.

The rise and fall of his chest increased. "Aurora, I…"

In a deliberate movement that appeared to take great effort, his gaze lifted to meet mine. The dark chocolate was almost gone, nearly overcome by sparks of red and orange, like burning coals ready to ignite.

My breath caught at the heat of that look. Something tangible and alive jumped across the space between us, something in a hot rush to infiltrate my body, pulsing with the beat of my heart, wild and strong and asking for more.

"I think…" His voice was rough, every syllable skating on sandpaper. He shook his head, his expression frustrated. "Was that…more of what you were looking for?"

More? I almost laughed. Oh, yes, it was more. More than I expected. And everything I'd imagined. At my silence, dark emotions flickered across the handsome lines of his face. His jaw tightened.

I touched a hand to his cheek. "I believe that was both more and," I took a shaky breath, "not nearly enough."

It took him a beat, but then a smile of satisfaction curved his lips, and when my hands slid up to tangle my fingers in the silk of his hair and pull him to me, he didn't resist.

I loved his sweet taste. The feel of his mouth as it moved with sensuous longing over mine. Warmth tingled along the back of my neck, shimmied down my spine. His arms slid around my waist as his mouth pressed harder. The tingling heat wrapped around my rib cage, sparking a fire that burned in my belly. My body arced against him, trying desperately to capture the feel of every part of him. His arms around my waist tightened. His hands started to roam, exploring my body—

He loosed his hold. I pressed closer, but his hands moved to my sides, his mouth pulled away.

"Aurora, this isn't—"

"Yes, it is." I didn't know what he was going to say, but I was sure I wouldn't agree because these feelings were too vitally important to my immediate emotional and physical well-being to do anything but act on them.

Ayden had his hands on my wrists, trying to disengage. "No, I really think—"

"Don't think." I kissed him to shut him up. "You talk too much." And I didn't want to hear it.

He started to kiss me back, then groaned and slipped his hands to my hips to push me away, so I reached up both arms and wrapped them around his neck. The move lifted my shirt from under his hands and when his skin made direct contact with mine, something snapped.

He became unnaturally still. The air thickened. A warm breeze spiraled around us like a coiling serpent. An intense energy seemed to ripple through his entire body. And then he moved.

One hand slipped under my shirt and around my waist, hot fingers splayed against my bare skin and crushed me to him. His other hand dug into the flesh of my hip and somehow, a moment later my back was up against a tree, the rough surface biting through my shirt.

His mouth never left mine. There was no relief, no holding back. His kiss was all-consuming, the only thing on his agenda. His lips bore down with a voracious intensity, demanding, unyielding. My chest tightened. Stomach constricted. My entire body was ready to burst, heart hammering through my ribs, veins unable to contain the torrent of blood. Heat filled my very core and pleasure raged, unstoppable, exhilarating, and rushing through every part of me.

While his body pinned mine against the tree, he ran a wide palm down my side, over my hip, my thigh, and back up. The other hand cupped my neck, my cheek, twisted in my hair. His mouth took control of mine. Hungry and hot. My lips parted and his tongue—

He ripped my arms from around his neck and jumped away. Literally, jumped back and put up his hands.

"Whoa! That is, ah…" He looked over his shoulder, breathing hard, face flushed. "You were right. I should go."

"Go?" Was he kidding? I had to lean on the tree for support. "Now?"

"Yep, yeah, yes," he nodded. "I told you I had that meeting thing."

"What happened to everything can wait?"

"Not anymore. And I, uh, we've had enough of…" his hand waggled in the air, "of this."

"Enough?" Great. Now I was repeating everything. "You've had enough?" And I couldn't stop myself.

"Because I don't want to— I can't—" He tried to smile but couldn't pull it off. "I'll call you. Later." He raked his hands through his hair, backing further and further away, looking lost and miserable, and leaving me with a cold and empty feeling.

"Call me?" I really needed to say something more effective, but I was so confused and hurt. Did I just get…played? He got me all hot and bothered only to *rebuff* me? Yes, that's what he did and— Wait, why wasn't I saying this out loud? Because I was a big wuss. No. Aurora you can do this.

I breathed in some courage and opened my mouth to speak just as a fire-breathing monster flew around the corner.

Chapter Thirty-Three

Eyes flashing a dark, cold, sharkskin gray, Matthias jabbed a hostile finger in my direction. "What the bloody hell was that in there!"

"Matthias," Ayden groaned, "not a good time."

"Like I care." Matthias started to rant at me but then took a double-take at Ayden. "What's wrong? You look like crap." He glanced from me to Ayden then looked nauseated. "Oh. Well, no wonder. But better she's kissing you than me."

"Matthias, shut up!" Ayden glared.

Heat pricked my cheeks. How the heck did Matthias know? What did Ayden say about me?

"Hey, mate, don't take your bad mood out on me. You signed up for this pretend boyfriend fiasco." The Aussie glanced pointedly in my direction.

"Oh, for— That's enough!" Ayden was furious.

I was toppling into the realm of humiliated.

"Whatever." Matthias stalked my way and made a show of wiping his palm down the cheek I'd kissed. "Don't you ever do that again. Disgusting. And don't give me any crap about getting Selena in trouble."

I glowered. "If you weren't such jerk, I might actually thank you because as much as it pains me, when you help protect my sister, it's hard to hate you."

His face screwed up. "Don't go all gushy."

"I said 'hard' to hate you. *Not* impossible."

"Good. Because I have no problem hating you." His eyes narrowed. "We're just lucky it was some idiot kid. *You* bring demons knocking on your door. *You* put her in danger. *You* should give her tools to keep herself alive. It's a wonder she's not dead already thanks to *you*."

I stepped back. Felt the blood drain from my face. I'd been hot, now I was cold…and going numb.

"Matthias!" Ayden shoved the Aussie hard enough to make him stumble. "That was a low blow."

"But true," Matthias said with satisfaction. "And she knows it."

Ayden moved toward me. "Don't listen to him."

I held up a hand to stop him and chose to let my legs give out. My back slid down the tree, and I plopped on the grass. What a fun afternoon.

"And you." Matthias flung a hand at Ayden. "Don't get too attached, because if there is *ever* a time when she is too much of a danger to Selena, or any of us, traitor or not, I'll drag her to the Mandatum myself."

Ayden glared at the Aussie. "You are unbelievable. After I saved your butt in there." A warm breeze swirled around Ayden bringing with it the luscious layers of fragrant scents from Mom's garden. "Get the hell out before I—"

"What?" Matthias spread his arms wide. "Gonna hit me again? Take your best shot, mate."

"Ayden, don't." I inhaled deep, but the garden's sweet smells didn't erase the sour coating on my tongue. "He's right."

"See," Matthias smirked.

Ayden ground out, "No. He's. *Not.*"

"You said it yourself." I reminded him. "Fido's on my side, and she could attack my family."

"Not the same." Ayden stood toe-to-toe with Matthias. "And the truth is he's just trying to pass his own guilt off onto you. Ain't that right, *mate?*"

The world darkened under the cloudless sky. Black spilled into the whites of Matthias's eyes.

"Guilt?" I glanced from one to the other, expecting the ground to crack from the tension rising off both. "About what?"

Matthias's nostrils flared and his lips curled into a toxic smile. "I think, my *mate* is referring to the fact that I killed my mum and sister."

Chapter Thirty-Four

I stood in our driveway. Ayden was in the street, eyes following Matthias's BMW as it screeched around a corner and disappeared. Ayden was completely still for a moment, then his body spasmed, fists pummeling the air, body spinning, feet kicking. It was the fireball flying from his hand and sizzling in asphalt that finally gave him pause. He looked around, worried, and saw me watching.

"Sooo..." I ventured. "You were serious? Matthias killed his mom and sister?"

"I didn't say that. He did. Because he's such a..." Ayden punched one more fist through the air, "friggin' *idiot*."

No argument here.

"Okay, but his mom and sister are dead, yes?" I knew his mom wasn't around, and she was definitely a taboo topic, but I hadn't heard any reasons why, and this was the first I'd heard about a sister.

"I can't say."

"Are you kidding? You can't just leave me in the dark."

Ayden rubbed his forehead. "It's personal. I can't talk about it. That's the deal."

"Like why Tristan lives with his grandparents and Blake with his Uncle Reece."

"Right. Whatever their story, they get to tell it." Ayden studied the empty street, face grim. "Even if they tell it in the *worst* possible way."

"Great," I muttered. "I love being on the outside of this wall of secrecy."

"Secrecy?" His tone was absentminded. "You're one to talk."

"Excuse me?"

"What?" He dragged his eyes away from the road. "Forget it." He glanced at his watch. "How about I take you for that coffee before I head off."

"To your big important meeting thing? Yeah, I don't think so, hot stuff." My ego still smarted from the recent rejection.

He blinked. "What's wrong now?"

"On our last outing there was a kidnapping on the menu with me as the main course." Did that even make sense?

"That wasn't my fault. It was Matthias trying to prove a point."

"That I'm a useless piece of crap?"

"Yes."

"What?"

"No!" Ayden's arms flailed. "You know what I mean."

"Do I?" I kicked my high horse and let the reins loose on a full gallop. "Maybe I'm secretive because you're secretive, keeping me in the dark, going off on 'meetings,'" I used finger quotes, "that you won't explain. And when you do finally show up you go all *hot-hottie-from-hottiesville* just before you give me the artic shaft, like some silly strumpet you mess with before you blow me off while you wait around for a real girlfriend instead of this pretend mumbo-jumbo we've," I pointed back and forth between us, "got going. And for dinner with her, I'd bet you'd show up."

Silence followed, broken only by my heavy breathing. Trenches furrowed across Ayden's brow.

"What are you talking about? You think I'm…" He looked like he was trying to translate an alien language. "And that there's another girl?"

"Yes!" I ground my teeth. "Okay, no. Not exactly. But there could be. I mean, you do this hot and cold thing. Just like *now*," I shot a hand toward my backyard, "when I have to beg you to kiss me and then things are…happening and then you *rebuff* me." There, I said it out loud.

"Rebuff you?"

"Quit repeating everything I say!"

"I'm sorry, but *rebuff* is what you took from that experience?" He choked a harsh laugh. "This is insane."

"What's insane is that you practically maul me," not that I minded, "and then run for the hills. It's like you don't want to get too close or even be alone with me."

Ayden raked a hand through his already-mussed hair. "Because I *don't*."

Oh.

I looked down at my chest, figuring there had to be a bullet hole. Or an arrow sticking out. Something to explain the pain. But then I realized it was just my heart. Breaking. Why did I ever think…

Idiot.

"That's, uh," I cleared my throat, "good to know."

"Not…" Ayden slid both hands back through his hair, then laced his fingers together, cradling the back of his head like he was trying to keep his skull from exploding. "It's… complicated. There's so much happening. " He dropped his hands and stepped toward me. "And to explain—"

"No, I get it." I jerked back and held up my palm. "It makes sense to keep your distance. Especially for when I become too dangerous and you help Matthias drag me to the Mandatum to save yourselves."

Low blow, I know. The result of a lethal combination of humiliation, pain, and paranoia. Ayden looked like I'd sucker-punched him. I suppose I did. I knew I should take it back, but my big mouth had yet to find an off switch let alone a rewind button.

Wondering how much of the something between us I'd just thrown away, I walked back into the house. Before he could see the tears. Before he could stop me.

Not that he tried.

Chapter Thirty-Five

Underneath the water just shy of scalding, the shower wasn't melting away the afternoon's manic misery like I'd hoped. Even the delicate floral scent of Jayden's fancy French shampoo offered no relief.

There was a knock and Mom opened the door.

"Special delivery," she said with aggravating cheer. "The coffee shop delivered your favorite. White chocolate raspberry mocha. Mmm. Smells good."

I moved the shower curtain and peeked out to see her set down the cardboard cup on the counter.

"Thanks. How'd you get them to deliver?"

"Wasn't me," she said. "According to the blond barista who brought it, Ayden got them to deliver by making it a condition for him buying a boatload — she used another term which I won't repeat — worth of coffee beans and various merchandise, including a cappuccino machine, and tipping them all heavily."

Of *course* it was a girl. I *bet* he tipped her heavily.

"Just leave it." I let the curtain fall and stuck my head under the water, half-hoping it would drown me into oblivion.

"Does this have something to do with you crying?" Mom said. "I noticed when you came in and raced up here. Want to talk about it?"

"Not really."

"Aurora—"

"Mom, please. Not now."

How could she ever understand? The secrets, the lies, the layers and layers of crap piled on my life. And everyone I loved bore the brunt. I scrubbed my scalp to rinse the suds then worked in some conditioner.

I heard Mom sigh. "Okay. For now. Look, I don't know what happened, but I see how you two look at each other. All the love and passion."

"Mom!" My warning tone was meant to stop further conversation. So why did she keep talking?

"Very bad things happened which frightened you, still frighten you, and that's understandable, but don't be scared of love." Her voice softened. "Love always beats fear, sweetie, but you have to let it in."

"Got it, Dr. Freud. Now, can I shower in peace?" I knew she meant well, but my pity party was best wallowed in alone.

"Fine. I'm here when you want to talk. I love you."

"Love you too," I said quietly as she left.

That part was easy. Loving my family. They were predictable and solid as a rock. But this other stuff? Too many unknowns.

Maybe I should shut down the pretend boyfriend "fiasco." Sure, it may be keeping me alive, but it was also killing me, because with each labored beat, my heart seemed to fissure a new crack, and eventually, it would shatter.

I tilted my head back into the shower's pulsing flow, breathing the steam, tasting the heat, waiting for relief to arrive.

"I require your assistance," a male voice whispered.

My mouth fell open. "Ahhgaluhg!" I gagged — near *drowned* — on a slew of water and lost my balance. The pink shower curtain proved no leverage whatsoever, and I ripped it down with me, rod and all, slopping into the tub with a *splash*, irritated *squeal*, and shuddering *thud*.

"Jay—!" I stifled a scream and hissed the second syllable through clenched teeth, "—den!"

"Have you sustained injury?" Jayden's face hovered over the tub.

"Not until you showed up!" I struggled to sit up. The plastic shower curtain crackled in protest as I pulled it to cover myself. "You can't come into my bathroom!"

"I needed to speak privately and the odds were probable that you would be bathing alone. Additionally, no one would interrupt you."

"And you didn't think that should include you?" I shoved the hair out of my eyes.

He cocked his head with a blank look. "It was the most advantageous way for us to be alone."

"That is stupid in so many ways," I fumed. "Besides, my mom was just here, you idiot."

"Then we must be expeditious in the event of her return. Come."

He offered a hand. I slapped it away. Then slipped trying to get up.

"Grrrrr!" I pointed at the door. "Go! Wait in my room." When he hesitated, I pointed harder. "Out! And close the door."

He opened his mouth then closed it, gave a sharp nod, and retreated to my room, closing the door softly.

My exit from the tub was anything but graceful. It didn't help I was furious. I wrestled the curtain off and dumped it, along with the fallen curtain rod, into the tub with a decisive clatter. Great, Dad just fixed the one in my bedroom and now I'd have to explain this. I snapped a towel off the rack.

Jayden spoke through the door, "Might I inquire—"

"No!"

"Excellent. I'm right out here if you need anything."

"You with a clue would be nice," I muttered, scrubbing myself dry.

He knocked. "What was that?"

"Jayden!"

"Right. I'll simply wait out here in your room."

With no clean clothes in the bathroom, my only option was to wrap the towel around myself, take a deep breath, and open the door.

There was a scream.

From Logan.

He stood just inside my open window. At the sight of me — and after the scream — he spun around and tried to duck out. In his panic, he miscalculated and slammed his forehead into the edge of the frame. The impact reeled him back. He stumbled and landed on his backside, holding his hand to his head, moaning.

"Aurora?!" Mom's voice shrilled from downstairs.

"I'm fine!" I yelled, then blew air between my lips and walked over to offer Logan a hand up. "Good thing you scream like a girl."

Cowering like a mouse facing a pack of ravenous leopards, he covered his eyes, rolled onto his knees, and crawled away.

"What are you doing n-n-naked? With Jayden?"

"Get a grip." I turned away to close the window and curtains. It was harder with one hand because the other had to make sure the towel stayed put. Otherwise, Logan might actually lose consciousness. "I'm not naked."

"Is anyone else naked?" Logan was sitting on the floor, back against my bed, shading his eyes with one hand and rubbing his forehead with the other. “Is naked a thing now that a girl’s on the team?”

Jeez, I hoped not.

I changed in my walk-in closet and reappeared wearing sweats to find both boys in my bathroom putting up the curtain and rod.

Good.

As I went about my hair care routine, Logan whacked Jayden on the shoulder. “It’s bad enough you do it to us. You can’t do it to girls.”

Apparently, Jayden pulled his “surprise” bathroom visits on all the guys. Which was supposed to make me feel better.

It didn’t.

“When I need to find each of you alone, the shower is the perfect location.” Jayden slipped rings on the rod, unperturbed by the scolding. I got the feeling he’d heard it before.

“No, the shower is *not* perfect,” Logan said with a rising level of frustration, “because—”

“I know.” Jayden flapped a dismissive hand through the air. “The naked issue. But naked is a natural state. I don’t possess lustful inclinations toward any of you. Your prime physical shapes should be a point of pride. And as for Aurora being a female, her status as a team member embodies her as an asexual presence.”

“Gee, thanks.”

“It wasn’t a compliment.”

“No kidding.”

“More of an observation on the agamic perception I have of you.” He stood on the tub edge and jammed the rod into place

“Jayden!” Logan slid the curtain back and forth a few times. “No one cares.”

Jayden said evenly, “My point is, being naked in my presence should not invoke such a heightened level of anxiety. It makes no logical sense.”

"Well, it doesn't have to," I snapped. "So take your logic and shove it. And don't let it happen again. *Capiche?*"

Jayden bristled. "I hear your unnecessarily hostile request, and will do my best to acquiesce."

"I'll take that as a yes. Now, let's grab some banana bread and do homework."

"No." Jayden grabbed my arm and dragged me out of the bathroom. "Since acquisition of Flint's treasure has proved impossible for an advanced civilization of enhanced humans with unlimited resources for well over a century, I've contrived a scheme to give Rose what he so desires without the encumbrance and time constraint of uncovering the treasure, thus avoiding your demise."

Homework could wait.

"Next time lead with that." I stopped to grab my shoes and hurried downstairs. "Let me tell my mom."

"Jayden already told her we're going to Blake's." Logan rode the railing down and opened the front door.

"Am I bait?" Not my favorite strategy. Besides, last time we'd tried it, disaster had ensued.

Jayden gave me a steady look. "No, you're the sine qua non."

I paused in the doorway. "You know, I hate it when you say things like I already know what they are."

"Noted," Jayden said then nodded and urged me toward the driveway.

Logan spoke over his shoulder as he hopped in his sleek, low-slung sports car. "He means his whole plan hinges on you."

"Great. No pressure. What do I need to do?"

"Use your ability." Jayden held the passenger door open for me.

I ducked in the backseat. "We gave up last week on sparking my explody power."

"I didn't 'give up.'" Jayden slid into the front seat and slammed the door just as Logan peeled out of my driveway. "I simply decided that we would wait for your ability to occur naturally rather than force it into a tumultuous state."

Sounded a lot like giving up to me. "How does my explody power work into your plan?"

"It doesn't." Jayden turned in his seat to face me. "If we find the demons that hired Rose, we'll use them to retrieve his sister then we'll eradicate said demons, and Rose will depart satisfied, leaving you unharmed."

I frowned. "I still don't understand how I help."

"Track the demons, Aurora." Jayden gave me a look that clearly questioned my intelligence. "You *are* the Divinicus Nex. That's what you do."

Chapter Thirty-Six

I kicked out a window, dove through the shattered glass, front rolled onto the road, and ran for my life.

I'd get home, grab a bag, and…then what? Where could I go? How could I hide? Not sure but they weren't going to take me. Not without a fight.

"Aurora?" Jayden snapped his fingers in front of my eyes. "Aurora?" He studied my face. "She seems to have devolved into some sort of catatonic state. She's very pale."

Logan punched Jayden's arm. "We weren't going to tell her we knew!"

"How were we to solicit her help while pretending she's not the Divinicus?" Jayden said.

"I don't know, you said you had a plan!"

"Yes. Confine her in the car then reveal we knew her secret."

"Oh, for—" Logan groaned. "Blake could've come up with something better."

My escape had been just wishful thinking brought about by my panic. Was I breathing? Didn't matter. I had to *move*. This time I did get out the window, wind slapping my hair against my face, lines on the asphalt blurring underneath me.

The car screeched and fishtailed. Jayden grabbed my waist and hauled me back in, hanging over the backseat to strong-arm me into place.

"*Blake?*" I could barely breathe. "Who else did you tell? Because you shouldn't because," I laughed, well, more of a rattling wheeze since air was scarce, "you sound crazy since Divinicus…es—or is it Divinic-i?—are always guys, and I'm pretty sure Jayden can now confirm I'm a girl, and I can blast demons which a Divinicus can*not* do which means I'm not it so you can call off that Mandatum extraction team because it will be a waste of their time."

"She's prattling," Jayden told Logan.

"Because you scared her. Next time I'll handle it." Logan sighed and caught my gaze in the rearview mirror. "Aurora, I'm sorry about Jayden's delivery."

Jayden released me and returned to his seat with a huff. "My delivery was sound."

"Aurora, only Jayden and I know. He figured it out when—"

Jayden cut in, "My suspicions were *confirmed* when she saved me during the altercation with Fiskick and Echo at the concert hall, but prior to that—"

"Yeah, we get it, you're a genius," Logan said, then told me, "I just heard the Kalifera call you Divinicus right before I killed it. But we didn't tell anyone. The rest of the guys can't know so they have plausible deniability in case we get caught hiding you and the Mandatum delivers consequences. We didn't tell Cacciatori so there's no extraction team, but we have to get rid of the threat of Rose. Does he know what you are?"

After a pause, I nodded. "Promises not to tell as long as I help get his sister."

"Like he can be trusted." Logan blew out a long breath. "And if he knows, the demons he's working with probably know too. But if we find the demons, get his sister, we can shut this whole thing down. It's a long shot, but…can you trust us and help track them?"

Well, gosh, such tempting options. I flopped in my seat and grumbled, "No."

The hope in Logan's eyes flickered out.

"Not because I don't want to, but because I can't. There's no control. I only find demons when they're within a certain range. And when I say *find*, I'm not searching, I just suddenly get the vision and know exactly where they are and how to get to them. Or, more often than not, they come after me. Like Fido."

Logan squinted. "Fido?"

"The blood contract demon," I said.

"You gave it a sobriquet?!" Jayden said. "Oh, Aurora, it's dangerous!"

"How far is your range?" Logan asked.

I shrugged. "A few miles? Usually less."

"I can work with that," Jayden nodded.

CHAPTER THIRTY-SEVEN

I squirmed. "This isn't working."

Jayden pursed his lips. "Because you're not engendering a tranquil state."

"Because I look like Frankenstein." I lifted my hands, dragging up the wires that were stuck all over my arms, head, neck, and chest with tiny sticky suction cups. Some blinked bright neon colors.

I was tipped back in what resembled a dentist's chair in the secret room at the Ishida house. The space was separated for two functions. On the other end, the windowless, rectangular space housed an extensive array of the latest computer equipment. The monitors alternated different shots from the surveillance cameras around town, and a couple had random documents left open. The half where I sat was set up like a gleaming, stainless steel, NASA-worthy intergalactic space station lab.

The ceiling was two-stories high like in the game room, but instead of swinging gymnastic rings embedded above, several pipes from all the extraordinary machinery zigzagged across in neat lines.

The odd scents from the rainbow of potions constantly bubbling in flasks atop Bunsen burners always wrinkled my nose. Glass jars held...specimens, and parts of specimens. Of the supernatural variety. I tried not so study them too closely because the bizarre and grotesque items along with claws, entrails, internal organs, and things with too many dead eyes — that I swear I've seen blink — freak me out. Call me squeamish.

Unfortunately, now I felt like one of them.

Jayden gave me a perturbed glance, then opened a refrigerated glass cabinet and looked over the multitude of vials.

"Perhaps a sedative would help."

"Nooope." I started to get up.

Logan put a hand on my shoulder. "Jayden!"

"Fine." Jayden grabbed a beaker, dumped out a thick, dark liquid into a sink, added water, then offered it to me, syrupy globs of olive green floating to the top. "Perhaps hydration would assist?"

"Ew." I waved him off, keeping a wary eye on the two long walls. They both had sliding doors hidden within. One led to the game room, and the opposite one opened directly into Ayden's bedroom.

"What if the guys walk in on us?"

"No one's around," Logan assured me.

"Relaxing is essential to meditation, Aurora," Jayden said. "Your strain of Divinicus power never ceases. It constantly scans your environment in the...background of your mind."

"Like on your computer," I said. "The anti-virus is always running, but you don't see it."

"That would be accurate," Jayden seemed pleased. "Currently, you only notice it when it locates a demon. A blip on your radar, in banal terms, and only with a demon at close proximity. Today, however, we attempt to have you not only perceive the scanning power but actively search the environment, expand the parameter, and focus on a definitive target."

"Gee, sounds simple." We were dead in the water.

"Just try to clear your mind." Logan started opening drawers. "We can set the brain scanner to help relax you."

"It's not a 'brain scanner,' but, yes, we could use the apparatus to induce a placid disposition. It should be here but…" Jayden swung out a cabinet and frowned. "Ayden's been using it."

He crossed the space and put his hand on a panel next to the door to Ayden's room and pushed a button. The door in the wall *swished* open.

Jayden started to walk in. Then froze. The room wasn't empty.

Ayden sat cross-legged on his platform bed surrounded by several ancient-looking books which were cracked open like he was studying for some test on archaic history. From a bowl in his lap he plucked a few corn kernels and tossed them into the air. Fire *whooshed* off his finger, the kernels popped into fluffy white puffs, he tipped back his head, and caught them in his mouth.

Wow. So much for his important, stressful, high-level Mandatum meeting thing. He was so full of it.

Logan's eyes went wide, and he stepped his small form in front of me.

Jayden sputtered, "W-what are you doing here?!"

"In *my* room? Some genius you are." Ayden continued fire-popping the kernels and catching them in his mouth. I'd be impressed if I wasn't so ticked off. "Dad sent Mom into town for emergency groceries. Whatever that is. So if you want something, call her."

"Dad's home?" Jayden disappeared into Ayden's room.

"Called from his office. I think. Why are you taking the brain scanner?"

"Yes, yes, carry on." Jayden scurried back into the lab grasping some sort of helmet made of braided silver wire with spiral tentacles and spikes poking out from the top.

Yeah, that wasn't going on my head.

Although I'd happily chuck it at Ayden. Big fat liar.

Ayden saw me and lurched up, forgetting the bowl in his lap. Kernels flew. "Aurora! What are you doing here?" He scrambled off the bed and headed toward us, eyes narrowing at his brother. "Jayden, whatever you're trying, don't you *dare*."

Logan slammed his hand on the wall panel and the door *swished* shut on Ayden.

I glared. "You said he was gone!"

"He was supposed to be with—"

The door *swished* open and we saw Ayden briefly before Logan punched the panel and Ayden had to jump back so the door didn't hit him as it closed again.

From inside his room, Ayden banged his fist on the wall. "Really?!"

"Lock the doors," Logan ordered.

"I'm *really* relaxed now," I said dryly.

"Place it upon her." Jayden tossed the helmet to Logan, then typed on a keyboard. "It's programmed."

"Whoa." I put up my hands. "What's that—"

Logan plopped it on my head.

My breath sailed out of my chest. A gentle hum thrummed over my scalp and the world around me slowed. Ayden banging on the door went from rapid thumps to the slow, dragging beats of a gong. Logan's movements seemed to lag a second or two. Very disorienting.

"It's oookay. You're saaafe." Logan's words were warped, slow, drawn out. "Nowww, close yourrr eyes and fooocus. Try thiiinking of Rose. See if yooou caaannn…" His voice faded.

Then Logan took a hatchet to my head.

At least it felt that way. Pain. Slicing through my skull. Exploding brain matter. I wanted to run but couldn't move. Wanted to scream but couldn't utter a sound. I was tethered to a torture device without means to escape. It was killing me.

"You must replace it on her head," Jayden sounded annoyed.

The pain disappeared. Most of it anyway. A dull ache still shadowed across my skull. That I could handle. My eyelids, heavy as concrete, fluttered open.

"She was making weird noises." Logan hugged the helmet to his chest, out of Jayden's reach. "And you just said it was making her brain-dead!"

"I said the computers lacked any reading of neurological activity."

"Yeah," Logan said. "Brain-dead."

"I'm not brain-dead." I yanked off the suction cups and wires with a *pop-pop-pop*. "Ow! But I will be if you put that thing on me again. It *hurt*!"

"See?" Logan hugged the helmet tighter.

"Who's dead?!" Ayden's voice muffled through the walls, followed by furious banging. "Open the door!"

Jayden brought his face close to mine and lifted my lids. "Describe the discomfort."

"*Discomfort?*" I shoved him off and slid out of the chair, snatching the helmet from Logan. "Give me that thing and don't you dare try that again!"

Red lights flashed. The computer screen filled with one giant red triangle flashing the word "OVERRIDE!" across the center. There was more thumping. This time, on the door to the game room.

Logan's voice rose. "Ayden's using the administrative password to get in."

Jayden rushed to the other end of the room and starting punching buttons. "But Ayden doesn't possess the administrative password. Only Mom and—"

The game room door *whooshed* open and a tall form stepped from the shadows.

"Father!" Jayden yelped.

Chapter Thirty-Eight

Even without Logan giving me a frantic "Stay quiet!" gesture, I knew not to utter a word. How could we explain my presence in the secret room? With a brain scanner? But we were going to have to come up with something because as soon as the Ishida dad turned around we were blown.

Wind tornadoed the room. Papers flurried like snow. A gale force blast sucker-punched my gut and shot me into the air. My back thudded against the ceiling, head banging on a pipe.

Someone said loudly, "Ahhh, ahhh!"

Glass shattered below. I started to fall. Something glinted. A dozen hunting knives flew up, ripped through my clothes, and embedded into the ceiling, effectively holding me in place. I glanced over my body. The knives had hit only fabric, outlining my form but missing any flesh. On closer look I saw the lethal looking curved blades were white, glittering. Frozen water.

Ice blades. Jayden's weapon of choice.

I still had the helmet in one hand. Gravity pulled down. Fabric stretched as my body sagged toward the ground. I tightened my abs and pushed my back against the ceiling, hooking my toes under a pipe and groping another with the hand not holding the brain scanner. I couldn't do it forever, but with Blake's psycho weight training, I should have the strength to endure for a while. Just had to get a handle on my vertigo.

"When did I become *father*?" Mr. Ishida rushed in and headed toward the computers.

There was no guessing where Ayden got those Himalayan cheek bones and T-frame physique. Mr. Ishida was a sharp looking guy. Raven locks were gelled straight back and ended in curls at the nape of his neck. He had a neatly trimmed jet-black mustache that curved into a thin, straight line down the sides of his mouth leading into a short beard that covered his sharp chin.

His ebony suit and crisp, white button-down shirt looked custom fit, and gave him the look of a cool, collected CEO. Or nasty mastermind villain. Until he smiled. Then his coal black eyes twinkled, and he looked adorable and harmless.

"Father. Ha. Ha." Jayden was taking great effort to *not* look at me, thumbs popping in and out of joint at a rapid pace. "Just a failed attempt at humor. *Dad*."

"Not failed," Mr. Ishida smiled gently. "I'm just distracted. Sorry." He batted a few flying papers out of his face. "Logan, what is all this?"

"I—I sneezed." Logan hid his panicked expression by whipping out his handkerchief and dabbing at his nose. The remaining papers fluttered to the floor.

"Oh. Bless you. Now, I've some business. I need privacy. What happened here?" Mr. Ishida bent. The beaker holding the water Jayden had offered me earlier had shattered on the tile floor. "No worries," he said and splayed a hand over the jagged mess.

The glittering shards of glass trembled and twitched, then like metal slivers reacting to a powerful magnet, they jumped into the air and hovered below his palm. He rubbed his thumb against his fingers in a circular motion. The glass pieces swirled in the air with a soft *clink*, then fused together, reforming into its original state. Mr. Ishida turned his palm up and the now undamaged beaker floated onto his hand.

"Perfect," he said after a close inspection, then tossed it to Jayden. "Be more careful, boys."

Oookay. Mr. Ishida had…superglue powers? This was new.

"Hey, did you boys have something to do with the hot springs?" Mr. Ishida sat in front of the computer screens and started typing.

"What hot springs?" Logan said.

"They're all over the mountain," Mr. Ishida said. "Been dormant for decades, but Reece said all the ones on their ranch suddenly started bubbling up again. Take Ayden, go find Blake, and check them out. My business could take a while, so best if you're gone. "

Just freakin' great. My muscles were already burning, and Jayden's knives beaded sweat. How long before they melted?

Jayden and Logan jerked a look at each other. I couldn't tell who was paler.

"No!" Logan blurted.

Jayden nodded like a bobble head, his hair bouncing erratically. "Perhaps your office would better suffice for business."

And since we didn't have enough of a crowd, Jocelyn Ishida, a stunning, petite female version of her one-year-older brothers, glided into the lab. She had the impeccable bone structure, flawless skin, and a glossy cascade of black-as-midnight hair, currently twisted into some complicated puzzle of braids. No wonder Matthias had a secret crush on her. Luckily, the poor girl hadn't a clue.

"Hey, Dad, can I go to the movies with Ashley tonight?"

"Get out!" Jayden pushed at his sister.

"*You* get out." Jocelyn pirouetted past her brother and skated deeper into the room.

Jayden grabbed at her.

My muscles screamed for release, and the ice blades were definitely starting to melt, the beads of water trickling down and hanging with quivering anticipation off the ends of the knives.

"Take it outside." Mr. Ishida sounded exasperated and started pulling drawers open. "Jocelyn, you can go if you take one of your brothers with you."

The pipes I'd been using to help hold me up suddenly wrenched. My added weight must've been loosening whatever was holding them in place so I let go. The ice blades kept holding me up, but the movement broke free several of the precarious droplets of water hanging off their edges.

Jocelyn and Jayden had been in a loud tussle directly underneath me, but she stopped and groaned at her dad. "Seriously? Ugh! They ruin every—" She flinched, then wiped at her cheek. "What the heck?"

She looked at her fingers, studying the water that had dripped from the melting blades and onto her face. Her head swiveled around.

"Nothing! Don't!" Jayden tried to shove her out again, but she twirled away from him and then…

Jocelyn looked up.

"Hi," I mouthed. Waved. Seemed the polite thing to do.

The knives pinged out from around my arm. My whole body lurched. I dropped the helmet. My hand flailed, reaching for the headgear before it clattered to the floor, but Jayden's hands flicked and the knives flew back up, pinning my arm as they stabbed my shirt against the ceiling and froze solid once again.

The helmet continued its descent. I watched as it rotated in a slow freefall. I cringed, holding my breath. Logan dived for it.

He missed.

Because Jocelyn caught it.

She gaped at the helmet in her hands. Then back up at me. Then at the boys, who were so spastically gesturing for her to be quiet you'd think they were swatting a swarm of killer bees.

"Everyone out!" From a drawer, Mr. Ishida grabbed a circular piece of grey metal the size and shape of a crown. It had sharp scalloped edges on the top with spikes and some kind of studs or jewels on the side. What was with all the bizarro headgear? The cabinet shook as he slammed the drawer shut. "I'm intercepting a call. I need to shut down the Holocom before it comes through."

A soft buzz thrummed the air.

Jayden practically stamped his foot. "A call from whom?"

How could this possibly get worse?

A woman's breathy voice reverberated throughout the room. "Madame Cacciatori. Paris."

That's how.

CHAPTER THIRTY-NINE

"Son of a—"Mr. Ishida slapped the metal crown thing on the counter with a violent *clang*, shoved to his feet, and buttoned his jacket, stabbing a warning finger at his children and Logan, his tone a razor's edge. "Not. A. Word."

Sophina Cacciatori, the Mandatum hunter in charge of tracking down the Divinicus Nex, and one of the people with the most power to ruin my life, shimmered into view.

On close inspection, her form was somewhat transparent and a bit shiny, due to some magical Mandatum science called Holocom which transmitted her 3-D image across space in real time, and into hologram form. In this case, while we saw her here, she was actually in Paris. France.

But that didn't make me any less terrified.

Not that she looked scary. In fact, she was an attractive woman somewhere on either side of forty, with strong features and a throaty laugh that I found rather infectious. Her thick brunette hair was pulled back in a low ponytail, and she wore a fitted jacket over a pale dress that loosely skimmed her voluptuous figure and showed off her, as Blake always remembered, "great legs."

Looking furious, Ayden flew in through the game room door, mouth open and ready to rant. At the sight of Cacciatori he stopped, eyes wide. Jayden pulled him over, but Ayden kept glancing around, leaning over, trying to glance under furniture, even open a cabinet in a nonchalant way.

Jocelyn surreptitiously tapped his arm, shook her head, then pointed up. Ayden lifted his eyes more than his head, and when he finally saw me hanging, he looked positively ill. He closed his eyes briefly, swallowed, then stared hard at Cacciatori.

"My goodness!" Madame Cacciatori exclaimed in a heavy Italian accent and smiled broadly around the room. "I am being given such an expansive audience."

You have no idea.

The guys and Jocelyn remained silent, taking heed to Mr. Ishida's orders. That's right. Smile and wave, boys, just smile and wave.

"Always a pleasure, Madame." Mr. Ishida gave a deferent nod. "And please accept my apologies. As I told your assistant, this personal…visit from you, such an important and extremely busy member of the society, is a waste of your valuable time. My wife isn't here and is currently unreachable, but I'll convey your request as soon as I'm able."

The boys shared a wary look.

"It is I who must apologize for the intrusion," Cacciatori said pleasantly. "I simply feared my assistant did not perhaps translate the dire nature of the circumstances and how much your wife is needed. Did he mention that Donal Jensen was seen? An exceedingly rare occurrence and an opportunity we cannot fail to take advantage of. As you know, the Council Directive Kill Order With Extreme Prejudice is still in place. He is considered a most dangerous threat."

"Yes. Your assistant conveyed the severity of the situation most eloquently, I assure you." Mr. Ishida clasped his hands behind his back. "As soon I establish communication, I'm sure my wife will respond promptly to your request. As she always does. Now if you'll excuse me?"

"Yes, of course."

Thank goodness.

Mr. Ishida had his finger on a button when Cacciatori stopped him and turned to the boys. "But I do have a question for the young hunters."

"Certainly. Jocelyn, let's go." Mr. Ishida gave the boys a warning look then exited with his daughter, a protective arm wrapped around her shoulders.

My body sagged, muscles losing the battle for contraction. Sweat dripped off my face. Water dripped off the knives. One or both dripped onto Ayden's head. He twitched, his hand jumping to his scalp, but he caught himself from looking up, and covered the movement by running his fingers through his hair.

"Have you had any progress on the Flint files?" Cacciatori asked.

"None, Madame," Ayden lied without hesitation.

"Unfortunate." She tapped a knuckle to her chin. "But there is hope. When we get the tracker back online, you will be notified immediately."

The boys stiffened but kept eyes on Cacciatori.

After a beat, Ayden said, "Tracker?" Putting good use to that whole repeating thing he liked to do.

"Trackers are electronically embedded in the files. A standard security precaution with our most vital documents." Cacciatori tipped her head sideways. "Did Father Bancroft not tell you?"

I stopped breathing. Tracker as in track the files down? Here? To us? I didn't know where the boys had the Flint files but the documents had to be somewhere close. They had been on my front lawn! If the Mandatum could track their progress, pinpoint everywhere they had been, I was toast. *We* were toast.

"No." Ayden's voice had an edge. "Father Bancroft must not have had a chance to mention it since our meeting was cut short." His eyes slid toward Jayden and Logan. "Due to an unexpected pressing matter."

Like my kidnapping. Super.

"What data did you reclaim before the tracker became inoperable?" Jayden said.

"It traveled west," Cacciatori said. "Over the Atlantic, toward the States."

Jayden interjected quickly, "Or Canada or South America, or even—"

"True," she agreed, "but we will have answers shortly. The files disappeared from my station here in Paris so it is a personal affront, and I must rectify this myself." Her eyes glittered darkly. "As you know, electronics are my…*forte,* so even if the files and the tracker have been destroyed, I can trace the ghost of the path they traveled until then. We will have answers in a matter of days."

"Wow, impressive," Ayden smiled wide. "How many days would that be?"

"Four." She paused, thoughtful. "Five, perhaps, but only if the one who disengaged it is of supreme ability. And if Gossamer Falls is their destination, tactical support teams can be at your doorstep in mere hours."

Yippee. Good news being that I wouldn't have to worry about that demon hoard stampeding my way in a week.

Cacciatori turned in a slow circle to survey the room. "I see perhaps you could use several of our latest upgrades." Her gaze remained eye level or below. At first. Then it started to lift. Higher and higher and…

My body trembled. I felt her eyes coming for me.

"You know what?!" Ayden blurted.

Blake burst into the room. "Madame Cacciatori!"

Matthias entered with Blake and noticed Logan's subtle chin-bob. The Aussie glanced up. His eyes turned to chipped ice, his jaw locked. His foot stepped in front of Blake's ankle, and he threw a subtle elbow into Blake's back.

Blake was grinning at Cacciatori. "You're a vision of beauty and— Oh! Omph!"

And the mountain came tumbling down.

Momentum took possession of his massive frame, and arms flailing, Blake stumbled and rolled and showed no signs of stopping. Like a supercharged ball in a pinball machine, he slammed into countertops, knocked over equipment, shot paperwork into the air, sent wheeled chairs shooting across the room to crash into tables and cabinets, rattling vials and glassware, and clattering microscopes and expensive looking machines off their shelves.

There was *clanging* and *banging* and a barrage of noise, and as he finally thumped to the floor, the holographic image of Madame Cacciatori stuttered and blinked out.

Blake sat up, grimaced, and reached underneath his butt. He pulled out the metal crown thing which had lost some of the pieces attached to the side, the top was bent, and the circular shape was seriously warped.

Mr. Ishida rushed in. "What happened?"

Blake said sheepishly, "Sorry, dudes, I think I broke it." He pointed at Matthias. "He pushed me!"

"Sorry?" Mr. Ishida breathed deep, grasped Blake's hand and yanked him up. "You…are," his face broke into a beaming smile, "brilliant!" He grabbed the sides of Blake's head and kissed his cheek.

"I am?"

"Dad, we can fix this," Ayden said.

"No!" Mr. Ishida snapped. "Don't touch a thing. Well, clean up but the Holocom *stays* broken. Got it?" Halfway out the door he stopped, a hand gripping the frame. His face faltered. "Not a word to your mother. Don't answer calls from Cacciatori. I'm leaving to talk to Bancroft. We'll figure something out. The Grants may have gone on this miserable mission, but…I have to agree with Tristan on this one, his grandparents are crazy."

Couldn't agree more.

After he left, the door *swished* closed, the knives disintegrated, and I plummeted to the floor.

A gust of wind stalled the brunt of my fall and I dropped into Ayden's waiting arms. He gave me a playful grin. "Hang around here often?"

"Ha ha." I squirmed.

He clamped his arms around my body and shifted me closer, whispering in my ear. "About earlier. We need to talk."

No thanks! Not ready! With a hard twist, I spun out of his arms, and landed in a less-than-graceful belly-flop on the hard floor. Not that any belly-flops were graceful. Mine least of all. Ouch.

He looked down at me, amused. "I take it you don't want to talk right now?"

"Or ever," I winced.

Ayden bent to help me up, but Jayden shouldered him out of the way. "Of course she doesn't want to talk about it."

Ayden frowned. "You don't even *know* what we're talking about talking about."

"I assumed you were going to ambush her with a barrage of questions about the tests we were running. Which are simply routine." Jayden had me up and was brushing off my body.

"Jayden, it's okay. Don't—" I used my arms to block him. "No, not the—" Not the boobs, Jayden, not the boobs. God, he was clueless.

"Then why all the secrecy?" Ayden knocked Jayden's hands aside. "Quit touching her."

Jayden scowled. "I should probe for injuries since you just dropped her."

"No probing," Ayden snapped. "I didn't drop her, she…jumped. Kind of."

Jayden gave his brother a disapproving look. "Since you have proven inept to the task, perhaps I should take over as her boyfriend."

"What?" Ayden and I said at the same time.

Logan rushed in to shove Jayden off and usher me away. "Don't listen to him. He's been reading relationship books to, ah, improve his social skills and thought he could use Aurora to experiment on." Logan made an exasperated noise. "I told him it was stupid."

Jayden looked offended. "I never—"

"Jayden!" Logan pointed to the computer screen that monitored the game room. Jocelyn was staring straight at the camera. "I think we've got more important things to worry about right now."

Jayden squinted at his sister. "Yes, the security breach."

CHAPTER FORTY

Inside the Ishida's pub-styled brass, wood, and leather infused game room, you would've needed a friggin' chainsaw to cut through the tension.

Situated in the back of the house, on the second floor, the vaulted ceilings and wall of windows offered stunning views of the lake and mountains, currently blurred from a slight drizzle misting over the scene. The weather mirrored the ominous overtones in the room. A cold wind howled, ushering in dark clouds of slate and asphalt, thickening the air with an earthy, wet scent fluttering in through several open doors to the covered balcony.

The adverse outdoor climate made the room all the more inviting with its cushy, overstuffed furniture and endless entertainment opportunities. From the carved mahogany billiards table, to the round, cherrywood game table covered in felt in the center, to dart boards, pinball machines, a jukebox, the home audio and theater system, and big screen TVs with your pick of an epic supply of video games and movies.

But at the moment, no one cared.

Under the oblong stained-glass Tiffany lamp hanging above the billiards table, Blake repeatedly gathered the colorful balls in his hands, then ricocheted them across the felt. They rumbled and cracked like the thunder and lightning threatening to erupt outside if the storm kept coming in.

Behind the gleaming brass bar, Matthias was on his second — no third — can of Milo, not even bothering to grab his usual glass from the racks on the mirrored wall behind him. Jayden's thumbs rolled in and out of joint with wet pops as he babbled on and on, and Logan had smoothed his tie so many times it was missing a layer of fabric.

I sat on the couch between Jayden and Logan. Careful to avoid Ayden's eyes. And *that* smile.

Aunt M was right. I was a hot mess. Best to keep my distance. I hugged myself, rubbing my biceps.

Almost immediately, I heard someone close the French doors to the balcony cutting the chilly draft, saw the logs in the hearth burst into roaring flames, and felt a chenille throw blanket being laid gently over my shoulders. Warm hands brushed my neck as they lifted my long curls and tucked the soft material against my skin.

So much for distance.

Ayden's fingers squeezed my shoulders. Fighting the urge to lay my cheek upon his hand, my body stiffened. He paused, then removed his touch, and in spite of the toasty coverlet, I shivered. As if someone cranked the furnace, heat suddenly radiated across the space and warmed my back.

I closed my eyes. Hot mess. Definite hot mess.

"Jayden, stop." Jocelyn held up a dainty hand glittering with rings. "You're doing that thing where you talk in circles using big words no one understands in hopes they give up asking and walk away." She lowered gracefully into an overstuffed leather chair. "What I did get is that she sees demons but no one can know because there's a threat. You have to protect her and I have to keep my mouth shut."

Jayden looked annoyed. "Affirmative."

Jocelyn's gaze flicked from me to Ayden. "And you're her bodyguard, not her boyfriend?"

Oh, thanks for pointing that out.

"Yes," I said before Ayden had a chance, hoping I didn't look as miserable as I felt.

The heat at my back vanished. Logan and Blake shot me odd looks.

"Really? You two sure seemed...cozy." Jocelyn twirled one of her braids in her fingers and frowned at her brother. "Then Ayden, why are you—"

"Joce!" Ayden's sharp warning whiplashed across the room. She flinched. "Enough questions. We've got some serious Mandatum problems. You know the family wants you out of the Mandatum business. It's too dangerous. Even Dad just had to lie to protect Mom. *Mom!* Of *all* people."

"Of course, I'd never do anything to hurt Aurora." Jocelyn snapped at Ayden then smiled at me. "You saved my life from Echo. I'll keep my mouth shut. Besides, it'll be nice to have a girl around to talk to. Help cope with these idiots." She glowered around the room. "But you guys know I hate being kept out of this stuff! I know more about the Mandatum than Blake!"

"Hey!" Blake protested.

"Okay." Jocelyn fluttered thick lashes at the big guy. "What are the names of the High Council members?"

Blake tossed a cue ball in the air. "Ahhh..."

Matthias rolled his eyes. "Mate, come on! You've got to know. They're the seven *leaders* of the Mandatum!"

"I know." Blake rapped his knuckles against his skull. "Give me a sec. There's that blonde chick."

"That was the assistant," Logan sighed.

"There's Madame Cacciatori," Blake said with confidence.

"No!" Matthias slammed down his can. "She's not on the High Council. She answers directly to them. She's in the intelligence division. Runs the Divinicus Task Force. You've got to know one name."

At Blake's silence, Matthias gave up with a growl.

"See?" Jocelyn smirked.

The doors to the game room burst open.

"My dad!" Tristan wheezed. "He's missing!"

Chapter Forty-One

"You're not making any sense," Matthias said as the rest of us all followed a frantic Tristan into the secret room. Jocelyn had left quickly, promising to stay home tonight.

"Really?" Tristan's freckles stood out against pale skin. "What part of 'my dad's been kidnapped' don't you understand?"

Me? Not much. Since this was the first I'd heard about Tristan having any parent who was alive.

"Kidnapped?" Jayden said. "I thought you just said his physician took him on an outing?"

"Yes," Tristan's head bobbed. "But it's some new doctor that I've never heard about."

Ayden's brow furrowed. "But this doctor works at Novo, right? And they sanctioned the release?"

"Yes! The idiots." Tristan's fingers pounded the keyboard. "After I dropped my grandparents off at the airport, I called Novo to check on my dad, and they told me he was doing so fantastic with this new doctor that the two of them went on a," his hands snapped into the air so he could use finger quotes, "'field trip.' Overnight! But there's no way my dad should be out…in the world. In his condition."

The boys shared concerned looks.

"Maybe you're overreacting, mate," Matthias said patiently.

Logan lifted his shoulders. "You do tend to think the worst."

When Tristan shot the boys a furious glare, Matthias took out his phone and headed for the balcony. "But I'll make some calls."

"Good." Tristan said. "I can't contact my grandparents until this stupid mission is over so I'm going to tap into Novo's security system and see what I can find on surveillance footage."

"Not a good idea," Logan said. "They'll track the hack and you'll be in some serious trouble. Wait to see what Matthias finds out."

Tristan breathed deep. "Fine. I'll see what I can find out without hacking."

"Dude," Blake put a meaty hand on Tristan's shoulder, "even I know Novo is one of the most secure Mandatum facilities there is. No one could kidnap him."

"What's Novo?" I asked.

"A premier Mandatum hospital," Jayden said. "It specializes in repairing those debilitated by Hallucinators. For years they have attempted to heal the brain damage Tristan caused, but unfortunately, even with their eminent level of capabilities, Mr. Grant's case has proven too severe for successful treatment."

The immediate silence was intense. Tristan froze from his fever pitch of activity and stared straight ahead.

Then the rest of the guys shouted in accusation, "Jayden!"

Jayden looked unperturbed. "It wasn't a recrimination. And we're all cognizant of the circumstances which—ah, I see my error." He glanced at me. "Aurora."

Great. Now I was the big mistake in the room. Better than the pink elephant. Barely. Tristan turned to me with blue eyes so haunted, my heart paused a hesitant beat.

I nodded. "I'll leave so you guys can talk."

Odd-man-out? Not my favorite position, but this was family and that took priority over my feelings being bent out of shape.

I was halfway to the door when Tristan started typing again. He cleared his throat. "It was after the demon attack when we were kids. The one that killed Garrett. Herman's brother."

I stopped and turned.

Ayden caught my eye, adding, "The one at the waterfall where our powers were activated early in order to protect us."

Like I could forget that horror story. "Right. You guys were only around…eight years old?"

Ayden nodded. The back of my neck prickled. I remembered seeing my first demons around that age. No attacks, just the occasional glimpse out of the corner of my eye that would send me screaming into my parents arms. Not good for a little kid. Gave me—

"Nightmares." Tristan let out a shaky breath. "I had bad ones. But even awake I freaked. Constantly imagined monsters and violence."

"We all felt that way," Logan said and the other boys murmured agreement.

"But I didn't know how to control my powers." Tristan's voice had a raspy edge. "So everything I imagined I accidentally forced into my parents' minds. I was literally driving them insane. We were alone, isolated in a safe house in Europe. My dad sent my mom away. Thought he could handle it, but he stayed too long trying to protect me. I caused too much damage."

Whoa. Talk about guilt. "And your mom?"

"She's fine." His smile was weak. "I see her pretty often. But in short doses. After what I did, I won't risk anything long term."

"Which is why you live with your grandparents," I said. "They're good people." Scary, but good.

"You have no idea." Tristan rubbed the back of his neck. "They're the only reason my Dad is alive. I could have literally turned his brain to mush if it went on long enough. But luckily they found us in time."

"Not luck," Ayden said. "You called them. You saved your dad."

"From death, maybe." Tristan's eyes were clouded with misery. "But he lost touch with reality. He's been at Novo ever since. Doesn't know me, my mom. Nothing. If he speaks at all, it's gibberish." Tristan wiped at his eyes. "What I did was…unusual. Too dangerous, especially in someone so young. The Mandatum wanted to take me away, isolate me, but my grandparents…refused."

"Threatened the friggin' Mandatum," Blake said with admiration. "Don't know with what, but that's what Logan's mom said."

"Which was supposed to be a secret," Logan muttered.

Tristan smiled. "My grandparents found a way to deal with…my issue, and with their help and the Mandatum training, eventually I learned control, and we came back here."

When Matthias returned, Tristan jumped to his feet. "Well?"

"It's legit," Matthias said. "I talked to the director of Novo himself. He's actually really excited about your dad's case. This new doctor came in a few weeks ago from overseas and has had a lot of success with your dad. He's having conversations, been asking about his family. Asking about you." Matthias almost smiled. "He's remembering. Everything."

Tristan dropped into his chair, arms hanging limp at his sides. "Why didn't they tell us?"

"They're being cautious." Matthias's voice was steady. "They're not sure how permanent his recovery is and were afraid seeing his family too soon would cause him to regress. This field trip — to another secure Mandatum facility, so don't worry — is a way to have him experience a different environment, see how he reacts, and hopefully, strengthen his ability—"

"To cope with new situations and environments," I said. "It's something they did when I was afraid to leave the hospital." Then I added quickly, "Not that your dad's afraid, but if he's only been at Novo for so long, it makes sense that they're trying to acclimate him to other places. Which also means they think he has a chance to get out of Novo at some point. That's good news."

Jayden gave me a surprised look, "Actually, I'd concur with that assessment."

"See, dude, you overreacted," Blake slapped Tristan's shoulder. "It's *all* good news."

Tristan huffed a little breath, then smiled. "When can I see him?"

"It's delicate, mate," Matthias said with sympathy. "They want you to sit tight for now. Said they'd call in a few days when he gets back. Let you know his status. But either way, I made them promise you could visit soon."

Tristan rolled his eyes. "I'm just supposed to sit around and wait?"

"Between hidden tunnels, long lost treasure, and a Mandatum tracker that could blow us out of the water, I think we can keep you busy," Logan said.

Tristan blinked. "This is why I can't leave you guys alone for even a few hours."

Chapter Forty-Two

After we got Tristan up to speed, he and Blake got busy. They sat at the computer console creating a map of the previously unknown tunnels with Tristan entering coordinates based on Blake's verbal directions and notes scribbled on paper. The rest of the boys had disappeared for various errands. We were supposed to call them when the map was ready.

"Make me another." Tristan handed Blake his coffee mug.

Tristan was on his third cappuccino from the new machine gleaming behind the bar. It was an elaborate affair of hammered copper and brass, the size of a child's doll house and full of so many domed cylinders it reminded me of a fairytale castle.

"Make your own, dude." Blake eyed Tristan's shaky hand. "And you should probably switch to decaf."

Tristan *banged* his mug down and kept working.

Sitting next to Blake, sipping my own yummy brew, I'd just finished sharing what I remembered about the layout of the tunnels that Logan and I had wandered through. Blake added my recollections to his many pages of sketches.

"Impressive," I said with sincerity, admiring not only his artistic talent but the extensive level of information. "You got all this without going *into* any of the tunnels?"

"I can read the earth, babe," he grinned. "Almost as well I read women, and once the veils were broken—"

"Veils?" I frowned.

"A type of cloaking device." Tristan said. "Still not sure how Flint pulled it off, but all these years it kept the tunnels invisible to even the strongest of earth Mandatum hunters."

"But not me," Blake said with pride.

I gave him a dubious look. "You said Fido breaking through the wall broke the veils and *that's* why you could finally 'see' the tunnels."

"I said that *could* be the reason. More likely, it was just my day to be *awesome*." He sang the last word then pointed at the computer screen. "Dude, that's off three degrees." He turned back to me. "Anyway, now all I had to do was touch the walls and ground *outside* the tunnels, and I can literally read through miles of the terrain. Get a type of geological map in my head. Then I give techno-boy here the coordinates." He thumped Tristan.

"And I do the important work," Tristan said.

"No way, dude." Blake said. "My skills got all this without anyone having to go in the tunnels with that crazy gal spouting off threats and trying to kill anything or anyone Mandatum." He thought for a moment. "But she does have a sexy voice. I'll bet she's hot."

"No, she's cold," Tristan said without taking his eyes from his task. "As in stone cold. She's dead."

"Ew," Blake cringed. "Not a good visual for my fantasies."

Tristan smirked. "None of your fantasies are good visuals."

"Ha! If you were *in* my fantasies—"

"I'd want to kill myself."

"That's not what I meant."

I shook my head. "Tristan, why do you think she's dead?"

"Killed herself 'cause she's in Blake's fantasies."

I laughed, happy about his lighthearted mood.

Blake swatted the back of Tristan's head. "Hurtful, dude."

Tristan kicked Blake's chair so it rolled a few feet. "I'm sure her voice is just a recording Flint made with one of his gadgets. And that would've been over a hundred years ago. So, yes. Dead."

Logan entered the game room. "Is it ready?"

"Almost," Blake said. "Where's Jayden?"

"In the kitchen." Ayden said, following close behind Logan. His clothes and hair were soaked, dripping a trail of water behind him as he hauled in a large metal footlocker.

He carried it by thick leather straps attached on either end, and I could tell it was heavy because it was like a wet T-shirt contest in here. The drenched fabric clung to every sculptured line of Ayden's torso and revealed in detail how his muscles flexed to hold the weight. It was glorious. If you were into that sort of thing. And based how my breath caught at the sight, I was.

Ayden regripped the handles and like ripples on a pond, sinew flowed under his skin. "And my dear brother is apparently way too busy to help get the Flint files which were in the boathouse in the cache he designed which is, of course, underwater and which *he* can get to without getting wet. But the rest of us? Not so much."

Logan paused at the balcony doorway. "I told you I could help with that."

"Don't think so." Ayden dumped the trunk on the floor and shook himself like a dog.

"It will just take a second," Logan persisted.

"Let it go, Logan." Ayden said. "I'm good."

He started to lift the hem of his shirt to wipe beads of water off his face. As the fabric peeled up off his stomach, ready to expose some serious skin, a turbulent blast of air came out of nowhere. It tornadoed around him, whipping over his body and flapping his clothes.

I jumped and almost bit my tongue because… I *might* have been licking my lips when the gust hit. Go figure. The whirlwind lasted only seconds.

Unfazed, Ayden let go of his shirt and glared at Logan. "Seriously?"

But the white-haired wonder ignored him, already working the balcony railing like a world class gymnast on the balance beam.

Ayden raised his voice. "I don't like this new little trick of yours." His hair stuck out all over his head. He used both hands to slick it back which made him look older. And kind of…sexy dangerous.

He caught my stare. Something registered in his eyes, and he gave me a slow, wicked smile. Heat licked up my spine and lashed a deep blush across my cheeks. I jerked my gaze away, a hand to my throat because it seemed like something threatened to strangle me.

"Aren't we, ah," I coughed to remove the squeak from my tone and reboot my vocal cords, "worried about the tracker in the files?"

Good girl, Aurora, focus on the threats to your life, not your heart.

"Get that out of here!" Tristan gawked into the game room, tipped so far back in his chair he would have fallen if Blake hadn't caught him. "Cacciatori could be tracing it!"

"Not right now." Ayden sat on the trunk and tapped his knuckle on the edge. "Jayden says this particular metal alloy will weaken the tracker. Or something. It'll slow Cacciatori down. Buy us that extra day or even more because—"

"He's so supreme?" Tristan butted in with a high-strung hint of sarcasm. "He'd better be right. I'm not about to get my dad back and have him visit me in a Mandatum dungeon."

I started to laugh at the dungeon comment, but studying the rest of the guys' faces, I realized he wasn't joking. Fantastic. If we didn't hurry, we'd all be in dungeons. At least I'd have company.

I stood and paced, picking up a beaker, pinging it nervously with my fingernail. I paused when I realized it was the broken one Mr. Ishida had put back together.

"He's a Revertor," came Ayden's voice immediately behind me.

Startled, I dropped the glass, but he reached around and caught it easily, his chest touching my back. At the contact, heat skittered across my shoulders. My eyes swept sideways, traveling up the length of his bare arm, watching rivulets of water upon his skin meander down through the contours of his muscles.

His warm breath skated over the back of my neck. The damp aroma of the lake clung to his clothes, but the scent of sandalwood still lingered beneath. He lifted the beaker and twirled it in the light.

"See, not a crack." His voice rumbled next to my ear.

And under my skin, ready to infiltrate my heart and crumble any resolve to keep my distance.

I snatched the glass and moved away. "What are you doing?"

"Telling you something you didn't know. It's called *sharing*." He followed my retreat, smiling. Like a cat. A Cheshire cat. Too knowing. It made me twitchy. "My dad can kind of…rewind the damage on inanimate objects. I told you the hunter thing is genetic. We have lots of powers in our family line."

Despite my irritation, I was interested. "You don't get the same powers as your parents?"

"Sometimes none at all," he shrugged. "Like Jocelyn."

"Don't forget your dad's a smuggler too," Blake said. "Way more cool."

Ayden laughed. "Sometimes, yes. But retired. Semi."

"What did he smuggle?" I had to ask.

"My mom for one. Smuggled her out of one heck of a jam." Ayden leaned in close and lowered his voice. "And according to her, hijacked her heart at the very same time."

His eyes, dark and playful, wouldn't let go of mine. I felt the intensity building. He moved to tuck a strand of my hair behind my ear, but I batted his hand and whirled away.

"Tristan, aren't you done yet?" I said.

"Because the nagging is so helpful." Tristan spun his chair and faced the middle of the room. "But, yeah. It's showtime."

There was a hum. Lights flickered. Then the magic happened.

CHAPTER FORTY-THREE

As if someone was drawing at super-speed using a laser light-stick, a miniature 3-D holographic rendering of the town of Gossamer Falls came to life in mid-air. Hovering just above eye level and measuring six feet at its longest length, the hologram shimmered and glowed in wavering shades of white, blue, and green.

In this fantastical image, the lake took center stage, the jagged shoreline broken up by off-shoots of large bays and small coves. Upon its shores, the surrounding community's buildings, roads, parks, and forest emerged in full detail. And it all seemed alive.

A breeze fluttered the leaves of the trees, water flowed through the winding streams and steep gorges, and the pounding currents of the waterfall poured over the cliff's edge, crashing into the deep pools below in a billowing, sparkling mist. Only things missing were miniature cars and people moving about their daily lives.

The shape of the lake was basically an oval, lying lengthwise from east to west, tucked in a long valley with the mountains jutting up around it. Starting on the west end was the main town with neighborhood houses and various buildings, such as the country club. This section spread clockwise to the north and east, covering about two-thirds of the northern perimeter. Then the mountains took over, and at the east end, directly opposite the town, was the waterfall with the portal behind it.

Continuing around the lake, curving down and clockwise on the south side, signs of civilization were sparse. Blake's dude ranch had his house, the barn, and several outbuildings, including the guest cabins. Also located in this section loomed the imposing Gothic drama of Flint's old house and the various smaller buildings on the estate. The rest of this mildly inhabited south end was covered with endless acres of the uninhabited forest and pastureland belonging to Blake's family.

While we all stood in awe, Matthias had arrived. He patted Tristan's shoulder. "Very nice, mate."

Blake scoffed, "Please, he had the easy part. I provided what you've all been waiting for."

He stuck his meaty paw into the middle of the holographic image and swiped his hand down. The model of the town's surface remained above, but Blake's movement pulled forth another hologram directly below. The underground layer.

In the same glowing lines of holographic light, a massive network of tunnels appeared. They spidered out underneath Gossamer Falls in a complicated layout of intersecting passageways that ran up, down, or leveled off. Some were straight and some were curved, with several sharp turns and even a few spirals. Honestly, it reminded me of Selena's ant farm.

"That's amazing," I murmured.

"Told ya." Blake grinned. "Watch this."

As he touched the hologram in various ways, things moved, allowing him to manipulate the luminous image. He could spin it completely in both directions. He could enlarge and reduce the whole illustration or just a particular area. He could separate an entire section out for closer study, highlight a section within the hologram, or turn things different colors. It was pretty cool.

"This is straight-up creepy." Ayden angled his head to get a closer look. "All this time and we never knew. Flint's tunnels don't just run from behind the waterfall to the portal like we always thought, they run—"

"Under the entire town." Blake was near quivering with excitement.

"Some even lead out." Tristan pointed at a few channels snaking out of the town under the mountains.

Blake shouldered Tristan aside. "Did *you* find the tunnels? Ah, no. *I* did."

"I don't care who found what," Matthias snapped. "One of you start talking."

Blake pointed at the flickering image of our high school sitting on the south side of the lake. "The tunnels originate at Gossamer High, Flint's old tower of doom."

He traced a finger along the tunnels and rotated the image, highlighting the passageways where they ran around the left edge of the lake to the main town and the majority of homes and neighborhoods. Like where I lived.

"They break up into hundreds of short, narrow tunnels under the town," Blake continued. "Connecting a lot of buildings together. Then they get longer and bigger as they go across the upper lake to the north under the country club, private school, and rich people houses." Blake spun the hologram and drew our attention to a corridor that ran under a large structure. He touched the building and widened his fingers. The house expanded in size and was easily recognizable. He told Ayden, "Like yours, dude."

Ayden reached out and touched the building, narrowing his fingers to revert it to the smaller size.

"Yeah, well, I'm not the one whose family practically owns the whole mountain."

"Just a few thousand acres." Blake laughed and thumped Ayden which knocked him into Tristan. "Because we were too smart and had awesome supernatural powers so the bloomin' Brits couldn't steal it from us. No offense, Matthias."

The Aussie made a face. "But I'm not— Never mind."

My brow furrowed. "Brits?"

"I'm part Native American, babe." He tapped his cheek. "Didn't you notice my swarthy complexion?"

Ayden snorted. "Swarthy?"

"That's what Uncle Reece calls it." Blake waggled his brows. "Sounds sexy. 'Cause we are. So is the fact that some of my family was on this mountain way before the settlers showed up. Makes you want to jump me, right now, huh, babe?"

"Focus, Blake," Matthias growled.

"You're just jealous. Sorry, chickadee," he said with a wink. "You'll have to jump my sexified, swarthy self later. When we don't have a crowd. Unless you're into that. Because I'm totally cool with group—"

"Blake!"

"Alas, duty calls." Blake offered me an apologetic look and turned back to the map. "There aren't many tunnels that go past the mountains and cliffs. See, nothing in the northeast fringes near your house, Matthias. But they start branching out again at the portal. Over here, babe." Blake spun the hologram and reeled me to his side to point at the lake's coves on the far east end where the iconic falls crashed and misted opposite the main town.

I knew how to read a freakin' map, especially since this 3-D one was idiot proof. But I bit my tongue. Blake was so happy nerding-out.

"This big tunnel here goes from the falls around the far end of lake and all the way back to the high school. But here's the weird part."

"It hasn't been weird yet?" I smiled.

Blake grinned back. "That big tunnel along the far end has all those little off-shoots going away from the lake. That's my ranch. It covers all the land around the falls and the high school. Those tunnels come up to nothing. Just forest and pastures. But here's the weirder part." He enlarged a tunnel wall and pointed at what looked like pieces of machinery. "Most of the tunnel walls have gears and stuff built into them."

I remembered the pieces of metal flying out when Fido broke through. "For reinforcement?"

"It's more than that." Tristan took a closer look. "It's some sort of working machinery. Could run stuff like the lights and the fireballs. And whatever other contraptions Flint built into his security system."

"He also built a secret access to the church, and a lot of the original buildings." Ayden pointed at the main town then dragged a finger through the pale lighted tunnels at the west end. The ones that curved up into buildings turned red.

I made a face. "Bet it made it easy to kidnap and transport his murder victims without anyone ever seeing him."

"Chickadee, that's not even the creepiest part. Look." Blake gave a dramatic shiver as he poked at two tunnel intersections, his touch turning them bright yellow. "Almost all the tunnels eventually meet at two locations. The high school and the portal."

"Why would he build so many secret tunnels to the portal?" Tristan said.

Logan shrugged and leaned closer to squint at the map. "They never found the bodies of Flint's victims."

Silence saturated the room because…

I cringed, "Ew, he threw the bodies into the portal?"

"Sick and efficient," Ayden said.

Logan walked slowly around the hologram. "You didn't find the rooms?"

Blake frowned. "What rooms?"

"The treasure he stole." Logan loosened his tie. "The Mandatum says it could fill three cargo trains. But other than the portal cave there aren't any open spaces. Where could he store it?"

"I think some stuff is still hidden from my ability." Blake enlarged an area underneath the school. "Here seems to be part of an open space. Has a bunch of mechanical stuff."

Logan shook his head. "It's not big enough."

Blake expanded the hologram around the mountains. "There are some gaps and dead-ends here. I could try mapping the ones that head out of town."

"How does Rose expect us to search through all this?" Tristan flung a hand at the map, then paced frantically, arms flapping. "There's a hoard of demons coming. And Cacciatori. And tactical teams. We don't have that kind of time!"

"You can't search it anyway." I met their quizzical looks with a steadiness I did not feel. "It has to be me."

Ayden shook his head. "Absolutely not."

I wasn't crazy about it either, but…

"When Logan and I were in the tunnels, the security system tried to kill him, but not me." I lifted one shoulder. "I don't know why, but I'll be safe." I hoped.

"Forget it. Flint was a serial killer." Ayden's look was dark. "With his super nerd ability he could invent crap way ahead of his time. Like Da Vinci. But a big difference is that Flint actually had the means to build the stuff. Those little flaming spiked things are probably the least of our problems."

Matthias nodded. "Agreed. Until we know more and have a plan, nobody," he raised his brows at me, "goes anywhere near the tunnels. We need to go over the Flint files right now to see what we can find that can help us with the search."

"The risk is too prodigious." Jayden arrived carrying a plate of fresh-baked cookies. "We must give the documentations at least another night in the alloy to further mute the tracker's efficacy."

Tristan groaned. "More delays?"

"Fan-bloody-tastic." Matthias blew out a frustrated breath. "Fine. We could use a good night's sleep." He pointed at the map. "Tristan, print out copies of that so we can all get familiar."

"I'll put the image on everyone's cell phone." Tristan sniffed the air. "Are those chocolate oatmeal bars?"

"Your favorite." After slapping Blake's hand away, Jayden presented the treats to Tristan. "A laudatory jubilation to venerate your father's reclamation. And further proof that I am propagating more emotional frivolity in my endeavors."

Because that sounded so frivolous.

A doorbell blared over and over, like some kid was poking away with relentless intent.

"Who the bloody hell is that?"

Tristan brought up a security feed of the Ishida's front door. The uninvited guest had a baseball cap pulled low to hide their face, but nothing could disguise the huge belly.

"Aurora!" Aunt M screeched in stereo, echoing from the computer speakers and through the front door and up the stairway. She jabbed the bell a few dozen more times.

I checked the time and pushed through the crowd of boys. "Crap. I'm late for dinner."

Logan gave Jayden a troubled look. "Didn't you tell her family we were at Blake's?"

"Confirmatory." Jayden said.

I paused my rush out of the room. "How the heck did she know I was here?"

"I told you there's something weird about M," Tristan said. "*Now* do you believe me?"

Matthias wiped a hand down his face. "Weird that a woman who specializes in security was able to track her nitwit niece? No, mate. I think that's the most normal thing going on around here."

Chapter Forty-Four

Darkness blurs, lightens to green shadows, then solidifies into trees. Oak and pine. Moonlight filtered by lacy wisps of clouds dips through breaks in the branches.

Blood-tipped fangs snap at the mists slithering through the night. Enormous pupil-less silver eyes stare though me. They belong to one of the almost-hellhound demons as it stands feral and wolfish on long thin legs. A thick layer of fur mottled with dirty shades of rotting wood and dried mushrooms spew out in a wiry mass, matted against the curved, spiral horns that spike out along its spine and tail.

It lowers into a crouch, tongue lapping across bared teeth.

"Oh, excellent," Rose steps out from behind a tree. "Now you're on high alert. Where was this ferocity last night?"

More silver-eyed hounds slink out from the forest to encircle Rose, growls slobbering the air. With a graceful leap, Rose grabs a low tree branch and swings himself up, out of reach of shredding teeth.

"Where is my stone?" A woman's voice, flat and emotionless, carries down from above.

Her human form sits poised on a tree branch, too high in the cloaking shadows of night for me to see her as much more than a blur.

"Safe." Rose snaps. "Unlike the Nex. Where were you? A demon got past your hounds and almost killed her!"

"The rogue was getting too close," she says, unconcerned with Rose's angst. "I was compelled to lay a false trail in order to distract him. But time is short."

Rose climbs to stand on a thick branch and leans against the trunk. "The Nex found the tunnels."

"But the hunters prohibit her from entering." Her voice grinds artic cold. "Once again men prevent a woman from reaching her true potential."

Rose scoffs, "They act to keep her alive."

"Fools. Flint's tunnels are designed to protect her. The girl requires fewer champions and more incentive." Her voice takes a dangerous edge. "A circumstance I am happy to facilitate."

"No!" Rose seethes. "Your bloodlust ruins everything. I will handle it."

"You had better, or bloodlust will prevail." She shrugs, "Regardless, I can search for the treasure on my own."

"Now who plays the fool? Neither of us can enter."

The woman laughs and stands, the silhouette of a bow pulled taut in her hands. "Are you concerned that I no longer have use for the Nex?"

Rose gives a bored look to the arrow aimed at his head. "Harm her without my consent, and I will assure delivery of your stone to the Mandatum. Or worse. Let's not forget who has the power in this relationship."

The hounds snarl.

"Yes," the woman lowers the weapon. "There are many vipers in this pit."

Rose scowls with dark intensity. "I swear I will end them all once I get my beloved back. I just need to open—"

I woke to darkness. And a weight pressing my chest. My hands lashed out. Fur slid between my fingers. Silver eyes glinted and a low growl rumbled the room. A creature of death.

Or not.

"Helsing!" I held my cat high. "Sleep on your own bed!"

He *meowed* and squirmed out of my hands, bounding into the shadows.

"Spaz."

On the ride home with Aunt M, I'd had to endure a Dump The Hex Boys lecture. Other than firmly declining an invitation to have Father Bancroft give me an "earful" about staying away from them, I didn't engage in the conversation. I was too worried about the plan the boys were trying to come up with to infiltrate the tunnels without getting themselves killed.

After dinner, I'd excused myself and gone to my room, using Jayden's meditation techniques to induce a Divinicus vision. I'd tried for hours, but after zero luck, I'd fallen into a fitful sleep, frustrated at my failure. Or maybe not. Because I'd like to think that after I'd tumbled into slumber, my efforts had kicked-in this dream-vision thing. Either way, I'd had one of these before, and ignoring it had almost cost Jocelyn her life.

Not this time. I'd convinced myself that these visions were clues that my kooky Divinicus ability managed to fetter out of my subconscious, or whatever, and I needed to act. We were running out of time.

The numbers on my digital clock glared in the darkness, confirming the hour at a little before one in the way-too-early morning. But despite my groggy state, I rolled out of bed and changed into dark street clothes and Luna's hoodie. Then, after a brief sneak into her room for a final essential, I slung my backpack over my shoulder and headed downstairs. By the time I hit the kitchen, I had a plan in my mind, but when I went to open the door to the garage, it was locked.

"No." I thumped my forehead against the doorframe.

Aunt M had put on a deadbolt so no one could enter until she was finished with her stupid project. It was probably booby trapped with alarms too if I were to try and break in.

"Told you not to go in there."

I yelped at the voice. "Aunt M!"

"Too many live wires. It's dangerous." M shuffled over in her robe and dumped Helsing in my arms. "Your stupid cat was scratching at my door. If you think you're sneaking out under my watch, think again."

"I'm not sneaking." I was so sneaking. "Everyone knows I leave early for workouts."

"Not this early."

"Couldn't sleep." At least that part was true. "I'm taking your advice and going on my own."

"No Hex Boys?" M's mouth twisted with suspicion.

"I'm Hexless. But I do need my bike." I set Helsing down. "Or I'll have to call one of them for a ride."

She wagged a warning finger. "Don't you dare. Wait here." She pulled a key from her pocket.

"What about the wires? Getting zapped would hurt you and the baby."

"I'm immune." She unlocked the door, slipping into the darkened garage. Moments later she squeezed out with my bike. As I wheeled it to the front door, M waddled beside me.

"Glad you're doing more without those boys. You need to join a club like you did before. Make new friends."

"I'll look into it," I lied. A normal student routine hadn't entered my mind for…I don't know, forever?

"How about that trip you were planning? Where was it? Austria? Spain?"

"No, it was…never mind." That all seemed a lifetime ago. I missed those carefree days of utter ignorance.

"Tell me where then," Aunt M said. "I've got offices worldwide, and if I don't have one where you want to go, I'll get one." When I smiled and shook my head, she rushed on. "London, Rome, Athens. Or Paris! Even I like that one. "

Sure. Great plan, dumped into the waiting arms of Madame Cacciatori.

"Thanks, but no." I opened the front door and poked my head out. The lights were off at Tristan's. Good. I sidestepped out. "I'm not interested in traveling anymore."

Aunt M followed me onto the porch, wrapping her robe tighter against the bitter chill. "But wasn't that the point of becoming fluent? I'd set you up to intern for a semester. And the summer. Or all year!"

"You never wanted me to go anyway," I whispered, gesturing for her to keep her voice down as I pulled on a knit cap and gloves. It was way colder than I expected. "See? I'm taking your advice left and right. Besides, I've found a new hobby. Staying healthy."

More like staying alive, but close enough. And it was more of a full-time job.

"Wish you'd make homework your hobby," Aunt M said. "I could tutor you. Or Bancroft. He's actually quite knowledgeable. And more patient. I can take you to see him when you get back."

"No thanks." I gave her a kiss on the cheek. "See you after school. Oh, and, if that mailman comes back, shoot him with your tranq gun. A lot."

She grinned. "That's my girl."

CHAPTER FORTY-FIVE

In the middle of the night, murderer's mansions-turned-insane-asylums-turned-high schools were creepy. Go figure.

Aunt M had dropped us off at our Gothic manor of a school only once so she could check their security. She had been…unimpressed, to say the least. Which wouldn't have been so bad if she hadn't gone on a very loud rant in the office about all the security flaws. Embarrassing at the time. Super handy when I decided to go all cat burglar.

Although, the beginnings of my journey were less than pleasant.

Slogging my bike through fog thick as slime was bad enough, but halfway through my ride a light snow had started falling. The flurry seemed to deaden sound, adding an eerie edge. A damp freeze eked through my clothes and stung my face. I skidded on slushy puddles on the slick asphalt and blinked frozen condensation off my lashes, the headlight on my bike struggling for enough visibility in the filtered moonlight to keep me from crashing.

Fun times.

But at least the air smelled fresh, and after nearly hurtling into the fifteen foot tall iron high school gates, because my paranoia of being followed had me looking over my shoulder way too often, I'd stashed my bike in the shrubs lining the stone wall. Then before my fingers made official popsicle status, I pulled out the lock pick set Aunt M had given me for my twelfth birthday and popped open the padlock on the chain holding the gates closed. Since Ayden's handcuff routine in the storage room under the concert hall, I'd been practicing. Nice to see it pay off.

Hands tucked underneath my armpits for warmth, I raced down the driveway, snow crunching underfoot, breath puffing out in pale bursts.

I only went down twice going up the slippery stairs before making short work of the pins and tumblers on the front door lock, then shoved through. I cringed at the loud squeak and *thud* as it closed, but the place seemed empty. And was oh-so warm. I pulled off my gloves to alternately blow on my hands and rub them together.

The three-story entrance foyer had an expanse of marble that spread to the grand staircase. To my right and left the room disappeared into shadows, but through the massive round window above the doors, moonlight flickered from behind ghostly tendrils of clouds and cast a bright circle of silver on the stairs. The place smelled of disinfectant, like the floor had been washed after the grunge of high-schoolers had left for the day. Now it was just me and a heavy silence echoing off the walls and high ceiling.

Something cut through the moonbeams. A dark shadow flying outside landed on the bottom ledge of the window, forming a predatory silhouette. I flattened my body against the door.

The shadow moved. A gargoyle? There were tons of them located along the upper perimeters of the school, and I always thought of them as protective. But perhaps tonight I was the enemy and one of the grotesque sculptures had come to life to strike me down. An unwelcome intruder to be slayed without mercy.

The gargoyle made a sound. "Hooo-hooo."

I sagged with relief.

On further study, the "gargoyle" might have been an owl. Two more shadows banked in and landed next to the first, the forms melding together as a trio of eerie hoots floated through the night. Then something with an impressive wingspan glided across the light and let out a shrill screech.

Every one of my hairs stood on end. Time to go.

I kept the flashlight flickering over the walls and floors, and when no goblins fell into the spotlight, I headed up the stairs, feeling the weight of the owls' stares on my back as I climbed through the silver shadow of the moon. Navigating through the endless hallways, I wondered if any of Flint's victims managed to escape his torture only to get lost in this labyrinth and recaptured again. What a psycho. How many more secret doors were hidden?

The illumination from my light kept a constant vigil, but any threat could burst without warning from the surrounding darkness. For an empty building, it made a lot of creaks, squeaks, groans, and moans.

Nerves on hyper-alert, I jumped and twitched so often I looked like a Mexican jumping bean. Which would mean I had some sort of squiggly worm trying to pop out. Not a great analogy. Especially since it reminded me of that sci-fi movie that made me scream every time when the wormy alien pops out of the guy's stomach and then the wormy alien thing grows into a giant slime alien thing with a hundred-and-one mouths full of a million-and-one pointy fangs and—

Oookay. I was way more freaked out now. Didn't think that was possible.

Heart pounding like it was ready to crack a rib, I picked up the pace. As I passed by the alcove where the walls inside had turned metallic and attempted to cage me in, I tried the door. Just for kicks. The handle resisted, was locked, and I moved away, figuring I didn't have time for side trips.

Behind me, something clicked. I whirled. And watched in rising horror. With a long, grumbling creak, the door to the alcove opened. All by itself.

It was dark inside. And silent. I froze, shaking with anticipation of some imminent attack. Blood pounded in my ears. My flashlight's trembling beam washed over the room. It was empty. But was it? *Something* opened the door. Could be hiding behind it.

I backed up, step by freaked-out step. When I was almost running, I turned and booked it to the library, pulling off my backpack and digging out the library door key I'd taken from Luna's room. Hands shaking, it took several rattling attempts to insert the shiny skeleton key and turn the lock so I could burst in and slam it shut with a thundering *thud* that shook the floor beneath my feet.

I raced around flipping on desk lamps because I'd had enough of the scary dark, then I headed toward the back and almost made it to the Flint section when something darted in my peripheral.

Stomach fluttering, I dropped and hunched against a bookcase then peeked through the volumes. A shadow slunk a couple rows over. I wiped my sweaty palm on my jeans and tightened the grip on the flashlight.

A demon? No, because then my Divinicus senses would be tingling. In *theory* anyway.

Rose? Wasn't sure. Flint's ghost? These days, it was possible.

Anyway you sliced it — just hoped I didn't bleed — this was turning into a very…

"—bad, bad idea." I whispered the end of my scary thought because hearing the sound of my voice was supposed to make me feel better. Still waiting for that to kick in.

I hunkered low and backed up. Slowly. If I could make it to the secret door —

A hand clamped on my shoulder. I screamed.

CHAPTER FORTY-SIX

I threw an elbow back. It connected. I heard a grunt, then turned with a kick to his side. Came back for a punch, the flashlight gripped in my hand for extra power. He blocked, caught my wrist and twisted. The flashlight clattered on the shelf behind me. He slammed me back against the bookcase, my body pinned by the length of his, one of his hands holding my wrists above my head.

"Nice. But faster follow through next time."

"Ayden!" I wheezed. "What in the wormy alien world are you doing here?!"

"I'm not even going to pretend I understand that reference. But hey, you attacked me." The glow of the fallen flashlight highlighted his sly grin. "Gotta say. It was kind of hot. Ready for round two? Or shall we take a break." He nuzzled my neck. "You smell so good. I vote break."

"Oh, no." I shoved him off. "You don't get to do that '*I'm so sexy and adorable you can't be mad at me*' thing."

His look turned to pleasurable astonishment. "You think I'm sexy and adorable?"

"No!" I lied, then slammed my palms into his chest. Ow.

His grin widened. "Oh, no. You said it. You meant it. You can't take it back."

"Get away. *Go* away." I grabbed my flashlight and stormed off toward the Flint section.

Ayden groaned and followed me. "No, this is good news. Besides, I'm not letting you walk away again. Let me explain, because earlier, at your house, that wasn't what I meant."

"Don't worry, I got the message."

I came to the door at the entrance to the Flint section, yanked on the handle and pushed. Then thumped into the door. Of course it was locked. I tried Luna's key. Didn't work. Ugh! Life clearly didn't want to give me the satisfaction of a dramatic exit, ending with slamming a door in Ayden's face.

I knelt, withdrew my lock picking set and got to work. Diving into a serial killer's maze promised to be a lot more fun than letting my heart fall to pieces.

Ayden leaned against the doorframe. "You know how our emotions are tied to our supernatural ability."

"You get angry, you catch fire. I've seen it. Old news. Leave."

I paused my work to shove him, but he just sidestepped and paced a half-circle around me. He swallowed audibly before continuing.

"Not just angry. *Any* intense emotion. Most of which I've trained extensively to deal with, but this particular…circumstance hasn't come up before, and I don't want to hurt you."

"What circumstance would make you hurt me?"

He wiped a hand down his face and muttered into his hand something I couldn't decipher. Then he smiled so tight it was almost a grimace.

"When I *want* you, when things get *hot* between us, I get…" He lifted his hands in front of himself, and they burst into flames.

I felt the heat from his hands, caught the burning scent. There was a beat of silence. Then as the last pin on the lock pinged to unlatch the door, gears of logic clicked into place inside my brain.

I stood, dropping my tools as I let out a long, expansive, "Ohhhh. Huh. So you've been avoiding being alone with me because—"

"Because I have a hard time controlling myself when I'm around you." He jerked his fiery hands to emphasize the point. "Got it?"

Yes. Yes, I believe I did. As I processed the news, a warm feeling trickled over me, healing together some of those fissures in my heart. I felt myself smiling.

"Anyway…" Ayden, actually blushing, snuffed out his hands and leaned against the frame again, looking equal parts uncomfortable and relieved. "Enough about that. Let's get back to me being sexy and adorable."

"Not a chance," I said. "You should have told me." Yeah, Aurora, because you're always so upfront about everything. Shut up, Aurora. No, *you* shut up. "Why are you here?"

"So glad you asked," he said with a sly wink before hurrying off.

"How did you find me?"

"Please," he said with disdain from somewhere in the shadows. "One, you had that look in your eye." He sauntered back into the light carrying two metal traveler coffee mugs and handed me a shiny lavender one. "And two, Matthias told you not to. So, of course, you'd head for the caves via the library's secret door. I made coffee, drove over, waited outside your house, and followed you on your bike."

I hated being so predictable.

"So you're here to stop me?" Uh-oh. I'd have to ditch him. Make a run to the secret door. But first, I needed an energy boost. I clutched the warm mug and took a sip. Yum. "Is this—?"

"Your favorite? Why, yes it is." He *clinked* his mug against mine, looking very pleased with himself. "White chocolate raspberry with extra whipped cream. I made it with the new machine. Jamie gave me the recipe."

"Jamie, the cute blonde who giggles every time you walk in?"

He raised a brow. "Jealousy? That's promising." He tipped his mug in a gesture of triumph. "But I only know her as Jamie, the kindly barista who helped me impress my girlfriend. In a bold move of creative genius, I added a pinch of freshly ground cinnamon —did you know it came in sticks? — and sprinkled white chocolate shavings on top. What do you think?"

That this guy couldn't be for real. But I took another sip and said, "Bold, creative genius paid off."

"Excellent," he beamed. "And no, I am not here to stop you. Simply lend support in my official bodyguard capacity."

My expression was wary. "Then you should've offered me a ride. I was freezing my butt off on that bike."

"Your backside looked perfect…*ly* fine." From under his thick lashes, he gave me a mischievous look. "I made a point to watch closely. It's one of my favorite parts of your body to guard. Along with your chest, let me add, before I get accused of further neglect."

I rubbed my eyes to help cover the blush. "No excuse. Should've picked me up."

"And miss all the sexy intrigue? Not a chance." He reached to trace a finger along my jaw. The gesture was unexpected and hit me like an electric charge. I choked and almost snorted coffee. A smile tugged at his mouth. "I love this secret late night meeting in the romantic library."

I swallowed down the coffee snot and smirked. "I was getting a more creepy vibe."

"Work with me." He glanced around and turned his voice all smooth and mysterious. "Bathed in a magical glow, you overwhelm me with your stunning beauty, making me forget all reason and lending just the right atmosphere to bear my soul and entice you into a compromising position."

"Or set me on fire."

He sighed with dramatic disappointment. "You're not helping me set the mood. I have so much to teach you."

I rolled my eyes. "Bring it, oh masterful one."

"Bring it?" He cocked a brow. "Wow. That's almost on par with your earlier use of the term 'strumpet'. But I'll have to 'bring it' another time." He leaned in and slowly brought his mouth to hover over mine. He spoke in a low rumble that slithered fire underneath my skin. "Because as much as I'd love to kiss you, right now, deeply and *ever* so thoroughly..." He brushed back my hair and stroked my cheek softly. "I've learned my lesson. Slow is the name of the game. We've got all the time in the world. And I plan to take advantage of it." He licked his lips, his voice husky and full of promise. "Very big advantage. Later."

He dropped a light kiss on my forehead then swung open the door to the Flint section and strolled toward the back, swirling his mug.

Waiting in the doorway, I breathed in deep then exhaled to clear my head, trying to steady…everything. As I watched him move with such easygoing grace, well, let's just say that speaking of backsides, I was a serious fan.

I found myself staring.

"Quit ogling me, Lahey," Ayden ordered over his shoulder. "We'll deal with your licentious thoughts later. Right now, we're burning daylight, and first period waits for no one. Follow me."

I laughed. Follow him? Not a problem.

"By the way," he paused to sip his coffee, "you said the tunnels won't hurt you, but I'm Mandatum, so how do you plan to keep them from trying to kill me?"

Oh, right. That might be a problem.

CHAPTER FORTY-SEVEN

In the Flint section, I climbed to the upper level shelf and pulled books aside to uncover the spiral. "When the flaming spikeballs attacked, I told them to stop, and they just did, so I'm thinking that same strategy will work if they come after yo—Whoa!" I shrieked. "What are you doing?"

"Helping you up," Ayden said.

I looked down. "No. You're grabbing my butt."

"No," Ayden said mildly, "I'm simply providing support. *This* would be grabbing your butt." His hands moved. I squealed. He grinned. "See the difference?"

I pursed my lips. "Ayden."

"Fine." He hauled himself up beside me and latched his arms around my waist.

I frowned. "What now?"

"I'm just making sure you don't go through without me this time."

"I'm not sure this is a great idea. What if the voice doesn't listen this time? Or something else attacks?"

"You'll save me and demand sexual favors in return. Or so I hope." He jerked his chin toward the wall. "Let's go, lusty wench."

Smiling despite my trepidation, I hovered my hand over the double spiral. Felt heat. Goosebumps on my skin. A rush of air, and this time I actually saw the bookshelf and wall swing back into darkness. A *click-clank* and that web of metal tentacles shot out, wrapped around us both, and *whooshed* us through.

We were dumped on our feet into darkness as the door closed, but lamps quickly sprung to life illuminating the dank, musty tunnel.

"Nice work," Ayden looked impressed.

Sally Security's voice echoed off the walls, "Mandatum intruder."

"Or not," I told Ayden, then shoved him behind me and shouted, "There is no intruder!" A flaming spikeball puffed to life. "Stand down! About face! Cease! Desist! Abort!"

The spikey fireball started its chainsaw rotations. Ayden reached from behind me, arms bracketing each side of my face, his palms facing out toward the threat, and produced a band of fire. It connected from one hand to the other, blocking me from the attack. I felt the heat on my face and smelled the burn.

"Get down!" he ordered.

"No!" I grabbed his wrists and shoved his arms out wide. Breaking the ribbon of fire. "Scrub the mission!"

The spikey ball shot toward us. Ayden's hand grabbed the back of my hoodie and started to sweep my feet out from under me, ready to blast Flint's mini fire grenade.

I screamed at the faceless woman. "Terminate! Do it...*now*!"

The fireball skidded to a stop in front of me, snuffed out, and dropped to the floor with a whiny *ping*. Lucky, since I had cleaned out my repertoire of clichéd halt commands. I kept myself between Ayden and the fireball as it collapsed into a small, smooth orb, and rolled toward us. I kicked it, but it skittered right back. Irritating. But at least it wasn't attacking anymore.

"See," I said, "*I* can protect *you* for a change."

Ayden spun me around and grabbed my jacket, pulling forward to lay his mouth firmly on mine. The kiss was deep and deliberate, jumbling my thoughts, stealing my sanity. Then he stepped back, breathing hard, hair tumbled over his forehead, chocolate eyes shimmering with mischief.

I stared, swallowed hard. "What was *that?*"

"Partial payback on your lecherous demands for saving my life." He adjusted his jacket. "But the rest will have to wait. I'm here on bodyguard duty so quit trying to seduce me and let's get to work." He saluted. "Lead the way."

Lips still tingling from the…vigorous contact, I glanced around the empty tunnels before picking up the deactivated spikeball still following me around and shoving it in my pocket.

Ignoring Ayden's questioning look, I said, "Right. Give me a minute to remember," or come up with it in the first place, "all the details of my super safe and sane plan."

He raised his hands in supplication. "No hurry. I'm just the muscle, here to follow orders."

"If only." Although I had to admit, the muscle was pretty sweet.

"Try me." He bowed in a courtly fashion. "Give me a command."

Kiss me you fool! Oh, wait. He'd covered that. Not that we couldn't go there again but — stay on track, Aurora.

Take off your shirt! Yeah, my hormones were raging.

I sighed and scratched my head. "Can you whistle?"

Chapter Forty-Eight

Ayden's hands rested lightly on my thighs. "Your super safe and sane plan was to wander the tunnels of a serial killer riding his pet demon?" His hand moved over the bulge of the spikey ball in my front pocket. "And his mini firebombs?"

I sighed. "Last I checked, bodyguards are the strong and *silent* type."

At Ayden's whistle, Fido, my trusty centimole demon, had come scuttling at hyper-drive. I almost didn't dodge the enthusiastically slurpy doggie lick she swung my way.

Now, Ayden and I were atop her neck, tucked behind the snapping antennae in a convenient cove just big enough for a couple of people to sit in safely, as long as they had a loose meaning of the word *safe*. He'd slung my backpack over his shoulder so he could scoot close behind me and give directions using the map on his phone. I steered by pulling on Fido's antennae. So far, so good.

She bustled along with ease and purpose, smooth as a monorail, Victorian lamps illuminating a few seconds before we reached them to light our way. I was darn proud of myself.

"We're not wandering," I reminded him. "We're going to that gap Blake talked about. Be patient."

"I'm nothing but," he assured me then slid his arms around my waist. His warm body pressed close.

"So, uh, this…fire issue. Is it normal?"

I felt him smile against the nape of my neck. "Actually, it's very common in our circles— the Mandatum. It's just never come up for me before. But now that it has, I'm getting help."

"What kind of help?"

He took a moment to answer, fidgeting uncomfortably behind me. "In learning how to control it so when I'm around you, in a certain way…assuming you're interested, then I won't hurt you. So when I've been off somewhere, unavailable, that's where I've been."

My mouth opened and closed a few times. "To, like, a therapist?"

"Not exactly." He let out a long breath. "It's someone who's been through this before and successfully controlled it."

"Is it Bancroft?" I was dying at the thought that he'd been talking to a priest about us, but would a priest have this problem? Maybe he hadn't always been a priest.

Ayden snorted. "He wouldn't help. Like your aunt, he'd be happy for another reason to keep me away from you."

"What does he have against me? And what is up with the two of them working together?"

"Nothing. And I don't know. From his end, he's being protective." Ayden said. "Historically, hunters and civilians getting close is risky for both sides. Exposure for us, physically dangerous for them—"

Fido banked a sharp right. Ayden's arms squeezed me in a rib-breaking grip. When she stopped short, we jerked forward then back.

My voice echoed in the darkness, "Now we'll make some progress."

The lights in the room started *ca-chunking*, lighting the space to reveal…

A dead end. Great.

Ayden dropped his chin on my shoulder. "Nice work."

I flicked him an irritated look. "Blake said it might be hidden."

He shrugged and swung off Fido, then reached for me, guiding my descent so I slid against him with aching slowness. When my feet finally touched down, our bodies were flush against each other, and I was finding it way hotter in the cold, damp cave than I expected.

I wiped my brow. "Guess we'd better start searching."

"Right," he said, his voice raspy. "For those spirals that literally open doors for you." He turned away and surveyed the room. "Any ideas where to start, Lady Croft?"

Before I could provide an answer—not that I had one—my mind careened out of my body as a vision took over.

Wind rushed through my ears, then died out into an unnatural silence. Fido and Ayden became smaller as I flew backwards, retracing our steps. The walls blurred into a haze of brown shades. Then jagged streaks of quicksilver shimmered as I drifted to a stop. The streaks consolidated into round orbs.

Eyes of silver. Menacing. Moving up and down as an entire pack of not-quite hellhounds barreled toward me.

Flaming spike spheres spit from the lamps, rocketing toward at least a few dozen dog demons. But just before the orbs made impact, the hounds dropped into the ground, as if the rocky earth was nothing more than swamp water. The spheres exploded like grenades against the stone, turning the tunnel into a warzone. Dust clouded, chunks flew, leaving burnt black craters in the ground, but the demons were untouched. Bursting out of the ground several feet away, they kept running.

With grace and agility, they jumped, ducked, darted, and, as a last resort, dived back into the earth. A few were hit, leaving the slime-ridden, leathery remnants of their blasted bodies on the walls before the mess vortexed into the ground. Many got clipped, the telltale yelps giving it away. But most moved forward, ready to tear us all to pieces.

I cringed when the pack hit, more like flowed, over me, and I felt only an odd prickling. Then my body zipped back, and I came to in the arms of a frantic Ayden.

"Tell me what's wrong!" He was shaking me hard. Brushing back my hair. "Aurora, what's happening?!"

I steadied myself with my arms around his neck. Tested my legs. "Nothing. Jeez, I'm fine."

"You're not *fine*."

I shoved out of his arms and ran to the wall. We were in a type of cul-de-sac, the lamps circling its rim to light the space. Other than that, nothing.

"It has to be here, Ayden. Remember, that's what Blake said. Mechanical things. In the walls." I ran my hand over the rough stone. Mingled in the damp, musty air of the cave, I swear I could smell wet dog.

Fido became suddenly alert, her nose pointed toward the tunnel. She chittered. Her nose lifted. Sniffed. Her head dropped and she let out a low rumbling growl.

"Aurora, talk to me." Ayden spun me around to face him.

"I think," yes, *think*, Aurora, "I have — because of the blood contract — some sort of mental connection with Fido and she senses something bad is coming. And we have to find a way out. Now!"

Some emotion raced over his features too fast for me to read, then his face turned grim.

He nodded. "Gears. Mechanical things. Something has to open up..."

We both looked at the lamps and said, "Levers."

"You start pulling. It only opens for you." Ayden faced the tunnel and his arms *whooshed* into flames. The sounds of explosions echoed. "I'll hold them off. Hurry."

No, I was planning on slowing down, might even take a cat nap. I ran to the nearest lamp and started yanking. Fido scuttled and coiled her long body to block the entrance to the cave.

The howls shrilled, and the sounds of their rabid, panting breaths were close enough to reverberate down the walls and crash into the open space. My hands tremored and slipped repeatedly until one of the lamps snapped under my grip.

"Ayden!" As I released and staggered back, I spotted a double spiral etched in the lamp's metal.

Things *clunked* and *cha-chunked.* Beside the lamp, wind shot out and dust burst from the wall. A ten-foot diameter ring cut out of the stone then *thumped* backwards, and the circle of rock rolled out of sight, leaving a gaping hole. A doorway. From the other side, steam hissed and heat blasted as if some dragon was about to appear. Through the murky darkness, *crunching* and *pounding* beat a chaotic rhythm.

A vision flashed ugly and quick through my mind. I shoved Ayden sideways and used the force to push myself back, skidding hard on my butt. From where he'd stood seconds before, a hound burst from the ground, jaws snapping.

All around, demons spurted from the earth like a wolverine horror movie, tongues flicking hungrily over glistening fangs. Ayden and I had quite the little army between us.

"Aurora!" Flames licked up Ayden's arms as he turned his back on the demons behind him to fight through the ones between us.

"Protect *yourself!"* I said. "They won't hurt me because they're working with Rose!"

The closest hound lunged at my throat.

I kicked its head sideways. "Never mind! You can help!"

The demons converged.

Chapter Forty-Nine

Fido struck fast as a viper. Her jaws snapped around a hound. A startled yelp. Bones cracked. Fido swallowed the demon in one gulp. Flint's spiked fireballs burst from the lamps and sliced through the air, ignoring Fido as she ate more demons. The fiery bombs converged like rabid locusts on the wolfish hounds, but the hellions just dipped into the earth. The ground exploded around me as if someone kept setting off land mines.

I stayed low, ducking from pelting debris, hoping I didn't run into a flying spiked ball. Dust blanketed the air thick as steel wool leaving a grainy taste in my mouth. Our world smelled on fire.

"Ayden?" I swatted at the clouds of grit, looking for him.

"Get to Fido!" he commanded.

I turned as he emerged from the smoke, throwing fireballs at the hounds creeping around me. A vision flashed, but I'd already spotted the silver eyes of a hound behind him, molded into the ground, looking like a crocodile lurking just under the surface of a swamp.

It lunged. I screamed a battle cry and raised my arms, running at full speed, thinking my blasty power would make an appearance. Any second now… Any second… This *exact* second would be fantastic—

I tackled the demon hound mid-air. Pain pierced my shoulder. We smashed to the ground. The variety of lethal prongs spiked out along Lassie's body and embedded into the ground on impact, stopping it dead. Momentum flung me off. I tumbled onto the cratered battlefield. Lassie was pinned to the stone floor as I scrambled to my feet and felt warmth leaking down my chest.

Blood. Awesome.

The hound ripped itself free, sending dirt and rock flying, then lurched up onto its paws. One of the horns dripped red from where it punctured my shoulder. So maybe tackling the spikey urchin wasn't the best idea.

Lassie leapt over me to attack Ayden. I fell back, swung my legs up, and buried a solid two-footed kick into its stomach. The demon sailed high then tumbled sideways away from Ayden as I followed my momentum into a somersault backwards onto my feet. Smooth. Professional. Where was Matthias when I needed to gloat?

I turned around. Lassie attacked. I barely caught its throat before it slammed me onto my back, snapping fangs inches from my face. I choked on the vile stench of its breath. Claws tore into rock on either side of my head. My arms strained and burned, elbows swung out to keep the claws from ripping out my brain. Spittle splattered and drooled down my arms. So gross.

"Ayden!" My muscles were losing strength. Fast. Lassie's dagger-filled mouth snapped closer.

A sharp heat pierced my gut. Pressure compressed my body. Lungs constricted. Then in a flash, my skin lit up like a radioactive glow stick, veining out in a throbbing, bright light, releasing the weight strangling my body. The rush of power flushed all fatigue from my bones. Energy thrummed anew up my arms, pooled into my palms.

Beneath my hands Lassie started to smoke. Its rabid jaws froze mid-snap. It tried to pull away.

"Oh no." I tightened my hold. "Let's cuddle."

Embers rained like fireworks. The sickly scent of burnt fur swirled with scorched flesh. White light crackled from my fingertips across Lassie's face and snout. Alarm flashed in its silver eyes, then all their light blinked out.

As the body slumped onto mine, it shattered to dust, the powdery grime tornadoing down past me and disappearing into the ground.

I smiled. "Like a pro."

I patted my hands over myself. My shoulder stung. There was blood. The rest of my back was one Amazonian agonizing bruise. I had drool soaking my arms, dirt ruining my hair. I still glowed. No clue how to turn off that nuclear switch, but didn't matter because I'd finally turned it back on. By myself. Without Jayden's science mumbo jumbo.

I heard growling and looked up. Ayden was surrounded. Demon dogs kept coming up out of the ground. But not a single one had an eye on me, instead choosing to converge all their blood-lusty attention on Ayden. Fantastic. I wasn't being attacked. *Why* wasn't I being attacked? I was a little offended.

My hands still glowed, but my power hadn't actually blasted out. I held out my arms. Tried to gather the energy.

Flames crashed across the floor, scorching the hounds in spiraling waves of inferno. I gagged at the sickly, sweet stench of burning fur and flesh. A tall ring of fire bled up from the floor and encircled me. I flinched back from the raging heat.

"Stay still!" Ayden yelled.

Sure, like I could move anyway. Fido scuttled up the wall to hang from the ceiling.

Like flamethrowers, fire jet-streamed off Ayden's arms. His shirt was shredded with claw marks, his perfect skin scratched and bleeding, but he strode with purpose through the lake of flames looking like some diabolical fire-breathing demon, wild and uncontrolled, scorching everything in his path, hot, angry colors reflecting deadly across his skin. Whimpers shrilled as the demons tried to dive back into the earth.

Other hounds leapt above the fire. Ayden jumped a round-house kick that dragged a trail of flames in his wake and lashed a demon in two. Before he touched ground, his other foot kicked an arc of flames that cut apart another two hounds half burrowed in the ground. He landed in a deep lunge, and the fire surrounding me disappeared.

He held out a flameless hand, his grin fierce. "How was that for strong and silent?"

I gaped. Ayden stood above me. Ash snowed the air around him. He looked like a fierce warrior, all dangerous and battle ready and sexy, muscles glistening.

"Demon infestation," a woman's voice echoed. "Proceed to sanctuary."

I slapped my glowing hand into Ayden's, and he pulled me up. At least she hadn't said *Mandatum*. Flint's remaining spikeballs buzzed down the tunnel and out of sight. Tiny pipes *popped* out beneath each lamp. A gurgling sound filled the air.

"Proceed to sanctuary."

I pointed at the gaping, dark hole in the wall where the stone had opened a doorway. Steam billowed, crushing noises thundered through.

"Let's make a run for it," I said.

Ayden doused his flames, swept me into his arms, and ran through the sea of fire. Hounds jumped from the ground at us. Some disappeared in a tornado of black smoke and a sharp scent of sulfur as the fire overwhelmed them, but one made it through. It howled in defiance, flames scorching its paws as it barreled ahead of us toward the opening in the wall.

As it passed the threshold, there was a violent *whirr* and large spinning silver discs flashed from the frame of the doorway. The hound was brought to a halt so sudden it was almost comical.

The overgrown circular buzz saws, which had shot out from the stone doorway, whined to a stop, and after a moment's pause, the hound's body slid apart in pieces. As the broken flesh slurped downward, a web of electricity pulsed the entryway a brilliant blue, incinerating what remained of the hound before it even got the chance to fall to dust.

"Whoa!" Ayden skidded to a stop.

"Holy crap!" I practically climbed onto his shoulders.

The pipes underneath the lamps burped loudly, then vomited a surge of sickly, green liquid that rushed down the walls and splashed fast and thick onto the floor. The hounds came back up through the ground, then yelped and yowled in agony as they touched the goo. Their fur smoked and their bodies distorted, folded in on themselves as the fluid melted through them, disintegrating them before our eyes.

"Buzz saws, electricity, *and* acid?" I seethed. "Are you freaking kidding me!"

Ayden shot me an exasperated what'd-you-expect look. "Genius. Serial. Killer."

Acid pooled, eating up demons and ground. When it hit Ayden's flames, it boiled into a noxious gas that burned our eyes and throat and made us cough.

"Fido!" Ayden yelled.

There was nervous, insistent chittering. The centimole scuttled directly above us, hanging from the ceiling, head dropped like a demented claw machine ready to catch her prize.

Ayden said, "Tell her to—'"

"Get us out of here, Fido!" I said, then hacked up a lung. My eyes watered against the stinging vapors.

Chittering what I hoped was a yes, Fido clamped us in one of her antenna claws, flung us hard. Then let go.

Above the flames, the deadly fumes, the acid, and disintegrating hounds, we jettisoned toward the opening in the wall. Where the buzz saws and electricity and whatever other tortures Flint's psycho mind had cooked up were ready to welcome us.

CHAPTER FIFTY

We hit ground. Ayden held me to his chest as he took the brunt of the fall on his back, cushioned somewhat by my backpack he still managed to wear. We skidded to a stop. Dust clouded all around, obscuring what little light filtered through the entrance.

I coughed. Blinked away the grit. We seemed unscathed. Limbs still attached, but Ayden wasn't moving. Terror speared my gut. I patted my hands over him with mild — okay, *major* — panic. No obvious life-threatening injuries.

"Ayden, talk to me. Are you okay? Ayden!"

"Not sure," he groaned. "Maybe you should keep copping a feel. In fact, you should go a little lower."

"Don't scare me like that." I whacked his shoulder which flared pain hot and sharp deep in my own shoulder. "Ow."

"Crap." Ayden sat up and took my arm gently.

I frowned at the puncture, shimmering with rivulets of blood. "Think Coach will let me skip P.E.? Already got my cardio."

A loud *click* vibrated the air. The buzz saws rotated to life and fed back into the wall. Then, like a missing puzzle piece, the circular stone doorway slid back into place, shutting us in with an echoing *hiss.*

Victorian lamps sputtered to life.

"No!" I ran over and kicked the wall. Slapped it silly. Ow. Stupid. "Is there a lever or spiral or something?"

I turned to demand Ayden's help, but he was looking around, gawking, visibly stunned.

I followed his gaze. Awe overwhelmed me too.

"Oh. My. God." I could barely breathe. "Flint doesn't have treasure. He has a weapon of mass destruction."

Lamps stuttered and slowly lit the space. Ayden and I stood on a narrow ledge with a lackluster bronze guardrail. Beyond that, the world vanished into a never-ending dark pit of doom, swirling with steaming mist. How far down? Fifty, maybe sixty feet. Couldn't say for sure, but we gawked nonetheless, craning our necks at the wondrous space.

Flint had somehow hollowed out the mountain, and we stood in the center of its massive, mechanically crazed core.

Golden light reflected off a chaotic puzzle of glittering, rusted gears and rods connected up and down and around the walls. Pipes gleamed copper, gold, and silver as they snaked an intricate maze up the sides. Gauges, bolts, and meters stuck out at odd places, sometimes attached to metal or wooden boxes sprinkled on the walls like fleas. At the bottom far below, a forest of machines billowed steam and sparks.

Gears groaned. Pumps hissed. Belts zipped. Chains rattled. Pistons pumped. It was a sauna, humid and hot, my clothes already sticky, my skin glistening beads of sweat. It smelled of wet earth and old metal.

Rising high dead-center was what had to be a death ray. A transparent cone filled with a writhing, pale blue fog.

We walked across a metal walkway that jutted out from our ledge, across the chasm to a circular room encased in glass. Inside, the air was dry and cool. It smelled stale, but still a welcome relief.

Rimming the room were old-school versions of the Ishida's control tables, making the place look like a Victorian age spaceship.

Brass typewriter keys. Copper buttons looking like unscrewed bolts. A series of gleaming switches begging to be flipped alongside old radio dials and gumdrops of lights blinking red, yellow, and green. Where paneling was missing, wires wormed around turning gears. Above the desks were oxidized green handles mounted in rows and columns. A metal grate hung with rusted tools.

I said, "If Rose gets ahold of this, he'll blow some city off the map."

Ayden winced as he shrugged off the backpack and let it *thunk* to the floor. "I don't think any of these are weapons."

I pointed to the central canister. "Do you *not* see the smoke-filled deathray?"

"It's a cooling or ventilation tower." Ayden bent over one of the metal desks. "Leads the steam out of here, not smoke. This is a control room."

"Oh." I craned my neck up, then down to scrutinize the giant metal-machine creatures chugging in the factory below. "Like it powers everything? The tunnels, security?"

Ayden nodded as his fingers trailed over the machinery. "And probably the school, his house, back in the day."

"How?"

"I'm guessing water power," he said. "From the gorges, rivers, waterfalls. This is amazing, but," he pulled his hands from the controls and checked his watch, "we've got to get out of here. School's going to start and your family will start asking questions."

"One of these has to open that door." I went to jab a button.

"Whoa!" Ayden caught my wrist. "Don't touch! All those machines down there, even if they hadn't been neglected for a hundred years, might be unstable and explode."

"Ooookay." I frowned and fingered a handle sticking out of the wall. It broke in my hand. Swell. "Since when do you know anything about engineering?"

"I try to ignore Jayden, but some of his babbling sinks in." Ayden squinted at the buttons and switches.

I gently pulled another handle. A long and narrow drawer slid out of the wall. Something glittered and quivered. I reeled back.

"Stop touching things!" Ayden swept me behind him.

A display case sprung out. Silver rimmed edges framing two pieces of glass encasing a crisp cream-colored map.

"I think it's the layout of the plant below us," Ayden said.

I swiveled it around. "Town's layout is on the other side. Look at the waterfalls and behind it, the portal."

Ayden's face was grim. "Why would he draw a double spiral over the portal? There isn't one there. We knew about the ones at school, around town. No idea what it is. I researched the symbol, but there's nothing in the Mandatum history books."

I squinted at the map. "I don't see any mention of the treasure vault. Or sanctuary."

"We'll have to look later." Ayden raked his hand through his hair which had lost a lot of its spike to the humidity. And demon attack. "Check the other drawers. I'll look for a way out."

A few drawers later I found a series of books with titles such as *Centrifuge Chillers, Pneumatic Air,* and *Associated Pumping System.* Meaningless. Boring. Until…

The small leather-bound book had no title, but engraved in the bright clasp holding it closed was the double spiral. Inside, crisp pages were covered with an elegant handwritten script, easily read, if I recognized the language. I didn't.

On second glance, I did recognize three words. *Divinicus Nex* and *Bellator.*

"Find something?" Ayden said.

"Not sure." I put it in the bottom of my tattered backpack that Ayden had left on the floor, then stuffed some of the other books we found on top. "I'll give these to Jayden." If there was a Divinicus connection, I was betting he could figure it out.

Three drawers later—

"Elevator manual!" I held it high.

Ayden looked around. "There is no elevator."

Chapter Fifty-One

Ayden pulled open the metal-latticed doors, then turned the handle of the door behind it and motioned for me to exit the elevator first. I walked out and turned around. Even without the flashlight, I knew where we were.

The high school. Specifically, we'd just stepped into the hallway from the very same alcove which I'd stumbled into when I was trying to hide from Ayden and Blake. The one where the stone walls had transformed into metal, and some buttons had appeared out of nowhere, and the latticed metal had tried to "cage" me in. According to Flint's maps and diagrams, the tunnels and school were riddled with them.

Ayden chuckled. "This was the creature trying to eat you?"

"How was I supposed to know?" I backhanded Ayden's arm, but instantly regretted the move when we both winced.

He took my hand as we gimped ourselves outside, through the fog and down the high school driveway, ducks quacking in the distance as the day readied to emerge from its slumber. While Ayden relocked the padlock and chain on the iron gates, I went to grab my bike, the sweet aroma of honeysuckle strong as I pushed aside the heavy vines climbing up the stone wall.

The bike wasn't there.

I looked around, confused. "Must be searching in the wrong spot."

I turned to check a different area, but the distinct click of a gun cocking and a flashlight beam flooding me in a spotlight sent me into freeze mode, heart thundering.

Chapter Fifty-Two

An authoritative voice commanded, "Hands up and turn around slowly."

I did so, then squinted and brought one hand down a little to shield the light directly in my eyes. I couldn't see much more than a vague silhouette of a man, but there was definitely a handgun. Pointed at me.

Fantastic. Who wanted to kill me now?

A shadow rushed from the side. The flashlight knocked to the ground and the goon was suddenly kissing dirt with Ayden's knee in his back, the gun pressing against the base of the man's head.

"Don't move," Ayden growled.

There was a beat of silence then the man said, "Ayden?"

Ayden peered to better see the guy's face. "Walter?"

"Son of a — Yeah, you idiot. Get the hell off me."

Ayden stood and helped the *officer* up. Yeah, it was one of Sheriff Payne's deputies.

"Sorry, man." Ayden dusted off Deputy Walter's uniform and handed him back his weapon. "Didn't realize."

The deputy holstered the gun and looked at me. "The Lahey girl, right?"

"Yes, sir," I nodded. The Lahey girl who was going to get seriously grounded when the Lahey parents had to bail her out of jail. And Aunt M. Oh, dear God, I'd never hear the end of this.

Ayden put a hand on the deputy's shoulder. "Walter, I can explain. This isn't what it looks like."

"It never is." The deputy breathed deep, looking anything but happy. "Did you guys do any damage?"

"Nope. You'd never know we were there."

A new voice rumbled out of the darkness. "I've got this, deputy."

The deputy's hand jerked to his holster, then stopped when he saw the man emerge from the shadows.

Spurs jingling on red leather cowboy boots, Rose moseyed out dressed like an old-time sheriff. Long, golden curls draping out from a wide brimmed western hat, he sported a brown leather duster coat, jeans, shirt, and vest, complete with a shiny sheriff star pinned to the chest. The two revolvers holstered at his hips captured most of my attention.

I froze, anticipating a gunfight worthy of the OK Corral, but, taking his hand off his weapon, Deputy Walter stood straighter and nodded respectfully.

"Sheriff Payne," he said. "Good evening, sir."

That was...odd. Rose looked nothing like Matthias's dad. Especially in this get up. I kept my mouth shut and shot Ayden a questioning look. He shrugged, looking as confused as I, and moved in front of me. Rose used a knuckle to tip the front of his hat up, then hooked his thumbs in his belt.

"I'll take care of these young'uns. You go about your business." Rose hitched his pants up, "And let's not speak of this again. Savvy, partner?"

Oh, jeez. This was a bad spaghetti western.

But the deputy just nodded again, said, "You got it, sir," and headed down the street where, now that light began to dawn, I saw his cruiser parked, my bike sitting next to it.

As the deputy drove off, Rose touched the brim of his hat in acknowledgement.

Watching the deputy salute back, I asked, "What was that?"

"He messed with his head," Ayden told me over his shoulder, then drenched his voice with suspicion as he tilted his head at Rose. "Since when does a Joat have that kind of Hallucinator power?"

Rose unleashed a smile so dazzling I was sure the sunrise was delaying its appearance, too embarrassed to try to compete with the brilliance.

"You flatter me young hunter." He bowed slightly. "However, it is the gentleman's pathetic weakness of mind which allows my meager powers to appear great. But on to more important matters. What did you discover? I await with bated breath." His hands rested on the butts of the revolvers in the holsters.

Ayden's arms moved out from his sides and his hands lit on fire. Rose raised his brows, then very slowly, his hands, palms facing out.

"Forgive me," Rose said solicitously. "I mean no threat."

"Forgive me, I *do*," Ayden countered. Fire licked up his entire arms. "You need to start answering questions."

"Another time perhaps." Rose sighed, and in a swirl of pink smoke, he disappeared.

Just *poof*. In *pink*.

Ayden and I stared. Crickets chirped. Ducks quacked. Swans honked. And even an owl hooted.

"Uhhh," I finally mustered after I lifted my jaw off the ground. "Is he supposed to be able to do that?"

CHAPTER FIFTY-THREE

"I told you if I don't come home my parents will freak." My whisper sounded loud in the morning silence as Ayden and I crouched outside our backyard gate. Despite the arrival of the sun, our breath misted in the cold air as we continued to argue.

"And I told *you*," Ayden insisted, "if you show up looking like *that* your parents will freak even more. Come on, we'll call from my house, say training went late. You can clean up, and I'll take you to school."

He started to turn back toward his car like we'd settled the matter.

"But I wasn't supposed to be training," I reminded him. "Aunt M will go on high alert. Plus, if they think training leaves me looking like this," I gestured over my body, "with all the cuts and bruises, that will be the end of it."

But what could we do? Sneaking in my bedroom window was out since too many of my family were milling about upstairs. Even if I could slip in and ditch the ripped clothes, tackle the bride of Frankenstein hairstyle, and clean off the overall sewage stench, there was still the matter of multiple injuries. I was a supernaturally fast healer, but not supersonic.

My parents would notice. And freakage would ensue.

Ayden paused, his expression mirroring my frustration. "We'll think of something. Here, let me…" He wet the hem of his shirt with his tongue. "You've got dirt and —"

When he tried to wipe my face with the spit-soaked fabric, I shied away and gave him a look. "Really? What am I, two?"

"The argument could be made," he scowled, but dropped the shirt. "Fine. I'm just trying to help. You can't hide this. And if they think the guys and I are involved," he made an effort to quell his rising voice, "your parents will never let you spend time with us again. Watch out!" Ayden tugged me down out of sight.

I peeked through the fence. Dad jogged around the side of the house in sweats just back from his morning run.

Ayden was right. I couldn't hide this and if they thought — wait a minute. Ohhh, yes. He *was* right. A calculating smile prowled onto my mouth.

Ayden shook his head. "Aurora, whatever you're thinking, don't. We can try something else. Anything else."

I snatched up dirt, leaves, and twigs and littered them all over my hair and clothes. "You're brilliant."

"No. I'm really not."

"I know what I'm doing."

"Nothing good ever comes after that statement."

"Have a little faith." I stood and gathered my bike.

Ayden pawed at me to keep me down. "He'll see you!"

"Go home." I spoke through the side of my mouth. "I'll meet you at school. I'll be late, but don't worry."

Ayden reached for me. "What are you doing?!"

I banged my bike through the backyard gate before he could stop me. From the sounds behind, Ayden's faith was in crisis, but I ignored him.

"Dad!" I shouted.

"Hey, sweetie." He waved. "How was the ride?" He took in my appearance and turned the color of glue. "Oh, my God!"

CHAPTER FIFTY-FOUR

Someone nudged me awake from the kind of dead-to-the-world sleep I hadn't enjoyed in days. No dreaming, no nightmares. It was glorious.

"Miss Lahey?"

A man's voice. Didn't recognize it. Who dared disturb my slumber?

The side of my face still rested on my arm, but my eyes opened, and after a moment, focused on Logan. Since when did he sound so old?

Something cut through my vision, and my second period teacher was leaning over me.

"I understand you were late this morning because of an accident." His voice seemed far away. "You do look a bit worse for wear. Your parents requested we call if you showed any signs of fatigue. I think this qualifies."

"No." My head shot up. Too fast. Ow. I winced. Pain. In my head, arms, shoulders. Oh, heck, pretty much everywhere.

Logan flicked his fingers at his lips. I got the message and wiped a web of drool hanging from the corner of my mouth. That got a hearty snicker from my classmates.

"I'm fine," I slurped. "Just a little tired. My dad checked me out at the hospital, nothing's broken, and I have no dizziness or nausea, no signs of concussion. Please don't call them. I'd like to stay."

The teacher looked doubtful. "Some might say wanting to stay at school *is* a sign of concussion." The class rumbled a collective chuckle. "But fine. If you feel poorly, you'll let someone know?"

"Absolutely."

My face was hot. From pain or embarrassment, couldn't be sure. I felt a cool breeze come out of nowhere and saw Logan's fingers moving surreptitiously. I smiled my gratitude.

I stayed awake through the rest of the period, mostly due to Logan slicing an artic breeze my way when consciousness faltered. The ending bell was like a razor to my head. I rubbed my temples as my classmates meandered out.

"Sure you're okay?" Logan put my books in my backpack and led me out. "Ayden told us what happened. He's kind of…worried. The tunnels are no place to go alone. Especially for…" he lowered his voice, "a Divinicus. You should have called me or Jayden."

"Divinicus." I stopped, remembering the book I found with the double spiral on the cover. It was still in my backpack which I snatched from Logan and started rummaging through. I found the mechanical manuals on top and handed them over. "Have Jayden take a look at these." I kept foraging for the smaller spiral covered one. "And there's another I'm hoping he can translate…"

If I could find it. I should clean this thing out.

"Hey!" some girl waved sharply as she cut into the room.

Glasses, brunette, eyes dark, big and exotic. I knew her, but there was a monkey wrench lodged in the gears of my brain.

"Crap, what's her name?" I said.

"Natasha," Logan said without hesitation.

I raised my brows at him. The little ghost blushed and adjusted his coat.

I smiled. "Well, well, well."

"Is Matthias taking you to gym today?" Natasha asked.

"I hope not," I said.

She frowned. "Know where he is?"

"Bet Logan could help you find him." I clapped the little guy on the shoulder. "Right, Logan?"

Logan gawked with eyes worthy of Bambi staring down a rabid T-rex and lost what little color his cheeks had moments ago. He opened his mouth. And squeaked. Like a field mouse.

It was painful to watch.

"No time," Natasha said. "I've got debate practice through lunch." She pulled a slip of paper out of her pocket and held it out to Logan. "Can you get this to him?" Without waiting for an answer, she tucked the paper into his breast pocket, patted his head, said, "Thanks!" and left.

He stared after her.

I shook my head. "Explain to me how *Jayden* was the only one who almost failed his Seduction course."

"Logan." Ayden's voice cut across the room, so harsh in tone, Logan flinched. "I've got it from here."

I turned and smiled, closing my backpack. "Hey."

Ayden didn't smile back. He waited in the doorway, seemingly oblivious to the fact that he was blocking most of it. He wouldn't move. Students had to contort themselves past him, but no one complained since his demeanor suggested he might snap their necks if they dared.

With a hard frown and nostrils flaring, his dark brown eyes flickered over me, assessing, cold. Logan nudged me forward. Silent, Ayden took my backpack, then my elbow, and led me away.

"I'll come with you," Logan offered, but one brutal look from Ayden stopped him in his tracks. "Or not," he muttered then gave me a faltering smile. "I'll, uh, see you at P.E."

I tried to smile back, but Ayden already had us weaving through the crowded hallway.

Studying his profile, since he wouldn't look at me, Ayden looked haggard, the angles beneath those Himalayan cheekbones more pronounced than usual, almost sunken, and dark circles hung beneath his eyes. He may have splashed some water on his face and through his hair, but no shower or shave.

You'd think after a visit with Bancroft and his insta-healing powers Ayden would look better, more caffeine-infused than coffin-ready.

Based on the dirt and some leftover demon body part splatter caked to the denim, the jeans were the same he'd worn last night. Or was it this morning? He'd changed his ripped T-shirt to one that he probably borrowed from Tristan since it was too small, clinging to every muscle of his torso.

He smelled of sweat and leather. Somehow still not unpleasant.

Unlike his mood. He was angry, wound tight, body rigid, as if every movement had to be controlled so he wouldn't detonate.

"Morning," I said in a cheery voice, hoping to penetrate the gloom. I hadn't seen him since the backyard so maybe he didn't know how well my plan had worked out. "My dad took me to the hospital for a check-up. X-rays, the whole nine yards. You know how he is. But I'm good. Superficial stuff. Except for the puncture on the shoulder." I tapped a finger near my collarbone and rolled my shoulder. Felt a dull pain. "But that only needed a couple of stitches."

He stared straight ahead, eyes scanning the crowd. A muscle ticked in his jaw. When he finally spoke, it was in a frigid tone. "I know."

Wow. Two whole syllables. I felt like rolling my eyes, but refrained. In his present grumpy state, it didn't seem like he'd appreciate the gesture. I plastered on a smile.

"Did you also know that I told my parents that I went bike riding in the mountains and took a terrible tumble off the trail and into the stream?"

"Nope." His mouth hardly moved.

Uh-oh. Syllable length deteriorating. Not a good sign. This was ridiculous. "Gosh, have I been a bad girl?"

Dark humor settled over him. "Don't play with me."

"Funny," I said coyly, "I thought you liked it when I played with you."

"Aurora, I'm being incredibly patient," he ground out.

"'Incredibly' may be stretching it," I said.

His fingers tightened on my arm and heat rippled off his body in waves. The rims of his pupils glowed orange. So I did what any sane individual would do when handling unstable explosives. I yanked him into a utility closet amid a pungent aroma of highly-flammable cleaning supplies and jumped in with him.

"Hey!" Ayden stumbled back, sent a mop clattering to the floor, and finally *thumped* against the shelving that lined the back wall.

"What's the big deal?" I shut the door and leaned against it, arms folded. "As far as I can see, it's all good. My plan was brilliant. Now they want me to always have workout buddies. Like you guys." I made a face. "Or Dad. But that's not the end of the world. Lucian and Luna were also offered up as sacrifices, but I can ixnay that."

"Aurora." He was fighting for patience.

"What?" I was fighting a growing irritation at the fact that he didn't appreciate my genius. "Crisis averted. Except for all this brouhaha." I made a gesture to encompass his attitude. "Jeez, relax."

"You still don't get it." His words were clipped. "Even after last night, our talk in the library and the colossal blunder you nearly walked into on your own—"

"I take offense to the word *colossal*—"

"—you are still shutting me out!"

"—and to the word *blunder.*"

He leaned in close enough for me to see a vein throbbing in his temple and dried blood smudged along his hairline. "Instead of being with you at the hospital, I had to hide and skulk around the emergency room like some delinquent, eavesdropping, scared to show my face because I didn't know what you'd told your parents. Then I had to trail you again here and wait hours before I was close enough to make sure you were okay."

"First of all, I thought you'd go to Father Bancroft while I was at the hospital. And second, if you've been following me it wasn't even one hour." I smirked. "We'll have to work on your sense of ti—"

He slammed his hand into the edge of a shelf. The metal dented.

"This isn't a joke! And I can't go to Bancroft. He'll ask too many questions." He backed away, his hands coming up to squeeze the sides of his head like he was trying to keep his brain from exploding. "Our regular avenues of help are cut off. Everything's off balance. I'm scared to death. Then you keep throwing yourself into danger while I blunder along, scrambling to protect you, but I can't." He slumped against shelving, rattling plastic and sloshing liquids, bringing a scent of bleach through the air as his voice became haggard. "Because you keep treating me like…*I'm* the threat."

His dark chocolate eyes closed, but not before I saw the pain they held.

Ah. *That* was the big deal.

My own irritation with his behavior started to dissipate. Because his anger wasn't an element, it was a compound. See, I pay attention in science. An emotional compound of fear, helplessness, and hurt because I didn't trust him. The pain from that wasn't hard to imagine given that it wasn't that long ago *I* was out of the loop because he didn't trust me.

He was silent but for long, slow breaths. I reached out and slipped my hand in his. He didn't open his eyes, but his fingers entwined in mine.

I leaned my shoulder against his and said quietly, "I'm sorry."

After a long moment, he shook his head and said in a rough voice, "Never mind. What's important is that you're alright. Your dad fixed you up nicely."

I squeezed his hand. "He can fix you up too. Let's call him."

"He'll ask too many questions. And getting him involved could put him in danger. Neither of us wants that. I'll be fine."

We sat in quiet silence, then he gathered me to him, arms wrapping tight, head resting on mine.

"When you're Mandatum," he said, "the one thing you can always trust is your team, and you're supposed to be on ours now." He kissed my hair, then took my face in both his hands and pulled back so he could look into my eyes, his expression intense. "You've got to trust that we've got your back, trust *me*, and quit keeping secrets and going off on your own halfcocked. Understand?"

"Yes," I said.

And I did. Intellectually. It was just putting the trust factor into emotional action where I was having trouble.

"But you're wrong about one thing." I wagged a finger. "This time I was fully and completely cocked." I finished with a confident nod.

Ayden made a choking sound. Sputtered then laughed. Once he managed to gain control, his head tilted sideways and he gazed at me. Then he lifted one brow in a highly suggestive slant.

"Fully and completely *cocked*, is it?" Ayden said. "My, my, my. Miss Lahey, the things you say."

Oh.

A blush thundered my cheeks and rolled down my neck.

"Uhhh, that didn't come out right. I meant…" Really, Aurora? My hands slapped to my face and slowly slid down, hoping to wipe away the mortification. Wasn't working. I gave him a pleading look. "You know what I meant."

"Oh, well," he blustered with mock dismay, "I'm thinking all sorts of things about what you meant, and I am absolutely *scandalized*."

"Ayden!"

"Fine." He glanced heavenward, his head shaking slightly, an exasperated smile tugging at the corner of his mouth. "But when this latest crisis is over, you and I are— "

"— having a serious make-out session!" Blake burst through the door and filled what little was left of the tiny closet. He grinned with satisfaction. "I told them I'd find you. Can I join in?"

"No." Ayden elbowed us past the big guy and led me down the hall toward third period, his arm around my waist. "Get your own girlfriend."

"Why can't we share? You're such a prude." Blake lumbered behind us. "Besides, you two aren't for realsies anyway so she's fair game. And I'm the best gamer in town."

Ayden snorted. "Even if you had game, which you don't, she's not fair anymore."

I gave him an odd look.

He blustered, "Uh, I mean, of course you're fair."

"Just fair?" Blake said. "Weak, dude."

I smiled.

Ayden glared at the big guy. "I meant were dating, idiot."

"You sure about that?" Blake stroked his chin thoughtfully. "'Cause I know a *gorgeous* gal like babe wouldn't want to date a guy who's stupid enough to think she's only fair. When did you ask her? Officially."

Ayden shrugged. "I didn't ask…exactly. Blake, this is none of your business."

"Nope. Not official then," Blake said. "She's still fair game. Come to papa, chickadee."

When Blake made a move to put his arm around me, Ayden slapped a palm on Blake's chest. "Back off. She's not—"

"Ow!" Blake yelped and jumped back.

I smelled burning. Blake put a hand to his torso where his flannel shirt was blackened and burnt.

Ayden turned pale. "Jeez, man. I'm sorry."

He started to brush at Blake's shirt, but the big guy pushed him off, nonplussed. "Don't worry about it, dude. I'm tougher than I look. Unlike you. Big baby."

He started to move off, but Ayden stopped him. We were almost to my classroom. The door was open and kids jostled us lightly as they headed down the hall and inside as the warning bell rang.

"You're right," Ayden said.

"Course I am." Blake folded his arms. "About what?"

Ayden glanced around, sparing a mildly irritated glance at Blake, then he faced me and spoke softly. "Apparently, I forgot to *officially* ask you this last night — or this morning, whatever — and I'm in a bit of a time constraint, so sorry for the lack of…finesse in my delivery, but, uh, don't know how else to say this so…" he lowered his voice further, "will you be my girlfriend?"

A snorty chortle of laughter escaped before I clamped my hand over my mouth. Blake made a couple of "tsk, tsk," sounds.

Ayden cringed. "Yeah, yeah, like I didn't already know that sounded lame. But I'm under a little pressure here so…are we a go? No more pretend. You and me together. For—"

"Realsies?" I said, then choked with amusement.

He groaned. "You're not helping. A simple yes or no is all I need."

I stifled a smile. "Does that mean we're going steady too?"

"Ha ha. I'll take these laughs at my expense as a yes." He turned to Blake. "See? Official."

"Still kinda iffy because you totally butchered that proposal," Blake said with a disapproving shake of his head. "But I'll have to coach you later. Right now Matthias wants us all at your house to go over files and books and do the basic treasure hunting stuff. He's been calling you all morning. Tristan's in the office taking care of getting us out."

"I can't leave early," I said. "I practically just got here."

"Sorry, babe, don't think you were invited."

I huffed, "What do you mean I'm not invited?"

"Tell Matthias, I'll be there *after* school," Ayden said firmly. "*With* Aurora. I'm not leaving her alone."

I gave Ayden an encouraging nudge. "Go. You're exhausted. Clean up and rest at home then get me after school. I'll be fine."

"I'll stay here," Blake offered. "Watch over her like she was my own girlfriend, which based on your sloppy seduction skills, I still claim she is. She'll be safe with big, bad me." Blake laid an arm across Ayden's shoulders. Ayden winced at the contact. "Much better than wimpy Fireboy here."

"Fine," Ayden said. "But I'll be back. Soon."

"Hopefully with your meager awesomeness restored." Blake poked a finger through the holes Ayden had burnt in his shirt. "Dude, you owe me a new shirt. Make it silk. Ladies love touching silk. Almost as much as they love touching me. Show him, Aurora."

Ayden spun me away from Blake to slip a warm hand on my neck and kiss my cheek. "Take care of her," he told Blake and headed down the hall. His steps were wobbly enough that he bumped into three people before he made it to the corner.

I stared at his back, worried. "Blake…"

"I'll get Logan to drive him home, babe." The big guy ruffled my hair. "Be right back."

I smiled and meandered into the classroom.

Someone yelled, "Hi-ya!" and sliced a sword directly at my throat.

Chapter Fifty-Five

I swung my backpack and knocked the weapon from my attacker's hands. It clattered to the floor, and I saw it was actually the teacher's wooden pointing stick. Hey, when it was swinging in a blur in my peripherals, it *looked* like a sword.

The class erupted in exclamations with my teacher shrieking the loudest.

"Mrs. Lahey, I didn't allow you to wait for your niece so you could engage in violence, not to mention the flagrantly inappropriate use of classroom teaching materials!"

Aunt M eyed her with distaste. "And that nitwit attitude is why you'll be first to die."

The class said things like, "Oooooo," and "Burn."

My teacher's jaw dropped. Along with, most likely, my grade. Which was something I did *not* need.

"Proper tactics and training are essential." Unperturbed, Aunt M nudged a toe under the pointing stick lying on the floor and flicked it skillfully up into her hand so she could twirl it as she continued to address the students, pacing in front of them like a drill sergeant. "The best opportunity to keep someone on their toes and battle-ready is a surprise assault when they are at the lowest point of exhaustion because *that*—" She spun to face her rapt audience and point the stick at them. They all jerked back in their seats. "—is when the enemy attacks. You'll all do best to remember that if you want to survive."

The students started clapping and hooting.

I smiled weakly at my stunned teacher. "It's been a...difficult pregnancy."

Aunt M snorted. "Don't make excuses to the dead dame walking. I'm providing a *useful* education."

The class went, "Oooooo," again.

Oh, jeez.

"She's just leaving." I grabbed Aunt M's arm and dragged her toward the door saying, "Before you decimate my GPA further."

"Don't blame that debacle on me," M said.

She tossed the pointer to the teacher who squeaked in surprise then fumbled and dropped it with a clatter. The class laughed. The teacher didn't.

Aunt M looked at her and muttered, "Useless," then turned to me. "Let's have tea."

I blinked. "What?"

M looked impatient. "I'm here with Father Bancroft helping him deliver to the drama department some of that medieval paraphernalia he likes to collect. He's loaning it as props for their next production."

Right. Some Shakespeare play. Bancroft being a collector of medieval artifacts wasn't surprising. After the Kalifera attack at the church, the boys had taken me to his personal quarters to recover, and considering the heavy, carved furniture and ancient battles depicted in paintings and tapestries, it made sense.

My aunt smiled too brightly. "Join us for tea in the auditorium."

And let the two of them hammer me about the horrors of hanging with the Hex Boys? Not to mention, I'd get to be under the scrutiny of a Mandatum bigwig? No thanks.

So I said, "No thanks," kissed her cheek, and scuttled back into class. M tried to follow me, but my teacher shut the door in her face, then shook the pointing stick at her as my stunned aunt peered through the small window.

I grabbed my backpack and was returning the various contents which had spilled out when I noticed something missing. Oh, no. I dug frantically but—

"Looking for this?" came a voice from the rear of the room. It was Luke Something or Other who sat to my right. He held up the book with the weird spiral on the front and odd language written within the pages.

As a starting linebacker for the varsity team, he resembled a refrigerator and had a talent for smashing things. He was pleasant enough and paid me little attention except to copy the occasional test answers off me. At this point in my academic career, not his smartest move.

I was almost to my seat when Mika from gym class, the shy school newspaper slash gossip guru who sat behind him, grabbed my wrist.

"Hey," she said with quiet urgency, "tell Matthias I'm helping take care of his…problem."

I almost laughed and asked, "Which one?" but she seemed serious. So, having no idea what she was talking about, I nodded solemnly and replied, "I'm sure he'll appreciate it."

Yeah, right.

As I sat down, Luke the Linebacker smiled and handed me the double-spiral book. It looked small in his hand.

"Thanks," I said with genuine relief.

He nodded and the teacher began her lecture, writing on the board as she spoke. I left the leather-bound book on my desk and started copying the teacher's notes.

"It's a fascinating elixir of ancient languages," Luke the Linebacker said quietly.

There was an odd lilt to his voice, but I didn't pay much attention until he reached over and tapped his pencil on the leather spiral-covered book. Then he touched the pencil to his cheek as if pondering some great mystery.

"I recognize Latin, of course, but this manufactured language brews within the complex elements of Etruscan, Lepontic, Camunic, as well as Ancient and Demotic Greek."

"Demonic Greek?" That sounded scary. How would this guy know?

"I said, De*mo*tic, little dove. Nothing to do with demons."

The breath froze in my chest, sending icicles to stab my gut. I turned toward him slowly. And stared. When he finally faced me, I could see the whole of his eyes shimmering pink. The same color when a certain someone *poofed* in and out of existence.

"Rose," I breathed.

He smiled, showing lots of teeth.

"Hello, dove," he said in that odd voice. Like it was coming from a radio.

"How are you doing this? *What* are you doing?" My gaze flicked around the room at the unsuspecting crowd before settling nervously on Luke the Linebacker. Who wasn't Luke the Linebacker at all. At least, not in this moment. "Are you here? Somewhere? Don't hurt him. Or anyone."

"I'm not in your proximity," he said mildly. "But since this body is, I can commandeer his mind as a temporary vessel. I will leave all unharmed. Now, as for the manuscript you have acquired, the language inside was fashioned by an individual possessing an inordinate capacity for words. I imagine it to be Flint's favorite Scriptor. Such a unique gift that one possessed."

"A what?"

Not-Luke the Linebacker said with annoyance, "Have you not read the files?"

"Been a little busy," I shot back, feeling on edge because this wasn't creepy at all. It was freaking terrifying. "You know, trying to do some *psycho's* bidding so he won't kill me."

"Miss Lahey, do you have something to say?" the teacher asked.

I jumped, knocking my notebook off the desk. "No, ma'am."

By the time I picked up the book, Mika was running her index finger slowly down Not-Linebacker's spine. He turned to her. Her breath caught, her eyes glazed over, and a small moan escaped her lips. She leaned forward. He flicked his fingers and turned away. Mika flopped back, looking dazed.

"What the heck?!" I hissed. "I said don't hurt anyone."

He chuckled darkly, "Trust me, she felt no pain. Perhaps I could show you?"

"No thanks, Romeo. Just show me what you know about this gibberish." And get out of this poor kid's head. And my classroom. And my life. Ugh!

"Pity," he shrugged. "However, this *gibberish* is anything but. I believe it to be a code used as a secret communique amid a unique few who understand its encryption. You can't translate it?"

"Other than Divinicus Nex and Bellator, no. Can you?"

"Alas, not. But I think *you* are supposed to."

"Why?"

"Because Flint targeted you years ago."

"Again, why? How could he know me? I wasn't even born for another hundred…" My voice trailed off as chills goosebumped over my body. I spoke slowly. "He was targeting the next Divinicus." I shook my head trying to break free some answers. "But still, why?"

"Read the file," he said then turned to Mika who had started touching him again.

The door burst open and Blake strode in holding a bundle of individually wrapped flowers and wearing a red cape that didn't make it much past his shoulders.

"Hey, dudes and dudettes, greetings and deliveries from the King of Courtship, the Principal of Passion. Principal, get it? 'Cause we're in a school. Okay, let's see who my first love victim is." He shuffled through a stack of pink notecards.

Rose, in Linebacker's body, had been doing the hand flutter thing at Mika when Blake waltzed in. The interruption had made Rose turn toward the front, and in that instant, Mika made her move.

She launched out of her seat with a throaty cry. Her entire all-in-one desk/chair was flung sideways, colliding into another student with a crash and yelp as she threw herself onto Not-Luke the Linebacker, crashing him and his desk to the ground. She wrapped her arms around him then latched her lips onto his like a bloodsucking leech.

The room erupted in sound. Shrieks, catcalls, more crashing desks, the teacher pushing her way through the crowd, and above the din I heard Blake say, "Dang, I'm good."

CHAPTER FIFTY-SIX

"That's the stupidest thing I've ever heard!" My hands strangled the air wishing for Matthias's throat.

"That's what I think any time you open your mouth," the Aussie said dryly.

After Ayden had picked me up from school, we'd gathered in the Ishida's game room. I'd let Mom know I was doing homework and promised to be home for dinner. We had the place to ourselves because Mr. Ishida had surprised his wife and daughter with a trip to the theater in Los Angeles, and an overnight hotel stay. The boys were sure it was his continued attempt to keep their mom distanced from whatever the Mandatum needed from her.

The orgy in my class had broken up almost as quickly as the linebacker's eyes had stopped glowing pink. He'd been a bit confused, but not unpleasantly so, to "wake up" in a hot liplock. Mika was all kinds of embarrassed and flustered. Last I knew, they were both sent to the principal's office.

Ayden sat on the opposite end of the couch flipping through a file propped up against my legs lying across his lap.

Tristan was inside the secret lab using the multitude of monitors covering the walls to run some sort of algorithm to compare and find connections among the images of the pages he'd scanned from

Flint's books as well as the files. Documents were flipping across the screens at light speed. On his feet and in constant motion, Tristan's fingers flew across a small army of embedded keyboards, touch screens, and floating hologram thingies that included new ones of Flint's underground, water-powered, steam pumping, electrical plant chugging away like magic.

Matthias waved the scrap of paper that Natasha had given Logan. "What the hell am I supposed to do with this?"

"You don't know what to do with a girl's phone number?" I snorted. "Someone please explain how Jayden was the only one who flunked the Seduction course."

"*Almost* flunked," Jayden corrected. He hung upside-down from the rings in the vaulted ceiling, pencil in hand, reading the double spiral journal in order to decipher the code. "*Blake* was evicted entirely."

At the pool table, Blake had been skimming files, then stacking them in neat piles based on "correlating subject matter." He grinned, "I'll call her for you!"

"A girl in my history class had a note for you too, Matthias," Tristan said. "It's in my backpack."

"Keep it. Bloody hell." Matthias crumpled the paper and tossed it toward the fire.

But before the discarded note could disappear in a flash of flames, a gust of wind caught it and swirled the paper into Logan's hand. He stuffed it inside his blazer, grumbling, "I'll deal with it."

As he retreated outside to the balcony, the boys shared a look but said nothing. Moments later Logan was walking the railing while papers from the Flint files literally hovered in the air as he read them.

So cool.

And then there was Matthias. So *not* cool.

"You should be thanking us for getting all this info," I said, taking a break from math to wave an arm at Flint's control room manuals scattered about. "And finding the center of Flint's magical universe. It was a success, not stupid, and as soon as I'm done, I'm helping."

"We can do without your kind of help," Matthias said. "You defied a direct order and endangered a team member which is the definition of ultimate stupid." He grabbed a pile of documents and spread them out on the bar with enough force to knock a few off. Not that he noticed since he was too busy trying to kill me with his scowly stare. "*This* is classified. For Mandatum eyes only. Just shut up and do your homework." He glared at Ayden. "Why didn't we drop her at home? Or off a cliff?"

Ayden didn't look up from his file. "Thought this would be more romantic for the two of you rather than gagged in the trunk of your car."

"Might upgrade to bottom of the lake next time," Matthias growled. "We need to come up with a plan before we go running off to the tunnels like morons again." He looked at me. "Or moron. Singular. Meaning you."

"Yeah. I got that." I chucked a wad of paper at Matthias's head. "But I'm the one on borrowed time. And the one who needs Flint's treasure before Rose decides to kill me."

"Hey." Ayden lifted his head from the file he was reading. "I told you we're not going to let that happen."

I stood and paced, hands flinging through the air. "Sure, sure. But he could remote mind control someone to murder me. Like some killer drone swooping in. And he can *poof*. In *pink*. Can all Joats do that? 'Cause it's a neat skill, and he could just, you know, *poof* in with a gun, shoot me dead, and *poof* out before anyone can stop him. Kiss, kiss, *bang*, *bang*, *poof*, *poof*, I'm dead."

Ayden caught my hand and guided me back to the couch, dark chocolate eyes brimming with confidence. "Trust me."

"And me." Tristan held up futuristic looking handcuffs with dials and buttons and lots of things glowing. "These are state-of-the-art. Will neutralize any hunter or demon's ability. We slap these on and he's not disappearing again."

Ayden's lips curved into a lopsided grin. "And don't forget, you've got a few moves of your own."

I ignored Matthias's snort.

Blake looked like he had an epiphany. "Hey, babe, we should get you some boots. Short skirt. And lots of leather to complimentarily accent your luscious lady parts."

Ayden raised a brow. "I'm good with that."

As I thumped his shoulder and went back to homework, Ayden's smile turned grim. "But Rose is no Joat. They're never much good at anything and his powers are way more than good. And I've never heard of one with the ability to teleport."

"That would be the *poofing* you spoke about, Aurora," Jayden said from above.

"I know what teleport means."

Matthias opened a file. "What do we do if we find Flint's treasure? If Cacciatori finds out, hell, we're better off if it stays buried."

"But, dude, we'd be heroes," Blake said wistfully. "Fortune, fame, the ladies falling at our feet."

"And the whole Mandatum descending on Gossamer Falls." Matthias rifled through papers. "Not that we're any closer to finding it. I've got Flint's background here, something about a sister who was Mandatum too, and he had a big interest in anything Divinicus related. Maybe that's what caught Cacciatori's eye. There's some footnote about a cover story on his 'true purpose.' What's that about?"

"It's not much better on my end," Tristan called from the computer room. "I have a serial number on the tracker we found in the demon, but if I try to access the report on what hunter last signed it out for use, the *entire* Mandatum will know I'm hacking their records. Which would expose us and Aurora."

"Well, in that case, some questions are best left unanswered." I rapped my pencil against my knee and tried to focus on homework. "What are linear systems of equalities again?"

"Inequalities," Jayden corrected.

"I could do it with an untraceable, non-Mandatum computer," Tristan said. "But the only computers sophisticated enough to hack their systems without a trace are ones designed by them."

I penciled in an answer. "Which means my best bet is finding that weapon before her hounds hunt me down."

"Her?" Matthias said.

I grimaced at my paper. No, that was definitely not the right answer. I erased, again, careful not to rip the page which had become dangerously thin.

"Rose's accomplice." I rubbed my scratchy eyes. Numbers were blurring together. "Didn't get a good look at her, but I had a thought that maybe her demon dog was actually trying to save me from the gorilla demon which then got me thinking maybe she's the 'she' Fiskick was working for, but then the dogs tried to kill us last night so I'm not sure. " A yawn cracked my jaw. I let my head fall back to stare up at Jayden. "Hey, bat boy, could you try explaining this again using very small words?"

Matthias snarled, "When did you meet Rose's partner?"

I hid another yawn behind the back of my hand. "Who said I met her?"

"You just did," Ayden ground out.

I looked at him, confused. He'd stopped reading, and was watching me with a harsh, near hostile expression. Then my sluggish senses clued into the sudden silence. Palpable and quivering. Outside, still reading, Logan remained unaware, but Blake had stopped organizing, Tristan came out of the computer room, and Jayden hung upside down, wearing a frown, which looked like an odd smile.

They were all staring. At me.

"Oh…" Crap. I should've just gone home. I sat up and rubbed my eyes hoping to wipe out the exhaustion and knead in a pinch of common sense. "I didn't…exactly…meet her, I…"

"Had a vision," Ayden said quietly.

My stomach wrenched. Dear God, he knew I was the Divinicus. How? Where did I blow it? I glanced nervously at Jayden who looked as appalled as I felt.

So I blustered, "Pfft. What? Vision? Why would I have a vision?"

"Or a dream." Ayden stood abruptly, knocking papers in the air. "Whatever you call it. Like that thing you had when you saw Fiskick and Echo talking about hurting Jocelyn."

I breathed a little easier. But not much. Ayden's expression wrestled between anger and hurt as his fingers curled into fists.

"I should've known. It's one of the reasons you went to the tunnels that night. I'm right. And you chose not to tell us. Again."

I laid my book down. "I can explain."

"Spare me the bloody drama," Matthias said tiredly. "Just tell us what you saw."

For once I was happy to do Matthias's bidding, avoiding Ayden's glare as I gave the details of Rose and the mystery woman's conversation. Minus the Nex talk, of course.

When I finished, the Aussie rubbed his temples. "What a nightmare. So we have a woman with demon hounds who wants some stone that Rose has, but they both want the treasure, and she's distracting some 'rogue' and there are more players in this game."

"Vipers in the pit, she called them," I said.

"And she uses a bow and arrow?" Tristan returned to the secret room. "I'll put this all in the computer. See if it comes up with anything."

"I completely understand what you've been through." Two somersaults later, Jayden landed on his feet, snatched my wrist, and pulled me up. "Some tea would settle your nerves. To the kitchen! We'll get Logan."

"Hey, guys!" Logan flew in from the balcony, so animated that his cheeks actually had some color. "You are not going to believe this. It's Flint. He was—"

Outside something crashed louder than a NASCAR pileup and sent the whole gang running.

CHAPTER FIFTY-SEVEN

At the end of the Ishida's driveway, Rose struggled with the mountain of garbage cans and their contents which was piled on top of him.

"Well, this is embarrassing," Rose said with a smooth chuckle.

Matthias and Ayden pounced on Rose, shoving him down and slapping on those super shackles that would squelch his ability to teleport.

Wow. Impressive. We just nabbed my supernatural assassin.

Blake caught my shoulder and reeled me back between him and Tristan as Rose sat up amid the trash. The rest of the boys circled him, eyes glowing.

Logan's fingers twitched and a whirlwind swirled around the outside of our perimeter creating a wall that would suck up anything that crossed its path. Flames licked up Ayden's arms. Matthias's shadow whips unfurled from his hands and danced like cobras swaying to the music of the charmer's flute. Knives of serrated ice glinted with lethal threat in Jayden's hands.

"Calm down, gentlemen." Rose sounded bored. "I came to talk, not indulge in murder. Unfortunately, it was dark and I encountered some unexpected wildlife which gave me a start and," he shrugged, "I am at your mercy."

Matthias cracked one of his whips. "Get up and get in the house."

"As you wish." Rose wrinkled his nose, picked a banana peel off his lap, and stood in the last faint beams of sunset.

"Whoa!"

"Is he wearing a leather cat suit?"

"Holy Mother!

"Dude!"

The guys all quickly averted their eyes and raised their hands to further block any chance of catching a view. Anything to *not* see Rose in his painted-on leather one-piece that left absolutely nothing to the imagination. Their reactions were pure entertainment.

"Stunning, right?" Rose spread his palms as far as the cuffs would allow.

"Oh, I'm stunned." Ayden looked ill.

Rose looked down at himself with admiration. "Not many males can pull off this look."

"*No* male can pull off that look."

"Actually, his finely sculptured physique would be considered the perfect complement for this type of anatomically revealing attire which accentuates his—"

"Bloody hell, Jayden, shut it!"

"Dude, this is so not right."

"I feel like it's looking at me."

"Feel like what's looking at—? Oh. *Oh!* Ugh, now I feel like it's looking at me too."

"How can it be looking at both of us?"

"Are you serious?"

"I'm gonna be sick."

"Someone please gouge out my eyes."

"He might as well be naked."

"Already did that," Rose said dryly and gave me a suggestive wink. "Ask Aurora."

"What!"

Now the crowd had eyes on me.

I frantically shook my head. "No, no, no. It's not what you think. He was in the water with most," my hands circled over my abdomen, "stuff covered."

"Most?" Ayden almost shrieked. The orange-red flames on his arms flashed blue-white.

"Trust me." I gave him a look. "You've just seen more than I did."

"Alright, stay put Rose." Matthias kept his eyes up. "But cover yourself."

"And exactly how am I supposed to do that?"

"Right." Matthias waved a hand at the boys. "One of you cover him up."

"I'm not touching him."

"Me neither."

"Un-uh."

"Grow up, guys." I kicked a fallen trash can toward Rose. "Put that in front of you."

Rose righted the container and placed it in front of himself. It covered what needed to be covered, and the guys visibly relaxed.

Rose sighed with weary amusement. "While my anatomy is impressive, what should concern you is our quest. Have you found Flint's treasure?"

"Why do you want it so much?" Matthias said.

"I only require one item. A stone. About so big." His hands formed the shape of an egg. "It hums with life. Within its confines the colors pulse and vibrate, constantly changing. It's a weapon which can be used to get my sister out of hell. You can keep the rest of the treasure. Keep the stone for all I care. Once I get my sister, I have no further interest in it."

"Why should we help you?" Tristan wanted to know.

Rose pressed his palms together as if in prayer. "Because I'm Mandatum. We help our comrades, do we not?"

"We can't find any record of you. You aren't a Joat," Ayden said. "What are you?"

"One that can help you. That's all that should matter." Rose was losing patience. "Those who want Aurora dead will only send others if I fail. I am offering to help you destroy them for good. Even help uncover the traitor in the Mandatum. In return you are asked to rescue a mortal from demons. An *innocent* mortal who is only in danger because demons desire Aurora dead. His hands clenched. His voice shook with emotion. "Indeed, isn't this just the type of crusade you have pledged your lives to endeavor?"

The resulting uncomfortable silence seemed an indication that Rose had some kind of point. If he was telling the truth.

"This stone," I said. "How can it get your sister out?"

"So happy you asked." He bowed slightly. "It gives the bearer the ability to open any portal. From *this* side."

The boys shook their heads.

"Impossible," Jayden said emphatically. "In the centuries of Mandatum history, no one has ever opened one from this side. Ever."

"You know only what the Mandatum tells you." Rose's voice oozed with condescension. "This stone was found centuries ago and considered too powerful. So all evidence of its existence was erased from the archives. The stone has been kept hidden, left in the care of a small sect of individuals, the responsibility passed down through generations."

"If there was something like that, we'd know, dude." Blake glanced around. "Wouldn't we?"

Rose lifted a shoulder. "It's just another example of a truth the Mandatum does not want you to know. Just as you have found the truth regarding Flint."

Matthias folded his arms. "What truth?"

"Have you not read the file?" Rose quelled his sharp, exasperated tone, and ground his teeth in irritation. "Flint never stole any artifacts. Never killed anyone. He *saved* thousands of lives. He used his estate here to run an underground railroad for Mandatum hunters and any member who wanted to flee the society."

"There's no substantiation for such pronouncements," Jayden said firmly.

"Not in the briefing of lies given to the likes of you." Rose started to pace but stopped when the boys shouted for him to stay put. "Oh, for the love of— That's why I wanted you to see the *original* file. So you would know the truth. See their lies."

"You're the liar," Tristan said.

"Actually…" came a quiet voice, "he's not."

We all turned to Logan.

He shrugged. "He's right about Flint. I was reading it in the file before he showed up."

Rose wore a smug expression. "Bravo, young Logan. Perhaps you could enlighten your fellow hunters."

Logan shook his head. "No. You tell us your version first. I'll see how truthful it is."

"As you wish," Rose agreed. "The Mandatum didn't willingly let people leave the society. To get out, you had to flee, and if you were found, well, let us say, you were better off dead."

"It's not like that now," Ayden said.

"Really?" Rose raised a brow. "Would they let you just walk away? And if it's so different now, why do you hide the extent of your powers to avoid being forced into the Sicarius?"

Or in my case, into service as the Divinicus. I didn't rebut his claims. And neither did the Hex Boys.

Rose stifled a smirk and continued. "Believe what you will about today, but in the late nineteenth century Flint hid people until it was safe to go out into the world. He provided false documents with which to start new lives. He never *stole* artifacts. Hunters happily paid Flint for their freedom from an oppressive tyrant. That's how he acquired his treasure."

The Hex Boys turned to Logan who nodded, looking grim.

Rose shrugged. "Honestly, I don't care about any of that. I'm just pointing out that your society isn't as benevolent as you would like to believe. When they found out what he was doing, they tortured Flint for information and the whereabouts of those he had helped, the treasure, and especially the stone, but rather than give anything up, he took the punishment and went insane for his troubles."

I looked at the boys. "Does the Mandatum still do that?"

"Of course not," Tristan said sharply.

"At least not that we know of," Logan muttered.

That was reassuring.

"Find the treasure," Rose said. "Use the stone to set my sister free. Then use it all as leverage to set yourselves free. But do it with haste because while I've grown rather fond of Aurora, and although it would be bittersweet, I *will* kill her to save my family."

"You're hardly in a position to make threats," Matthias said.

"You still don't understand the game we are playing." Rose looked disheartened. "Perhaps some…incentive would best spur you on with more enthusiasm of purpose."

Didn't like the sound of that. Or the cold glint in his eyes.

"Hmmm." Rose laid a slender finger along his jaw as if deep in thought, then he turned to me. "I believe the loss of a beloved brother should hone my point."

Fear sliced razors across my gut. Then my eyes settled on the handcuffs. “Threaten all you want. You’re not getting anywhere near my family.”

“Thank you.” Rose’s smile took a malicious curve. “These will come in handy.”

As he raised his arms, his skin shimmered translucent, and the super high-tech shackles dropped through the air. Rose caught them before they hit the ground, then he dissipated in a swirl of pale pink smoke.

Wow. Impressive. We just *lost* my supernatural assassin. And let him loose on a new target.

Matthias turned paler than the moon. “Aurora, where are your brothers?”

CHAPTER FIFTY-EIGHT

I slipped around a corner, cursing whoever polished the hospital floors to such a slick shine.

"Aurora, wait!"

I couldn't see Ayden. I'd left him in the dust when I'd jumped out of his car before he'd had a chance to park.

Back in the yard outside the Ishida home, Logan had launched into the air like he'd been shot from a cannon and flew across the sky to check on Lucian at my house. Jayden had Supermanned into the air too, heading for the hospital daycare where Dad was working late.

And, no, I didn't know they could fly like that. Logan made sense, kind of, using air and all, but Jayden's had something to with manipulating molecules. I didn't understand, nor did I care. I was just happy for the speed.

In cars and providing backup, Matthias and Blake had followed Logan while Tristan and I had dived into Ayden's car where I'd never been so thankful for his death-defying driving skills.

But deep down I knew it didn't matter how fast we all were. Nothing beat teleporting. My worst nightmare — my family taken because of me — could already be a reality.

I banged open the hospital daycare door to a dizzying mash of bright colors, tiny furniture, sprawled toys, and cartoon animals spattered across the walls. Not a single child in sight.

A kindly grandma type greeted me. "Miss Lahey?"

"Oron," I said between ragged panting. "I'm here for my brother."

"You just missed him."

"No." My stomach dropped into freefall, ready to take my knees out on the way.

"The nurse just took him to your dad." She smiled. "They're going home shortly."

"Nurse?" I said.

"Quite the attractive blonde," she chuckled. "And so charming."

And dangerous. Stupid, psychotic Rose.

I tore out of the room and collided with Ayden.

He spoke quickly. "Lucian's safe. The guys have your house secure."

My emotions twisted into a gut-wrenching mess of happy, relieved, and terrified.

"Rose has Oron," I choked out then pushed off him and raced through the halls, tears streaming, searching for my dad because maybe, just maybe I was wrong.

But Dad's office was empty. Just a desk with patient files and pictures of a happy Lahey family which I'd officially ruined. I sagged against the door frame, tired, scared, angry, not sure what else, but none of it good.

Ayden grabbed my shoulders. "I'm sure Oron's fine. Jayden would never let anything happen to him."

"Where is Jayden? He should have beaten us here."

"There's my elusive daughter!" Dad waved from a nurse's station up ahead. "Haven't seen you enough lately."

I raced forward. "Do you have Oron?"

"Thank you," Dad said to a woman behind the desk as he passed her several folders. He turned to me and frowned. "Nurse is bringing him now. What's wrong? Have you been crying? Again?" He shot an openly hostile look at Ayden, who, under the glare, visibly flinched.

"No, Dad, it's…I've, ah, got to tell you—" I choked on a way to explain that his son was kidnapped, lost in the clutches of an assassin because I was some supernatural freak and a selfish coward, unwilling to give myself up long ago to save my family.

"You look a little too rosy." Dad put a hand to my forehead. "Any dizziness? Let me check your shoulder. Could be infected."

"Dr. Lahey, there you are," said a woman behind me. "I've got a precious delivery for you."

I knew that voice. I turned slowly, jaw dropping.

The woman was average height, thirties, pretty, but made more memorable by her ever changing costumes. Instead of typical nurse's scrubs, her blue uniform was dotted with floating white feathers and fitted to her lovely figure. Her hair swept down in a braid, simple but for how her blonde locks changed color and bled into teal at the ends, matching the uniform and the identical shade of her eyes.

"Gloria?" I gasped.

Sure she was missing the wings, but it was definitely my guardian angel. She had a sleeping baby with a mess of red curls in her arms. Oron. I nearly collapsed in relief.

"Aurora," Gloria nodded at me.

"You two know each other?" Dad said.

Gloria smiled. "I was here when she was in the hospital during her coma. Are you ready to take Oron home, Dr. Lahey? Or should I return him to—"

"Home!" I took my baby brother from Gloria, holding him to my chest like he was sack of diamonds and everyone else was part of a heist. "We're going home. Right, Dad? I'm fine. Just a little tired. Let's go."

"Yes, ma'am." Dad laughed and gave me a salute. "I can examine you there. Let me collect my things from the office."

"Take Ayden and show him those tumor photos. I'll wait for you at the nurse's station. Gloria and I need to catch up." I grabbed her arm and dragged her down the hall out of earshot, then hissed, "Where have you been? I've got an assassin threatening me, my family. Name's Rose."

Gloria shrugged. "Not ringing any bells."

I huffed. "You'd think the Divinicus Nex would get a better guardian angel than this."

Gloria narrowed a disapproving look. "No one can get to your family on my watch."

"He threatened to take one of my brothers."

"Impossible," she said firmly. A moment later her mouth twisted sideways, and she tilted her head. "Unless…"

I clutched Oron closer. "Unless what?"

"Are you sure he threatened to take *your* brother?"

My stomach was back in freefall. "Where's Jayden?"

Gloria offered a sad smile. "Not my job." Then she ducked around a corner.

I heard a rush of feathers like a thousand doves fluttering down the halls. When I caught up, Gloria was gone. I would have screamed in frustration, but Oron was sleeping on my chest in utter peace.

Tristan raced up holding a computer pad and looking grim. "Where's Ayden?! Jayden never got in here. Look at the security feed."

I watched a grainy video of Jayden walking toward the Emergency Room entrance. As he passed a parked ambulance, the back doors opened, and an EMT wearing a ball cap hopped out. He bumped Jayden off balance, then slapped Tristan's futuristic, power-stopping handcuffs on Jayden's wrists.

Jayden threw a punch and a kick, but Rose sidestepped, caught Jayden's fist with his own, looked directly at the camera, and even had time to wink and tip his ball cap before they both disappeared in a swirl of pink smoke.

Chapter Fifty-Nine

Clouds smothered the moon, and in the dark outside my backyard gate, I glanced expectantly toward the forest. Nothing yet. I still wasn't sure this was a good idea, but it was all I had.

The boys were out trying to hunt down Jayden, which is what I should've be doing, but Dad wouldn't leave the hospital without me, so I was home.

Going crazy.

After dinner I'd tried phoning for some progress, some way I could help, but I'd only reached Matthias.

"Stay home and out of the bloody way," he'd snapped and hung up.

Stupid son of a jackal.

With a plan born of desperation and guilt, I'd snuck into Tristan's room, still cluttered from the guys' stuff when they'd slept over to watch out for Rose. It was easy to find something of Jayden's. His orca-covered surfer shorts had lots of bright colors. Then I'd gone outside to the edge of the woods behind our house and started calling for Fido.

Hey, I had a supernatural protection detail with a nose the size of a space shuttle at my beck and call, so why not use her?

I puckered my lips and whistled. Okay, *tried* to whistle, but could only crank a few decibels. I tried Ayden's snazzy technique using two fingers in my mouth with even less success. So it was back to whispering as loud as I could. So slick. And when that didn't work, I was about to stab my palm to get some blood when it occurred to me that I already had plenty of other wounds. So, fighting whimpers, I jabbed at the stitches on my shoulder until blood oozed.

Shortly after, I heard the cracking and smushing of foliage. Something big was on its way.

I smelled fresh, upturned earth and was poised on alert, ready to run back into the safety of the protection wards the boys had put around the house, when Fido bustled through the forest on her bazillion spindly legs. She heaved to a halt like a locomotive, the back seeming to stop about an hour after the front. I weaved and bobbed to avoid the slobbery lick she lapped my way. Her six eyes blinked as her head cocked sideways, and she made that chittering noise that rumbled the ground beneath my feet.

After an awkward pat on her face, I pressed Jayden's shorts against her nose. She probably couldn't smell much other than her own putrid breath.

"Come on, girl. Get the scent."

The centimole demon swung her massive head, clattering Mom's gardening supplies to the ground, and nosed around the rotting scent of the compost bin.

"Not that." I grabbed the fur on her neck and tried to pull her around. Not happening.

"Aurora, you alright?" Mom called from the back porch. "Putting scraps in the composter isn't supposed to be a hazardous waste event. Need help?"

"No!" I yelled, pushing Fido aside when she nosed through the gate to see Mom. "Just gonna see if I can find Helsing. Think he went after a mouse."

"Ok. Don't go far."

My bloodhound brilliance was going nowhere fast. I grabbed a whisker, thick and rough as the gym's climbing rope, wrapped it around my hand, and yanked her head up. Ready to scream, definitely near tears, I put the fabric bunched in my hand up against her nose again.

"Focus, Fido. This is a blood contract order." Wow, that sounded stupid, but I didn't know what else to do. "Find Jayden!"

For several moments she didn't move. Then I felt her hot breath on my hand as she inhaled deeply. Fido recoiled and stood tall, nose raised to the sky, quivering, no doubt catching the scent. I smiled. Matthias was going to eat glass when this worked. She squealed and reared up. I jumped back and nearly lost my footing when she dived into the ground. Debris splattered amid a mighty roar of breaking earth as Fido dove nose first into the ground and burrowed deep until she disappeared completely.

There was a rumbling underfoot that slowly faded. I stepped to the edge of the massive hole she'd created. It was starting to cave in on itself but was still big enough that it could swallow our mini-van.

Super.

I grabbed a shovel and started filling it up. Slow going. Almost useless since, to save pain in my shoulder, I could only use one hand, but better than being inside under the hawk-eye scrutiny of my family.

I'd freaked out Lucian by unconsciously petting him and Oron throughout dinner. That was after he'd accused me of readying for a sniper attack when I'd checked that all windows and doors were locked, and shut the curtains. Since I'd balked at coming home, Dad had told Mom that maybe I was indeed spending too much time with the Hex Boys. At least he was happy my puncture wasn't infected. I wasn't happy when he gave me something for the pain. I felt mildly groggy. Not a good idea when I needed to be top of my game.

Not that I'd set the bar very high.

I was walking a tightrope, and even on good days, my balance was sketchy. If we could just find the treasure. And this stone. Get rid of Rose. Then…what? My life would go back to normal? What a joke.

I'd been shoveling for a while when a branch snapped in the darkness. Too heavy for a woodland creature, not heavy enough for Fido.

"Rose?"

No answer.

Which was definitely worse than an answer, because I could feel a presence. Something was watching me. Something powerful. Energy rippled through the air. The silence morphed into the kind where even the subtle hum of nature ceased.

The hair on my arms raised upright as a chill of ghostly fingers crawled up my spine. My instincts screamed and ran away, leaving me empty and cold.

I gripped the shovel and took one tentative step back. Then another. Edging closer to the gate. I wasn't sure where the protection wards surrounding the house started. I should have had the boys mark it. I could be over the line and vulnerable, but surely the gate was safe, and I was almost there.

From the left, something broke fast from the shadows.

A man wearing a hat and long coat was all I could register before I slammed the shovel into his chest. He caught it, ripped it from my hands, and swung. I dropped to the ground. Felt the *whoosh* of air over my head as he missed.

I rolled sideways and kicked out his ankles. He thudded onto his back with a grunt. I jumped on top of his torso which felt anything but human — lumpy, hard, sharp things biting into my legs — grabbed the handle of the shovel that was now in his hands, and pinned it against his throat. I leaned forward, pressing hard. Ignored the scream of pain in my shoulder. The faint scent of alcohol — whisky maybe — gave me pause. I'd thought it was Rose, but the body didn't seem right. Older, thicker.

The man bucked, almost threw me off. I reeled back one hand and slammed the heel of my palm onto his nose.

A hand latched around my wrist. Beneath me something lit up in the darkness. Small round orbs blazed and cracked with an electric yellow light, like the wires in a light bulb powering up.

Eyes. Glowing eyes.

Holy crap, he was Mandatum. Part of a hit squad? Strike team?

Didn't matter. I needed to run.

Before I could pull away, energy shocked up my arm. Power. My power, coming to life.

Weightlessness wracked my body. I broke from gravity and my mind spiraled down the street in a vision. It seemed to be moving faster than previous ones. The world blurred to shades of black and grey. I glimpsed a tree, moonlight shining off water, just before I blasted through rock and stopped in front of…

Rose stood in a cave, a firm hand on his tall, lanky prisoner standing near the glittering pool of aqua marine water. Jayden wore the super shackles that squelched hunters' powers. The ones which had been so ineffective on Rose earlier.

Rose was rolling his eyes. "Cease with the unnecessary heroics. Disarm the security. Help me and I will help you."

Fido rumbled into the cave. Rose did a double take, and for the first time, a glimpse of fear flickered across his smug, handsome features. "How in Hades did that get out?"

Fido's growl shuddered the walls and rippled the surface of the turquoise pool shimmering under the sharp, iridescent stalactites.

That's my girl.

Jayden looked equally worried. "It's volatile."

"Then you better disarm the system before it gets hungry," Rose said with urgency.

"And alert the team of my whereabouts?" Jayden's eyes narrowed. "I will not collude with whatever treachery you have planned."

"Perhaps I simply plan your freedom."

"I don't want it." Jayden wrenched from Rose's grip. "Not at the expense of their lives."

Fido slunk closer, antennae snapping.

"I desire *my* life, so disarm the system or send an alert. Do it now." Rose shoved Jayden.

In a blink, my mind raced back from the vision and rammed into my body. My gaze cleared and locked onto the freaky yellow orbs beneath me.

Wait…What…oh, right, I was in a fight with some crazed hunter. Crap. I felt more disoriented than usual. My sight was starting to swim. Breathing became a struggle, as if cotton balls were shoved down my throat.

I tried to pull away, but he had my wrists and jerked sideways, rolling us both over so he was on top, pinning my wrists to the ground. He was heavy. And strong. I brought my knee up. Hit something hard, sharp, felt like metal, which only sent zinging pain down my leg. I was losing steam. Losing the fight. Just…losing. Muscles collapsing upon themselves. My shoulder burned with hot pain. All my energy was escaping from my body. I felt like a balloon losing air, and I couldn't tape up the hole before I deflated into nothing. I opened my mouth, tried to find enough breath to scream.

A yowl shredded the night. Not me. Not human.

In my peripheral, a shadow leapt through the air and latched its snarling mass onto my attacker's face.

The man let go of me to roll away and rip off the rabid beast clawing his skin. Muscles slack, I flopped like a ragdoll and rolled sideways, attempting to crawl away. The man jumped up and bolted into the dark. I sucked in a strengthening breath, coughed, and staggered to my feet, holding my arm close to my chest. Movements beyond sluggish, I fumbled the back gate open and stumbled inside.

"Dad." I meant to yell but it came out a hoarse whisper.

My knees trembled. I collapsed on our garden swing and face-planted into the cushions. Black blotted my vision. What the heck did that hunter do to me?

The swing jiggled under new weight. Something soft rubbed against my cheek. A gentle *meow*.

Van Helsing. Of course. The rabid beast who'd come to my defense.

He curled against me and ripped out another yowl, somewhere between the guttural howl of a jaguar and a siren's piercing wail. The same sound he made when, as a stray, he'd found me in a filthy alley, broken, beaten, and dying.

An unsettling thought beat through my mind as I blacked-out.

I had my own personal banshee.

Chapter Sixty

Nightmares chased me awake.

I was lying on softness and wrapped in warmth, the last dregs of sleep paralyzing my limbs.

"Don't you dare send a team," Aunt M's voice roused me. "If I pull out, that only leaves Bancroft to watch…"

A door closed, and I couldn't hear anymore.

I remembered Mom finding me on the swing. She'd screamed for Dad who, after making sure I wasn't comatose, carried my groggy self upstairs to my room. Even only half-awake, I saw they were furious with fear. Dad redressed my puncture which had opened up completely and was bleeding profusely. They'd both berated me for not getting enough rest. I was asleep before they'd tucked the comforter around me.

I dragged my arms up, my shoulder only a mild ache, and rubbed eyes with lids that felt lined with sandpaper. My bedroom was blanketed in the dead of night. Van Helsing curled in a neat ball on my chest lost in dreams, where I'd like to be. Instead, something plucked the strings of my mind and nagged me awake.

"Ken, I think…through something and…but if those Hex Boys…"

Through my closed door, M's hushed voice carried in and out from the hallway. Then the door creaked like she was leaning on it from the outside and…

"I already asked, and they won't consider visiting, let alone leaving for good. The last time we talked them into moving closer, Aurora almost died. They won't listen to us again even if…" The door creaked, and I lost her voice again.

My head throbbed, a strumming in my brain that suddenly flashed taut, urging me to remember something…important…

I shot up, ignoring Van Helsing's grumble as he tumbled off my chest, and groped in the shadows on my nightstand. I found a phone and dialed. The vision's connection to Fido was still strong.

"Aurora?" Logan answered.

"I know where Jayden is," I whispered and hopped out of bed.

"Jump out your window," Logan said.

I paused. "Uh, I said I found Jayden, not that I'm suicidal."

Logan hung up.

A soft *ping* came from my front window. I edged aside the curtain. Logan hovered mid-air.

Oh. Sure. That's normal.

I opened the window. Behind me, the bedroom door opened. I dived for my bed and yanked up the covers.

"Aurora?"

I remained still.

"Just a minute, Ken," M whispered. "I thought I heard somethi— Ahh—!" She cut off her near shriek, then hissed, "No, it was the stupid cat. Give me a minute."

Through slitted eyes, I saw M shuffle over to the open window. I held my breath, waiting for a startled cry regarding a flying Hex Boy. She looked out, then closed it and the curtains before rearranging the covers around my shoulders and heading for the door.

"Yes, I heard you. Cat burglar. Ha ha," M whispered into the phone as she left my room. "What? No, I won't back off. She tore open the wound on her shoulder somehow. Was so tired she fell asleep out in the cold. Could've caught her death."

If she only knew.

"Protection is what I do, Ken. I swear, those Hex Boys are bad news, and I will bury them, one way or another before I let anyone harm a hair on…"

Her voice faded, and I waited until I heard her bedroom door close before I was back in action.

I hopped on one foot, tying my shoe, and hissed out the window, "Logan!"

Logan tornadoed up from below. "Where's Jayden?"

"The portal." I shrugged into my jacket, relieved my shoulder felt nearly numb. I remembered Dad giving me something. Pain killer probably.

"Already looked there. His security code was used to get in, but no sign of him. We keep getting alerts, but there must be a glitch. "

"Don't know about that, but I can still feel them with the Divinicus connection, so let's go." I leaned out the window. "Where's your car?"

Logan glided close and held out a hand. "I've got a better idea."

Chapter Sixty-One

Logan did *not* have a better idea. Sure, flying with nothing but a pint-sized albino's super wind powers keeping you from splatting to the ground miles below may be considered fun by plenty.

Just not me.

Especially since Logan bobbed, weaved, and even barrel-rolled us through the tree tops. Then the forest gave way to moonlight glinting off the tall, thundering waters of Gossamer Falls. Logan swooped down over the beach and headed a course directly through the crashing water. I readied to get soaked, but a gesture of his hand brought a fierce wind that parted the waters, and we sailed through with only light moisture dampening our skin.

We landed in a small alcove illuminated by the jittery hold on my flashlight. Water dribbled down mottled gray rock. Wind whistled mist against my skin. The falls crashed a dark curtain behind us, glinting silver when the moon peeked at our backs, the air wet and musty. It seemed to be a dead end.

"Where's the entrance?!" I yelled over the thundering water.

Logan stuck his hand in a cavity in the wall, then withdrew, blood trickling thread-thin down his finger. Rock split and retracted to reveal a keypad. Logan punched in the code and stepped back, pulling me with him.

The ground shuddered, stone crumbling small pebbles as the wall split open a doorway. We stepped into a cavernous room lit with an eerie green glow from some organic material on the dripping wet walls.

"Glow-in-the-dark algae," Logan said. "Jayden swears it shouldn't exist here but…"

"Cool." I started to move down the only tunnel, but Logan held up a hand. I frowned. "What are we waiting for?"

"Us," growled a voice at my shoulder.

I whirled, juggling the flashlight until the beam landed on, "Matthias!"

And Ayden, Blake, and Tristan.

"Get that bloody thing out of my face." Matthias smacked down my flashlight.

I scowled at Logan. "You called them?"

Silent, he suddenly found his cuff links very interesting.

"Of course he called us." Matthias yanked me aside. "*We're* his team."

Ayden barely spared me a glance as he shook water from his jacket and headed down the tunnel. Did he blame me for Jayden's plight? Probably. I did.

"You're all the backup I'd need, chickadee." Blake ruffled my hair as he passed. "I still don't get why we're here. *A*-gain. We tore this place apart already. Jayden's not around."

"But Logan said she had Fido track Jayden here." Ayden hit me with a cold look. "Although she didn't think to call *me*."

"And give you false hope? No," I said, feeling guilty. It wasn't exactly a lie but…ugh, I hated all these secrets, I just wasn't sure the truth was a great idea either.

"Cameras are off for some reason." Tristan had a translucent computer tablet in hand and was using his jacket to wipe off water droplets. "The portal's closed. Aurora can go in, but it's safer if she waits out here."

"A hunter attacked her at her house." Logan motioned for me to go forward. "She stays with us."

Matthias yanked me back again, disbelief and outrage swirling comically on his face. "You've got to be kidding."

"Rose?" Tristan asked.

"No," Logan said. "But Rose could have sent him."

Ayden turned around, pale and worried. "Are you alright?"

"On a scale of one-to-important, that doesn't even register right now." I pushed past them down the tunnel.

"It's a bloody waste of time," Matthias said. "Logan, hold up. Tell us more about this hunter."

I raced ahead of the boys and almost slipped when the tunnel narrowed and my feet hit slick metal. The floor had dropped away and changed into a catwalk. Large glowing stones embedded in the wall at regular intervals gave light, and through the grated steel at my feet I saw rushing water below lit with some blue light swirling in the currents. There was an earthy scent and the air tasted wet. Droplets clung to the railing I used to steady myself as I kept running.

I reached a glossy door that swished open on my approach. Across the threshold, I entered another algae-lit cavern, crossed another catwalk, and finally reached the solid ground of a tunnel that opened to the portal where I skidded to a stop next to Fido.

She nudged me and chittered nervously, staring at the portal and the body in front of it lying battered, bleeding, and unmoving.

Chapter Sixty-Two

Jayden looked bad. Propped up against the portal wall, eyes closed, chin dropped to his chest. His long black hair was matted in clumps and fell over most of his face, but I could see blood streaming down his forehead. He still wore Tristan's handcuffs, but it was the bazillion pounds of chains lassoed and weaved tight around his body then anchored around the massive boulder that was going to make it tough to set him free.

"Jayden!" My voice bounced over the cavernous stone.

His head lolled from side to side, eyes fluttered, and the knots in my chest loosened. He was alive.

The metal net that Fido had broken through was nowhere in sight so nothing blocked my path as I raced toward him. Jayden saw me and struggled to become alert, eyes widening, head shaking in staccato bursts. I'm sure without the hot pink gag tied around his mouth, he'd be saying something brilliant, but it just came out as garbled nonsense.

"Don't worry, the guys are coming," I assured him.

The ground and walls shuddered violently. On the surface of the bubbling pool, the reflection of the stalactites hanging above blurred, and I was knocked off my feet.

Jayden became more frantic, fighting against the chains. The stone wall behind him, the portal itself, began to change. It became fuzzy, distorted, like looking through a camera going in and out of focus.

Hmmm. Just spitballing here, not being a portal expert or anything, but I'd put that in the "not good" category. It was almost as if the portal was trying to — I gulped — open.

Now? With Jayden right there, ready to get sucked in.

My mouth went dry.

"Guys, help!" I yelled over my shoulder.

There was a piercing *snap-crackle-pop* of stone and another nerve-rattling shudder, and a long crack opened across the portal wall. As it lengthened, light burst through. Deep red and menacing. The color of blackened blood. The beam washed the cave in its gory light as the crack opened wider and wider by the second.

It was dangerous to go near it. The thing could break wide open and let loose a torrent of lava, demons, ghoulies, genuine fire and brimstone — whatever the heck that was — and who knows what else. The smart move was to stay far, far away.

But whoever said I was smart?

"Aw, screw it," I muttered.

I scrambled to my feet and sprinted across the space, ignoring Jayden's frenzy of muffled protests. I jumped over the boulder wrapped with chains then skidded on my side. Dust flew. My feet hit the wall. Solid rock, thank goodness, but the crack spidered new fissures. More deathly red light seeped through.

Jayden groaned and rolled his eyes.

"Oh, shut up." I yanked out the gag, then the saliva-soaked fabric stuffed in his mouth. Yuck. "How do I get the cuffs off?"

"Get out!" Jayden shouted as he planted his foot against my stomach and shoved, vaulting me back.

In midair, my skin suddenly illuminated. As I thudded to the ground, sparks flew from my fingers and morphed into lines of white electricity that spiked out in jagged streaks directly toward the portal. When the currents hit the wall, the portal fractured like a hammer shattering glass.

And the lines of current stayed connected.

As hard as I yanked and tugged, grunted, groaned, and screamed with effort, I couldn't pull my hands away. It was as if they were tethered to the portal.

Ayden arrived out of nowhere and jumped in front of me. He grabbed my wrists, and wrenched them sideways, then with a grimace, fell to his knees. The streaks of electricity from my hands cut out. I flexed my fingers. My skin still glowed and tingled, but I was free, had control.

"You…okay?" Ayden coughed and put a hand to his chest, seemed to have trouble breathing.

I nodded. "What's wrong?"

"Nothing," he said quickly. "Let's help Jayden."

Matthias bellowed from the catwalk, "Ayden, Aurora, get out of there now! The portal's opening!"

Gee, ya think?

"I got this!" Blake raised his hands.

The chains around Jayden rattled and started to stretch, releasing him. Then, across the cave, a cotton candy cloud burst beside Blake. An elbow materialized and slammed into his chest, rocketing the big guy back like he'd been hit by a cannonball. Jayden's chains *clinked* and fell limp.

The pink mist cleared with no culprit insight. Logan and Tristan rushed to Blake who wasn't moving. I really hated Rose and his parlor tricks.

Flames exploded on Ayden's hands. He grabbed a length of chain that still imprisoned his brother. As the metal turned red hot and softened, Ayden pulled it apart. I looked at my hands, still glowing, then grabbed the links. In my fingers, the loops of metal heated and became as pliable as cooked noodles. Odd sensation, but helpful.

"Ayden, get her *out*," Jayden boomed. "It's a stratagem!"

"A what?" Ayden said as we shredded apart the molten chains.

"A…a…" Jayden actually struggled for words. "A trap!"

The portal kept disintegrating. New fissures appeared bringing more rock pelting my back. Wind whipped my red curls across my face. The smell of earth was strong and mingled with the burning metal. Air with a noxious scent of sulfur whistled and hissed through the cracks, as if a giant waited on the other side of the portal ready to suck us in with one breath and crunch our bones in his massive jaw.

One panicked rip of my hand shredded the last of the chains. I felt immediate relief and just as quickly my skin's light snuffed out. Good thing because otherwise I'd burn Jayden when I helped carry him out. Panting, I turned to Ayden, but he wasn't there. He was…

"No!" I screamed.

Jayden twisted free, links dripping off him as he dove to his twin, fallen and half-buried under rock. With a storm of curses, Matthias ran toward us, the rest of the guys following. I crawled for Ayden.

A cloud of pink blinded me. I batted it away but hit flesh instead of smoke.

Rose caught my wrist. "Took your sweet time, dove."

Tristan shouted, "Look out!"

I thought he meant Rose, but a bubbling noise made me turn.

Through one of the cracks something bright orange-red and thick as cookie dough oozed out.

Magma.

It sizzled hot, steaming, and ready to drop on Rose and me. Slid down the stone as if the portal was a volcano about to explode. I lost my breath as Rose slammed me back against what remained of the shattered wall. And directly under the oncoming lava.

"Stop!" I yelled and tried to pull away, but the whack-job trying to murder-by-molten-earth was inhumanly strong.

A black whip cut through the air behind Rose. Just as it was about to wrap around his throat, Rose gracefully ducked his head sideways. The whip snapped harmlessly at the air.

Rose smiled and yanked my hand down, palm flat against stone. Heat flared on my skin.

"Best of luck." He threw me a kiss and disappeared into dust like the darn Cheshire cat.

I ripped my hand away from the wall and saw…

"Uh-oh."

Rose had put my hand over a double-spiral carved into the stone.

Searing heat scorched my cheek. The glob rolling down the collapsing wall dribbled small dollops of lava onto my sleeve. I squealed and batted at the sizzling fabric, then turned to run when a black whip encircled my waist and tugged me out of the magma's path just as it splattered to the floor.

The whip disappeared. With one wave of his arms, Blake cleared the fallen rocks. Jayden and I helped a groggy Ayden to his feet. I glanced back at the double spiral, then raked my eyes around for doors opening or tentacles reaching to pull me into some hidden passageway.

Good news?

None of that happened.

Bad news?

The floor opened up.

CHAPTER SIXTY-THREE

I fell. Fast.

Cold water soaked my back as I slid, racing down and gaining speed. Like riding the tubes at the waterpark I'd been to with my family last summer. But this was pitch black. And no guarantee of a safe landing.

I sloshed this way and that, skimming up one side and then the other. My hands reached out in a useless attempt to slow myself down and just made my rocking motion worse. I almost spun a three-sixty. I wanted to scream but was too afraid of drowning from masses of splashing water.

I wanted it to stop.

Then I shot out of the tube and wished I was back in because some worse horror was probably waiting to gobble me up with extreme prejudice. And chomping of sharp teeth.

I flew through the air then dropped, splashing into even colder water. Deep. Freezing. Still dark. Bubbles caught starbursts of faint turquoise light. I pumped my arms, kicked frantically, broke the surface, and sucked in a loud breath.

Something splashed next to me. I screamed and swam away. A head popped up.

"Ayden!" I treaded closer as he flipped hair and water from his eyes.

We were in a large pool with sheer walls on three sides, one of which had holes where we'd come shooting out. More glowing algae spidered eerie light across the walls, ceiling, and even networked underneath the deep water until it faded to pitch black. A mass of thick roots or vines entangled with the algae, some dangling from the ceiling like streamers, others clinging to the walls.

Someone splashed beside us then came up sputtering, "All her bloody fault!"

Oh, yay, Matthias survived.

A duet of shrill screams cut off his colorful rant. Blake shot into view, Tristan clutched in his arms. Their shrieks drowned out when they cannon-balled right on top of my favorite Aussie. Logan was next, arms flailing.

Jayden swan dived. No splash.

"You alright?" Ayden caught my hand.

"Not when what's in the water gets us!" Tristan splashed a spastic swim for the jagged shore. "There's probably some monster down there waiting to eat us! Or leeches!"

"Leeches?!" I kicked hard, fast, and frantic for the jagged shoreline.

Matthias spit water. "Bloody loon."

"Fine! Get eaten by Jaws," Tristan said.

I crawled up the rocky ledge, using the thick roots lining the sides to pull myself free of the water. Our rocky beach funneled into an algae-illuminated tunnel which looked much safer than the murky waters of death. I helped haul Ayden out and waved for the rest of the guys to hustle.

"Mandatum infiltration," intoned a voice.

Super. Sally Security was back. "Shut up!"

"Love that sexy voice." Blake heaved out of the pool. "Not as sexy as yours though, babe."

He grabbed Tristan and Logan and lifted them out like they were bags of soggy marshmallows. Matthias ignored my hand and climbed out on his own. Jayden was flipping and diving under the surface.

"It's very refreshing!"

"Come on, Flipper," Matthias said.

"We're all going to die!" Tristan shook off the water. "We can't get out. There's no food." He spun, slapping at seaweed on his back. "Is it a leech? *Is it?!*"

"Calm down." Ayden slapped the slimy green plant of Tristan's shoulder. "We'll be fine."

The water in the pool started to bubble and churn, gaining speed and swirling into a whirlpool that caught Jayden in its vortex. His arms flailed as he went under.

"Quit messing around," Ayden said.

But when Jayden finally surfaced, he looked confused and scared. "I can't g—"

The current accelerated and pulled Jayden under again.

Matthias snapped out his hand. "What the bloody..." He repeated the motion, but no whips unfurled from his fingertips.

Blake reached an arm up, grasped air, then flung it down. Frowned. Repeated the move. Logan spiraled his hands then glared at them when nothing happened.

"*Now* would be the time to save him!" I said.

"My powers don't work!" Blake dropped to his knees and patted the earth.

"Same here, mates." Matthias glared at the dark tunnel like he could scare the shadows into moving.

"What's going on?" Tristan grasped both sides of his head.

Ayden pointed at the water with one hand while trying, and failing, to ignite the other. "We need to get him out of there!"

No kidding. I grabbed one of the roots and pulled. It didn't budge. Blake brushed me aside, grabbed a bunch in one hand, and ripped them out, then sifted through until he found one he liked.

He flung it out to Jayden. "Grab on!"

It landed close, but Jayden missed. Blake tried again. And again, but Jayden kept missing, disappearing under the water for longer periods.

Ayden tied a root around his waist. "I'm going in. Someone hold the end."

"He got it!" Blake yelled triumphant.

Jayden wrapped the root around his arm. Blake snapped it taut then backed up and planted his feet. "Everybody pull!"

I ran behind Ayden as we all latched on and pulled. Sweat beaded into my eyes as we strained in the musty, humid air, dragging Jayden through the heavy current and closer to shore. He kicked the last few feet.

Even had one hand on the rocky edge when a monstrous beast burst from the water.

CHAPTER SIXTY-FOUR

At least a part of it.

An enormous tentacle, the size of the giant redwoods you can drive your car through. It flung over our heads. Seaweed hanging like ripped tendons, the twisting appendage snapped the air, drenching us with dank smelling water.

We ducked. The vine in our grip slipped forward. Something speared the ground next to us. I jumped back from the…giant metal blade?

Yep. With this up-close and way-too-personal view, I saw the creature was all metal. A huge mechanical squid, the deadly limb constructed of interlocking metal plates that narrowed at the end to a sharp, steely harpoon. Which, after stabbing into the rock next us, seemed to be stuck.

Ayden pushed me into Logan's arms. "Get her out of here!" Then he ran to the shore, Matthias right behind him.

Logan and I ran toward the tunnel. A shadow swiped overhead. Hanging seaweed slapped my face. I tasted dirty water, stumbled. A tentacle slammed into Blake. He flew through the air, then thudded and spun out on the rocky ground.

I started to go to him, but Logan cried, "Get down!" and pulled us both to the ground as more and more tentacles whipped through the air.

Gears groaned. Joints creaked. Metal squealed. The pool's surface frothed as the multitude of scaled feelers surged from the center of a growing whirlpool where currents swirled into a dark pit. Over the crashing tides, the loud *whir* of blades echoed, like someone had just turned on a colossal garbage disposal.

Ayden and Matthias yanked Jayden out of the water and the trio ran, Matthias shouting, "Move, move, move!"

Logan and I reached Blake who was being helped by Tristan. Something hissed past and rock exploded at Tristan's feet. A harpoon speared the ground. The tentacle groaned, trying to twist free. Behind us, a dozen more snaked up, poised, ready to attack.

Someone shoved me forward and I sprinted into the tunnel, arms raised like that could somehow stop the ginormous, harpoonified, robo-squid.

The tunnel curved and zigged-zagged, and when the sounds of whirling rapids and whipping metal limbs faded, we stopped. I flopped next to Jayden sitting on the ground, head in his hands.

Matthias leaned against the wall beside him, panting. "Everyone okay?"

"I think," Tristan gulped and clutched his chest, "I'm having," lots of wheezing, "a panic attack."

"When are you not?" I said.

Ayden collapsed beside his brother, flicked and snapped his fingers, rubbed his palms together. "Still nothing. Crap."

"My powers were…impeded." Jayden heaved deep breaths, long black hair dripping off his face. "I don't understand."

"I do." Matthias glared cold gray eyes my way. "Way to go, moron. You broke us."

"Oh, shut up," Ayden said wearily.

"Yeah," I said, but honestly didn't know if Matthias was wrong.

"Check your cells." Ayden pulled out his phone and they all followed suit, walking around to see if they could find a signal with the waterproof devices. No luck.

"Fascinating." Jayden trailed a finger along the wall where water trickled down. "I'm sure it's temporary. Perhaps Flint invented an elixir to put in the water as a security measure to nullify hunters' attacks."

"So quit touching it!" Tristan slapped Jayden's hands away from the wall.

I stood and jogged in place to generate some heat because my wet clothes were making my teeth chatter. "Where are Blake and Logan?"

Screams bounced off the walls, morphing into battle cries as the two Hex Boys barreled down the tunnel and stopped.

Matthias scowled. "Where did you get that?"

Blake and Logan wore medieval knight's helmets and wielded long, shiny broadswords. Well, Blake wielded while Logan teetered and stumbled under the weight.

Blake flipped up the visor, revealing a grin from ear-to-ear. "Guess who found Flint's treasure!"

Chapter Sixty-Five

Moving deeper into the tunnel, Logan dragged the tip of his sword on the stone, leaving a trail of sparks until Blake stole it and balanced both blades on his shoulders. The algae thinned out to nothing on the ceiling, but the guys kept a steady pace into the darkness.

Tristan hooked his arm through mine. "I've got a bad feeling about this."

"Then don't attach yourself to the albatross," Matthias growled from the infinite black.

"Almost there," Blake said with bubbling cheer.

Moments later I felt the air change, become less dense. We'd moved into open space.

Ca-chunk-chunk-chunk-chunk. Victorian lamps sprung to life until the whole place was illuminated in a soft yellow glow.

The room spanned out so vast the farthest end was still in dark, but what was visible glowed with exquisite, and seemingly infinite treasure. Stairs on either side led to a second story that wrapped around the perimeter and was equally burdened with acres of ancient riches.

On one side of the entrance, suits of armor — two of them missing the helmets and swords that Blake refused to give up —

stood ready for battle. On the other, stood a heavily carved mummy's sarcophagus, its colorful paint chipped and dulled over the centuries.

Everything else was more mainstream treasure type of stuff.

Crates and trunks piled everywhere bursting with extravagance and history. Some were open, revealing a cache of glittering jewelry of rich deep colors, ornate exotic boxes, pieces of clothing from centuries past probably taken from some kind of royalty, small statues, shiny and grotesque weapons, and lots of things I didn't recognize other than to fathom that archeologists and thieves would be drooling.

There were urns twice my height, vases, marble tombs from ancient temples, furniture longing to be returned to some castle, and massive pillars which looked like their last gig was holding up the Parthenon.

Statues stood everywhere. A few beautiful, most creepy. Demonic creatures. Wings, horns, fangs, claws. And several grotesque gargoyles like the ones guarding the school.

In the center of the room were large wooden tables inlaid with metals and precious gems. Dusty scrolls and more golden artifacts littered the surfaces. The whole place blossomed with the bounty of long lost treasure.

I turned to the Aussie. "Still an albatross?'"

The gate behind us slammed down, blocking our only known exit. Like a guillotine.

Matthias scowled. "Definitely."

So much for my victory lap.

Muscles straining, Blake tried to pull the gate up but other than an inch or two, it didn't budge, even when the other boys helped.

"We're supposed to find some little rock in all this?" Tristan whined.

Yeah. Wasn't looking good. I shrugged. "At least we don't have to fight any more whacko security or mechanical monsters."

Something zipped past my head, aimed for the Hex Boys. They dropped or dove out of the way. A spear *twanged* as it embedded into the grate of the gate and wobbled from the impact.

In a cornucopia of fury, arrows, spears, darts, and crossbow bolts sliced through the air. Matthias yanked out my ankles. I thumped on my back. The flying death projectiles *thwacked* into the sandy soil around our feet and *pinged* off the walls.

"You just had to open your big mouth," Matthias growled.

I dove behind a trunk overflowing with fine fabrics. Ayden scurried beside me.

Matthias rolled behind a crate and inspected a tear in his jacket. "Oh, come on. It's brand new!"

"Not our biggest worry," Ayden snapped.

"I'm hit!" Tristan cried from behind a tomb.

Logan whacked Tristan's shoulder. "It's just me!"

"Oh. Never mind!"

"We need the high ground!" Jayden called from behind a mountain of crates barely covering him and Blake.

I peeked out. On the second floor walkways statues had come to life, shooting with sharp weapons and plenty of determination. Ayden yanked me back.

"High ground's taken," I said. "Sally Security! Abort! Shut down! Cease—"

Metal arms wrapped around my shoulders. One of the headless knights wrenched me up into the line of fire. I twisted and kicked, but all that got me was a possibly broken toe.

"Blake!" Ayden yelled.

Blake tossed one of the swords across the ground. Ayden said, "Jump!" I grabbed Sir Gala-had-a-head's arms and lifted my feet high. In one continuous move of impressive grace, Ayden caught the handle of the blade and swung it in a wide arc, cutting clean through the knight's knees.

Shrapnel and bolts flew as the knight *clanged* to the ground. I rolled away, watching oil spurt like black blood from the severed limbs. The knight's armored hands clamped around my ankle, dragged me across the ground. Ayden swung again, and with a screech of metal on metal, stabbed the sword into its belly. The knight convulsed once then stilled.

"Way to save the damsel, dude!"

I scurried out of the open and hunkered behind the wooden sarcophagus. "What are they?"

"I think," Ayden panted, "Flint somehow mechanized some of the artifacts."

"Evil frickin' geniuses." I shook my head. "I hate those kind of guys."

"Aurora!" Jayden shouted from behind his cover. "You can demilitarize the vault!"

"Small words!" I shouted.

"Turn off security!" Ayden said. "How?"

"I translated it!" Jayden held up the double spiral journal and tapped the symbol on the cover. "This graphic formation indicates that there is a sensor which—"

Splinters exploded as an arrow hit the sarcophagus in front of me and burst through the wood. I threw my arms across my face and slammed back into the wall, staring weak-kneed at the deadly tip of the arrow that had penetrated and stopped only centimeters from my chest.

"Don't need to know *how* it works!" I shouted over whatever Jayden kept blabbering.

"Understood." Jayden flipped frantically through pages. "This journal lists the locations of the locks and their purposes…"

Flip, flip, flip.

Blake peered over his shoulder. "What language is that?"

"There's a deactivation lock beside the Buddha statue from an emperor of the Liao Dynasty," Jayden said. "But…it's nine meters tall which is three stories and I don't see anything resembling that here so perhaps there's another treasure room which would mean —"

"Jayden!" Tristan snapped. "Is there one in *here?!*"

"Give me a— Yes!" Jayden tapped a page. "That wall behind Alexander the Great's tomb."

I followed his line of sight. "You mean the marble tomb several *hundred* feet away?"

Please say no, please say—

"Yes."

Crap.

Chapter Sixty-Six

I huffed a deep breath. Then two more. Trying to suck in courage, leaning against the ancient Egyptian sarcophagus for support.

While Jayden had climbed a tall stone pillar to scout the area, the rest of the guys huddled somewhere off to my right discussing the strategy to get to me to the sensor lock thing. The plan entailed Ayden and me sprinting across open space while avoiding Flint's mechanical psycho assassin squad and their deadly UPFOs — Unidentified Pointy Flying Objects.

Easy, right? So why did my breathing crack

No, more of a creak. Wait. That wasn't me.

The lid of the Egyptian sarcophagus swung open with a shuddering *thud*. I caught a foul stench then something gruesome curled around the edge of the wood. Fingers. Long, leathered, peeling like dry, rough bark, nails yellowed and browned, one hanging by a thread of frayed linen. Or gnarled flesh.

I gulped. "This is so *not* happening."

But sure enough, an oh-so-super-gross, mummified corpse of some ancient Egyptian royal staggered around the corner and turned its blank, bandaged face toward me.

There was moaning.

It was mine.

I swung my leg into its stomach, felt the bones crumble. King Tut stumbled, powdery bits of flesh crumbling from the hole in its gut, but he kept coming.

I scrambled around the sarcophagus and kicked it hard. It teetered but didn't go down. The mummy turned toward me. I backed up a few paces then ran full-tilt, launching myself high and latching onto the painted wood coffin like a baby koala on her mama. When it rocked forward again, I leaned my weight into it and, in way-too-slow motion, it toppled over.

As I rode it down, the lid closed and the full weight of the Egyptian tomb crashed onto the mummified remains. With a bone rattling impact, it smashed the should-be-long-dead royal into a cloudy mess of linen, gears, sparks, and dust. I rolled off and averted my face, trying not to breath in some bizarre virus. Or ancient curse.

A spear exploded the dirt next to my hip. I rolled sideways.

Something gray circled above. One of the granite gargoyle statues had taken flight. It made a sudden U-turn and tucked its wings like a falcon diving on its prey. Me.

I rolled again. The gargoyle bombed into the ground. Stone chunks exploded to pelt and bruise, frayed wires spun out like fireworks. One down, but more of his comrades were stretching their wings and clouding the air.

Along with a new shower of arrows. I was ready for a drought.

Scuttling away, I spotted a dagger, grabbed it, and leaned against a tomb of shiny black marble. In between pants, I spit out mouthfuls of bitter grit.

Tristan ran over in a hunched sort of waddle. "Get cover!"

With a grunt, he shoved open the top of the stone tomb, gripped my jacket, and threw me in. I landed on a pile of something hard and uncomfortable. I coughed and waved away the thick, grimy air.

Tristan slid the lid closed but for a crevice of space. When I blinked through the blur and dim light, my skin shriveled and crawled in on itself. I shrieked, high-pitched and horrified. I was nose to nose with the lipless, grinning face of the weathered skeleton of a long dead corpse.

Not that any corpse was ever alive.

My hands pushed through the tattered remains of a tuxedo, knocking aside a jauntily placed top hat as I scrambled off the bones. His arms moved. He reached to hold me in a...*death grip.*

Oh, yeah, there was my macabre sense of humor.

Dagger in hand, I chopped with a mad frenzy in my best re-enactment of the *Psycho* movie shower scene, with plenty of piercing screams — mine — but minus the blood.

The tomb lid slid off.

"Sorry!" Tristan yanked me out. "Didn't think that one through." He patted my shoulders. "You good?"

I swatted him off and glared. "Am I *good*?"

Someone had the nerve to laugh. "Nice one, mate."

Gee, wonder who.

From his perch atop the ancient column, Jayden shouted, "There's a weapons cache on the table near the tomb!"

He jumped down as Blake pushed the column over to provide more cover then dragged over a gilded, high-backed throne. I piled up crates until we were protected on all sides.

The rest of the guys somersaulted, back-flipped and dove to join us. Show-offs.

Jayden pointed across a long stretch of open space. "It's a clear shot."

The pathway he indicated ran between a hedge of treasure and a blank stone wall and ended at a giant table that housed a mound of weapons topped by a two-foot tall, bronze statue of a spear-wielding warrior on a horse. Beyond that was the tomb, and on the wall behind the tomb, I'd find the cavemanesque spiral etching that shut down the attacks.

Supposedly.

Just had to make the run through the line of fire first. Sometimes it was so awesome being me.

"Go on three." Matthias swung a crate of fine china plates over the pillar then dropped back down. Arrows flew overhead.

"I'm not fast enough," I said.

Ayden squeezed my shoulders and looked me in the eye. "Yes you are. Stay in front and I'll be right behind, covering you with this." He hefted the knight's shield. "Then I'll get to the weapons, throw some over to the guys, and we'll all cover you while you shut down the security and save the day."

He had such faith in me. It was so adorable.

And so utterly stupid.

Logan grabbed several small statues and scooted his back against the throne. "We'll provide cover for the both of you."

"And create a distraction," Jayden added.

"See?" Ayden smiled with encouragement. "No problem."

Nope, no problem. Just a colossal disaster.

"Don't worry, babe." Blake twirled a sword in one hand and a spear in another. "The only thing getting near your cute butt is me."

"Blake!"

This was nuts. I'd never make it. I'd trip, fall, become a pin cushion.

"One," Matthias said.

Sure, he was counting. Counting on me getting dead.

"Two." Matthias risked a peek to the second floor.

Tristan wrung his hands. "She's gonna die."

"Thanks," I glared. Didn't help hearing my own thoughts out loud. But somehow his lack of faith spurred my courage and a spunky desire to prove him wrong.

I sunk into a runner's stance. Ayden crouched behind me and lifted the shield.

Matthias gave me a nod. "Thr —"

"Wait." Ayden caught my arm.

Oh, thank God. I collapsed against the pillar, body trembling so hard I was near convulsing. Spunk was gone. Ran away screaming and took courage with it.

"Stay here." Ayden dropped the shield, gathered several china plates, and chucked them into the path we were supposed to take.

Gears cranked and rumbled. In sporadic locations along the empty wall chunks of stone slid away like opening windows. Then, with the hissing sound as if we'd disturbed a nest of seething king cobras, darts shot from the openings, shattering the plates before they hit the ground.

"Are you k-kidding me?" I wiped my hands on my jeans. "That's crazy."

"That's classic," Ayden said. The other guys nodded. At my blank look he said, "The shooters on the second floor want to chase us into that line of fire. The weapons cache is bait to encourage us to do just that."

I felt cold. "An ambush."

"Like I said, classic." Ayden shrugged out of his jacket.

"What are you doing?" I didn't think my heart could pump any harder. "We're not still *going!*"

"Not you. Just me." He smiled. "Don't worry, my mom sets up stuff like this all the time."

"It's true," Jayden confirmed. "And in this exercise, Ayden is the best of us all."

As the rest of the boys began throwing things into the path, which produced an endless stream of darts-o-death, Ayden stared with a rapt, almost trancelike intensity.

"What are we doing?" I asked Tristan as I grabbed a small chest and tossed it.

"The darts are triggered by motion sensors," Tristan said. "We keep throwing stuff to activate them so Ayden can study the layout and memorize their trajectory."

Ayden waved a casual hand. "You just have to read the position of the projectiles and navigate around them. No problem."

"Seriously? Your mom is whacked," I said.

"But in a good way," he grinned. "I'll get to the weapons, send some over like we planned, and someone else will get you across to shut security down. No problem."

He kept saying that. I'm not sure he understood what it meant.

"I'm ready." Ayden stood behind the throne, stared at the walls, bounced on his toes, and with his face a stark mask of determination, sprinted into the line of fire.

Chapter Sixty-Seven

It was a beautiful—and frightening—thing to watch.

Darts rocketed across in rapid succession while Ayden moved like he was working a gymnastic floor routine. He leapt, flipped, twisted, spun, and rolled. At one point he skidded on his knees, leaned back so far his head skimmed the floor, turned over, spun on his belly then was up again, contorting his body to elude the lethal punctures of a gazillion missiles of death.

Ayden slid underneath another table, and his final dive dropped him in the far end of the room, underneath the large wooden table where he was tucked between the slabs that held it up, and safely beyond the scope of the darts.

Ayden slapped the floor. "Yes!"

We all cheered. At least, I did when I could finally release that breath I held.

The darts ceased firing. A soft *clicky-clack* rustled up the alley followed by a *ding.* Almost like a grandfather clock prepping to chime the hour. We scanned the room for the source of the sound.

And found it.

On the table above Ayden, the bronze statue of the barbarian warrior moved. The stallion reared, legs pawing the air in robotic motions, steam billowing from its snout.

"Ayden, watch out!" I yelled and pointed.

Ayden looked for danger, but he couldn't see through the table above him where the warrior raised his spear.

"Move!" the boys shouted.

But too late. The warrior plunged his spear through the thick wood of the table like it was Jell-O.

Matthias swept his arms forward expecting to launch every shadow in the room into an attack that would demolish the statue. Blake slammed the ground with his palms and twisted like he could blast the table sky-high and shatter it into mere wood chips. Logan swirled his arms as if mixing a volatile vortex to tornado the threat into oblivion. Tristan squashed his head in hands, eyes hard in concentration trying to will Ayden into moving. Jayden snapped empty hands out to create a tidal wave that would annihilate all in its path to save his brother.

But it was all wishful thinking because nothing happened. We had no powers here. It seemed I was the only one who remembered.

I cocked back my arm, then shot it forward. My explody power didn't happen, but I hadn't expected it to. I didn't have the years of luxury powers-on-demand, which in this case, was an asset. So instead, I threw the dagger. It rocketed out of my hand and across the room.

Darts shot from the walls, trying to knock the weapon out of the air.

They missed, and the blade buried into the barbarian's gut, wrenching him off the poodle-sized horse which leapt off the table with a strangled, high-pitched whistle of steam and disappeared into the mass of treasure. Before he went down, the warrior plunged the spear through the table and out the bottom side, but only a few inches. I was way proud of myself.

Until I saw Ayden sprawled on the ground. Bleeding. And he wasn't getting up.

CHAPTER SIXTY-EIGHT

"Ayden!" Jayden jumped up, planted a hand on the pillar and launched himself out into the line of fire.

Matthias leapt and grabbed Jayden's shirt. Arrows and darts *hissed* and *whished*. Matthias hooked an arm around Jayden's neck and hauled him kicking and screaming back into our shelter. The bladed tips *pinged* off the pillar or *whooshed* overhead.

"Blake!" Matthias barked.

Blake, his face somber, took Jayden and restrained him in massive arms.

"I can do it!" Jayden screamed.

"So can I!" Logan said.

"Too dangerous!" Matthias ordered. "We'll find another way!"

Logan snapped off his jacket and loosened his tie. "I'm going."

"Dude, no!" Blake tried to grab him too.

Logan ducked out of the way. Jayden wriggled free. Matthias and Blake pounced on Jayden to keep him from running blindly into the darts. Logan lowered into a runner's stance.

"Tristan, stop him!" Matthias said.

Tristan and I lunged. Grabbed Logan's legs. Held on. He struggled. Fear pounded blood through my head, ready to explode from my veins as I looked around for something, anything to help Ayden.

"I'm okay." Ayden's head came up.

I breathed relief. Took his sweet time letting us know.

Ayden pushed off the floor.

"Careful!" Tristan shrieked.

Ayden paused and cautiously avoided the spear poking through the wood as he sat up and leaned against the table base. I couldn't stop staring at the blood on his shoulder, screaming red against his white shirt.

"Take it easy, mate. We'll be right there." Matthias turned a hard look on Jayden. "We've just got to come up *with a plan* before we go running around halfcocked and getting killed."

"Cut me," I said.

"What?" the Hex Boys around me all stilled.

Matthias's eyes narrowed. "I didn't imagine that, did I?"

"Ayden, throw us a knife!" I said.

"No!" Tristan and Jayden shouted.

"Yes!" Logan countered.

Ayden nodded. "Good plan!"

"Good?" Tristan blinked. "Are you two having a fight?"

Some clanging. Darts hissed. A knife with a gold filigree handle thudded into the back of the throne above Blake's head. I moved to grab it.

Blake plucked it out first. "Babe, you're not thinking straight."

"She never is." Matthias snatched the knife and held it out to me. "But right now that might work for us."

I smirked. "Careful, Aussie, that almost sounded like a compliment."

I reached to take the knife, but Matthias caught my wrist, reeled back his arm, and stabbed the blade into my hand.

I screamed. The Aussie laughed.

Okay, it was only a prick. On my finger. But his serial-killer plunge and deranged look of delight got my heart pumping.

A drop of blood oozed.

"You're a jerk." I pulled back, but he wouldn't let go. "Hey!"

"Hold on." He looked around, paused a beat, then wiped my bloody finger on the floor.

"Oh, thank you." I wrenched my hand back. "If I get the Black Plague, I'm infecting you first."

Something rumbled louder than the fight. The floor shimmied. The UFPOs stopped spearing through the air because even Sally Security noticed our newest arrival.

From the darkness at the far end of the room, Fido slid out on her overabundance of legs. At the sight of me, she lifted her head, opened her mouth, and from the deep recesses of her belly, she bellowed a fierce T-Rex-worthy roar.

Sally Security renewed her attacks. Arrows and darts got caught in Fido's fur or simply bounced off her skin. But the spears hit hard, and I flinched in empathy every time they struck. Fido snarled and snapped, took hit after hit but wouldn't back down. When a nasty looking gargoyle swooped down from above, she caught it in her pincher antennae, shook it hard, and slammed it into the wall. It shattered in a raining ooze of oily goo that drenched the rest of the statues.

Nothing like having my own homicidal diva of a demon.

Tristan whimpered, "We are so dead."

"Nope," I smiled. "She's our saving grace. Fido, over there!" I pointed to Ayden.

As she glided over us to get to Ayden, I jumped up and ran.

Someone yelled, "Wait!"

But I didn't.

Instead, I darted beneath Fido's belly, using her wall of scuttling legs as cover from the darts. When we reached the table Ayden was under, Fido curled her body around it while I weaved out from her legs and lunged into the tiny alley of space between Alexander the Great's tomb and the wall. With a jerky side-step and using shaking fingers to feel over the rough stone for the etching, I moved along, praying a dart didn't explode out of nowhere.

Heat flared under my hand. A double-spiral, chest high. Thank goodness.

Beneath it the stone cracked vertically, then two small doors swung open. Inside was a hollowed out copper box with a green button which was lit up, a red one which wasn't, and a bronze lever. I yanked. The green light died as the red flickered on.

The lights went out. Followed by ear-piercing screams.

The lights flickered back on.

I found my breath and screeched, "Did it work? What happened?!"

"You idiot!" Matthias bellowed. "You killed them all!"

Chapter Sixty-Nine

"It wasn't funny," Tristan said.

Blake yanked a spear out of Fido's side. "It was a little funny. But a whole lotta mean."

Matthias smirked at me. "Only time I wish I could've seen your face."

He, Tristan, and Logan were trying to open the gate with weapons they took from the cache on the table.

The lever had turned off the security. Best guess was that the lights turning on and off was some kind of reboot, shutting the mechanized treasures down. The screams had been mostly Tristan and Logan being terrified, and Matthias's comment was him scaring me to death which solidified his jerk status.

Like there was ever a question.

With a pathetic whimper, Fido slumped onto her belly. Her large mottled tongue started licking her wounds. Blake hopped onto the table, petting her affectionately with one hand as, with the other, he pulled out the weapons that had made it past her plated armor and embedded into her skin.

Ayden sat on a wooden trunk, Jayden hovering beside him. I was on my back on the ground in front of them, knees bent. Relieved and exhausted.

"Jayden, I'm fine. Stop it. I don't need to take off my shirt." Ayden pushed off his brother's attempts to look at the wound on his back. "The tip of the spear just nicked my shoulder. Nothing deep."

Jayden was clearly concerned. "But you collapsed. I can better assess the wound if you take off your shirt."

A sudden image of smooth, taut muscle flashed through my imagination. I propped on my elbows for better viewing because it suddenly dawned on me that Ayden was the only Hex Boy I had yet to see shirtless — he was the only one I'd felt-up so I had an idea — a problem that would be corrected in mere seconds. I tried not to salivate too heavily.

"No," Ayden said. "Just lift it up in the back."

Suddenly playing the shy schoolboy? And he wouldn't look at me. Hmmm.

While Jayden checked out the wound, Ayden nudged my shoulder with his toe. "So did I totally impress you with my ninjistic dart-evadement skills?"

"Absolutely," I said. "You also took twenty years off my life. Sure you're okay? You should take off your shirt."

Ayden raised a brow.

Too obvious? Probably.

"You know." I shrugged. "For medical purposes only."

There was *clanging* and *banging* then Matthias said, "It's no bloody use."

"Good." Blake pulled the last dart out of Fido and grinned ear-to-ear. "*Now* do we get to go treasure hunting?"

No one had a better plan so…

We'd been here for what seemed like hours. Currently, Ayden and I were scouring the paperwork on a heavy wooden table for clues that might hint about a stone. The rest of the guys were scattered around the room. When I tossed aside another sheet of parchment like it was Lucian's dirty laundry, Ayden caught it one-handed, wincing slightly before unrolling it with great care.

"Oh my God!" he exclaimed looking over the elegant script. "This was signed by King Louis the ninth!"

"Nerd," Blake chuckled from somewhere across the room.

"Aurora," Ayden said, "maybe you should look at things that are…less fragile." He set the document aside like it was a precious artifact.

Okay, so maybe it was, but a lot less precious than my life.

"Fine. I'll go through more chests of jewels." I looked around with despair. "But this seems so hopeless."

"I'll help." As Ayden pushed off the table to stand, he grimaced and reached a hand to his chest. At my worried look, he started to shrug, then thought better of it and stilled. "I told you, it's nothing."

He kept saying that, but something wasn't right. Jayden had inspected the spear wound and deemed it a "minor puncture" that was "not life-threatening," although, the "anomalous stippling" around the injury was "disconcerting," and he wanted to get home to the lab for some tests. Ayden's movements made it clear he was in pain, but he remained tight-lipped and wouldn't let me get close enough to check it out myself. I was worried.

There was a crash.

"Stupid bloody— Blake!" Matthias yelled. "I can't reach! This stupid no-powers business — ugh! There's another room over here. Tristan follow me."

"Why me?"

"Hurry up. Everyone keep looking for an exit."

We'd checked out the back where Fido had emerged from, but it was a maze of a dozen dark tunnels branching out in different directions that nobody wanted to risk getting lost in just yet. When I'd tried to get her to "go fetch" us an exit, she'd rolled over to get her belly scratched. My demon whisperer techniques needed some work.

In the back, we'd found some cool looking construction machinery. Flint's weird, warped versions of modern day equipment. Tractors, bulldozers, tunnel drillers, and much more. If push came to shove, we could dig our way out with the same machines Flint had used to make this place.

I yawned and tripped over a fallen urn as I followed Ayden down an aisle. I was cold, wet, exhausted, covered in dust, trapped, exhausted, banged up, *exhausted*, and, best of all, lacking the one thing that would keep me alive. Rose's precious stone.

Treasure hunting sucked.

In my peripherals, an angel statue moved. I squealed and dived for cover. I was about to yell for Ayden to do the same when the angel spoke.

"Aurora?" Jayden popped out from behind the statue.

"Jeez!" I growled. "Don't do that. I thought another statue had come to life to eat me."

Jayden shook my arm. "We require your assistance to discern if there is an egress."

I was too tired to ask for a vocab lesson.

"Go. I got this." Ayden nudged me away then turned to sift through another treasure chest.

Jayden lead me through the labyrinth of luxury antiquities to a far off chamber where Logan waited by a wall.

"What am I digressing?" I rubbed my eyes.

Jayden frowned. "Nothing, you haven't said a thing."

"Touch this." Logan tapped a double spiral carved on the wall.

"It's Flint's symbol for the Divinicus and Bellator." Jayden held up the journal. "The more commonly seen circular, smoothly curved spiral denotes sensors that react to you, while the more geometric, quadrangular spiral marks sensors that react to the Bellator. Together they'll react to either one."

"This is the only one we could find close by," Logan said. "See if it opens —"

"An egress." Jayden seemed excited. "I already told her."

At my blank look, Logan clarified, "Exit."

I slapped my hand on the Divinicus/Bellator symbol. Heat flared. Something rumbled beneath it. I jumped back and watched the top layer of rock on the wall just…disappear.

In its place was revealed a mish-mash of metal that looked part massive puzzle box, part Fort Knox vault door. Thick rods, rectangular bars, gears of various sizes, sliding bolts, knobs, handles, levers, all conjoined in an intricate and massively complicated deadlock machination. Then, like some enmeshed cluster of serpents, it unraveled before our eyes with more rumbles and a series of *whirrs*, *clicks*, *clacks*, and sliding metal. Finally, with a colossal sigh, as if we'd awakened a giant sleeping for a zillion years, the door rolled open.

"Welcome to the sanctuary," Sally Security intoned.

Coughing on dead air and dust, we gazed into darkness.

"Well?" I said.

Logan gave me a weak smile. "It likes you best, so…"

"Tag. You're it." Jayden smiled. "See how I'm learning playful colloquialisms. It refers to the game of tag and your turn to —"

"Yeah, I get it." I gave him a level look. So much for big, bad demon hunters.

I took one tentative step forward. Then another, ears and eyes stretching their limits to reach through the dark and silent space, nerves twitching, on edge. As I crossed the threshold, lights flickered on. I squealed and reeled back, crashing into Logan and Jayden.

"Don't stop," Jayden urged. "We're on the brink—"

"Of getting shot by poison darts," I snapped. "Maybe. I don't know and neither do you. Don't rush me."

Jayden made an exasperated noise, but Logan put a comforting hand on my shoulder.

I moved deeper into the room, almost having to push through the dense atmosphere. A faint smell of ozone twitched my nostrils. Thick, dry air crawled over my skin bringing a chill that made me shiver. I initially flinched as Victorian lamps *ca-chunked* to life, but then the space illuminated and my head swiveled up, down, and sideways.

"Holy crap," I breathed.

The far end of the room was still in darkness, but I could tell it was massive and reached about four stories high. Stone walls were carved with numerous words, neatly organized in columns and rows. I couldn't read it but guessed the language as Latin.

Lines of bookcases made of carved rock rose up across the center of the room, each shelf stacked with volume after volume of books. Mostly leather-bound. All old.

We walked down the aisles, necks threatening to dislocate as we craned to take it all in.

Sure it was impressive, but I sighed. "Great. More crap to look through."

"What is this place?" Logan sounded awestruck.

"One heck of a library." Blake turned in circles.

Jayden jumped. "When did you get here? You're supposed to be looking for Rose's requested stone artifact. You're the earth expert."

"I'm letting Matthias yell at Tristan for a change."

"Go back!"

"No. I'm tired. It's too hard. It's like trying to find a potato chip in a bag of sand."

I ran my fingers across the leather spines, noting titles in Latin. Some also had ranges of dates listed, all of centuries past.

A light flickered from the front of the room. By the time I made it past the last aisle, the glow had become stable. There was no exit, but despite my exhausted — did I mention that? — state, I recognized cool when I saw it.

It was like a small apartment. From a different century.

Front and center was a huge desk. It looked old and French. There was a seating area, a small kitchen that housed an old-fashioned iron stove and a granite sink with large metal water taps. Nearby, a small pine table with two chairs sat across from a doorway that led into darkness.

Further back, one corner held an enormous clawfoot tub. In another, near a full-length gilded mirror, was a brightly colored collection of vintage Victorian era fashion. Racks of gorgeous dresses in vibrant hues and yards of shimmering fabric. Shelves of elaborate hats decorated with feathers, lace, and ribbon. Rows of dainty shoes and boots.

Tucked against the wall was a four-poster bed draped in heavy tapestries. It had an enormous, extra fluffy mattress covered in pale lace. Way less picky than Goldilocks, my weary body ached to rest on that pretty pile of dust. If only for a minute. Or twenty.

I yawned as I passed the desk, glancing at something resting on top. I stumbled. My heart vomited to my throat and I bolted, screaming with gusto.

Blake caught me by the waist.

Logan dropped into a hunter's stance, arms up like he held an invisible bow, fingers grasping at nothing. He scowled. "I hate this."

Jayden frowned briefly at his empty hands as Blake moved me behind his bulk.

"What is it, babe?"

I pointed and gagged. Logan and Jayden stalked to either side of the desk, fists up, ready to strike. Then they looked at each other and relaxed.

"Hardly a danger," Jayden said.

"Didn't say it was dangerous," I finally managed. "That was my 'It scared the crap out of me!' reaction."

Jayden leaned over the desk, studying the object of my horror. "A skeleton. Female. Sixties, I'd guess."

Why would any teenage guy know that?

"Who is she?" I slapped my cheeks, trying to keep my eyes open as the adrenaline faded. Didn't work. I leaned against Blake who ruffled my hair.

The skeleton sat in the chair, slumped over the desk, like she'd laid her head down for a nap and never woke up. Empty eye sockets stared at me, gray hair, surprisingly long and thick, draped behind her. The remnants of a blue dress hung off the bones. A gold chain was around what was left of her neck, a gold pocket watch hanging upon it.

From underneath her bony hand, which still had a silver and black fountain pen entwined within, Logan picked up a leather bound book and flipped it open. "Pages are blank."

"Fantastic." I felt like chucking something so I grabbed the book.

Heat zapped into my hands, up my arms. Words, sounds, and images jettisoned toward me, blurred, then stabbed into my eyes, burrowed into my head. Towers, cold steel bars, cloaked figures, faces lost behind dark hoods. *Run!* My brain sizzled on overload.

I dropped the book. But the wave of visions kept crashing. I clutched my skull. Opened my mouth to speak, but a torrent rushed into my head. Everything went black. And I gave in to the relief of unconsciousness.

Chapter Seventy

Run! Now! Before they realize what you carry! Run! Now!

The words danced in my head, over and over. Filling the darkness.

Someone cradled me against a solid chest. Voices nudged me awake.

"Place her on the bed."

"No. It's old. And a dead lady slept in it."

"She wasn't deceased when she slept in it. She perished at her desk."

"Close enough. I'm keeping babe."

The arms around me tightened.

"Fine. Logan, more water."

A squeaky creak. A rush of water. I tried to talk.

"Babe moved!"

"I told you her vitals are fine. Give her a moment. This will help."

Cold water splashed on my face. I sputtered. Tried to slap it away.

"Babe's awake!"

"Calm yourself."

"*You* calm yourself, logic boy," Blake said. "I'm a passionate guy. I get to be upset. Especially when my best girl collapses after making words magically appear in a book." Blake jiggled me. "Babe?" My eyes opened. "She's back!"

He was big on announcing the obvious.

I blinked, expecting pain considering the brain malfunction I had before I blacked out, but…

"I'm okay." I patted Blake's shoulder.

He started to set me in a chair, but I squirmed onto my feet. Bounced on my toes. I was feeling strong and kind of…tingly. I didn't want to sit. Or stand still.

Logan held out a pewter goblet. "Jayden says the water's fine so drink up."

I raised it high and downed the fresh tasting cold liquid in one gulp then slapped the goblet down on the table. Jayden put a hand on my forehead. "No fever. Any pain? Nausea?"

"Nope." I pushed him away, stretched, wiggled my body. "But Elizabeth's diary sure packs a wallop. Wow."

"How did you know her name was Elizabeth?" Jayden said. "After you touched the book, words appeared on the page and we only just read that it belonged to—"

"Elizabeth Grace Flint." I tilted my head sideways to crack my neck. "Nathan's sister. He built these caves for her to hide from the Mandatum because she knew too much."

"About what?" Blake asked.

Run! Now!

"So hot in here, huh?" I gathered my hair up and fanned the back of my neck. "About the usual stuff. Scandal, sex, a cover-up. And the fact that the Mandatum murdered the last Divinicus."

Chapter Seventy-One

"You're making no sense." Jayden was frantically flipping pages in Elizabeth's diary. "The Flint files mentioned a sister, but there's nothing in here about murder."

"Trust me. There is. Because whatever's in there," I pointed to the book, "is in here." I pointed to my head. I waved off Jayden as he opened his mouth. "When I touched the diary—"

"The words lit up like invisible ink coming to life," Blake said.

I rocked on my heels. "Right. Then all the info rushed out and straight into my head."

Logan glanced at the other two boys. "Elizabeth. She was a Scriptor?"

"You're reasoning is sound," Jayden nodded. "They're the only hunters that can communicate the written word into another's mind."

"But across different time zones, and after they're *dead?*" Blake shook his head. "I've never heard of a Scriptor doing that."

"You've never heard of Ernest Hemmingway either," Logan said.

Blake made a face. "That jerk from third period?"

I scanned the room like a stone skipping on water until my gaze settled on a far wall. I ran to it and slapped my hand over one of the Latin carvings. Stone rumbled, the smooth surface cracked in a rectangle, and a drawer slid out from the wall. I pointed to the leather bound books stacked inside.

"These are more of her diaries during the years that she was here in Gossamer Falls. But those — Blake lift me up."

Hands on my waist, Blake raised me up to sit on his shoulders. I braced a hand on the wall, put a foot on his shoulder, pushed off his head with my other hand, put my other foot on his other shoulder, and managed to stand up surprisingly steady. At this height I could touch some of the higher writings. I ran my hand over a carving to my left. More rumbling and another drawer unrolled from the rock.

"More diaries," I teetered on tip-toe, Blake remaining rock-solid beneath me. "This and another level have ones from when she was living with the Divinicus. In Europe mostly, but they traveled a lot for security reasons. And those," I pointed to the uppermost levels then moved my finger around the room "are the diaries written by or about all the other Divinicuses — or is it Divinic-i? — over the centuries. A complete history."

Jayden's eyes tracked slowly over the room. He swallowed hard and cleared his throat before speaking in a hushed, reverent tone. "You're telling me that we have…the *Divinincus Nex Chronicles*?"

I patted the stone. "Guess so."

"But that's impossible." Jayden's thumbs popped in and out of joint. "You're talking about something the Mandatum guards with the utmost secrecy and security."

"Whatever." I shrugged. "Moving on. Blake, catch." I jumped into the air, legs straight, toes pointed, and dropped into Blake's waiting arms.

"Nice, babe. We could be cheerleaders together."

"Sure." I popped from his arms to my feet, darted over to the tall stone bookcases, and swiped my hand over the spines. "These are re-creations of all the books Elizabeth ever read. Including, but not limited to, Mandatum stuff. Things like history, accounting records, personnel files. Things that would be in—"

"The Mandatum archives." Jayden was barely breathing as he wandered in a daze to the aisles of books, neck craned to stare at the sky-high shelves. "She stole these? For that alone they would come after her. How could we not know this was missing? It would be catastrophic to the society. And how did she get to all this top secret information? Only a very few on the highest levels have access."

"She didn't steal it," I said. "She re-created it. She had a photographic memory of everything she saw or read. Books, documents, images, people. Even anything auditory like conversations or music. Whatever she experienced was in her head forever and she spent years writing it all down. Well, not always *writing*, exactly." I rotated my fingers around my temple. "Sometimes she could kind of think it onto the paper. I'm not quite sure how that works. Yet. I've got to read, read, read. More, more, more."

"No way a normal Scriptor could do that," Blake said.

I grabbed a book, but before I could open it, Logan snatched it from my hands. "Maybe later."

I frowned. "Why not right now?"

"You seem a bit…wound up," Logan said. "I'm still confused. She was a fugitive hunter?"

"Maybe. I need to read more, but…you're right. Later." I glanced at the books, then closed my eyes, fingers pulling at my hair. "She…she…"

Run! Now! So much jumbled in my brain, desperate for release. Lines of information, sayings, titles, names, locations, they kept popping up faster than I could piece them together. *Run!* It felt like spiders crawling under my skin. I scratched my palm.

"Babe, you alright?"

"Sure. Fine." I breathed deep. Fisted my hands. This was *awesome*. For once I knew more than they did. I could finally get a handle on all my Divinicus Nex crap. I had knowledge, and access to more. But first I had to…to…what? Sort through what I already had. Organize the information ricocheting around inside my head.

"Not a fugitive." I tucked my hair behind my ears, concentrating. "Elizabeth was with the Divinicus for years as his biographer."

Jayden nodded. "Every Divinicus has one, but why did she come here and create this?"

I filled my cheeks with air then blew it out, shaking my hands to relieve the tingling. "The Bellator set this up with Nathan Flint because the Mandatum was going to kill the Divinicus's kid."

"What!" Jayden shrieked.

"The Bellator," Blake said patiently. "That's the hot girl hunter who has the special supernatural connection with the Divinicus. They share an emotional and physical bond, and she becomes his lifetime protector and companion. Really dude, try to keep up."

Jayden's hands clenched into tight fists, which he shook at Blake. "Of course I know what a Bellator is!"

"Then quit asking stupid questions."

"But Aurora is talking nonsense!" Jayden almost screamed. "The child of the Divinicus and Bellator is sacred."

"Exactly," I said. "Which makes a child created from Elizabeth's affair with the Divinicus blasphemous."

Jayden's head trembled from side to side like he was short circuiting. "Elizabeth couldn't be pregnant with the Divinicus's baby because the Divinicus is only ever sexually intimate with the Bellator."

I rubbed my eyes. So itchy. "Which is why Elizabeth was a dead woman walking. Broke all the rules when she fell in love with the Divinicus. Even though the Bellator was heartbroken, she couldn't let them kill the baby." I rapped my knuckles on Blake's shoulder. "Help me get more books down."

"Maybe you should grab Ayden." Logan gave the big guy a push.

"Yeah." Blake shot me a strange look before jogging out.

"But I need— Ugh." I wiped my sweaty hands on my jeans. Images suddenly flashed in my head, showing me where I'd get the answers to my questions. "Column forty, row five, volume seventeen twelve." I tittered a laugh. "Oh, that's so much better than tracking a demon."

"Aurora!" Jayden slapped a hand over my mouth. "We agreed you'd kept your abilities a secret."

I pushed him off. "Secret, schmeetrit. Don't you see? That's why the spirals react to my touch. This place was made for the Divinicus." Grabbing his shirt, I yanked our faces close. "This place was made for *me!*" I laughed. "Isn't that great?"

"Perhaps you should sit," Jayden said.

"No way. It's awesome! This is *my* sanctuary now. The last Bellator didn't want to kill a pregnant woman or her soul mate's child, so she had a place made to hide and protect all of them. Not just *her* Divinicus, but every one after him. So I could be free. Wow. Bellators fix everything. Where's mine? I'm thirsty." I ran over to the sink, turned on the faucet, shoved my mouth into the stream of water, and guzzled. Then I stuck my head under the flow. "Ah, feels better. Weird that an underground cave is so hot." I pulled my head out and shook it to fling off the excess water. "Look, I'm a dog!"

Ayden came running in. He looked good. Really good.

Color in his cheeks. Hair gelled and mussed to perfection. Jeans fit just right and that awesome leather jacket with the scars and imperfections from his being a big, bad, sexy demon hunter. Not to mention that knowing smile flip-flopping my stomach.

Although, he wasn't wearing it now.

Frowning, he glanced at his brother. "What's wrong with her?"

"Nothing." I ran over and snaked an arm around his neck. "Especially now that you're here, sugar lips."

My fingers slid into his hair, pulling his mouth against mine. He tasted yummy. Minty. And all mine. But he pulled away.

I planted a bunch of kisses on his face and neck. "Helloooo, gorgeous."

Blake said, "She must think you're me."

Ayden pulled my head back and lifted my lids with his thumbs. "Her eyes are red. Did she take something?"

"I gave her water." Logan smacked Jayden. "You said it was fine."

"It's not the water," Jayden said.

"Maybe it was when babe got hit with the book?"

"Who hit her with a book?" Ayden sounded like he was ready to hit someone. I kept kissing him.

Logan whacked Blake then told Ayden, "No one. Blake meant the information from the book somehow hit into her brain. All the sudden she just *knew* stuff."

"Then babe started acting like she was on some high-octane caffeine, sugar-rush combo with an adrenaline chaser."

Ayden listened with growing anxiety as the boys' related events, which was *boring*, so I pushed away and skipped down the aisle.

"Aurora!"

I raced ahead of Ayden and climbed a bookcase, swinging off it one-handed. "Look, I'm a monkey!"

"Come down!"

"But I haven't figured out what went wrong yet." I grabbed back onto the shelves. "The Bellator smuggled a pregnant Elizabeth — let's call her Lizzy, makes her sound spunky — to her brother, Nathan, in Gossamer Falls and later, the Bellator and Divinicus also planned to escape here. To this place." I swung off a shelf again to gesture toward the room.

Below, Ayden growled, "Aurora, quit doing that!"

"Spoiled sport." I latched back on. "Nathan built this as a hideout. Eventually, he would've gotten them all new names, new documents, new lives. But…"

"Did they get discovered?" Blake asked.

"Don't encourage her," Ayden said as he and Logan climbed up after me.

"I don't know." My foot slipped. Chin cracked against stone, but I caught myself from falling. Tasted copper. Blood. Had bit my tongue. Didn't hurt. I kept climbing. "She writes about it. Must be here." I scuttled across the shelf and then up, up, up!

Jayden pointed to the walls. "I thought you indicted that her diaries were in those drawers over there."

My head jerked around. "Oh, right!" I jumped down.

"Jayden!" Ayden was annoyed.

"Sorry. But this allegory is fascinating."

Blake steered me away from the wall. "Got her."

"No!" I struggled against the big guy, looking over my shoulder at the masses of information just waiting for me to absorb. "There's still so much I don't know."

"Come on, babe." Blake pulled me along. "Tell us what happened next to Nathan and Elizabeth."

"Lizzy," I corrected. I scratched the back of my hand. Then my scalp. Lots of itches. "Nathan hid her child, but the Mandatum captured and tortured Nathan to insanity before he told Lizzy where he hid the baby so Lizzy hid here until…" I glanced over Blake's shoulder at the corpse. "She looks sad."

"Probably because she's dead," Blake said.

When Blake turned to glance back too, I slipped out of his arms.

"Babe!"

Ayden scowled. “Blake.”

“She tricked me.”

“So alone and scared. “ I zoomed past the skeleton, grabbed a midnight blue gown, and held it against me in front of the mirror. “Nathan captured. Her child missing. She searched for years, using the sanctuary as her base.” I grabbed a hat dripping with feathers and veils, and plopped it on my head. “Hiding out in the tunnels, selling off pieces of the treasure when she needed money. But no baby. Eventually, she couldn’t travel and…she died. And that’s all I know until read, read, read!” I twirled and nearly fell.

Ayden caught me. “Not happening.”

I stamped my foot. “But I have to.”

A sudden, sharp pain blossomed in the back of my head. I rubbed it, trying to relieve the building pressure, a vise tightening around my skull. Didn’t help. Got worse. Pinpoints of light edged my vision. My knees gave out.

A gaggle of noise made things worse. The guys were talking. Getting louder. Arguing. Every word an icepick chipping away at my skull.

“And there’s no way to get her out!” Ayden shouted. “You were supposed to be looking for an exit!”

“There’s one in the back.” I pointed toward the mini-apartment. “Another elevator.”

“We don’t even know where it leads,” Jayden protested.

“Has…several exits.” I hissed air through clenched teeth, sorted through the blistering inferno of information. “Closest one…tunnel…near the falls.”

“Babe knows what she’s talking about.”

“It’s old!” Jayden sputtered. “The mechanics could break down. We’d be trapped.”

Inside my head was a minefield. Every new sound setting off a fresh explosion, sucking all energy. My eyes squeezed shut.

Something tickled my nose. I rubbed it away and my fingers came back with blood. Not the best sign. But better than leaking brain matter.

"I don't care." Ayden was losing patience. "Get the guys. We're leaving."

"Please stop." My gut twisted. I wrenched away to fall on my knees and throw up.

At least I didn't pass out. Although that might be preferable to what felt like an axe-wielding psycho running around in my head shredding soft brain tissue. Or Ayden slapping my cheeks as he held my face. His expression vacillated between fear and fury.

"Her eyes are crazy red."

My heart accelerated. "Changing color? I'm transforming?" I pinched my face. "Into what?"

"No," Ayden said soothingly, brushing aside my hand and caressing my cheek. "I meant they're bloodshot. Relax. Take this." Ayden pushed something through my lips. A mint. Then he lifted me in his arms and kissed my forehead. "We're getting you out of here."

I started to rest my head on his chest, but his shirt was wet. And he winced with every step.

"What's wrong?" My mouth ran dry. Suddenly my pain didn't matter. "Oh, God."

"It's nothing," he murmured.

No, it was something. Soaking through his T-shirt.

Blood. And lots of it.

"You're hurt." I squirmed. "Ayden, stop! Put me down."

He dropped on one knee. Then, quite unceremoniously, he dropped me. But I couldn't complain. He couldn't hear me if I did.

He'd collapsed onto the floor.

Chapter Seventy-Two

"Ayden!" My hands hovered, afraid to touch him.

Blake rushed over and with one yank, ripped Ayden's bloody shirt up the middle.

My breath sucked in.

His chest was peppered with red welts, some black in the center, not so much bleeding as oozing. Jagged purple lines ran in between the welts, like some macabre version of connect-the-dots.

Jayden skidded to his knees, then gingerly inspected the injuries.

"This can't be." His lips thinned. "It looks like he's…burned."

"When the lava came out of the portal it splattered," I said. "Maybe it hit him."

"Even lava doesn't bother him. Nothing with heat does."

"Are you sure? Maybe it's special lava because it's from the Waiting World because he was fine when we were melting the chains after he stopped my fingers from zapping—" A cold realization stabbed through my chest. I flopped on my butt. "Oh, crap. It was me. I-I-I did this." I scooted away.

"Babe, calm down."

I pointed at Ayden, my hands shaking like I held a jackhammer. "When he knocked me aside to cut the connection, the explody stuff was zapping from my fingers and must have hit him in the chest. But I never thought…he didn't say…I'm so sorry." I crawled back over and smoothed the hair from his forehead. "Ayden. Wake up. Please."

He was hot, starting to sweat, shivering. And even if I didn't see the look in Jayden's eyes, it was clear we didn't have much time.

Chapter Seventy-Three

We rushed down the tunnel leading from Lizzy's room and found the latticed metal elevator where, like a size-ten foot in a size-five sneaker, we squeezed in. Logan climbed up and hung from the side, moving his hands in odd motions. Blake was cradling Ayden like his wounded friend was made of fragile, paper-thin glass, and without a word spoken, the rest of us gave him as much room as we could.

Face smooshed against the metal, I punched buttons on the control panel before Sally Security had even finished asking me to, "Enter destination request."

When I felt the weight of questioning looks as to how I knew the proper code, I avoided eye contact because, hey, I had no friggin' clue. I was running on knowledge that came from a place I couldn't explain. If I was wrong, we'd find out soon enough.

And they could kill me then.

With a *clang,* jolt, and belch of oil, metal, and something acrid — probably terror — we started a crickity-rickety journey up, riding in silence thick as C-4 and just as volatile.

I was an emotional schizoid.

Sometimes I felt empty. Gutted, hollow, and numb. Then I'd look at Ayden, vacillating in and out of consciousness, and a zillion icicles, honed to razor sharp points, stabbed mercilessly through my body, leaving me cold and writhing in nerve-shattering pain. Then I'd wipe sweat from my forehead with shaky hands and realize I was still hyped-up from whatever the sanctuary did to me. Or I could be flooded with guilt — and shock — over putting Ayden at death's door.

Burning the Hex Boy who was *unburnable.*

No one was saying it, but they had to hate me at that moment. Know I did. And I got the niggling feeling that they might even be a bit scared of me.

Hey, I scared myself.

Could be why my breathing became halted. Then energy rippled through my insides, splashing with violent fury like a stormy sea on jagged cliffs. My hands prickled, and when I looked down, they started to glow. I quickly stuffed them in my pockets.

A wind swirled around the cramped space and Logan blurted, "My powers are back," just as the elevator jerked to a stop, the door opening to let us stumble out into a tunnel.

"Finally!" Jayden flung a few ice blades then hustled to Blake and checked Ayden's injuries.

With the sound of gears turning, the elevator simply disappeared, covered over by weathered stone, smooth but for a small, inconspicuous carving of a double spiral.

In the distance, we could hear the thundering water from the falls, and using the hologram tunnel map on their phones, Logan and Matthias led us out. I jogged on the other side of Blake, hands hidden, afraid to touch Ayden, as I watched Jayden work. Eyes a murky blue-green, he hovered his hands over Ayden's chest wounds.

"Jayden," I swallowed hard. "I'm so sorry. What can I do? I didn't mean to hurt him."

"The burns appear superficial." Jayden's words were clipped, cold, sterile. He frowned. "Other than he *shouldn't* be burned, they're normal and not life-threatening. Certainly wouldn't cause him to react like this." As one hand ran over Ayden's shoulder, Jayden jerked as if bitten. "Oh, no."

My stomach lurched. "What?"

"Shh!" Jayden placed a palm on Ayden's neck then, with an increasingly grim expression, he moved it gently along Ayden's collarbone and over the wounded shoulder. "It's not the burns." His Adam's apple bobbed. "It's the toxin."

My brows knitted. "What toxin?"

"In his blood!" Jayden blurted then seemed surprised by his outburst and reeled his composure back in. "I can read the plasma composition. It's tainted. Point of origin is the spear puncture."

I rasped, "The blade was poisoned?" Jayden nodded gravely, and I nearly collapsed. It wasn't me. But my tiny sense of relief lasted only an instant. "You can fix him, right? With your watery powers. Just suck it out!"

"It's not that easy." Jayden's nostrils flared while his hands worked on the wound, eyes swirling brighter as a pale vapor lifted off Ayden. "I am extracting as much as I can, but a fatal dose has already infiltrated his blood stream." He flinched when Ayden's body spasmed. The vapor cloud dissipated. "That's as much as I dare. Now the best I can do is slow his blood flow to diminish the toxin's acceleration through his system."

At the word "fatal," my mind nearly shut down. I blinked back tears. "That will buy us time to save him?"

Jayden nodded. "The faster we get him to the lab at the house, the better. Blake *move!*"

We hit turbo-boost and soon raced into the cave illuminated by the glow-in-the-dark algae which put us in sight of the backside of the waterfall. The roar was deafening. Mist rose from the pounding waters and took on the eerie green glow.

Jayden burst into a dead run.

I stumbled when the vision hit. It was quick. Tristan pulled me upright. I recovered and ran forward, yelling, "Jayden stop!" but it was too late.

He parted the waters of the falls and walked right into an ambush.

Chapter Seventy-Four

I sprinted after Jayden anyway, screaming things like "Stop!" and "Ambush!" but the crashing din of the waterfall drowned any warnings. Logan caught my arm and shoved me back into Tristan who, despite my struggles, kept me in place as the white-haired wonder drew his bow and fired.

The arrow missiled for Jayden's back, aimed to sever his spine in two.

What the heck?!

Clueless to the danger, Jayden barreled toward the opening of parted water. From Matthias's hands, shadow whips snapped out. They licked through the air and wrapped around Jayden's waist then he was yanked off his feet and hauled backwards into the cave.

The arrow sailed over the fallen Jayden and headed directly at the leader of the ambush.

Rose.

Standing just outside the falls, wearing a smug smile, he tilted his head, showing mild interest in, but zero concern for, the arrow rocketing toward him. He didn't even attempt to move as the arrow speared his heart.

Kind of.

When the arrow hit his chest, Rose's form simply wavered like smoke from a chimney, and the arrow passed harmlessly through, dissipating in a pale white puff as it buried into the sandy beach behind him.

"Evening, boys. Aurora." Rose shimmered into a more solid looking shape standing with feet planted wide, a thumb hooked into the front pocket of dark jeans that were tucked into knee-high leather boots. His shirt was a white, billowy affair, cuffed at the wrists with an open V-neck that showed off his tanned, toned chest. His long waves of golden hair were pulled back and tied in a black ribbon. Very much the pirate.

He reached out a leather-gloved hand. "Find what we need?"

"Call off your demons," I said. My vision had shown six winged monsters perched on the waterfall above and seven more landlubbers lurking just out of the line of sight.

Blake's head bobbled. "What demons?"

"Love to," Rose shrugged and folded his arms. "But if I do that, you'll come out and stop searching."

"Who said we didn't find it?"

We all looked at Ayden who had spoken despite being barely conscious as he leaned against Blake.

"Got it…right here." Ayden's voice had a weird gurgle. He hacked a wet cough.

"Excellent." Rose held out a hand.

Jayden practically ripped apart his brother's clothes. "Where is it?"

"Have him," Ayden wheezed a long rattling breath, "come in here and get it."

Jayden clutched his twin's shirt. "You don't have time."

"Very…dangerous." Ayden spoke slowly whether for emphasis or because he was deteriorating. "He couldn't," he winced, "get in. Tricked us."

"In where? Tricked how?" I shook my head. "It doesn't matter. Blake, can you sense the stone on him?

Blake whispered, "He doesn't have one," but set Ayden down and helped Jayden rifle through his pockets.

Rose whistled. "I'm waiting. And I'm not a patient man. I do hate assassinating anyone before breakfast. Tends to ruin the appetite."

"Don't…go…out." Ayden struggled to get up, but lost the battle and flopped back. "Not…human."

"I get it." With trembling hands, Tristan pushed me behind him. "Rose can't get in anywhere."

"Aurora's house," Logan said, readjusting his hold on the bow and arrow and aiming directly at Rose. "And only in the school after the shields went down."

The boys were solving some puzzle I couldn't comprehend.

Jayden moved in front of his fallen brother. "He never intended to break into our home."

"He bloody wanted us to catch him outside." Matthias stared at Rose with awe. And a growing anxiety.

"Cat suit was a brilliant distraction on my part. You boys are so repressed." Rose's grin lit up the night. "Took you all long enough. And now you're one man down. Tsk, tsk." Pink smoke curled from his fingers. His eyes began to glow.

"Everyone back in the sanctuary!" Matthias shoved us back.

I stayed put. "Ayden will die if we don't get him help."

Tristan tugged on my arm. "Rose isn't human."

"Then what is he?" I snapped.

Out on the beach, a tall, trench-coated man emerged from the mist, arms slightly away from his sides, hands open, like he was about to engage in an old-fashioned gunfight in the dusty main street of a tumbleweed town.

Beneath the lowered brim of a tattered fedora, he had the profile of a hatchet. Harsh angles, sharp lines. Pale eyes glittered so cold they looked like they'd been chipped off a glacier.

He stepped alongside Rose. A gun held steady in his hand, the muzzle pressed firmly against the non-human's golden hair.

"He's a god," the man said.

Then he pulled the trigger.

Chapter Seventy-Five

I jammed my hands over my ears, the *bang* ricocheting through the cave. Tristan threw us both behind Blake's bulk.

Logan readied to shoot his arrow, but Matthias knocked his arms down.

"Bloody perfect timing, Jenny!" Matthias slammed into the stranger with a back-slapping hug.

I peeked around. Rose was nowhere in sight.

"Don't thank me yet, godson." The man — Jenny? — stepped back, pulled out another automatic weapon and pointed both guns up. Six shots fired. Demons screeched, and the connections I'd had with them from the vision vanished. "Didn't kill him. Just scared him into teleporting to safer waters for a spell."

"Gone, even temporarily, is all we need," Matthias said. "My mate's down."

Jenny, with an Irish brogue thick as Aunt M's porridge, was tall and extra bulky. But that was due to his vest of death.

A custom-made affair of lethal.

It held eight guns holstered down the front of his torso in two columns. Another two guns hung below his armpits from shoulder holsters. Two more off his hips. His belt dripped with a variety of sheathed knives. Was that a grenade?! And either a very long knife or a short sword was strapped to one thigh. A sawed-off shotgun strapped to the other. The hilts of two more sharp items poked out from his back, criss-crossed behind his head.

"Jenny?" Tristan shrilled. "*Actual* rogue demon hunter Jenny? One of the Mandatum's most wanted for treason, murder, larceny, extortion—"

"Shut up!" Jayden shoved Blake forward. "Get Ayden in the car!"

"Man down?" Jenny said as a demon slunk from the water behind him. He whirled, pulled the trigger once and turned back to us, not bothering to watch the hellion scatter into black dust and vortex into the ground. "Knife? Gunshot? "

"Poison."

"Hurry, Blake." Jayden flicked a hand at Ayden lying on the ground, unconscious once again. "The most logical conclusion is that the tip of the spear was dipped in a Curare poison, but there are *several* Curare poisons which originate from South America, so in order to formulate an antidote I'll have to use the lab to narrow it down to either tubocurare or—"

"*Or…*" Jenny pushed his way past Blake and dropped on one knee next to Ayden. From inside the depths of his frighteningly overstocked coat, he extracted a fat syringe with a needle the length of Texas. "We could just take care of it now."

In one swift motion, he used his teeth to rip off the cap of the needle, stabbed the needle into Ayden's chest, shoved the plunger down, and then pulled the whole thing out. Ayden convulsed once and was still.

"There." Jenny stood, capped the needle, and replaced the empty syringe into his coat, "Should be right as rain."

I hinged my jaw back on and slapped at Jenny's feet. "What did you do?!"

Jayden looked ready to faint. "What was in that? We didn't even make a diagnosis on the chemical compound!"

"Didn't need to," Jenny shrugged. "It's my own concoction. Takes care of most everything."

Jayden sputtered, "Mo-*most* everything?"

"Relax, aqua man. Shouldn't take long."

"Ahhhh!" Ayden screamed and jerked up into a sitting position, knocking me aside in the process. He leaned over, heaving deep breaths.

"See?" Jenny looked bored.

"Are you crazy?" I crawled back to Ayden, put my hand on his burning hot cheek.

Jayden kneeled next to his brother and shot Jenny a venomous look. "If you have caused any permanent damage, I will…I will…cause you an interminable amount of duress."

Ayden caught my hand with his. He looked up. His eyes swirled bright orange.

"You'll be fine," I said.

Ayden threw me onto my back and jumped on top of me. His mouth attacked mine, his hands pinning my wrists against the sand. Whoa!

His weight lifted and I was left stunned.

"Um…" I touched my stinging — not in a bad way — lips.

"Sorry, lass." Jenny was holding Ayden at bay with one hand gripping his jacket. "Forgot about that particular side effect."

Ayden looked somewhat disoriented, but was settling down, his eyes returning to dark chocolate. Jenny shoved him aside and hauled me to my feet.

"So, Matty, this is your newest team member?"

"I never said that."

"Didn't have to." With the squint of a scalawag, the man eyed me up and down in a clinical sort of way. "Donal Jensen. Call me

Jenny." He had my hand in the rugged boulder of his iron grip and he shook it vigorously, sandpaper skin chaffing my palm. "Quite the looker. But useless as a chocolate teapot unless you can fight. I hear you have some power issues."

"I guess." Hmmm…Didn't Cacciatori mention "Donal Jensen" and "kill order" in the same sentence? I looked around for help, but other than Matthias, the rest seemed as stunned as I.

"I'll take care of that." Jenny turned to Matthias. "Your Dad know you're rumbling with the Greeks?"

CHAPTER SEVENTY-SIX

Jenny was in his fifties. Maybe. Hard to tell. Partly because of the scars shining in an ugly marriage across his face and throat along with a few fresh scratches down his cheek. He must have been handsome once. Until life's masochistic amusement cut plenty into the weathered marble of his skin, and no doubt the tattered soul within. He put his hands on his hips, pushing back the coat. Metal glinted.

Was that a machete?

We'd moved onto the beach outside of the falls so Ayden could get some fresh air and recoup. His head lay in my lap, his eyes closed. Doing my best to ignore the dried blood on his shirt, I stroked my fingers through his soft hair while my other hand kept touching other parts. Shoulder, arm, hand, face. Anything to stay connected. Anything to assure myself he was here and alive.

"Jaysus. You young pups know nothing," Jenny growled.

To be fair, he growled everything. His voice grounded out every syllable like a chainsaw on concrete.

He looked down his hawkish nose at the boys. "Not your fault, I suppose. Mandatum likes its secrets. Especially likes to keep mum about the gods."

"So," Matthias said, "when I called you about helping with her powers and mentioned Rose, you knew he was really Eros?"

Tristan's fingers had combed his blond hair to a scattered mess. "We've been hanging out with the Greek God of Love?"

"And desire," Jenny said. "Also goes by Cupid. But either way, Rose is one of his aliases. Thinks he's clever mixing up the letters. Everything from their myths are true. And when you described him, Matty, it wasn't a leap. You made my day." He slapped the Aussie on the back. "I've been tracking the S.O.B. since he came out of the Paris portal, killed a few good hunters by the way, and headed for North America. It all fit. Now I'm just waiting for him to hook up with Aphrodite."

"His mom." Oh, yay, I knew something. Eros, Aphrodite. Mythos and real life were colliding. My head hurt.

"Yes, lass. Word is Aphrodite finally came out of hiding and was the one who got Eros out of hell a few weeks back. She needs him to help with some master plan to open portals and unleash a demon army of epic proportions in order to— "

"Go all dominatrix on the world?" I said.

"Colorfully accurate, lass." Jenny scratched his cheek, opening the fresh scratches and smearing blood. "But I only care about capturing Aphrodite to use her as bait to get to Artemis." He fingered a knife on his belt.

"Bait?" Matthias said. "Why would Artemis come for Aphrodite?"

"Revenge." I shrugged. "They hate each other. Something about being responsible for killing each other's favorite guys. I think."

"Both poetic and smart," Jenny smiled. "You must be Irish."

Matthias scowled. I scowled back.

"The trouble I've had tracking Artemis is that the Goddess of the Hunt is a diehard loner," Jenny said as he paced across the sand. "She doesn't need or want anyone or anything but to be left alone.

She's been hiding out, staying under the radar, but she hates Aphrodite with a passion born of centuries of malice, and if I offer her up, Artemis won't miss the opportunity for revenge. I'm sure of it."

"Why didn't you tell me?" Matthias looked wounded.

Jenny dropped a hand on Matthias's shoulder. "Because, boyo, couldn't risk you calling a Code Olympus before I could get here and take care of things myself."

"Wait a minute." My head was spinning. "Code Olympus?"

Ayden winced as he lifted his hand to rub his eyes. "Any time the gods show up, protocol dictates the Mandatum is notified. Teams — plural — of the highest level of Sicarius guards are dispatched to take care of them."

I felt cold. Mandatum. Here. In abundance.

"Because going up against them, without backup, well…" Tristan chewed off a fingernail. "Gossamer Falls and everything in it could end up a pile of ash."

"Worlds have been known to disappear," Logan said with a dismal air. He'd taken out his pocket handkerchief and kept refolding it.

I swallowed. "So the gods really are gods?"

"No," Jenny said with disgust. "They're demons. Deadly and more dangerous because they're the most powerful. And smart. Not sure where they came from, but with their charm and stunningly *human* good looks, the vile guttersnipes were able to convince people that they were the gods the humans *already* worshipped."

"Wreaked havoc and took all kinds of advantage." Tristan dropped to the sand like his knees just gave out.

"You know the stories, Madame Mythology," Ayden said. "They're a nasty group. The Mandatum took down most of them centuries ago. The few that are left, especially Aphrodite and Artemis, are on the Mandatum's Most Wanted list. Eros got out a few weeks ago when we were at the Alfred Hitchcock marathon." His brow creased deep furrows. "Why didn't I make the connection?"

"None of us did, mate," Matthias said. "It's not like we have a current photo."

Jayden nodded. "And his costumes functioned to distract us from his true form. Clever."

"You said 'Cassanova' escaped." I slapped my forehead. That was the night I had my Divinicus Nex vision of Rose, uh, Eros. "And opening the portal for Aphrodite's army is why Eros wants that rock. There is no sister to save."

Jenny snorted. "Just playing on your sympathies. They love to manipulate. Especially with family." Jenny's pale eyes glittered. "Walk away. Take your loved ones. I've got nothing left to lose. I'll handle this. I'll take them all down. "

"Or die trying." Matthias shook his head. "We're not abandoning you."

"That's guilt talking, boyo." The Irishman readjusted his hat. "Don't trouble yourself with a corpse. Artemis killed me eight years ago." Jenny bared his teeth and in a voice so cold he should've exhaled frost. "I'm just trying to return the favor."

Matthias looked sad and shaken. They all did.

"Why do you want her dead?" I asked.

Jenny finished reloading his guns and took out a cloth to give them a buff. "Artemis had been hunted for centuries. But my team and I were the only ones who ever got close. So to distract us off her trail, she killed my wife and daughter." His tone was frighteningly matter-of-fact as he sighted down the barrel of a weapon then replaced it in its holster.

I felt a chill. Then frowned. "Killed your daughter? That's weird."

"Weird?" Jenny gave me a dubious look. "Perhaps you don't comprehend how demons operate, lass. They slaughter innocents."

"I know." I scratched my head. "But according to myth Artemis is the protector of young girls. It doesn't make sense that she would kill one."

Jenny laughed bitterly. "Demons make sense? You've got a lot to learn. Self-preservation. *That* makes sense."

"I guess," I said quietly. "And I'm sorry. About your family."

"Don't cry over me, lass." He twisted an ugly smile. "This is good news. I've spent eight years and broken every Mandatum rule to hunt that butcher down and this is the closest I've ever got." His hands went to the hilt of a short sword. "This time, I won't miss."

The ground shook underneath us. Waves splashed onto the shore. Jenny put his hands on his guns. I stood and helped Ayden to his feet as a massive demon burst from the water.

Jenny pulled his weapons, pointed, and fired.

At Fido.

"No!" I screamed and threw myself in front of her.

Muzzles flared. Light blasted. My hands raised. The bullet hit me. But not like a…a bullet. It was more like a freakin' *freight train!*

The force lifted me off my feet and slammed me backwards through the air, stealing oxygen from my lungs, control from my limbs, and consciousness from my brain.

Lights out.

Chapter Seventy-Seven

My body felt heavy and thick as I thudded to the ground.

Squishy, lumpy, smelly ground. With a red sky and black clouds above.

"No, no, no!"

I jerked up into a sitting position. Dead bodies everywhere. Layers of them. Ranging from supple and fresh from the embalmer, to decomposing skeletons with flesh sliding off bone. They covered every inch of the ground.

Heck, they *were* the ground.

Welcome to the Waiting World. Population, me.

"There you are, sailor!"

And one perky angel.

She stood to my right in full costume, per usual. A classy, white sailor uniform dress, complete with a navy blue squared-off collar that tied in a bow at her chest, and a crisp white hat sporting a little golden anchor. Her sensible navy pumps hovered just above the oozing graveyard of human rot. Her eyes were the same tropical sea blue as her hair tucked in a neat bun at the nape of her neck.

Subtle was not in my guardian angel's vocabulary.

"Where did you come from?" She did a little tap dance and ended with a twirl. "Not that I'm complaining. I love it when you visit."

"Gloria," I whispered her name, but my volume quickly rose. "Where have you been?!"

"Out and about." She waved a dismissive hand before offering it to me. "But enough about me, how have *you* been?"

I grabbed her hand and yanked myself up. Globs of gunk stuck to my bare legs, sliming down my calves because I was in some flimsy dress, although this time I had ankle boots to keep the ooze from between my toes, but then the slime seeped down my legs *into* the boots and the ooze pooled around my feet and…*squish squish.*

I shivered.

"How have I been? You are the worse guardian angel *ever*!" I stormed about in my fury.

Squish squish.

"Who do I talk to about this ridiculous choice of attire? Ankle boots in a knee-high swamp of *that!*" I jammed my hands toward the ground, then folded my arms in a huff. "Seriously. Worst *ever!*"

"That's a bit dramatic. And unfair." She put a hand on her waist and cocked one hip. "Because honestly, who do you have to compare me to?"

She had a point.

But I still managed to huff with indignation, "Well, if you're the best there is—"

"I like to think so," she beamed.

"Then why did I just get shot? Oh, jeez." My hands frantically patted over my body searching for holes gushing blood. "Am I dead?"

"If you don't want to get shot, then you shouldn't go jumping in front of bullets." Her tone was overly patient. "Aurora, I can save you from many things, but not from yourself. And you didn't get shot, you were shot *at*. A significant difference. Besides, you didn't need me. You handled it quite nicely." Her smile was brilliant.

"Really?" I flopped my hands around at my surroundings. "Exactly how is ending up in this literal hell hole brilliant?"

Gloria pursed her lips. "Check your hand."

I raised both of them. One was clamped in a rigid fist. It took some work to uncurl my fingers.

"Is this…?" I stared in awe at the small piece of metal cradled in my palm. "I stopped a *bullet?*"

Gloria walked — glided — over. "No silly. You're not superman. Or woman. You activated your ability's defense and bounced into the Waiting World before the bullet hit you. It came along for the ride but it has no power here. You're safe."

"Safe?" I went to tuck the bullet that I *stopped* — don't care what she said — into my pants pocket but I wasn't wearing any pants — stupid dress — so I stuffed it my bra instead. At least that was still there. "The Waiting World is not safe."

Gloria made a snort-chuckle sound. "Compared to being shot by a bullet it is."

Hungry howls carried over the rotting landscape. I saw several dark, hunched bodies in the distance creeping my way, their leathery skin stretched over skeletal forms.

"Sure. Until I get eaten by ghoulies."

She shook her head sadly and sighed. "One day you'll understand." Then she leaned over to pick through the bodies.

Ew.

I gritted my teeth. "Why don't you explain it to me now? Why didn't you tell me I had a Greek god slash demon on my tail? Can't you just go all ninja on Eros and get rid of him?"

"All *ninja?*" Gloria's laugh tinkled like wind chimes. "Oh, I've missed our little chats. You're very funny. No dear. Limitations, remember. I explained all that."

"You didn't explain diddly squat." I slapped my hands to my sides because stomping my foot was just too…squishy. "Saying there *are* limitation doesn't explain *what* those limitations are. Big difference."

"Because that's a limitation. Oh, there you are my beauty." Her eyes glittered with pleasure. With her thumb and forefinger, she delicately grabbed the tip of a finger bone from the sea of corpses and pulled. The rest of the hand and an entire arm slithered out with some totally gross wet noises.

Double ew.

Gloria kept her eyes fixed on the limb that had tendons and muscles hanging in a stringy, gloppy mess. "All you need to know is that I'm keeping up my side of the bargain. You're family's safe. Eros." She made a sound of disgust, like a hairball got stuck in her throat. "Thinking he could get past my work. The hubris. Now, you'd better get back to the Hex Boys before they have any more of a fit."

"Finally." The sooner I was out of here the better.

I waited. She ignored me. Too enraptured with the grossalicious hand. It started moving, dead fingers grasping open and closed. She giggled.

"Gloria?"

"My apologies." She stood straight, shoulders back, and using the hand not holding the creepy, half-dead arm, she gave me a sharp salute. "Aye, aye, captain." She relaxed. "Now off you go." And she went back to studying the arm, lifting it high, flicking aside slimy, hanging parts to carefully inspect the area that had been ripped from a shoulder.

"Off I go? You need to fly me out of here!"

She looked confused. "I don't fly you—" Her expression cleared. "Oh, I see the misperception. Sometimes you can be very…" she thought for a moment, "I believe 'thick' is the appropriate term.

A metaphor which implies your brain matter is too dense for intelligent thought to —"

"I know what thick means!"

"Oh, good, I got it right."

"Can you just vamoose me out of here!"

"Touchy, touchy. Okay, one last time, my dear. She tucked me under one arm and *whooshed* open her massive wings — white with nautical navy blue stripes. As we twirled into the blackened sky, I refused to think about the severed limb she still held in her other hand, which I swear was trying to latch onto me.

If I was thinking about it, that is. Which I wasn't.

"But remember this." Gloria continued in a grand voice. "Only when the mighty willingly fall into the depths of their fears can they truly be reborn to the freedom of their greatness."

"Whatever." My stomach was doing the queasy thing as we climbed higher. Don't look down, don't look down, don't look... Heights. *So* not my thing. I swallowed down bile. "So is dressing-up a thing with demon gods too? Eros seems to like it."

"Does he now?" she said slowly. "Well, I suppose imitation is the *sincerest* form of flattery." She didn't sound flattered. "I'll have to find a way to show him my appreciation for his...tribute."

Okay, now she just sounded creepy.

But I didn't have time to ponder because she yelled, "Anchors aweigh!" and tossed me through the dark clouds and into a blinding, bright —

Uh oh.

CHAPTER SEVENTY-EIGHT

Water. All around me. Dark. Frigid.

I panicked, sucked in a short breath before I could stop myself, gagged, sputtered. Probably because I didn't anticipate being dropped in the *Arctic Ocean*. What was she thinking?

I pumped my arms and kicked, swimming toward a light. Not *that* light. I hoped.

The light of the moon on what better be the surface of the freezing water that Gloria thought fit to—

I saw some sort of movement, near the moonlight, then something blocked it. Despair threatened to join my already overwhelming terror. Then, suddenly, hands tugged at my arms and I was abruptly yanked out of the water and dumped on sandy ground.

On all fours I gagged, threw up the water I'd inhaled. Tasted much worse this time around. Breathing returned, ragged, but steady, and a comforting hand rubbed my back. Through the wet clumps of my hair I saw the forest. The lake. Good. I was still in Gossamer Falls, on familiar ground. My head turned to my savior, ready to thank them.

I screamed. Lurched away.

Demon god Eros, still in that ridiculous pirate outfit, put a steely grip around my ankle and dragged me back across the sand. He jumped and landed the length of his body on my back, pinning me down.

"I know this looks bad," he said into my ear.

I think we'd skipped past bad to downright horrific. Pressure and heat surrounded me. A light flashed. From me. Eros yelped. His grip loosened. I shoved him off and kicked his side for good measure.

"Ow!" He rolled across the beach, then sat up and rubbed his arms and chest. "What was that?"

I sat up, hands out, but the power that had vibrated over my skin was gone. Nothing glowed. I tried to conjure back the energy. Didn't happen.

Crap.

I felt kind of stupid with my hands out, so I acted like I was brushing sand off them and glared. "More to come unless you stay away."

He raised his palms in surrender. "I never planned to kill you. All of this is not what you think."

"No kidding. *Eros*." I spat. "With you nothing has been what I thought. Save your sister? What a crock."

"It's my wife."

"Oh, now it's your wife." I'd been doing a kind of backward crab-crawl away from him but paused. "If that's true, why tell me it's your sister?"

He shrugged. "I believed you could relate better to a sister in peril. Be more sympathetic to my pain. More disposed to assist. Conversely, you would see a wife as a threat and bear less inclination to help."

"Threat to what?" I looked around not so subtly for an escape.

"My affections, of course." He sighed. "When you fell in love with me, as all women do."

I snorted. "Fat chance."

"Yes, your lack of ardor was most unexpected," he said thoughtfully. "Eons of precedent have proven my charms universally irresistible. My mere presence can incite the passions of those in my sphere. As demonstrated by the couple in your classroom. And young Selena's amorous suitors."

I glared. "That was all you?"

"Purely unintentional," he said casually, as if the ends justified his selfish means. "Although, my presence has proved beneficial to the Lahey family finances."

"Say what?"

"The townsfolk have been buying an overabundance of flowers thanks to my influence. You're welcome." He gave a short nod. "And now we will work together to free my beloved wife from her wretched torture inflicted upon her by Aphrodite."

"You're a piece of work. The answer's no. I'm not falling for—" I stopped short, my brain making connections. "Wait. Wife?" I shook my head as the pieces fell into place. "As in *Psyche?*"

"Just like in your mythology books." He fiddled with the lacy cuffs of his puffy-sleeved shirt. "Only Psyche is no mere mortal. She was Mandatum. A hunter."

"Okay, now you're just talking crazy."

"Yes." His smile turned wistful. "It was crazy. Which is why I acquiesced to my mother's lies. But love doesn't always make sense. I, of all people, should know that." He closed his eyes briefly. "I was a fool then but no more. You can help me make it right, little dove. When Aphrodite tricked Psyche into Hades to win me back, she never escaped. No happy ending like the myth. I've been trying to rescue her for centuries. You're her only chance, Aurora. *Please.*"

I sucked in a long breath and knew what I needed to do. "Okay."

Eros jerked, his face contorting in surprise. "Okay?"

"With all of hell gunning for me, I'm not missing the chance for a demon god to owe me one. Big time. Help me up." I extended a hand.

Eros smiled, relief relaxing his frame as he closed the distance and towered over me.

I focused, tried to get my outstretched hand to glow again, but felt nothing.

Plan B it was.

I threw a fistful of sand in his face. Eros blocked with an arm, but too late. He cried out and reeled back. I kicked out his ankles. He thumped down. I jumped up and took off into the forest.

Eros liked to morph his sob story into something that seduced out my sympathy. Not this time. Fool me once, and all that jazz. My only regret was that I hadn't blasted him. No, my powers only got into gear to burn-up my unburnable boyfriend. Typical.

"Ayden!" I screamed and launched over some prickly bushes. "Fido!"

"They're too far away," Eros's voice came from just ahead.

I skidded to a stop, dead leaves and dirt flying. Couldn't see him. I backed up against a tree.

When Eros spoke, he sounded closer. "Our time is limited. You must listen."

I sprinted at an angle for the beach. A few strides would have me on sand. The lake lapped at the shore, the moon's reflection dancing on the dark surface. I thought about rainbows and puppies and took a couple of calming breaths trying to suck in some energy.

"Running won't help any of us." Eros sounded well behind me. "Aphrodite wants the Nex as her pet and she is relentless. I'm not the first she has sent. Fiskick, hired by the Mandatum traitor to kill you, was secretly working for my mother and tasked with retrieving you for her."

Hmmm. Memories of another abduction attempt were not helping my puppy and butterflies vibe.

I was steps away from the beach when he appeared immediately in front of me. I darted sideways, stumbling onto one knee, recovered and huddled behind a tree. I wiped a line of sweat from my brow and glanced around. Eros stood far across the sand at the water's edge, arms crossed over his chest. He wasn't even breathing hard.

"When Fiskick disappeared, I'm sure courtesy of you and the Hex Boys, she turned to me," he said. "I only agreed to help her because she promised to rescue Psyche. It's what she does. She'll leverage your family, the boys, whatever it takes until you have no choice but to do her bidding. You'll help her build her army of demons, then destroy the Mandatum, and the world."

I knew I'd go to the ends of the Earth to protect my family. But would I be willing to *end* the Earth? To end humanity? Or enslave it to the likes of demons?

"And if I don't?" I said.

"Then she will kill you."

Yeah. Kinda figured.

"As long as she resides in this world, you and all you love are not safe," he said. "Get the stone. Get my wife. And I will help you be rid of her forever." He turned and looked straight in my direction with eyes that so many through the ages have found irresistible. "I have a plan."

So did I. Hunched low, I slunk in the direction I was pretty sure Logan's car was parked. And hopefully, close by was a battle-scarred, trigger-happy Irishman who I could use as a human shield while he dealt with this mythological madness.

Hey, I didn't say it was a long-range plan. At this point, just making it to homeroom tomorrow would be a cause for celebration. Until it was time to turn in homework. Man, I was never going to be a senior.

A cloud exploded in front of me. Before I could back-peddle, Eros grabbed my hand. Something scraped my finger. I slammed an open palm at his nose. He jumped back before impact, hands up in supplication.

I stared at the ring he'd shoved onto my finger. The metal band hummed against my skin and beams of light suddenly shot out from the oval stone. Strength surged up my arm. Not good. I think.

"What is that!" I yanked off the ring and threw it onto the sand.

Once off my finger, the stone stopped the light-up routine but still glowed. Big as an egg, it shimmered with iridescent blues, greens, and dark pinks, stunning in their beauty, swirling through the jewel as if it held a complete galaxy within. Sparkling stars, shooting comets, twinkling planets, brilliant suns, and spirals of effervescence.

"It is yet another show of good faith." Eros kept his distance. "It gives you great power. Just what every Divinicus needs. Similar to the stone you must find but...different. Take it with you to the treasure. It should help you locate the stone we require. They share a connection."

I pointed to the ring. "When you do surprise stunts like this, I don't trust you! Besides, why would you help me?"

"Because it helps me."

"Now that makes sense."

"Aphrodite is a monster. I care not to be enslaved to her any more than you wish to be enslaved by the Mandatum." His gloved hands curled into fists. "What do I care about armies and ruling the world? I am not the God of War."

"All you do is lie, threaten, and manipulate." I backed for the beach thinking making a swim for it would be better than trying to outrun Eros in the forest. "And since when have you shown a sign of good faith?"

"I led you to the treasure. I've kept the traitor and their demons at bay while I've warned you of the coming disaster. And…and…I kidnapped Jayden!"

"Kidnapped?" I blinked. "That's something the villain would do!"

Eros glanced into the woods. "We haven't time for me to explain all I have done or the intricacies involved. You must trust me."

"No I mustn't." I shot back.

"Then believe this." His eyes of green jade glittered with desperation and fear. "If we do not find that stone before Artemis and Aphrodite arrive, it's over. For all of us."

"Whoa." I stepped back. "Who said anything about Artemis? And her and Aphrodite together, isn't that—"

"Apocalyptic? You have no idea." He cocked his head, listening, then turned and shouted into the forest. "Over here, lover boy!"

Crashing sounds, then Ayden burst from the forest onto the beach.

CHAPTER SEVENTY-NINE

In one swoop, Ayden lit up his arms and blasted them like flamethrowers. Eros *poofed* out of sight and popped up yards away, safe, unscathed.

Ayden kept firing as he raced across the sand to stand in front of me, facing Eros who had evaded every shot by teleporting all over the beach. *Poof, poof, poof.*

"You alright? Did he hurt you?" Ayden asked over his shoulder. "When you disappeared with Fido, I thought you were shot."

"Me too, but I'm fine. Long story." I was still tingly from the ring. Part of me wanted to grab it and get some power pulsing through my body, but the part that didn't trust Eros or anything he gave me won out. "But Eros didn't hurt me."

"And I won't." Eros bowed deeply. "I mean no harm, young Ayden. I even found your lady love first and pulled her from the raging waters. You and I both aspire to her safety and well-being."

Ayden glanced back at me.

"It's true," I told him. "At least about pulling me out."

"Forgive me, Eros." Ayden's tone held a snide edge. "But since you already threatened to kill her, I'm a little skeptical."

"Just a playful ruse."

"Playful?" Ayden laughed. "Why would I believe that a demon god would *aspire* the safety and well-being of the Divinicus Nex? That's crazy."

A cunning smile slithered onto Eros's lips. "So you do know."

I froze. Then my head swiveled slowly to study Ayden's profile, jaw set, lips pressed in a hard line.

I finally found my voice. "Which one of them told you?"

"No one told me." Ayden ground out the words, anger clipping the syllables. "*You* should have told me."

"Then how did you know?"

"How could I *not* know! We're trained to look for this kind of stuff. Granted, the girl aspect threw me at first. But come on!"

"Why doesn't anyone think to tell me they know?"

"Maybe some of us were hoping you would trust them enough to confide in them instead of being so paranoid and thinking I'd — *they'd* betray you. But I — *they* are really tired of waiting for that to happen and I — they — ah, screw it." Ayden kicked the sand. "Why didn't you trust me? I kept waiting and waiting, trying to give you every opportunity to reveal your big secret. But I got nothing!"

"That must have been frustrating," Eros said with great sympathy.

"It was!" Ayden said, then glared at Eros. "You keep out of this! But seriously, Aurora, did you really think I'd turn you in? Or I couldn't handle it? That it would scare me off? That's so insulting."

"Indeed," Eros said. "Perhaps I might suggest more open commun—"

"Shut up!" Ayden and I yelled. He shot flames at Eros.

The demon *poofed* away and reappeared on the opposite side. Ayden leapt around to stay positioned in front of me.

"What?" Eros looked flabbergasted. "Love and romance are my areas of expertise. I can help. And this is good." He made encouraging gestures with his hands. "Go on. Let's get it all out in the open."

Ayden tried to barbeque him again, *poof,* then turned to me. "You'd think you'd know by now how I feel. I mean, I'm willing to take control lessons from my *mom* just so I don't kill you when we…I…you know."

Eros popped up on our right, nodding with compassion. "I understand your discomfort."

"*His* discomfort? What about mine?" My voice squeaked. "Your *mom?*"

"Yeah, my *mom,*" Ayden snapped. "And it's a long and embarrassing story that I don't want to get into right now." He huffed. "If you don't mind."

"Seems a good place to stop." Eros rubbed his hands together. "I suggest you kiss and make up for now and we'll pick this up later. Perhaps *after* we've suppressed the unleashing of the whole demon apocalypse issue."

"We are not on the same side!" Ayden's entire body suddenly *whooshed* into flames as his hand shot out with a narrow but blazing blast of fire.

This time Eros didn't turn to smoke. But his sleeve did.

Flames caught on the frothy white pirate shirt, burning through the material and across Eros's skin.

Ayden clutched his chest and dropped on one knee, groaning. His flames blinked out. I moved toward him but saw Eros raise his eyes, furied with shock and outrage. The demon god looked ready to attack.

I snatched the ring out of the sand. Power surged again. Beams of light shot from the stone.

"Back off," I warned, either the power of the stone or my own fury boiling my blood.

Don't know what the ring did, but judging from Eros's expression just before he blinked out in a pink puff, I was holding some sort of nuclear bomb. He reappeared at the far edge of the forest, staring a murderous glare toward Ayden.

"I'll forgive you this once, hunter," Eros growled. "For you are protecting your lady love. As am I. We *are* on the same side. You will see."

"Doubtful," I spat.

Keeping my hand up, light still shining from the brilliant stone, I stepped closer to Ayden who remained down. I didn't know how to use the ring or how it would fare against the most powerful type of demon, but if Eros made one move against Ayden, I was willing to go down fighting.

I lowered my voice to a menacing rumble. "You'd better start helping rather than being a deceitful, selfish monster, or I'll call the Mandatum myself, cry 'Code Olympus' so fast and loud the Sicarius will bury you back in hell before you know what hit you. And whatever happens to Psyche…" I rolled a cold, indifferent shrug. "Well, that's on you."

I readied for a godlike wrath, but instead, a weary sorrow bled into Eros's green eyes.

"As it always has been," he said softly. Then he nodded. "As you wish."

And he was gone.

I chucked the ring into the sand and felt its energy drain from my body.

Ayden sat up. "That was gutsy. And hot. No wonder you're my hero."

I knelt beside him. Mostly because my knees gave out. Threatening supernatural demon gods was harder than it looked.

"What's wrong?" I said.

"Burns." He grimaced with pain. "Are they supposed to hurt this much?"

Fresh blood blossomed on his shirt. My skin iced. I fought to keep my expression neutral.

"Probably. But I know what to do." I swallowed hard and helped him to his feet.

Wincing, he put his arm over my shoulders, then looked down and frowned. "Did the God of Love propose to my girlfriend?"

"Not hardly." I picked up the ring half-buried in the sand. It lit up in my hand, then dimmed when I put it in my pocket. "I'll tell you later. Since we're being all honest, I should give you the heads-up on my guardian angel."

"Cute." He chuckled, but then saw my face. "You're not kidding."

"Nope. Oh, and I sent myself to the Waiting World. And stopped a bullet." Don't care what Gloria said.

"What?" he stumbled. "If you were in the Waiting World, why did you disappear instead of going into a coma like last time?"

I gave it some deep thought and came up with the brilliant conclusion of, "I have no idea."

He laughed. "Okay, tell me what you do know. I'm all ears. By the way, you asked *'which one'* told me you were the Divinicus. Who else knows?"

CHAPTER EIGHTY

It was still dark, only an hour or so before sunrise, as I hustled with Hex Boys in tow down the side of my house to the door to the garage. I rattled the knob. Locked. Stupid Aunt M and her *surprise*.

"Blake, open it," I said briskly.

Surely his powers included opening metal locks.

He glanced at the rest of the boys.

"This isn't a good idea," Ayden said. Again.

"I must verbalize my concurrence."

"That's all you've been doing, Jayden." For once I understood him.

"Involving outsiders is an ill-advised plan." Jayden barely contained his frustration. "I told you I could take care of the injuries. At closer inspection they're not that alarming. Frankly, I believe he's simply hypersensitive because he's never before had acquaintanceship with burns and the magnitude of malaise they incite."

Blake laughed. "Jayden just called you a baby."

The back of my eyelids itched with exhaustion. I'd had enough.

"Exactly, Jayden," I hissed. "He's never had burns, but somehow *I* burned him. And while Father Bancroft always fixes you guys with his healing power, he's skedaddled out of town, and you couldn't go to him anyway because you can't explain how Ayden could suffer an injury he's not supposed to be able to suffer without explaining *me* and you can't do that otherwise I'm in more danger, sooooo this is all my fault, my mess, and I'm going to fix it, which means using my dad because no matter how smart you are, he's been a trained physician for longer than you've been alive and short of magic healing powers, he's the best man for the job, so you will all wait in the garage while I get him." I inhaled a long breath and used every remaining ounce of energy to shoot all the boys my nastiest stare. "Now, shut up and follow along. Or I will make you pay."

They all shut up.

Except Blake.

"Pay how?" he whispered. "'cause I could totally be into this whole dominatrix thing you've got going on. Are we talking whips, leather, and handcuffs or—Ow! Logan, dude, you are seriously repressed. Want Aurora to spank you? Ow! That really hurt. Have you been working out?"

"I hate to say it," Matthias said with obvious reluctance. "I mean I *really* hate to say it, but she's right. He should be checked out by a professional. We just have to come up with a cover story."

"Already got one. Blake?" I gestured to the door.

Blake fluttered a hand. There was a click. I turned the knob and entered expecting the aromas of a construction site — metal, wood shavings, oil, paint — but it smelled clean, polished.

Huh.

Before I could tell them to beware of loose wires, there was a hum and lights flickered to life. Things started moving. I stumbled to a stop. Someone bumped into me. Then I stared open-mouthed at what used to be our garage.

Chapter Eighty-One

"She built this herself?" Tristan's voice still pinged with awe. "Incredible."

We were all checking it out—except Blake who'd started pumping iron with the weights in a far corner—but Tristan had been drooling over Aunt M's ridiculously complex system like a kid in a candy shop.

When the lights first came on, it just looked like a bunch of sleek, built-in cabinets. But as we watched, panels slid away, shelving and desktops seemed to feed out from the walls, and in moments, we were looking at an incredible computer setup that looked like it could monitor space satellites.

On Mars.

Several individual computer stations, another at a large desk with a couple of big screens on the wall, and all sorts of storage along with printers and oodles of electronic devices, most of which I didn't recognize.

"Wow," Tristan said as he and Jayden opened a cabinet and checked computer components. "This is next, *next* generation super-computer stuff."

Jayden nodded. "But how could she procure technology which shouldn't exist?"

"I think she builds it herself." I shrugged. "It doesn't look that different from other computers."

"But it is. Inside." Tristan carefully closed a cabinet door. "You know what this means?"

"My aunt went insanely overboard?"

Tristan's eyes sparkled with excitement. "That, *and* this system is not only faster and smarter, almost Artificial Intelligence kind of stuff, it's also," he paused as if waiting for a drumroll then whispered the next word like it was the answer to the universe, "*untraceable*. Even to the Mandatum." He dug in his pocket and pulled out the Mandatum tracker that had come off the lava gorilla demon. "I can find who last checked this out."

"Finally, some good news." Too exhausted for enthusiasm, I motioned for Ayden to take a seat. "Wait here. I'll get my dad. Tristan, hack away."

"With pleasure." Tristan rubbed his hands together then cracked his knuckles as he sat at the big desk, Jayden hanging over his shoulder. Tristan tossed the tracker to Logan. "Find the serial number."

I looked around. "Where's Matthias?"

The door to the kitchen burst open and Aunt M cried, "Ah *ha!*"

Tristan spun, fell out of the chair and onto his back, then raised his hands. "Aurora said I could touch it!"

Logan dropped the tracker and joined the rest of the boys who were backing toward the door.

"What are you doing here?" Aunt M demanded.

"Sorry," I said. "I didn't mean to ruin the surprise."

"No, I mean…" Aunt M roamed squinty eyes across the group, then jabbed a finger at me. "You didn't sneak out?"

I paled. "Well, duh. I'm right here."

Not exactly a lie.

"Oh." M pushed her glasses up her nose. "Ummm, might want to go tell your parents that. I already sounded the alarm."

"M!"

"I saw an empty bed," she said unapologetically. "Teenagers are rash, self-indulgent, and irresponsible. They don't consider the long-term consequences of their actions on themselves or others, so I thought you were out doing something stupid with your boyfriend." She lifted a shoulder. "Or kidnapped."

I heard the thumping of angry parent feet above. Great.

Aunt M gasped. "Holy hackers, Batman."

Tristan's hands were up again. "I didn't do it!"

M gave him a pained look as she waddled past and tried to lean over, her hand reaching down.

For the tracker.

I scurried over and picked it up. "It's nothing, Aunt M. I'll throw it away."

"Don't you dare!" She snatched it from my hands. "Oh, it's off." M laughed with more than a touch of hysteria. "Didn't think I brought any of these with me. Pregnancy. Fries the brain."

"This thing is yours?" I tried to snatch the tracker back, but M stashed it the one place I wouldn't go. Her bra.

"One of my many patented devices. Nobody else has them. Or can duplicate my special blend. I'll take care of it."

She headed back into the house. With the only credible lead I had on the traitor who was trying to assassinate me. The boys shared my panicked look.

"M, wait!" I rushed after her through the kitchen door.

Dad, his hair sticking out in every direction, was grabbing the phone. "I'll call Sheriff Payne!"

"Then Interpol!" Mom screeched. "They might have her out of the country by now!"

"Dad!" I caught his wrist.

Dad stopped mid-dial. Mom dropped the car keys and purse.

"Oh, yeah," M said as she passed them, "Aurora was in the garage."

Dad gave her a hard look. "You didn't think to check before waking me up telling me my daughter was off making me a grandfather?"

"How could I know she'd be ruining my surprise by playing with my work of art? She failed her computer class."

"I got a B!"

"B-*minus*. That's failing. And that would look good compared to what your grades look like now thanks to the Hex Boys."

Oron's wails carried through the house.

"Fantastic." Mom flung off her jacket and trudged upstairs.

Dad's voice was rougher than his morning stubble. "M, you've seriously got to—"

"Pee." Aunt M patted her stomach. "Baby on my bladder." She waddled out.

I went after her, scrambling for a plan to get the tracker back, but Dad stepped in front of me and caught my shoulders.

"We may have overreacted," he said. "But let's turn this into a positive opportunity to have a little heart-to-heart. I know we've had *The Talk* before."

Oh, no.

"Dad, I've really got to talk to Aunt M." I side-stepped him.

He blocked me. "And your mom's been encouraging you to be open to your feelings and trust the love."

"Yeah, we covered all that."

"But I just wanted to say that sometimes, at your age, love can often be confused with," he looked me dead in the eye, "lust."

Oh, God.

"Dad, please," I choked.

He wandered the kitchen. "I was a teenage boy once, too, and I know how they—"

"Ew. Just stop." I glanced at the door to the garage. It was closed. But…did I hear snickering? "You don't have to worry."

"Not that Ayden's a bad guy. But he *is* a guy and you're a beautiful girl and in the heat of the moment…"

If he only knew the irony of that statement.

I slapped my hands over my ears. "Lalalalalalala."

"Fine, fine. But you know what I'm saying. I want you to know that you can talk to me about anything. Even…" he took a deep breath, "sex."

"*Dad!*"

I opened the door to the garage, ignored the boys' vast ranges of amusement — of course they'd heard every humiliating word — and pointed at Ayden, slumped and pale, his shirt stained dark red.

"He's bleeding."

Ayden's smile was weak. "It's nothing, sir."

Dad's face went eerily neutral.

"Well, son, good thing you're a doctor. Oh, right. You're not. I am." Dad's voice was rimmed with steel. "Which makes you the patient and me *in charge*. Aurora, get my medical bag. Boys, get him in a chair at the table." Dad went to the sink and started washing his hands. "Because I'm willing to risk my entire career on the rash diagnosis that *that*," he indicated Ayden's chest, "isn't nothing."

Chapter Eighty-Two

With Oron asleep on Lucian's shoulder, the Lahey clan, minus Selena and Aunt M, along with the Hex Boys, minus Matthias, formed a quiet semi-circle behind Dad to watch him put the final touches on Ayden's wounds.

This wasn't how I'd dreamed of enjoying the sight of Ayden's half-naked form. Nope, the fantasy hadn't included the gaping crowd. And for that matter, it didn't have Dad treating Ayden for Aurora-inflicted, life-threatening injuries.

I felt like a walking death-ray.

But I felt a whole lot better with Dad caring for the injuries. I knew he'd save the day.

So with worry somewhat assuaged, I bit my lip and let my gaze travel over Ayden's shirtless physique, a welcome distraction from the sinking abyss of guilt.

As Dad worked on the wounds, which were mostly concentrated on his upper chest, Ayden tensed often, giving me a delightful view of the multitude of muscles that ripped his body into knee-weakening gorgeous. Sculpted biceps. Broad shoulders. Abs worthy of Michelangelo's chisel.

And that skin. I remembered the feel. Taut. Smooth. Warm and springing to life under my touch.

A faint heat stained my cheeks at the memory. When I realized Ayden had been watching my appraisal, my blush raged to inferno levels. I kept my eyes averted for the remainder of Dad's ministering.

Dad snapped off his plastic gloves. "You can put your shirt on now."

Crap. With the peep show almost over, I risked another glance — gaping stare — at Ayden's below-the-neck eye candy. Hey, a girl's got to take her kicks where she can. And Ayden half-naked definitely kicked in a serious chemical reaction.

Dad eyed Ayden's bloody shirt. "Then again, maybe not."

Mom said, "Lucian, go get one of your shirts."

"Sure, but, uh," Lucian shifted from foot to foot, "I don't think it will fit him. Might be…" He resettled Oron and said softly, "A little small. Maybe."

Luna snorted. "Ya think?"

"Shut up!"

"This'll be fine." Ayden reached for his shirt, but Mom whipped it away.

"Not a chance. Kids, upstairs and help me find something."

At their departure, Dad closed up his medical bag. "And these injuries are from a—"

I jumped in quickly. "Like I said, it was Jayden's super-duper laser thingy, which went crazy and Ayden got caught in the crossfire." I smiled tight, nerves wracked by Dad's stoic face. "Right, Jayden?"

Jayden ground his teeth, looking like he'd be happier chewing glass. "Right."

Ayden, Logan, Tristan, and Blake covered their mouths to hide the smiles at Jayden's expense.

"And with their parents out of town, they called me to come see you," I said. "Because you're the best there is."

Appealing to Dad's vanity couldn't hurt.

"Uh-huh. Okay, first of all, Mr. Smart Stuff," Dad settled a stern look on Jayden, "no more dangerous experiments."

"Understood," Jayden gave a stiff nod. "Because I now realize that despite my genius level IQ, a super laser—"

"Super-*duper*," Ayden corrected.

Jayden shot his brother a scathing glance. "A super-*duper* laser…*thingy* is apparently beyond my scope of cognition to control safely, and my days as a reckless operator of such high-level equipment are at an end."

Dad nodded, pleased. "Second, I'll need to treat the wound regularly so—"

"Done, sir," Ayden saluted. "I'll report to your house morning and night."

Dad glanced from me to Ayden. "How is that different from the last few weeks?"

"Dad!" I blushed.

He stood and picked up his medical bag. "And third, I'm taking you to the hospital right now for some tests. Make sure there isn't any internal damage."

The roaring litany of protests from the Hex Boys bordered on madness. They sounded like a gaggle of grannies, but Dad was having none of it.

"Sorry, gentlemen, that's the way it is, or right now, I call an ambulance and everyone's parents. I'm sure the sheriff would be happy to provide a police escort to the hospital."

Ayden pulled me aside. "Aurora, do something."

"Sure," I nodded. "Hey, Dad. Ayden says you're right and that you two should take his car to the hospital. He'll even let you drive. Right, Ayden?"

Ayden wiped his hand across his mouth so he could mutter behind it, "Not what I meant."

Through the gritted teeth of my huge smile I said, “I know.”

“That sporty red number?” Dad grinned. “Sweet. Let’s hit it, kemosabe.”

They were headed to the car, Ayden wearing one of Dad’s bright, flowery Hawaiian shirts, when Aunt M’s Taser went off in the side yard, and what sounded like a body thumped against the fence.

Someone screamed for mercy.

CHAPTER EIGHTY-THREE

Aunt M was in a fencing stance and had a white-knuckle grip on her Taser. Despite her belly, she managed to bounce on the balls of her feet. Van Helsing stood beside her, hissing, his hackles raised.

"Gotcha!" she screeched. "Stay down, you limey swine or I'll zap you again! Someone get me my tranq gun!"

"Saints and sinners, woman. I'm no pervert!" Jenny lay on his back, coat open.

He'd lost most of the arsenal, now wearing only the two guns in the shoulder holsters. But his overall look was still serial killer-esque.

Matthias raced around the corner. "No worries! He's with me!"

Aunt M didn't budge. "What's the son of the po-po doing hanging out with this lawless looking cretin?"

Matthias arrived breathing heavily. "He's, uhhh, an undercover cop. Old friend of my dad's. Detective Jen…nings is in town to surprise my dad for…his birthday."

"Then what's he doing skulking around here?" M wanted to know.

Matthias swallowed. "He came with me…while I checked on Ayden, whooo is doing good, yeah?"

"Will be in no time," Dad said. "I'll have to call and wish your dad a happy birthday."

"No!" Matthias laughed awkwardly. "You can't."

Dad frowned. "Why not?"

"He can't think anyone knows because..." Matthias's brain was spinning its wheels, but finding no traction.

Since I was always happy to help out my favorite teammate, I said, "Because Matthias is throwing him a big surprise birthday party and Jen—Detective Jennings is the surprise guest so he has to hide and we can't mention anything about this otherwise we blow the surprise. And the best part is we're all invited. It's sometime soon. He's still pounding out the details, but promises it will be huge bash. Big, *big* celebration. Right, Matthias?"

The Aussie's smile could freeze over Gossamer Falls Lake. Twice. "Absolutely."

"I love surprises." Dad nudged M backwards and pried the Taser from her fingers. Then he gave Jenny a helping hand-up. "Nice to meet you Mister, sorry, *Detective* Jennings. I apologize about the misunderstanding." He lowered his voice. "It's been a...difficult pregnancy."

"Not a problem." Jenny shot an acid look at M. She sneered back.

"Party?" Mom popped her head out from an upstairs window. "Can I bring something?"

"No," I said. "Matthias has it all handled. He's a big party guy."

"Yep. That's me." Matthias shoved Jenny around the corner. "Aurora, I did have a couple of party related questions." He grabbed my arm and dragged me along. As soon as we were out of sight, he whispered, "Come over to my house after school so Jenny can check out your powers. My dad will be gone today so the coast is clear."

"Why do I have to stay away from your dad? I like him." So charmingly opposite from the Angry Aussie.

"Because you'll bollocks the whole thing up. As usual."

"That doesn't tell me anything."

"Shut it and listen up." Matthias glanced over his shoulder. "Just deal with the exploding-light-blast thing. Don't tell Jenny you can take trips to the Waiting World or...have vision dreams about demons."

"Don't you trust him?"

"Sure. It's just..." The Aussie's eyes flicked away.

"You kinda don't."

"He has his own agenda. Can be a bit...unhinged when it comes to Artemis."

"You're saying he'd use me to get to her?"

"I'm saying don't give him the chance. See you after school. Don't be late, or I won't remind him to switch out the real bullets."

The first light of sunrise crawled over the horizon. The start of another stellar day.

CHAPTER EIGHTY-FOUR

In the kitchen, wearing purple polka-dot rubber gloves, because Mom thought even the most mundane utensils should be brazenly garish, I dumped the cooking pot into the sink's soapy water and scrubbed with vigor. I stared out the window, but even the shimmering lights of sunrise and the garden's joyful beauty and exquisite scents couldn't brighten my mood.

After Ayden and Dad left, I'd tried for a quick nap while Luna showered. But while I should've been — no, I *was* — exhausted, when I closed my eyes my mind went into overdrive, replaying the crazy night, then seemed to stick on the vision of Ayden lying near death.

My gut wrenched every time, shocking my system with adrenaline. I became wired, edgy, ready to explode. The "what if" scenarios were endless. It all could have gone so…fatal. And the common denominator of disaster?

Me.

Ironic how Aunt M and Bancroft wanted us separated because they worried Ayden and the boys posed a danger to me when the truth was, *I* was the real threat. To all of them. I mean, jeez, I'd brought demon gods to their doorstep. Something even the

Mandatum considered so cataclysmic it called for teams of Sicarius, their most lethal killers. And the boys wouldn't even call for backup.

Because of me.

Maybe M and Bancroft were right…just for the wrong reasons. Maybe, after we got through this, I should consider keeping my distance.

"Come on! If we leave early Mom will buy us real breakfast." Lucian grabbed his jacket off a kitchen chair and grabbed his backpack, then mine off the floor. "Meet you at the car."

"No!" I dropped the pan and tore my backpack off his shoulder.

"What's your problem?" Lucian said. "I'm being nice!"

So was I. Just couldn't explain that I'd stashed Flint's flaming slasher spheres in my backpack. Given all the psychos gunning for their pound of my flesh, I figured I should be armed. Didn't think the mini-bombs would activate on my little bro, but better safe than at the hospital sewing on severed limbs. I chucked the bag under the table.

"Sorry. Got a…delicate…art project in there. Meet you at the car." I pushed him out before heading back to the sink. "Best brother ever!"

"Weirdest sister ever."

"Aren't you done yet?" Mom bustled into the kitchen and grabbed keys off the hook. "We have to go."

"I'm trying," I scrubbed harder. "But burnt oatmeal puts up a heck of a fight."

"Leave it to soak. Oh, Dad called."

My heart tripped over itself. "How's Ayden?"

"Fine. Dad ordered him to skip school and rest." Mom walked over to me. "So you two are okay? He's not the reason you're looking zombie-esque, is he? Because I'll—"

"No, Mom," I interrupted before she got to the homicidal threats. "We're good. I just haven't had much," let's call it zero, "sleep."

"Are you having nightmares again?" She looked worried. "Should we get you back to the therapist?"

"No." I patted her arm. "Just give me a few days to catch up." And stop a demon apocalypse without getting us all killed.

"Fine. For now. Meet you in the car. Hurry." She kissed my forehead and disappeared into the foyer. "Selena, what are you doing? No, you can't go naked. I don't care if Bubbles is naked, pick up your clothes off the stairs and put them back on. Yes, right now. Fine, you can wear your shirt backwards. M! Come on. Luna and Lucian are already in the van." The front door opened. "Ayden? What are you doing here?" I dropped the pot. Soap splashed in my mouth. "You're supposed to be home resting. Dr. Lahey's orders."

"And I will," I heard Ayden say. "But first, I was hoping I could drop Aurora at school."

"Why is there a Maserati in my driveway?"

"I left my car with Dr. Lahey. He seemed to like driving it."

"I just bet he did," Mom muttered. "Mid-life crisis here we come."

"So, about Aurora?"

"Not sure," Mom snapped. "You made her cry the other day. I don't like that."

I cringed.

"Neither do I, ma'am."

"But you fixed it?"

"I believe so."

"Mm-hmm." Mom sounded skeptical. "If it happens again, I may start removing body parts." Pause. "Meaning yours."

"Yes, I understood that, ma'am."

Mom laughed. "Just kidding, silly." Then she screeched, "M!"

"Jeez, you're like a banshee." Aunt M said.

"You waddle like a duck."

"You do know these raging hormones make me prone to violent outbursts."

"Take your best shot, Daffy. Ayden, Aurora's in the kitchen."

"But no hanky-panky," Aunt M warned. "Because *this* is what happens and it ain't pretty. You should see the size of my—"

"Ooookay, M, move it along."

"Calm down, banshee, I was going to say *feet*."

"Aurora!" Mom yelled. "Ayden's here."

Gee. Ya think? I tried to peel off the gloves which weren't doing much for my look, but…too late.

Ayden sauntered into the kitchen. Underneath the leather jacket, he wore a fresh T-shirt. A thin layer of bandages was visible through the fabric, but no seeping blood. He looked very much alive and way more than well. Downright gorgeous, in fact. My knees trembled. Goosebumps rippled over every inch of my skin. I had to work to control my breathing.

Calm down, girl. Distance, remember?

"Couldn't resist coming by for another poisoning?" I lifted the pot from the water. "Aunt M's oatmeal should to the trick."

"No," he said smoothly, "I couldn't resist coming by for you."

Goosebumps re-fired in triplicate. How could I resist that? More importantly, why would I want to? Because, Aurora, being around you could get him killed. You should back off. Starting now.

"You look good." Some might say edible. I gritted my teeth and went back to scrubbing the pot. "But Dad's right. You should go home and rest. I'll get a ride with Mom when she gets back."

"Crap," he muttered. "I knew you'd do this."

"Do what?" I turned my head and jumped. He stood right next to me.

"Blame yourself. You're probably even thinking you should break up with me, keep your distance. From all of us."

That was creepy. I looked down. "Might not be a bad idea."

"Forget it. Horrible idea. Not happening." Ayden took my face in his hands. "I know what you're going through. I did the same thing. Even ran away from home to protect them."

My brow furrowed. "Who?"

"The people I loved." His hands slid down to my shoulders. "When I was young, learning to control my power, I burned plenty of them. Now you burned me. It happens. We all go through this, Aurora. Some more extreme than others. Look what happened to Tristan."

I threw the sponge. "That just proves how dangerous it is!"

"Of course it's dangerous, but running away won't solve the problem." He tipped my chin up with his knuckle and forced me to look at him. "Won't work anyway. You're not getting rid of me that easy."

"Not unless I zap you into the Waiting World by accident."

"Then I'd just wait for you to come rescue me," he said easily. "Hopefully wearing some skimpy leather outfit."

I snorted. "Nope. It's usually some stupid dress."

"Really?" he said with interest. "Short? Low cut? Think I mentioned I'm a big fan of your…various body parts. Will there be cleavage?"

A giggle skipped from my lips. "Shut up."

"Laughter. Much better." He cocked his head and smiled. "Look, we have families to help us cope with all this, you don't. So, I'll be the one to tell you."

"Tell me what?"

His hands cupped my neck, thumbs stroking along my jaw, his dark eyes full of compassion and reassurance as he spoke in a low, confident tone. "It's not your fault. You are perfect. You will master your powers." He kept his eyes locked onto mine. "And I'll be there every step of the way to help, because we're in this together and nothing, absolutely nothing you can do will ever scare me away." He placed a soft kiss on my forehead.

I leaned into the touch and closed my eyes. "But it's so risky."

"But it's so worth it."

"But I shouldn't."

"But you want to."

Yes I did.

My heart was skipping, my stomach fluttered. Classic signs. Sure, while I hated that I hurt him, being away from him was way more painful than I wanted to endure. Wimp.

He studied me for a long moment. "The truth is you want me as much as I want you. Let's just deal with it."

Deal with it? I had trouble saying it out loud.

Those sensual eyes of warm chocolate brimmed with promise, kicking my emotions into a triple arc loopty-loo of longing. I breathed him in. The scent of leather, sandalwood, and…Ayden was a blissful combination.

I released the breath in a sigh. "You're awfully sure of yourself."

He chuckled, "No, I'm awfully sure of you." He slid a hand down my arm. "Could those be…goosebumps?"

"Uh." I licked my lips. "No."

He gave me a wry smile as his fingers stroked my skin. "The evidence would seem to dispute your statement."

Wow, even lawyer-speak sounded sultry when it rolled off those luscious lips. Yeah, probably should've taken The Fifth on that one. My skin was as bumpy as a book in Braille, confessing all I could not say. And his long, slender fingers read every word.

"I'll take that as a positive sign." His eyes roamed my face and eventually landed on my mouth. His lips parted slightly and a heavy breath slipped through. His head started to dip, then paused. He closed his eyes briefly, seeming to rethink the move. Then he stood straighter, lifting my wrist to showcase the purple polka-dot glove. "And these? Extremely sexy," he said, eyes sparkling with amusement.

"Yeah, they aren't—"

My voice shook, so I shut up and immediately ripped off the gloves as if they were on fire. Well, one glove came off easy, but then the free hand was so sweaty — probably because my core temperature was through the roof — that I couldn't get a grip on the stupid rubber no matter how hard I tried.

"Allow me," Ayden said, grasping my arm to stop the spastic movements.

Then, holding my gaze hostage, he started to peel off the glove. Ever so slowly, inch by excruciating inch. As my skin was exposed, the floral scented breeze rustling through the window chilled the beads of sweat.

I shivered, but not from the cold. Something low in my belly pulled taut, quivering. I swallowed, then parted my lips in the hope that doing so would make breathing easier. Not so much. My bottom lip trembled so hard I had to bite it to quell the motion. The movement caught Ayden's eye, and passion darkened his look.

Finally easing the glove free, he tossed it into the sink with a small *splish* of soapy suds, and when his eyes finally released mine, my body was in such a hot and heavy overdrive, I almost slumped against the countertop.

Okay, I did slump.

Ayden gently twisted my arm back and forth, studying it from the elbow to the tips of my fingers, seemingly enraptured by this ordinary part of my anatomy. He pulled in a breath and blew out a soft gust of hot wind that dried any remaining moisture. Razor sharp chills splashed over my body in waves. My eyes closed.

When I could finally lift my lids, Ayden wore a knowing smile. I watched, mesmerized, as he lowered his lips toward the sensitive spot just inside my wrist. His lips parted, then I felt his mouth moving against my skin. And his tongue, hot and wet.

He was drinking me in. Or sucking me dry. Didn't matter. The languid sensation from his touch spread throughout, melting me like sugar in hot tea. I was hooked.

His mouth traveled down my arm. Teeth lightly trapping my skin while his tongue swirled some seriously seductive magic. Nerve endings sparked to dazzling attention. When his lips reached the sensitive inside of my elbow, I jumped, then nearly collapsed with a weak shudder.

His cheek grazed up my arm and over my collar bone, faint stubble tickling my flesh. His mouth and tongue found the curve of my neck. My hand slipped into the silk of his hair, fingers twisting, holding him steady, afraid he'd abandon this monumentally important task and leave me wanting. And, oh, how I wanted.

His mouth moved to the hollow of my throat and around the other side, tracing a choker of heart-stopping kisses. Lungs struggled for purchase. But, honestly, if this was the price for not breathing, I was willing to pay. In spades.

My other hand grabbed the edge of the countertop because my legs had officially liquefied.

Ayden caught my waist, lifting me up. My arms wrapped around his neck. He snaked one arm under my shirt and around my back, crushing me against him. He raised his head, eyes almost black. Breath had either stopped altogether or was panting too fast for me to keep track of. Who knew? Who cared?

His palm moved deliberately up my side, tracing the lines of my body. Finally, cupping my neck, his hand guided my head down so our foreheads touched. His mouth moved closer to mine. Almost touching. Almost.

I felt his breath. Hot. Wanting. Coming in short, halting pants. Just like mine. And when I could stand it no longer, my arms tightened, closed the distance, and pressed my hungry lips to his. And that sumptuous mouth that had already delivered such magic to my body, now worked miracles on my lips.

It was like fire bursting into my bloodstream. My skin burned. His mouth moved over mine, slow then fast, hard then soft. Molding against me. Tasting. Taking. Tongues tangling. He wouldn't let up. Over and over again, spinning the tension in my core wire-tight, building to a need that ached for release.

Ayden made a strangled noise then lifted me into his arms and swept me across the room to the kitchen table, almost slamming me onto the wooden surface, lips never leaving mine, kissing me with a ravenous hunger.

I felt it too.

My hands shoved the jacket off his shoulders. He let go of me long enough to let it fall to the floor. The edges of his pupils glowed. A ring of fire, burning from the outside in. His hands grabbed my face, tangled in my hair as he kissed me long and hard, ravaged my mouth. Almost brutal, but I couldn't get enough.

I arched my body against him. He groaned. So did I. He held me tighter.

My hands slid under his shirt, fingers kneading the curve of his back, feeling heat, muscles rippling underneath. He was like a candy store. I was on a sugar rush. And had yet to have my fill.

I leaned back. His body followed, kept flush against me, his lips devouring mine. My back on the table, I felt the weight of him, his body hard, tense, unyielding. My own screamed for…I wasn't sure what. But skin would help. Skin and close contact. *Closer* contact.

I rode my hands up his back, crushed him to me, wrapped a leg around his thigh. I careened in a whirlwind of longing. Clear thought had left the building and desire reigned supreme. Hallelujah.

His hands slid to my hips. I pressed closer, felt the heat between us intensify. It was a tangible thing. A running connection that—

Ayden jerked away. I reached for him, but with an angry oath, he pushed off me and backed away.

I sat up.

"No," he put out a warning hand. "Stay back." His eyes weren't glowing, they were actually filled with flames. Wisps of smoke lifted off his shoulders.

"I'm sorry," I rasped.

"Oh, God." The words wrenched from him. "Please don't. I'm the one with the…" his hand spiraled in the air leaving a thread of smoke, "problem."

I wiped sweat off my brow, tried to catch my breath. "I wouldn't call it a problem."

"Really?" His hand raked through his seriously messy hair. "I almost lit you on fire."

"Almost?" I said with a sly grin. "I *was* on fire."

He covered his face in his hands, but at least he was laughing.

I suddenly remembered his wounds—because I could finally think straight. "Sorry. I didn't even think. Does it hurt?"

He had a look of comical amazement. "Hurt? Oh, yeah. But not in the way you're worried about."

A blush drenched my cheeks. "Want some water?"

His hands slicked back across his skull. "A hose might be better."

I fanned my face. "For you and me both."

I scooted off the table, but Ayden stopped me, his look serious.

"Aurora, I didn't mean to…" he swallowed, cleared his throat, "I shouldn't have…gotten carried away. I want to get this right so…don't, ah, let me make you uncomfortable…or anything."

"Oh, it was uncomfortable, alright." I offered a coy glance. "But not in the way you're worried about."

He arched a brow. "Miss Lahey, are you flirting with me?"

"Well, hot stuff, if you have to ask, I'm not doing it right."

His laughter rumbled low, slithering heat underneath my skin. I pulled him to me, backing him against the table, risking a literal firestorm as his lips laid upon mine with a burning promise of—

"That's how babies are made!"

I reeled back and knocked over a chair. "Aunt M!"

"Sex kills!"

"M, seriously." Mom walked into the kitchen and rolled her eyes.

My aunt patted her belly. "It killed my waistline." Then she cackled.

Who was the banshee now?

"Ayden and Rory sitting in a tree," Selena sing-songed, "making b-a-b-b-y-n-g."

"Mom!"

"Selena," Mom admonished. "That's not the right spelling."

"Thanks, that's helpful." I picked up the chair. "What are you doing back?"

"Forgot Bubbles," Mom said.

"And I have to pee." M left the room with a parting, "Told ya."

Mom gave us a long look. "You two might want to fix your hair." She picked Ayden's jacket up off the floor and held it out to him. "Before you get in Ayden's car and follow us to school."

CHAPTER EIGHTY-FIVE

Technically, it was *my* car. The Maserati was my wildly extravagant gift from Ayden's parents for saving Jocelyn from being blown to bits. It was also the wildly extravagant gift my parents wouldn't, technically, let me accept. At least I got to drive it occasionally.

Like now.

Good golly, Miss Mechanical Molly, this baby could purr. Like a jungle cat on steroids. Sleek lines, seductive curves, sinewy engine muscle. It wasn't a machine, it was a monument of mechanical perfection, responding to my every touch.

Much like I responded to Ayden.

We were almost to school and neither of us had said a word. Then Ayden finally glanced my way once too often, and we both burst out laughing. Ayden was first to catch his breath.

"So that wasn't embarrassing at all."

"Not at all." I lifted a hand off the wheel to wipe away tears. "You sure that didn't hurt?"

"Trust me, I have no complaints. In fact, I'd be happy for you to pull over right now and we can continue our…conversation."

I blushed. "Yeah, except my mom hasn't stopped watching us in her rearview mirror. Not to mention Luna and Lucian."

In the back of the van just ahead, my brother and sister kept pointing at us and laughing hysterically. I waved. Live this down? Not a chance.

"Yeah," Ayden grinned, "except for that."

We followed Mom through the school's massive wrought iron gates, and while she dropped off Luna and Lucian, I headed for the parking lot.

"I'll search through Flint information at home for info on the stone," Ayden said. "Then the rest of the guys will help after school while you meet Matthias and Jenny to work on your powers. Unless you want me there?"

"No. Better enjoy that yippie-kai-yay party on my own. But thanks." I parked next to Jayden's car and leaned back in the seat. "So what are we going to do if or when we find the stone?"

"Use it to take down the gods and save you," Ayden said, stroking a gentle hand down my cheek.

I smiled. Over Ayden's shoulder I saw the students happily starting their day in the misty morning air draped over the Gothic mansion, oblivious to the impending catastrophic wrath of demon gods.

I sighed with more than a little envy. "Ever wonder what it's like to be normal?"

Ayden slipped a hand over my neck and pulled me close, lips brushing mine as he spoke. "I'd hate it, because then I never would have met you."

Just before they closed, embers flickered in his eyes, then his mouth completely covered mine, sending my insides into a flip-flopping turmoil of excitement. I started to return the kiss.

"You're to be recuperating at home!" Jayden stuck his head through Ayden's window.

Ayden pulled away with a growl. "Just dropping her off." He rolled up his window.

"Hey!" Jayden jumped back to avoid being strangled.

I laughed and when the window closed I asked, "Did you tell him you know about me?"

"Never got a chance. When he's not berating me for not resting, he's going on and on about those stupid Flint manuals. He's driving me nuts." Ayden rested his forehead on mine. "So I want to mess with him first." Ayden's lips captured mine. Hot and hard.

"That is *not* recess from activity!" Jayden banged on the glass. "Dr. Lahey clearly stated— Agh!" Logan yanked Jayden back.

With any chance of a romantic mood irrevocably destroyed, Ayden and I got out. Rather than listen to Jayden's tirade, Ayden slid into the driver's seat of his brother's car, and skidded out of the parking lot while I booked it into school. Not that things got much better there.

Because math, my first and worst class of the day, was about to get worse.

Tristan and I, both exhausted, were minding our own business—a.k.a., dozing off in the back of the room— when Katie — super-tall, super-jock from my PE class — who sat in front of me in this period, rapped my head with a rolled up newspaper. I was about to use it as a pillow, when Tristan snatched it from under my head.

A second later he said, "Oh, no. No, no, no," and when I looked up he was holding the paper in front of my face. "What did you do?"

I blinked to focus and read the headline.

"LONELY HEART LONE WOLF ACHING FOR TRUE LOVE'S KISS."

Underneath was a photo of Matthias — probably taken off Mika's stalker wall — and a story she had written about how he was…well, the headline says it all.

Oh boy.

I told Tristan, "It wasn't me." Exactly.

"Yes, it was," Katie said over her shoulder.

"Thank you, Katherine," I gritted a smile. "So helpful."

She turned in her seat. "You told us Matthias was in the market for a girlfriend. Now Mika is hellbent on making sure he's happy even if it isn't with her."

"For heaven's sake," I said. "I didn't think she'd do a whole story about it."

Then Tristan started yapping about how this overt publicity was exceedingly bad, and Katie started yapping that I better not be messing with Mika. At that point my math teacher, Mrs. Likes To Make Things Complicated, got ticked off and brought Tristan and I up to the white board — because superstar-jocks were apparently immune to public humiliation — to suffer unwarranted embarrassment by giving us some ridiculously hard problem to work on.

Mrs. LTMTC rapped a finger against the white board directly in front of me. "Will you be starting this problem any time soon?"

Beside me, working on his own equation, Tristan jumped at her voice and dropped his dry erase marker. He looked around dazed and confused as if just woken from sleepwalking. Which was entirely possible given how exhausted we both were.

"You betcha!" I gave Mrs. LTMTC a hearty thumbs-up. "I love algebra."

"This is pre-calculus."

The class snickered.

"Right," I said.

"If you don't start studying you'll be *back* in algebra," she told me.

"How fast could I make that happen?" I muttered under my breath.

More laughter from the crowd. Guess I didn't mutter.

"Quit making it worse," Tristan hissed.

Mrs. LTMTC glared and brushed by us to address the class. About what? Not sure. Not sure why I'd drawn a smiley face as an answer either.

All of my precious brain cells were geared toward solving the complex equation of staying alive. No way, I could do a calculation with more letters than numbers in my current state. I was borderline delirious.

Scratch that. I was beyond delirious.

I uncapped the marker trying to remember her morning lecture, but since I'd been napping through most of it, I wasn't having much luck.

"If the Greek demon gods don't kill me, my parents will after they see my report card," I whispered.

"Let's survive the Code Olympus first. And quit putting Matthias in the spotlight. We're supposed to stay low profile." Tristan stifled a yawn. "How am I supposed to write the answer without a marker?"

I pointed at the one he'd dropped on the floor. As he picked it up, I asked, "You have the answer?"

"No. Is that a smiley face?"

Crap. I'd drawn another one.

I scrubbed it off then focused on the board. It was slightly blurry. I wrote a few things down.

"I just want to blast Eros and Aphrodite and go to bed," I whispered.

"Less talking, more solving!" Mrs. LTMTC said. "Miss Lahey, are those Roman numerals?"

"Is that the correct answer?" I said.

"No."

"Then those are *not* Roman numerals." I wiped the Roman numerals off the board.

She turned to answer a student's question. Whew.

Tristan looked relieved, then returned to his problem. "If you could just track Aphrodite and get us her location—"

"We could take her down. I know."

"Uh, no." He paused to yawn. "I was hoping she was far away and we could anonymously tip-off the Mandatum to send some *Sicarius* team to take her down before she ever got close to us."

"Oh. That makes more sense." After a yawn of my own, I nearly broke the marker as I scribbled on the board and huffed, "Don't you think I've tried? But I can barely track demons that are as close as here in Gossamer Falls."

"I know. That gorilla demon was almost on top of you before you noticed. Long-range detection is much more helpful." Tristan focused forward as he actually started to gain traction with the equation. Smarty pants. "I wonder why you're different," he said absently. "Maybe it's just a training issue. Wish I knew more about how the Divinicus visions work."

"That makes two of us."

I started copying Tristan's work. Not proud of it, but I promised the universe I would study in earnest later. However, Tristan was right, figuring out how to utilize my powers long range would—

Wait a second.

My hand paused the copying. My head swiveled toward Tristan.

I stared. "What did you say?"

"That I don't really know how your Divinicus visions—" Tristan froze. Dropped the marker again.

"Oh, crap," I said.

He *knew.* Fear iced over my skin. I was sick of living with the terror of being found out. Waiting for the hangman's noose of doom to strangle the freedom from my life.

I grabbed his shirt. "Who told you?! Who else have you told?"

Tristan's hands flew to shield his face. "Don't smite me!"

My grip loosened. "Smite you?"

"Pearl said you threatened to smite her!"

"I don't even know what that means!"

"Neither do I! But I don't know what a Divinicus can do!"

Mrs. LTMTC rounded on us. "My goodness!" She gave a quick clap and smiled. "You solved it! Wonderful. Oh, there's the bell. Don't forget homework tomorrow. "

Student's gathered their things and I moved aside as everyone, including Mrs. LTMTC filed out. Interesting because there had been no bell since class had another thirty minutes before it was over, *and* we had definitely not solved the problems.

After they left I said, "What just happened?" Then I saw Tristan's eyes glowing with swirls of amethyst. I slugged his shoulder. "That was you? Why didn't you do that before she dragged us up here?!"

Tristan looked aghast. "It's against Mandatum protocol. And *unethical!"*

I rolled my eyes. "Oh, for crying out loud. What good are your powers if you don't use them?"

"They're dangerous. Rules are in place for a reason."

"Like turning in the Divinicus to the High Council?"

"I'm not turning you in." Tristan massaged his face. "Who else knows? I thought I destroyed all the footage."

"Footage?!" I shrieked and it echoed off the walls of the now deserted classroom. "You recorded me doing Divinicus…stuff?"

"Shh!" Tristan looked over his shoulder. "Not exactly. I just watched enough of our surveillance video of you around town dealing with demons, and along with everything else, I figured it out. For the record, you let demons get way too close. Once we get the traitor, you're much safer under the Mandatum's protection. Have your own Sicarius guard, round-the-clock security, eat lobster, be safe."

"Be ripped from my family," I snapped.

"Mandatum would protect them too." Tristan said. "Probably. They're basically royalty along with you."

"Royal *prisoners*." I rubbed my temples against the ache that threatened.

"But—"

"I will smite you!"

"You don't even know what that means!"

"But I do," said Mrs. LTMTC as she walked back into the room. "And it is never pretty."

Tristan was speechless, but I caught on.

"Eros," I said staring at the teacher's glowing pink eyes. "Quit doing that to people. It can't be good for them."

He, Eros, as the she teacher, gave a tired smile. "In this case, I thought it necessary to help. I had her send the class to the library to study rather than cause a commotion when they attempted to access their next class too early."

"Oh," Tristan said, still a little wide-eyed and very wary. "Didn't think of that."

"Of course." Eros nodded. "I must compliment you on the impressive extent of your powers. You captured the minds of the entire room in a moment of stress and almost without thinking. It is not surprising that as an untrained child, you had such a devastating effect upon your parents."

There was a beat of silence, then Tristan's eyes glowed bright purple and he shouted, "Don't you talk about my parents, you son of a—!"

The teacher immediately hunched over, cradling her head, moaning.

I grabbed Tristan's arm which, like his entire body, was shaking. "Tristan, stop. You're hurting *her*, not Eros."

Tristan blinked. Focused. He turned to me. His eyes still had enough of a faint glow that my head felt a sharp, painful twinge, and

I winced. He looked terrified, grabbed my shoulders as the light in his eyes died immediately. "I'm sorry. I didn't mean to. Please."

"I'm fine," I assured him, the pain gone, then I glared at Eros, or…the teacher—gads, this was confusing—who had recovered. "Is there a point to this visit other than causing trouble?"

"Apologies." Eros spoke with what seemed like grave sincerity. "I meant no offense. And I take none. You are quite right about my maternal parentage. It is her deeds about which I am here to warn you. Aphrodite is almost done gathering her reinforcements for the siege upon Gossamer Falls. She will arrive in two days time."

The teacher's eyes turned normal and she blinked, confused, steadying herself with a hand to the desk.

"What happened? Is everything okay?" she asked.

I caught Tristan's eye and said what we were both thinking.

"Not by a long shot."

Chapter Eighty-Six

Matthias sent a message he'd meet me at his house. So after school, more than a little nervous, I started driving to a fun-filled afternoon with a Hex Boy who hated me and his bloodthirsty godfather with a death wish who planned to use real bullets to jumpstart me into fighting shape in less than two days when a demon goddess planned to unleash a demon army. Or kill me trying. Who wouldn't be thrilled?

I steered around the last of many curves to Matthias's remote, high-on-the-mountain location and upon arrival was sure I'd made a wrong turn somewhere because…

I expected Matthias's house to be loaded with cobwebs, dripping with bones of his victims, and generally covered in creepy. Probably because I figured it would match his pathological morose, glum, and downright nasty temperament.

I was wrong.

Surrounded by wildflowers and fruit trees, the two-story log cabin was compact, neat, and downright quaint. It was stained pale blond with hunter green shutters and had a covered porch that wrapped around the entire first floor, which boasted pieces of colorful outdoor furniture cushioned with bright floral prints. Bird feeders hung from the eaves where small winged creatures flitted about, including a lone hummingbird that sipped red liquid from a giant, hanging plastic flower, sunlight glistening off a kaleidoscope of iridescence feathers. From the weathered stone chimney, smoke curled a lazy trail heavenward.

I was wrong because I'd forgotten a very important aspect of the Aussie's life. The man who was standing on the porch. Even though he wasn't supposed to be here.

It was easy to appreciate Sheriff Payne's forty-something gorgeous exterior. He stood almost six-three, broad shouldered, square jaw, hazel brown eyes, and a million dollar smile. Honestly, ladies in town practically lined up to confess to crimes just so they could be interrogated by Sheriff Hunk and have a chance at a strip search.

But while the smile could light up a room — and the female population's libido — he socialized only with the Hex Boys' families. And the gold wedding band he wore kept would-be suitors at bay.

He ran a tight law enforcement ship, seemed to have a sixth sense, and consequently, what little crime ever nested itself in Gossamer Falls was quickly solved and shut down.

I gripped the Maserati's wheel, instinct screaming for me to pull a fast one-eighty and book it out of here. The boys had made it clear I wasn't supposed to talk to him. But it was too late for a great escape because seeing me, he bounded down the steps, delivering that high-voltage smile, slapped the hood of the car, and motioned for me to pull next to his SUV. My door opened before I shifted into park.

"Well, this day just turned into a right beaut! Welcome!"

And that heavy Australian accent only added to his charm. How could he be dangerous?

I smiled and waved, which in Sheriff Aussie language must have meant pull me into a bone crushing hug. Then he held me at arm's length, his look suddenly ominous.

"I know why you're here," he said gravely. "And I've got to say, this is a serious offense."

Crap, he was already on to me. I was going away. To the slammer. A deep dark dungeony slammer. I readied to make a run for it.

His face lit up. "A serious offense that you didn't come sooner!" He squeezed my arms. "Look at you, then. Color in your cheeks, sparkle in your eye. Is that for a certain young man?"

"Uh…"

"You are here to see Matthias, right?"

"Yeah, but—"

"I knew it!" He stepped back and shook a knowing finger. "I could tell something was up in the girl department. I am the sheriff after all. Hot-diggity. But where are my manners? Come in, come in." He led me onto the porch, babbling away as he ushered me into the house.

I gazed wistfully over my shoulder, looking for a way out without raising any red flags. If the guys had just *told* me why I should steer clear. Idiots.

"I'm out of practice." Sheriff Payne laughed and squeezed my elbow. "We rarely get visitors. Partly my fault. It's hard to be social and be sheriff. Never know who you might have to arrest, right? Matthias should be home soon. Can I get you some tea? No, I bet you're a lemonade gal. I make it myself. From our own tree. Sit. I'll get you a glass."

So far so good. He was so chatty, I wouldn't even need to talk.

He pulled out a chair at the pine table in the kitchen which opened up from the living room and offered a stunning view of the valley and shimmering lake below. The house was full of plaids and flannel, leather furniture and general guy appeal, although tidy and clean, with a few feminine touches like floral pillows and lace curtains. The walls were lined with shelves, all stuffed to the brim with books on top of books. The fire in the stone hearth warded off the coming evening chill.

How could the Angry Aussie ever be angry surrounded by this?

A blur of slobbering fangs and claws flew out of nowhere and attacked me. I screamed.

"Sadie, off!" At the sheriff's command, the demon sat.

I could still see its fangs.

And tongue.

Because it was smiling. Tail wagging a solid *thump-thump* against the wall, and admittedly, the look was friendly.

"You have a German Shepherd?"

Sheriff Payne scratched behind the dog's ears. "Belgian Malinois. She's French. Oo-la-la. Retired police dog, but," he touched the tip of her nose, "her sniffer still works like a champ. Doesn't it gorgeous." He ruffled her fur. "Don't like dogs?"

"I have a cat."

"Oh. Don't worry, she'll figure it out."

Sadie lay down, dropping her chin on her paws, soft brown eyes tracking my every move. Each time I glanced her way, the bushy tail swept the floor, but she stayed put.

The sheriff set my tall glass of lemonade down on an actual lace doily. He sat across from me as I took a sip. Definitely homemade and yummylicous.

He smiled. "So how long have you and Matthias been going out?"

The lemonade spewed from my mouth. And nose.

Not so yummy.

"Whoa!" Sheriff Payne jerked back then jumped up to get some napkins—actual linen. "Sorry. Didn't mean to scare you. I'm so used to interrogating, I tend to get right to the point."

Sadie's head had come up in the commotion, but it dropped back down. Tail sweeping with vigor.

I cleared my throat and patted my chin dry. "You didn't scare me. It's just…I'm sorry." This was awkward. "Matthias and I aren't dating."

"Oh." He sat back, his face thoughtful, shadowed with disappointment. "I was sure he had someone. But…you sure?"

I snorted, then did my best to cover it with a strangled cough. "Very sure."

"So much for my detective skills." He drummed his fingers on the table.

"Not that he isn't really handsome." I felt bad now and wanted to make it up to him. How could I go wrong complimenting his son?

"He is quite the looker." The sheriff had a faraway look. "Gets that from his mum."

Maybe some, but not all, Sheriff Hot Stuff.

"And he's so charming."

Who said that? Me? Oh, brother. Talk about a stretch. But the reference to his wife had the sheriff looking all melancholy.

"I mean he's just so gallant and suave." Now I couldn't shut up. "All the girls at school are dying to go out with him." That had some truth to it. "He's probably just trying to decide, you know, which one of the many ladies to date." That didn't.

I looked up from playing with my napkin. Sheriff Payne was giving me an odd look.

"You think Matthias is charming?"

"Sure!" I used over-the-top enthusiasm to cover the lie. Matthias so owed me for this whopper. "And generous and…gosh , I could go on and on. Just a ray of sunshine in everyone's day." At least Selena probably thought so. The sheriff still looked strange so I asked, "Is something wrong?"

"Not at all." He shook his head, but his expression morphed. The faraway look and melancholy vanished as he focused on me. I suddenly felt like a new-found species being studied by the mad scientist.

And knew I'd made some sort of terrible mistake.

I squirmed, started to rise. "Maybe I should go."

"No, please." The sheriff laid a hand on my wrist. The touch was light, so why did it feel like a shackle? I sat back down. His mega-watt smile was back. "Matthias should be here any minute. Why did you say you wanted to see him?" He settled back in his seat, arms crossed, eyes appraising.

Okay, definitely felt like I'd waded into quicksand.

"I didn't. Say." I fiddled with my napkin. Sipped lemonade.

He kept quiet, his expression genial, but both he and Sadie watched me closely.

Probably some interrogation technique. Stay quiet so the perp — that would be me — spilled her guts. The silence was a big open chasm that I had an overwhelming desire to fill. I pinched my mouth shut and looked around for a distraction.

"Oh, look." I jumped to my feet and grabbed a picture off one of those old library cabinets. The ones with lots of mini drawers that held index cards. "Is that Matthias? He looks so young. And who's—" Now, looking at the others in the photo, I didn't know what to say.

An eight- or nine-year-old Matthias with shaggy waves of hair tousled by the wind stood between a younger Sheriff Payne and a dark-haired woman. Who knew dark and morose Matthias could look so giddy and carefree with a brilliant smile that rivaled his dad's and the dimples in full force.

The woman had Matthias's eyes, blue so pale they stuttered into gray. She wore old-fashioned horn-rimmed glasses on a pretty face full of soft angles, and her wavy hair pulled into a severe, short ponytail.

On Matthias's shoulders perched a young girl, maybe five, whose arms were wrapped around the necks of the two adults. She'd been caught mid-laugh, eyes squinted nearly shut, mouth open in an ear-to-ear grin. She had the woman's round face, but her hair was straight and fawn brown like the sheriff's.

He walked over and stood next to me.

"That's Tilly, my wife, Matthias's mum, and Bindi, his sister. We were at the park near our old house on Sydney Harbor." He pointed. "There's the Harbor Bridge and the Sydney Opera House."

My fingers trailed over the glass. "What a beautiful family," I said softly. "And so happy."

"Thank you," he nodded. "Yes, it was devastating when we lost them."

My stomach churned like it was tumbling shards of ice. "Sorry. I didn't mean to…" Remind you of the most horrible time in your life? Nice, Aurora.

"No worries. Lots of good times to remember." With a delicate touch, the sheriff placed the picture on the cabinet and flashed a bitter smile. "Matthias wasn't always so…dark. He was a sweet boy. Always laughing. Pulling practical jokes."

Yeah, that one didn't track. But one thing was for sure. This happy, adorable, giddy boy did not kill his family.

"Adored his mum and sister," the sheriff continued. "I'm glad he spends time with Selena. Bindi wasn't much older than her when…things happened, so it's good for him."

"Selena adores her BFF, Matty," I smiled. "When he's with her he's like a different person. All sweetness and light. Hardly recognizable."

"I thought you said he was charming?"

I looked away from his wry grin. "Oh, he's, uh, *painfully* charming."

"Nice save," Sheriff Payne chuckled then his brow knitted. "Selena calls him Matty? Unbelievable."

"Is that bad?"

"No," he said quickly, but that melancholy look was back. "It's just…that's what we called him. But once his mum and Bindi were gone, he insisted on Matthias. The fact that he lets you—"

"Oh, no. Only the rest of my family gets that privilege. If I did it, he'd have my head." I grinned. "In the most charming way possible, of course."

"Of course," he grinned back. "But either way, it's a good sign. So make yourself at home. I'll be outside. You can wait in his room. Upstairs, second door on your right. Give us a shout if you need anything."

He pulled me into a quick hug and headed out. Sadie padded over to nuzzle her cold, wet nose in my palm then trotted after him.

I looked around. "Okay, that was somewhat…unusual." I let out a long breath and wiggled my shoulders to release the tension. "But you did good, Aurora. Whatever they were worried about, wasn't an issue. It's all good."

I gave myself a mental pat on the back and noticed the staircase.

Matthias wouldn't want me going into this room. Nope, breaching his private inner sanctum would be considered totally off limits. He'd freak.

I looked left. And right. Then bolted up the stairs two at a time, raced down the hall, and skidded into his open doorway.

That's when things got downright weird.

Chapter Eighty-Seven

I stepped in slowly, tentative, but an Aurora booby-trap didn't skewer me as I crossed the threshold. Things didn't start out weird. Just surprising.

Polished wood planks covered the walls and floor, with throw rugs placed here and there. The ceiling pitched up at a steep angle and held a large skylight. Artwork — looked like English landscapes of all things — hung around the room except where built-in bookcases covered one wall, the shelves holding books lined in neat rows and a few framed photographs. Across from a bay window with a window seat sat an elegant mahogany sleigh bed with end tables on either side holding matching Tiffany lamps of rich colored stained glass. There was an old trunk at the foot of the bed, and not far from the open door of a closet stood a large armoire.

Built into the far corner was a quaint, river-rock fireplace with a leather rocking chair in front that had a Tiffany floor lamp curving over the back. It made a great reading nook, evidenced by the book and coffee mug sitting on the hearth.

The room was clean, not a dirty sock in sight — so much the opposite of Lucian's disaster of a room — as well as warm, cozy, and inviting — so unlike Matthias's disaster of a personality.

The bed was made to military specks, crisp and smooth. I ran my hand over the quilt which smelled freshly laundered and was clearly handmade by someone with great skill. The soft fabric was worn in several places where a careful hand had stitched and patched repairs, some old, some new, but all done with fastidious precision.

The quilt design was a stunning, elaborate mural depicting three distinct Australian landscapes. Dry Outback, tropical rainforest, and sparkling coastline artfully blended from one to the other, with intricate details of flora and fauna so cleverly integrated, it was a delight to discover something new the closer you looked. The edge was bordered with framed blocks, each depicting a native animal. The usual koala, kangaroo, crocodile, platypus, along with creepy spiders, snakes, and lizards, as well as ocean animals, colorful birds, and several creatures I couldn't identify.

I moved to the end of the bed and opened the trunk. A pleasing floral scent wafted up. More quilts in a kaleidoscope of colors were folded neatly. On top of them was a well-stocked, velvet-lined wooden sewing box along with several books with blank covers.

I opened one of the volumes and found pages filled with handwriting. Each entry started with "Dear Mum," and ending with "I miss you. Love, Matty."

"Oh, jeez." I snapped the book closed.

Wow. Diaries. Matthias's deepest thoughts and emotions.

I could finally have some serious leverage—uh, I mean, finally understand his innate complexities. So tempting.

I opened up the volume I held, then closed it and checked a few more.

No, I wasn't reading them. As much as I hated him, that would be way too wrong. I have some scruples—yeah, I know, surprised even me—but I wanted to confirm a theory, and I did.

Matthias had started these diaries *after* his mom died. It was an accounting of his daily experiences since he lost her, as if he was away at boarding school and wanted to keep her updated on his life.

I replaced the diaries with care, closed the trunk lid, and flopped myself into the leather rocker, ruminating on the unfathomable depths of The Obnoxious One.

I rocked back and forth in the comfy seat. On each of the curved wooden armrests, initials had been scratched with a childish hand. My fingers traced over M.P. on the left and, with a sense of deep sadness, over B.P. on the right.

Ugh. This was getting to be too much.

Looking for a distraction, I lifted the mug off the hearth and sniffed. Tea, not coffee. The book looked old. I picked it up, read the title, and laughed.

"Yeah, right," I said to no one.

I opened the book. And stopped rocking. My jaw dropped, but I clamped it shut, afraid to drool on this precious gem in my hands as I delicately turned pages to confirm that…

Holy mother of romance literature.

It was Jane Austen. *Pride and Prejudice*. Published 1813. A *first* edition.

"No way." I slapped it shut. Then cringed. "Sorry." I petted the cover with reverence before setting it back on the hearth.

My wide eyes roamed the space and settled on the bookcases. I shot up and across the room so fast the rocker swung forward hard, caught some air, and *thumped* back. With mounting disbelief and confusion, my gaze scrambled over the titles on the shelves. I pushed aside some framed photos of a young Matthias and his family and pulled out a few books to confirm that…

Son of a gun.

I slumped my butt on a lower shelf and leaned my head back, trying to make sense of this revelation. The artwork on the wall next to the window caught my eye. I moved in for a closer look. Extravagant English gardens surrounded a grand manor house, but it wasn't a photo or painting, it was a framed, glass-covered, expertly crafted needlepoint.

I checked the rest of the "artwork" and sure enough. All needlepoint. Most were large canvases of majestic British mansions which somehow seemed vaguely familiar, but there were also a couple of very small works of koala bears done with more beginner-level, childlike talent.

I heard shouts from outside and dashed to the window. Too engrossed in my Goldilockyness, I hadn't heard Matthias drive up. Out front, he argued with his dad. Hands flew in all directions.

"Why wouldn't I invite her in?" Sheriff Payne sounded exasperated. "Reece is constantly grumbling about the boys always being at the ranch."

Reece? Oh, Blake's giant of an uncle who, along with Blake, ran their dude ranch. Hex Boys weren't big on me talking to him either.

"I don't go to the ranch." Matthias pulled his hair back. "He should tell them to leave if he doesn't like it."

"Of course he likes it. He'd like it even more if you were there too. And I'd like it if you guys were all here sometime. But they never come here. So when we get one guest. A girl even. A nice girl that you're hanging out with—"

"We're not hanging out."

"I know you're not romantic, but you have been hanging out. And despite what Bancroft thinks, *I* think it's great. As long as you're careful."

"How do you know we're not…romantic?" Matthias made the last word sound like a flesh-eating virus.

"She told me. Which is another thing—"

"*Told* you? You interrogated her? And asked about us being *romantic*?"

Yep, flesh-eating virus again.

"Yes, Matthias. I tied her in a chair in the basement, stuck a light bulb in her face, and tortured her until she talked. Goodness, give me a little credit."

"That's not what I meant."

"It was a friendly conversation."

"You don't have friendly conversations."

"Maybe I would if you ever had friends over to have friendly conversations with. She says you have lots of girls at school who like you. There's no rule that says you can't date."

"Are you kidding me?" The Aussie's voice hit a new high. "There are no girls."

"That did seem iffy. Which reminds me—"

"Is this about that bloody newspaper story? She'll pay for that, trust me. Where is she now?"

"In your room, but before you—"

"What!" His pitch could shatter glass.

Matthias turned to glare at his bedroom window. I jumped back and slammed against the bookcase. Did he see me? I wouldn't look, but heard feet running. A book tumbled down over my shoulder. I scrambled to catch it.

"Matthias, I need to talk to you about something!" his dad yelled. "Bloody hell."

Footsteps pounded up the stairs. I'd just finished shoving the fallen book in place when the Aussie filled the doorway. His frantic eyes swept the room as he flipped back the waves of hair that fell over his forehead.

"What did you touch?"

"Are you going to spray everything for cooties?"

His pale eyes narrowed. "Maybe."

"Then I touched everything."

"Very funny." Beneath his dry tone was an underlying thread of panic as his eyes kept darting to the trunk then the bookcases. "You're early."

"No, you're late."

"You should have waited for me outside. And never, *ever* have talked to my dad. I told you to stay away from him."

"Mr. Hospitality doesn't exactly take 'no' for an answer. You said he was supposed to be gone."

"He was. He's acting weird." Matthias was fidgety. "I think he knows something. What did you tell him?"

"Nothing. But you can tell me something." I stepped closer to the bookcase and ran my hand along the edge. He tensed. "About your…eclectic, shall we say, choice of reading material." My knuckle tapped my chin. "I kind of get the Greek epics, Shakespeare, Edgar Allan Poe — for sure — and even Mark Twain, but—"

"Samuel Langhorne Clemens."

"Who?"

"Never mind."

I knew there was an insult in there somewhere just wasn't sure where, so I ignored it.

"Anyway, what has me completely stumped is the complete library of classic romantic literature." I hoped my smile had a Cheshire Cat vibe. "There's Jane Austen and the Bronte sisters just to name a few. Even first editions of *Pride and Prejudice*, *Jane Eyre*, and *Wuthering Heights*."

He sighed and leaned against the doorjamb. "Your point?"

"My *point*? Come on. You have to admit these are some strange titles for any guy, but you? What's the story?" I laughed. "Get it? *Story*. Because—"

"It's none of your business," he snapped.

I meandered around the room, gesturing at the walls. "And these needlepoints?"

As soon as I moved, Matthias nearly sprinted to the bookcase, immediately honing in on the book I'd knocked over. He grumbled something under his breath, and taking the ancient volume from where I'd replaced it, he put it somewhere else. Its *proper* place, I'd guess. Then he took the photos I'd moved aside and arranged them in their original positions.

"Come on, Matthias," I said with a wicked laugh. "I've got you now. Spill your secrets."

I was all but rubbing my hands with glee thinking how I could use this knowledge against him when his shoulders slumped. His hand raked violently through his hair. When he finally faced me his expression was so desperate and defeated I almost felt sorry for him.

"The guys don't know. Aurora, please, don't tell them. *Please*. They'd never understand. I'm begging you." He dropped his face in his hands.

"Um." Oh, jeez, were his shoulders shaking? Yikes. "Ummm. Okay. Yeah, sure." Should I pat his back or something? No. He might bite. And I wasn't sure he'd had all his shots.

His head came up, his face red. He squinted a hard look, part suspicion, part fear, part hope. "Are you playing with me? You're going to tell them, aren't you?" He groaned. "Sure you are! Now everybody can have a good laugh at the sad, lonely, pathetic idiot."

"No, I promise." Keeping the Aussie's secrets? This was new. "I won't tell."

His expression turned to relief. "Thanks. I'll tell you sometime. And I'll tell them. Just...not yet." He stood tall, pulling himself together. "Besides, we have too much to do. Jenny's ready to check out your powers. And don't worry. Most people live through his training."

"*Most* people?"

"Yup. Let's go."

CHAPTER EIGHTY-EIGHT

Matthias changed in the closet, ditching the T-shirt, jeans, jacket, and boots for sweats and running shoes. "I think Jenny was kidding about the bullets."

Oh, that made it all okay.

He glanced up from tying his sneakers, his look smug. "Gonna chicken out?"

"Of course not."

Yes, please. Where's the official Chicken Out form?

"It's just that I've got to be home for dinner or Mom's got this whole Interpol thing happening."

He rose and slapped my back. "No worries, mate. You have my word. Dinner. On time. Let's hit it."

I followed him downstairs. Heading to my doom?

"Dad! Aurora and I are going out."

Sheriff Hottie came out of the kitchen, a dish towel flung over his shoulder. "Like on a date?"

I laughed. Matthias cringed.

"No, Dad. Like on a workout. And you wonder why I don't tell you anything."

"Come again, Aurora. I make a mean key lime pie."

"Yeah, yeah." Matthias grabbed my elbow and steered me out the door. "Actually, it is delicious. Wouldn't want to waste it on you.'

"Bye, guys. Have fun." The sheriff waved. "Love you, Matty."

"Love you t—" Matthias froze. Paled.

He turned to say something to his dad, but the sheriff had wisely ducked back into the kitchen out of sight. Which left me as the sole recipient of "Matty's" squinty-eyed glare. A creepy smile slithered onto his mouth, his voice cold menace.

"Let's go have some fun."

Chapter Eighty-Nine

"I'm not having fun!"

The switchback trail was near vertical, considered one of the most difficult hikes on the mountain.

"But you are keeping up. At least your training's done some good."

I was proud of myself for staying on Matthias's tail. With minimal wheezing. But it wasn't an accident. The guys had taken me up here several times.

Matthias stopped so fast I bumped into his back. He slapped a hand over my mouth, and ducked us out of sight off the path. "Quiet," he whispered, then snatched up a broken branch and shimmied it over the ground.

I heard voices just as the man and woman came around a sharp corner of the trail. The size difference was comical. Blake's Uncle Reece who could be mistaken for a grizzly, and Logan's mom, the petite dance instructor who barely breeched five-foot—in heels.

"So you lost the trail. Big deal." Logan's mom patted Reece's elbow, because that was as high as she could reach. "Maybe it was just some random hiker who didn't know that he shouldn't be going through your property. Maybe checking out the hot springs. Probably already gone. Too bad. I was in the mood for a rumble. Retirement can be so boring."

"A random hiker couldn't lose me," Reece said with indignation. "No, this was a hunter. A good one. I'll alert the others and restart tracking tomorrow." After they passed us, he pointed to the ground. "Look, Matthias and that Lahey girl were up here recently. Are they dating now?"

Matthias muffled a pained noise.

"She's supposed to be dating Ayden. Bancroft isn't happy. You know he's been complaining. Personally, I think it's been good for the boys. Logan's come out of his shell somewhat."

"I agree," said Reece. "A break from Mandatum and hunting is healthy. Although, there is a theory…"

The voices faded.

"They must be tracking Jenny." Matthias headed up the trail and I followed.

"Should we warn him?"

"He'll already know."

We picked up the pace and after a dozen more switchbacks, reached the top. A small, flat meadow surrounded by towering trees with a sheer cliff on one side, a heart-stopping drop into a rocky gorge of raging rapids. He walked close to peer over the edge. My knees tingled, suddenly weak. Heights. Not my thing.

"Be careful." I leaned over, resting my hands on my knees. "Where's Jenny? How is this helping control my ability?"

"Over here." Matthias gestured for me to join him. "I'll show you."

"No thanks."

"Want help or not?"

"Fine." I trudged over, using sideways baby steps. Sweat oozed from my pores.

Matthias held out a hand. After a moment's hesitation, I took it.

His other hand snapped around, gripped me hard, and with a great heave, he threw me off the cliff.

Chapter Ninety

Freefall.

Arms and legs flailed. Nothing to stop me. In seconds I'd be dead. Murdered by the Aussie.

Before I'd plunged a few feet, breath deserted my lungs. My throat closed. The white water below, the jagged rocks jutting through like spiked teeth of a ravenous monster, all rushed toward me, and I didn't even have the luxury of screaming.

I'd trusted him, and now I was going to die.

Icy wind whipped my face, but inside heat flashed. Pressure squeezed my body. My hands, grasping at nothing, began to glow and light shot out, hitting the water below, blasting it into the air like a geyser and shattering rock. But all I got was wet. Nothing stopped my fall.

I picked up speed, dropped closer to the river, the spray of the rapids tingling against my burning hot skin. Too frozen with fear to even close my eyes for the impact, I still flailed my limbs in a useless attempt to stop the splatter of my body on serrated stone poking through the river's rushing currents.

My hands glowed hot again. Maybe I could blast my way to China?

Something slipped around my waist. Tightened. With a violent wrench on my gut, my body jerked once, and I glided into a smooth arc over the raging rapids, cold water spraying my face as I sailed just inches above the jagged rocks of the gorge.

Suspended by a black rope, it swung me like Tarzan back up and onto the cliff where I was dumped in a quivering heap on a barren patch of rocky soil. I tasted dirt.

Frantic wheezing and choking finally expanded my lungs. My vision cleared. Matthias stood several yards away near the top of the cliff, feet planted wide, holding the other ends of the two ropes still wrapped around my waist. The ropes which had caught me mid-fall, and carried me to safety.

But not ropes. His shadow whips. And the Aussie looked extremely pleased with himself.

"How dare you!" I raged.

I tried to get up but failed. My legs were boneless. I flopped over.

The whips still squeezed around my torso. With a feral growl through gritted teeth, I made it to my knees and seized them with every ounce of strength I could muster. Beneath my glowing hands, the whips sizzled. I lifted them high above my head and yanked down with a fury, whipping the Aussie's weapons in an undulating snap right back at him. I felt heat and tingling across my shoulders, down my arms, then sparks fed out my hands and onto the black lines.

It was as if I'd lit a fuse.

White light crackled along the dark lines that tethered me to Matthias, devouring the darkness at a rabid pace. When it reached the end, an explosion of light and showering blue white sparks broke the contact between us and catapulted Matthias backwards through the air.

I groaned and rolled around clutching my belly. The whip had stopped my fall but it felt like my stomach had been wrung out by the hands of a giant, twisted till my guts wanted to spurt forth. Hair and dirt stuck to my sweat-streaked face. And I stunk. But considering the alternative, I was in great shape.

My mouth split into a crazed smile. “Take that, you Aussie dingo.”

I hoped that was an insult. I expected a snappy, remorseless comment from the heathen who nearly killed me, but there was only silence. That…wasn’t right.

“Oh, no.” I pushed to my hands and knees. “No, no, no, no.” Crawling was my only mode of travel, but it got me to Matthias’s prone, motionless form.

He was face down so I rolled him over. Shook him. He didn’t move.

“Don’t you dare!” Fighting panic, I laid my ear on his chest.

Th-thump, th-thump.

“Thank God.” I leaned over his face. Was he breathing?

“Try to give me mouth-to-mouth, and I will throw up.”

I sat back on my heels and let relief wash over me.

“You wouldn’t be the only one.” I blew out a heavy breath. “Jeez! You scared the dickens out of me.”

He sat up on his elbows, grimacing. “Since when do you care?”

“Are you kidding?” I whacked his chest. “No one would ever believe I killed you by accident. Your dad would lock me up in the clink faster than you could say, ‘Shrimp on the barbie.’” My hands patted over his torso. “And he still might if you’re hurt. Is there any damage? Burns?”

“Get off!” He slapped my hands away and checked himself out. “Seems fine.” His head fell back and he spoke loudly. “Told you it would work.”

"You didn't tell me anything!" My fists pounded on him. Sparks flew.

"Ow, those sting!" He pushed me off.

I studied my hands. The power was fading, but they still glowed. And felt…buzzy.

"Serves you right!" I railed at him. "You tried to kill me!"

"If I'd tried, you'd be dead, and I wouldn't have to listen to you babble." He sat up as I flopped down. "It was nice payback for the newspaper thing, but truth is, I just had to test my theory."

"By almost killing me?"

"Yes."

I barked a laugh. Then stopped, because I saw he wasn't kidding.

"Stay away from me." I scooted back.

"Relax, drama queen." He dusted himself off and sat up. "I just needed you to think you were going to die so your power would kick in. You're welcome."

"You're insane."

"No, lass." Jenny sauntered out of the forest. How he could walk with the weight of all those weapons was beyond me. "He just wanted me to see how you operated." He eyed Matthias. "Looks like that might've stung a bit, boyo."

The Aussie scowled. "Nothing I can't handle."

"And you didn't tell me she could grab your whips."

"Yeah, mate, didn't know that until just now."

"She's just full of surprises."

Matthias flopped on his back. "I've always hated surprises."

I gave them both dirty looks. "Think you two could tell me something I don't know?"

Jenny tipped his hat back on his head. "With hunters, our abilities are tied to our emotions."

"I *know*." Gee, so much for the expert.

"At its core," Jenny said, "your power is tied to your will. In your case, it comes out when you're in fear for your life. Your will to survive." He squatted down next to me and turned to Matthias. "But if the demon she protected last night was any indication, I'd bet good money it'll kick in if someone she cares about is threatened too. Her will to protect loved ones."

"See!" I shouted at Matthias. "You could have demonstrated without putting me in mortal danger."

Matthias twisted his lips in a demented smile. "Not nearly as much fun."

"Whatever. So how is all this brilliant knowledge supposed to help me control the explody thing?"

"Explody thing?" Jenny said.

I nodded. "It's a technical term."

"I see. Well, lass, that's what I'm here for. And it's time to find out."

Jenny yanked me to my feet. As he turned and walked away, he flipped a knife, more of a dagger, high into the air. While the glinting blade rotated in the sunlight, he shrugged his shoulders and let his trench coat fall to the grass. The arsenal strapped to his body was in full view. He held out an empty palm just in time for the dagger to fall into it.

In a blur, he spun around and threw it.

At me.

The knife rocketed at high speed. My adrenaline spiked, but either fear froze me too long, or I was just too exhausted to move, because my reaction faltered, muscles slowed. I started to dive right, but knew my sluggish response had cost me. I wouldn't beat the blade.

I raised my arms to at least deflect it from a dead shot between my eyes.

Matthias kicked my feet out, and I went down hard. “Jenny!” he yelled.

I sat up, breathing hard and fast. “Stop trying to kill me!”

“Would’ve just nicked you.” Jenny was unperturbed as he walked over, kicked the knife into the air and caught it. “Come on, girl, show me your skills.”

He walked away, jerking his head for me to follow.

Yep. Nothing but good times ahead.

CHAPTER NINETY-ONE

In no time, I was dripping blood, sweat, and tears.

Okay, not blood. And the tears? So far I'd managed to hold them back despite the mega-level frustration. But there was definitely sweat. Gallons of it. Not my dream day, but historically, I was more of a nightmare kind of gal anyway.

It wasn't all that dramatic. Jenny kept having me try to conjure up the blasting power. And I kept failing, producing nothing but a couple of sparks.

"Want me to throw her off the cliff again?" Matthias offered.

What a generous fella.

However, Jenny decided that I needed some adrenaline pumping action so we worked on some hand-to-hand combat. I didn't completely suck. The most fun was practicing various fighting techniques with Jenny's short swords.

But when I tired — telling myself it was the serious lack of sleep issue — I quickly lost little things like speed, agility, and overall cognitive function. And then the hits just kept on coming.

Jenny jabbed an elbow to my back. I flopped onto the rocky ground. And stayed there. Not really caring that dirt coated my sweat-stained cheek and drool dribbled from the side of my mouth.

Exhaustion claimed every muscle. And any part of me that wasn't numb was a flowing tide of pain.

"Get up." Jenny dug a boot toe into my hip. "We're not done yet."

"I am." My slurred words displaced a little puff of soil.

Jenny slipped his foot under my stomach and flipped me over. I groaned. Then I groaned again because the groaning hurt. And on went the vicious cycle of pain.

He jabbed the sword tip into the sand and crouched down, one hand on the hilt of the blade. "The only excuse for quitting is being dead."

I rolled my head sideways and spit out sand. "Does wanting to be dead count?"

Jenny's smile was diabolical. "You tell me."

The sword was suddenly swinging a graceful arc toward my torso.

I screamed, rolled out of the way, and once on my feet, threw the short sword that was somehow still in my hand.

Jenny bent his knees and leaned back in a contortion odd enough to qualify as some advanced yoga move. The blade passed him harmlessly.

"That's more like it." He pointed his sword at me, his mouth split into a wide grin. "*That* I can work with."

I dropped to my knees. I think it had something to do with the fact I could no longer feel my legs.

"No slacking, lass. The fun's just starting."

"Again. I am not having fun."

But I made it to my feet. Something cold was thrust in my hand. I blinked. Focused. A dagger.

Jenny slapped my shoulder, almost knocking me down. "Next, I want you to—"

I didn't care. Without looking, I rotated my arm and threw the knife. Just to shut him up.

Twang.

I had to squint to be sure, but darn if the knife hadn't buried its tip in the trunk of a tree. A goofy, lopsided grin curved my lips.

"I did it."

"That you did. Now go again."

And once I started, I didn't feel like stopping. Especially when I kept hitting target after target. Energy started buzzing inside me. Suddenly, I wasn't tired.

Jenny produced an endless supply of sharp things. Daggers, short swords, scythes, hatchets, machetes, some circular pointy thing. We walked through the woods finding new targets. Jenny occasionally provided a reassuring hand on my shoulder.

My insides were hot and vibrating. I was giddy. It was like on a long run when endorphins overrode exhaustion, and I felt I could run forever.

Jenny dropped a hand on my shoulder and tossed an apple high. When I reached for my next weapon, nothing was laid in my hand. But muscle memory kept my body moving, my arm reeled back, and my hand shot toward the apple. Energy rippled down my arm.

Light blasted.

The world exploded.

CHAPTER NINETY-TWO

Not the whole world. Just mine. And the apple. Like a fresh fruit grenade.

I dropped my hand and turned away from the brilliant light and sticky wet bits that splattered my face.

"Yes!" I jumped up and down. Punched the air. "Did you see that?" Adrenaline pumped. I felt so good! I wanted to celebrate. To hug someone but…

Jenny was terrifying and probably booby-trapped. And Matthias was…well, Matthias. So my jumping kind of dwindled. Along with my euphoria. Yippee.

Jenny lifted a shoulder. "Decent work, lass."

Matthias looked unimpressed. "About time."

Wow. Killer support team.

I looked at my hands. They glowed. And tingled. Hot. Alive. Maybe I shouldn't be so excited I was going nuclear. What if I couldn't stop? I started to shake and tucked them under my armpits.

"Get a grip." Matthias was annoyed. "You've been glowing for a while now." He turned to Jenny. "She tends to panic. Then choke."

Sparks trailing, my fingers pointed at the exploded apple bits. "Are you blind? I was just awesome!"

"It was *us*, by the way." Jenny tipped his hat at my perplexed expression and looked directly at me. His eyes were glowing a deep yellow. "I tapped into your power. Increased it. I needed you exhausted so you wouldn't notice. Otherwise you might have fought me."

An uncomfortable knot twisted in my stomach. "Wait. You messed with my power?"

"Just gave it a boost, lass." He spread his arms wide. "I can turn it up or down. It's what I do. My particular…charm, if you will."

"Your hunter ability? Well, it's not charming. It's…rude and—" I stared at his yellow eyes, at the scratches on his face, then stepped closer and smelled the whisky. I whacked his arm. Not hard, but he flinched. "It was *you*. Outside my house. You attacked me."

Matthias gave Jenny a hard look. "That true?"

Jenny rubbed his arm where I had touched him then shrugged, indifferent. "Just went to observe the lass you'd called me about. Saw her cavorting with a demon. She saw me and attacked with a shovel."

"I didn't—" see him until *he* attacked *me* but there was no reason for them to know I wasn't as battle ready as they thought I was.

"I took offensive action." He touched the scratches on his face. "More harm to me than you, child."

When he'd touched me that night, I'd had the vision of Jayden and Rose. Great, he could tap into my Divinicus vision power too. My uncomfortable feeling was turning into really ticked off.

I folded my arms. "This power tapping thing you have, don't do it on me again."

"Can't promise that, love." Jenny had the nerve to offer a playful wink. "And besides, we were a good team just now. I only amplified the power, it was your aim that hit the apple. A fine shot."

I wasn't always thrilled with being this freak of nature, but I liked being the master of my own freakishness. The fact that he could take control made him like some sort of body snatcher. I didn't like it, could see why other hunters would find him unnerving to be around. And why the Mandatum would want him put on ice.

"I'm a tad disappointed she didn't vanish again," Jenny told Matthias.

"So sorry." I hoped he slipped on the sarcasm pooling off my words.

"No need to get testy," Jenny said. "When I amplify the power it's easier for you to identify the feeling. Now you just have to remember it — like muscle memory — and you can access it again. Here, try it on your own."

He picked up a pine cone. Tossed it high in the air.

I blasted it without thinking—*bam!* He continued throwing rocks, pieces of wood. I took them all down. The energy radiated from inside—not one particular place—just coursing throughout. Tickling up my spine, zig-zagging across my chest. Even my ears tingled.

"And you're not doing anything?" I said.

"It's stronger when I touch you," he said. "And I can do it from a distance, but you have my word, I'm not doing anything now. Feel better?"

"Yes." And I did. Powerful. Finally in some sort of control. "So what now?"

"Have the boys recalibrated the shields around the town?" Jenny asked Matthias.

"They didn't have time to make them impenetrable to the level of the gods, but enough to slow them down and give us fair warning."

"Good. Then now, lass, you go home, practice turning it on and off, and get some rest. You'll need it." Jenny used the tip of a sword to hook first his coat then his hat off the ground and into his hands. "Aphrodite and her lot have buried entire civilizations. We'll all need to be on our game but especially you. Because you're our secret weapon." He slapped his hat against his leg then settled it on his head. "But no pressure."

CHAPTER NINETY-THREE

I stared at the ceiling until I heard Luna wake from her coffin. Then I stole the shower before she did, but it wasn't as relaxing as I'd hoped. At least we didn't have school today. Although that just meant I'd spend my weekend searching a dead lady's underground hideout. Yippee. But first I planned to steal the tracker from Aunt M's room.

We needed any clues to the traitor it could provide. Besides, M having anything Mandatum related freaked me out. Not that I could do much about her client list. Obviously a dangerous crowd. Maybe her paranoia wasn't so…paranoid after all.

I couldn't get a hold of Ayden. I'd hoped he'd help with my breaking-and-entering caper, but anytime I called, Jayden answered and said Ayden was asleep, assuring me that he was fine and would fully recover in a few days. Odd, because he sure seemed healthy and…vigorous yesterday on the kitchen table. I grinned.

Then it faded.

Crap. Maybe he had a relapse *because* of yesterday on the kitchen table. Maybe I was some kind of black widow.

Lucian knocked on my bathroom door. "Matty called!"

Speaking of poisonous vermin. "I'll call him back later."

"Fine. Next time he calls I'll mention you're too busy in the bathroom. Should I tell him number one or number two?" Lucian chuckled. "Must be two. You've been in there a long time."

"Lucian, go away!" Murder might do wonders to relieve my stress.

He huffed and clomped off. "Girls never appreciate bathroom humor."

After finishing up, I stepped out onto the mat and grabbed a towel, noticing a slight ache in my shoulder. I wiped steam off the mirror for a better look. The puncture was a bit ragged from yesterday's adventures, and stitches had torn, but it hadn't bled, and seemed to be healing well. The older scars around it that fed over my shoulder in jagged white and pink lines, the ones from the alley attack, were continuing to fade. The scar that wasn't fading much at all was the red line on my arm, a courtesy slice from a ghoulie's talon during my first stint in the Waiting World.

I wouldn't be wearing that strapless ball gown I didn't own anytime soon.

There was a *thump* in my bedroom. Then arguing. Towel tucked securely, I poked my head out.

Van Helsing sat on top of my dresser with an arrogant, green-eyed stare, and the tip of his tail twitching a haughty rhythm. That was normal. The rest of the scene was not. Or at least it didn't used to be.

"Are you kidding me?" I hissed.

Logan covered his eyes. "I told them it was a bad idea. Get back— Go— Stay in there!"

Tristan turned away and tried to shove Blake around so he wasn't looking at me, but that wasn't happening.

Blake waggled his eyebrows. "Now that's what I'm talking about, babe."

I hiked the towel tighter. "You can't keep doing this."

"I disagree, chickadee. I could gaze at you fresh from the shower over and over again."

Jayden frowned. "We thought we'd be in and out before you were finished. And bear in mind, I refrained from joining you in the shower again."

"What!" Blake's eyes bugged. Logan and Tristan thumped him repeatedly trying to get him to turn around. "Ow. Why didn't I get invited into the shower? Babe, I'm way more man than all of these guys put together!"

Jayden huffed. "Like the rest of you, she seems to prefer showering alone."

"One shower with me would change her mind. Ow! Okay, you guys are being mean."

"Is Ayden with you?" My heart skipped. "He seemed better yesterday."

"I told you he requires solitude to heal." Jayden wouldn't look at me. "You should give it to him. We agreed I'd act as boyfriend if the requirement arises."

Since when? But he seemed testy so I didn't push it. "You know I can't leave for the sanctuary until after family breakfast. And I'm getting the tracker from Aunt M's room so since you're here, you can help, but…why are you here?"

Jayden pointed to Blake who held the ring Eros had given me.

"I don't recognize this type of stone. Since Blake deals with earth, we thought he might be able to identify it without us having to run tests at the lab."

I perked up. "And do you?"

"Why, yes I do, milady." Blake's chest puffed out, hazel eyes twinkling. "I finally know more than genius Jayden. Let me savor the moment."

"Blake," Logan warned.

"Fine." Blake closed and opened his eyes. "Moment savored. But Eros is messing with you. This has to be a fake. They're too rare. And even if he did have one, he'd never give it up."

"Why, what is it?" I asked.

"It's a *replica* of an umbra stone." Blake held it up and rotated it. Sparkling freckles of sunlight caught in the facets and winked across my bedroom walls.

Tristan looked wary. "I thought the stone was just a myth."

"No, it's real," Blake said. "Hunters with Earth powers know all about them. Because we deal a lot with minerals, gems, and if we find one, we're supposed to protect it with our life and get it to the High Council immediately."

Jayden paled. "Blake, give it back." He tried to grab the ring but the big guy just lifted his hand out of reach.

"Keep away!" Blake grinned. "Babe, catch!"

I heard Jayden, Tristan, and Logan yelling "No!" Even Helsing let out a warning *yowl*. But of course I caught the stone. It was a reflex.

And a big mistake.

Which I realized almost immediately because the stone's energy stoked up from my hand and into my arm, filled my chest. I could cover that up, but the bright glow radiated from my palm, beams shot out. I might as well have been trying to contain a star.

I dropped the stone, but it was too late. It rolled on the carpet, streaks of light bathing the bedroom walls.

"Uh..." I breathed. This was going to be tough to explain.

"You?" Blake's eyes went huge and ping-ponged between the stone on the floor and me. "You're the Divincus Nex?"

I screeched, "What? No!" How the heck had Blake, of all people, made that leap?

Blake cradled his head in his hands. "But—it can't—you can't—" He spun once, then came back to point at me. "I knew it!"

His gaze bounced excitedly to each of the boys. "Jayden was right. It's her! She's a girl. The Divinicus Nex is a girl! It's Aurora!"

When Blake reached for the ring on the floor, Logan, Tristan, and Jayden launched their attack.

Chapter Ninety-Four

Since it didn't seem prudent to wade into a Hex Boy brawl at any time, let alone when wearing only a towel, I stood on the sidelines and watched them wrestle on the floor. Between grunts and curses, I gathered information.

"So an umbra stone activates, or glows, only when a Divinicus touches it?" I said.

Jayden sat on the back of Blake's thigh, grabbed his ankle, and bent it back. "Correct. Which is how he ascertained your Divinicus identity."

"Tag, babe," Blake muffled from under the pile. "You're it. Guys, let me up. I'm not going to turn her in. I think it's cool having the Divinicus as my girlfriend."

I rubbed my fingers together, remembering the feel of the pulsating force of the stone. "Blake, you sure you don't know what the stone does?"

Blake shrugged his torso and, sitting on his back, both Logan and Tristan lurched up like they were riding a bucking bronco.

"Sorry, babe. Like I said, they don't tell us much other than to get it to the High Council asap because the Divinicus uses it for some sort of extra demon-tracking powers. It's all pretty hush-hush."

My brow creased. "Eros said it would give me great power and help find the stone I need because they're similar. Have a connection."

The door opened. We all froze.

"Mom, this isn't what it looks like."

Mom put her hand on her hip. "It looks like a group of boys wrestling on the floor of your bedroom while you watch. Wearing a towel."

"Okay," I admitted, "it is what it looks like, but it's not—"

"Sexual?" She raised her eyebrows.

"Mom!"

Luna stuck her head under Mom's arm and sucked in a breath. "She's gone from a love triangle to a kinky sex pentagon."

Blake lifted his head. "Vote for Team Blake!"

Mom rolled her eyes. "Boys, vacate. Now. Aurora get dressed. And everybody head downstairs. Breakfast is on. I made quiche. There's plenty for all."

"First edible breakfast in weeks," Luna said.

Blake smacked his lips. "Yum!"

Mom checked behind the door. "Ayden's not here, is he?" I shook my head. "Then there's no lust factor. Although, your father may not be as easy going as I am. So, gentlemen, get *out*."

As she left, Mom dragged Luna away with her.

Blake shook off the other boys and stood. "That's offensive. I'm a very lustful guy."

"And a big blabbermouth." Logan whacked the back of Blake's head. "But remember you can't tell—"

"Ayden!" Blake shouted.

"Right," Tristan said, "or —"

"No, it's…" Wide-eyed, Blake jerked his chin toward my door.

Our heads swiveled.

Ayden filled the doorway, leaning against the frame, arms folded. "What can't you tell me?"

He arched one eyebrow awaiting a reply. The silence seemed ready to explode.

Ayden zeroed in on Blake. "Come on, Weak Link, give it up."

Blake blurted out, "Jayden was in the shower with Aurora!"

I choked. "What!"

"You idiot!" Logan thumped Blake repeatedly.

"Technically, that's true." Jayden said. "But only once."

Ayden's arms dropped. Along with his jaw.

Tristan jumped up and shoved Jayden's shoulder. "Shut up!"

I tugged the towel tighter. "Ayden, that didn't happen. Exactly. Guys, he already knows the Divinicus thing."

"Oh, good." Blake was relieved. "Secrets? Not my thing."

"No kidding," I said.

"You told *Blake* before me?" Ayden said. "Unbelievable."

Blake raised his brows. "What's that supposed to mean?"

I held up my hand. "I didn't tell anyone."

"Oh, my God! Why are you in a towel?" Ayden sprang forward and ripped off his leather jacket. One hand got caught in the sleeve, and he whipped his arm up and down trying to dislodge it. Finally free, the jacket slapped to the ground. Ayden snapped it up and practically dove in front of me in his haste to drape it over my chest and shoulders.

"Are you okay?" I said. "Don't hurt yourself. The chest wounds could open up."

"I'm fine." Ayden narrowed unpleasant looks over his shoulder as he tightened his arms around me, holding the jacket in place. "Why are you guys here? You shouldn't be here." He led us both in an awkward sidestep to my closet. "Take your time. Get clothes on. Lots of them."

He shoved me inside and closed the door. In the pitch, dark I reached for the light switch, but the door opened again.

"Sorry." Ayden's hand slid in, groping for the switch, found it, and flipped it on. "Don't come out until…lots and lots of clothes."

As I dressed, I heard the strain in his voice.

"A shower? What the freakin' hell, Jayden?"

"Not like that," Tristan said. "It was his usual shower surprise routine."

"On Aurora! On a girl! Mom and Dad will kill you if they find out."

"I've already been apprised of my error."

"If I don't kill you first."

"Whoa, Fireboy. Calm down."

"Blake, let me go."

"Maybe if you stop smoking."

"Yeah," Logan said, "you're about to light up."

"I'm about to light *into* all of you!"

"Ayden!" I exited the closet, giving my shirt a final pull over my hips and sprinted over to my bedroom door. "They're right. Calm down. You're going to have my whole family in here if you don't quiet dow— Ugh!"

The door burst open with enough force to throw me back against the wall.

CHAPTER NINETY-FIVE

Matthias flew into the room.

"Aurora?!" He stopped to look at the crowd. "You're here already? Good. All hands on deck. Where's Aurora?"

"Here." I pushed off the wall.

"Bugger!" Startled, Matthias jerked around then scowled. "Quit playing games. This is serious."

The Aussie stomped over to my dresser and started emptying drawers into a black duffle bag slung over his shoulder. The rest of us stared at each other, bewildered. Helsing, still on the dresser, arched his back and hissed.

"Shut up, cat. The rest of you, don't just stand there, help!" Matthias ordered as he continued his frantic assault on my wardrobe. "We've got to get out of here. Now!"

I marched over, snatched my bra out of his hands, and shoved it back in the drawer. Something *pinged* onto the floor.

"Is that a projectile from a firearm?" Jayden said.

Tristan paled. "Why do you have a bullet in your br—clothes?"

"Because babe is awesome."

Couldn't agree with him more. "I'll tell you later."

Before I could retrieve the bullet off the floor, Helsing jumped down, grabbed it in his mouth, and raced to tuck it under the purple pillow in his bed, where he also kept Gloria's feathers. Then he crouched, glowering, as if daring any of us to take it away.

Great. My cat was a hoarder.

I turned to Matthias. "What's your problem?"

"You talked to my dad." He said it as if I'd given U.S. nuclear passcodes to North Korea.

"You're still mad about that? I didn't give anything away!"

Ayden's gaze jerked to me. "When did you talk to his dad?"

"Yesterday. At their house."

Tristan groaned. "What did you tell him?"

"She lied!" Matthias's eyes were pale and wild as he kept wadding my clothes into the bag. "You *lied* to my dad!"

"What? I didn't lie."

"You must have." Matthias was breathless.

I smirked. "Well, maybe about you being charming."

All the boys went immediately still. Matthias shot me a sub-zero look.

"You told him I was charming? Are you an idiot?! Never mind." He jabbed a sharp finger at me. "Stupid question. Stupid girl. Stupid, stupid, stupid!"

I smiled grimly. "And there's the Matthias I've come to know and loath. You're being ridiculous. I'm not going to tell your dad that I think you're the biggest jerk on the planet."

"Yes!" Matthias was back scooping up clothes. "That's exactly what you tell him because it's the truth."

The rest of the boys muttered agreement.

"Oh, come on," I said, exasperated. "That's just mean. No parent wants to hear that about their kid. Even if it's true. I like the sheriff. He actually *is* charming."

"So tell him *he's* charming. Because it's the truth. And you always tell my dad the truth, or you don't tell my dad anything at all."

"Relax, dude," Blake said. "Just because he knows babe lied to him doesn't mean—"

"No!" Matthias cut in, frantic. "He doesn't know. *That's* the problem. I mean he does but…he doesn't."

"Oh, no." Ayden rubbed a palm across his face. "Are you saying that he couldn't *tell* she was lying?"

Matthias looked ill. "Bingo, mate."

"Oh, no," Tristan murmured. "This is bad."

"What's the big deal? Would you stop?" I yanked my bra away from Matthias again.

"No." Matthias grabbed it back. "Because you have to get out of town. Out of the country!"

"Why?" I stole the bra again and stuffed it in the drawer.

"His dad's a human lie detector," Ayden said. "That's his power."

"Fascinating!" Jayden was almost gleeful. "Yet another one you're immune to, so it seems. Like Tristan's hallucinating. And you can hold Matthias's whips. Perhaps you should try to drown me."

I looked at him. "Are you crazy? Next you'll want me to suffocate Logan!"

"Excellent," Jayden smiled. "I hadn't thought of that."

"What?" Logan backed away.

I shook my head. "I don't get the problem with the sheriff."

"Stupid!" Matthias said. My bra was back in his grip, flinging back and forth.

Ayden sighed. "The thing is the sheriff knows you don't think Matthias is charming so he knows you lied. Normally, that wouldn't be a problem, but in this case it is because when people are lying, he gets a reading from his ability—a sense, vibe, whatever you want to call it—that tells him it's a lie. But, apparently, when you lied his power didn't kick in. You're—"

"Immune," I said quietly.

"And no one's ever been immune! Now my dad's asking questions. Questions I can't lie my way out of. He knows we're hiding something. He's coming here to interrogate her. And us. Not good. We all have to disappear, mates. Pack your bags!"

"Calm down," Ayden said. "Let's think this through."

"And stop grabbing my bra."

"Huh?" Matthias looked down at the lingerie in his hands. His eyes bugged. "Ahhh!" He tossed it in the air and vigorously wiped his palms.

Blake caught the under garment. "Oh, yeah."

"Blake!" we all yelled.

"Give it back!" Ayden reached for it, but at the last minute pushed a hand through his hair and looked away. "To Aurora."

Tristan stared at the floor. Logan had his shirt pulled up to his forehead. Matthias kept wiping his hands on his jeans.

Blake held up my bra and studied it. "Babe, this is better than I dreamed. Lace is sexy."

"Blake!" I snatched the bra, threw it into my closet. "I do *not* want to know what you dream about."

"And stop dreaming about…any of that," Ayden added.

I rounded on Matthias. "I can't just disappear. My family would freak."

Matthias paled. "Your family. What if they can lie too?"

Tristan swallowed hard, his skin looking greener the more the hysteria rose in his voice. "If your dad figures out we've got a Code Olympus, he'll call in the whole Mandatum. They'll take us all out of here. Put us in the Sicarius." He spared a panicked look at me. "Aurora in some lab."

"That's not happening," Ayden said darkly. "Everyone relax."

"Let's relax after we get the tracker while everyone's downstairs for breakfast," I told him as I grabbed my backpack and headed into the hall. These guys were seriously cramping my burglarizing style. "You can be my partner in crime. I'm calling it Operation Bonnie and Clyde."

"Given that Bonnie and Clyde died brutally, I have grievous concerns about whatever this operation entails," Jayden said.

So did I.

CHAPTER NINETY-SIX

As I worked my tools on Aunt M's bedroom doorknob, the guys clogged the hallway.

"You're taking too long."

"Shut up, Aussie," I said, irritated because he was right. "You don't have to be here for Operation Butch Cassidy and Sundance."

"You're such an idiot," Matthias said. "They died in a hail of bullets. Which, if your aunt catches us, will happen to us too. Besides, this isn't a mission. Not that we name them anyway."

"D.B. Cooper?" I said.

Lucian came around the corner from the stairway and said, "Missing and presumed splattered on some mountain top." He grinned. "What kind of mission are you guys on?"

"Heyyy, brrrooo." I stretched out the words to give myself time for a brilliant cover story. Then the lock pick set clattered to the floor so I went with, "This isn't what it looks like."

Lucian folded his arms and stared us down. "Looks like you're breaking into M's room to find something she doesn't want you to have."

I made a mental note to never use that line with my family again.

"Tell you what," Lucian said. "Promise you'll look for my nineteen eight-three Nintendo Entertainment System and I'll cover for you."

Tristan's jaw dropped. "That's a collectible."

"Why do you think I'm freaking out she took it? But you'll have to hurry. Mom sent me to get you guys for breakfast." He hustled downstairs.

Ayden put the fallen tools into my backpack and said, "Blake." The big guy twirled a finger, there was a click, and Aunt M's door swung open.

Show off.

At first glance, nothing in the room jumped out as an obvious hiding spot because it didn't look like anyone lived there. Set between two windows, the bed was made to military perfection, there were no clothes left out, no dust on the end tables. No suitcase. No sign of M.

"You sure she's staying here?" Blake asked.

"We've only got one guest room, not dozens like you, Mr. Native American Real Estate Tycoon."

"Hey," Blake protested. "That's Mr. Swarthy Native American real estate tycoon to you. And for the record, our house only has one. The cabins are for the dude ranch tourists."

"And any hunters passing through," Tristan added. "But Blake's right. Maybe she moved into the garage."

I opened the closet to show them her signature blouses, skirts, and blazers pressed and hung in neat order. "She just likes to leave a minimal footprint."

We got busy scouring the room, but after a several minutes of searching, other than a couple of cool flash drives with tiny password keypads on one side and labeled "CLASSIFIED" on the other, we came up empty. Blake had completely given up, choosing to sit cross-legged on the floor, eyes closed like he was meditating. Incredibly helpful.

"Got it." Logan crawled out from under the bed, but my excitement died when I saw he held only Lucian's prize gaming toy.

Someone opened the door. I jumped.

"Time's up," Lucian said, then beamed. "You found it!"

Glad someone was happy.

"Bloody failure of a mission. Let's go." As Matthias moved past a window, his body suddenly jerked in spastic contortions just before he squealed like a girl and dropped to the floor.

"We're dead!"

Chapter Ninety-Seven

Through the window facing the street, I caught a glimpse of a sheriff's squad car before Matthias yanked my ankles out from under me.

Great. I could stay and risk getting found out and dumped in a Mandatum prison, or give up the search for the one thing that might get us the drop on the traitor who had me in his crosshairs. Being the Divinicus left a girl with such awesome life choices.

Lucian peered out the window. "Is that your dad?"

Matthias went for Lucian's ankles too.

I swacked him off course. "Chill out. Lucian, answer the door. Tell him we aren't here."

"He'll know Lucian's lying," Matthias ground out. "Or worse."

"Ah. Yes. That." I frowned.

Lucian gaped at me. "Did you steal another car?"

"No, I didn't *borrow* another car," I said.

"Woulda been cooler. Don't worry. I owe you." Lucian patted his game system and wheeled around for the door. "I'll get rid of the sheriff."

"No, no, no!" I grabbed at my little brother, but we Laheys are a speedy species, and Lucian had already sprinted out.

Ayden crouched low and waved us out the door. “Out the back! We’ll hide at Tristan’s.”

“Because the sheriff won’t think to look next door?” Tristan said. “Please!”

Matthias slapped Blake’s shoulder as he army crawled past the giant. “We’re going.”

“Uh-huh.” Blake remained in his reflective pose. “Right behind you.”

We raced down the hall and halfway down the stairs before a knock on the front door froze time.

“Coming!” Aunt M pushed her way through the kitchen door and into the foyer. “Don’t they teach you patience at cop school? Or just how to infringe on my inalienable rights?”

Lucian came out of the kitchen beaming. He pointed at M, then himself and gave us a thumbs-up.

At the appearance of my aunt, our group on the stairs had turned to stone.

Because *that* made us so inconspicuous.

But amazingly, M didn’t seem to notice. Helsing met her at the front door and stared out, tail twitching as she cracked it open barely an inch and gave an irritated squint.

“Ick. What are you doing here, Sheriff? You can’t come in without a warrant.”

“No official business today, ma’am,” Sherriff Payne’s polite cheeriness didn’t get Aunt M to budge the door.

“Then you should have no business here at all. Good-bye.”

“I was hoping to talk with Aurora,” Sherriff Payne said quickly.

“Aurora?” Aunt M had started to close the door, but she paused the motion.

Then she turned and stared. At *us*.

Oh, crap.

I sliced my hand back and forth across my throat and spastically shook my head.

She chewed on her lip, then reopened the door a crack, and returned her attention to the sheriff. "Why?"

"She's been hanging out with my son, Matthias, quite a bit. Thought I should come by so we could all get better acquainted."

"Why?"

"Why?" Sherriff Payne sounded confused.

"That's what I said, copper. How'd you become a government enforcer with lousy hearing like that?"

While she spoke, Aunt M moved her hand behind her back, untucked her blouse from her waistband, and very, very slowly pulled out…

A gun.

Oh, crap, crap, *crap!*

I made more frantic gestures, but M wouldn't look at me. The tension from the boys seemed like it was ready to explode.

I told them quietly, "It's only a tranquilizer gun," but as it came out of my mouth, I realized the absurdity of thinking that made the situation any better. Because if she shot the sheriff with any kind of gun, all hell would break loose, and it would have nothing to do with a demon army coming through some portal.

Sheriff Payne cleared his throat. "Is there any chance I could speak with Gemma or Clyde?"

Behind the door, Aunt M held the gun up next to her shoulder. "Why don't you want to talk to me? Is it because I'm fat?"

"You're not fat."

"So you're deaf *and* blind?"

While Sheriff Payne struggled to converse with M, Lucian snickered, and gestured for us to come down. Aunt M gave us a quick sideways glance and an almost imperceptible nod, flicking the gun barrel back and forth to encourage us to move along.

As we approached the kitchen I heard a familiar deep voice. I swung around, collided with the boys, hissing "Bancroft's here!" then frantically shooed them toward the other end of the house. They disappeared down the hall. I shoved Lucian hard, sending him stumbling through the kitchen door, whispering, "Keep them busy!" I turned around to follow the Hex Boys and make my great escape, but, instead, I uttered a strangled, "Aglck!" and skidded to a halt because my path was blocked.

By Trouble. With a capital T.

Chapter Ninety-Eight

Or in this case, M.

I bumped into her belly and would have fallen if Aunt M hadn't grabbed my arm. My eyes jerked around the room, scared. "Where's the sheriff? Oh, no. You didn't—"

"Shoot him? Nah. He's just cooling his heels outside. I can distract the nit-wit police in my sleep. Guess our breakfast chat is ruined. But I won't have him grilling my niece, so scoot out of here and take these." She offered the tranq gun then pulled out her Taser as well.

I backed up. "Aunt M, I don't think that's a good idea."

"Don't be afraid to use them. On anyone or any…thing." She slapped the weapons into my palm. "Because rest assured, I've got the means and mental acuity to get you out of any mess you ever find yourself in. Except being dead." She patted my shoulder.

"Thanks." I kissed her cheek. "Love you."

"Yeah, yeah. Get lost." She waddled to the front door and giggled like a mad woman. "I've got law enforcement to mess with."

Ayden came down the hall as I tucked the gun in the back of my waistband and Taser in my pocket. He raised a brow. "Weapons?"

"It's how she shows she cares. And at the moment, they're safer in my hands than hers."

Blake jogged up behind us wearing a huge grin. "You so owe me." He held up the tracker.

"No way." I gave him a hug, then took the small piece of equipment. "Where was it?"

"Hidden inside the light switch plate," Blake said. "Blended with the other components, so took me longer. Harder to isolate. But I keep my awesomeness status. Hugs are good, chickadee, but come on. Big kiss. Right on the smacker. You know you want to. I saved the day. Fireboy's going down."

"In your dreams," Ayden said and dragged me outside.

A light drizzle fell, dampening my sweatshirt. It was cold. Should have brought a coat.

The guys were waiting for us in Tristan's Suburban. Ayden jumped in the third seat with Matthias, Tristan rode shotgun, and I squeezed into the second seat next to Blake and Jayden. Behind the wheel, Logan gunned the engine and raced the truck through the winding mountain roads like it was a sports car on the autobahn. Beside us the forest was a blur even without the rain starting to come down harder and pelt the glass. Logan turned on the windshield wipers. I held on tight.

"What took you so long?" Matthias slumped in the backseat. "That was too bloody close!"

"I don't see what the big deal is." I turned to the Aussie. "Your dad can't tell I'm lying, so I'll lie. Play dumb."

"That won't be a stretch," Matthias muttered.

"I mean about any supernatural stuff. Like demons."

"But *we're* not immune," Matthias glared. "And after you, we're the ones he'll come at."

"We can't run from your dad forever," Ayden told him.

"Just for now," Matthias said quietly and gazed out the window.

"Won't matter, we're all dying tomorrow anyway," Tristan said. "There's no way to find the stone in time."

"We've got this one." Blake held up the umbra stone.

"While disheartening, Tristan's pessimism is justified," Jayden sighed. "I've been reading the spiral manual."

"Oh, give it a rest," Ayden groaned. "No one cares about complex filtration schematics, steam systems, hidden levers that control everything."

Jayden shot him a dirty look. "My point is, the treasure vault so effectively concealed beneath the lake, is of a large enough magnitude to make the chances of Aurora searching its entirety in time highly leveled against us."

"Guys, I was thinking…" Pretty much all night with thoughts that kept me awake and terrified. "That maybe you should call in a Code Olympus."

Logan nearly drove off the road.

"No way!" Ayden said.

"If it comes down to my freedom or everyone in town dying from a demonic war…" I swallowed. Took a deep breath. "I can handle a luxury cell." Better than thousands of deaths on my conscience. "Tristan said I'd get lobster every day."

"Until the traitor has you killed," Ayden snapped.

"Lobster's overrated," Tristan mumbled.

"Not happening, babe."

"Like I haven't already thought of turning you in?" Matthias slid me a calculating look. "Only a million times. If I thought it made us all safer, I would, but at least for now—"

Alarm bells from the boys' phones filled the car.

"Demons!" Tristan yelled. "They're breeching the shiel—"

The rest of his words drowned out as my vision jerked my mind out of the car. I didn't spiral far, but wished I had. Like a cloud of ravenous locusts, demons were on the move. And way too close. Demented creatures full of horns, wings, blades, claws, fire, spikes, blood. More than enough to fill the school gym.

Leading them all was a gorgeous blonde woman with a billowing white dress draping off her abundant curves, shapely legs peeking from thigh-high slits. Next to this supermodel stood Eros.

He caught my eye, almost as if he knew I was watching, and said to the woman. "So glad you could make it early, most exalted and beautiful one. Ahead of schedule by an entire day."

"Am I early? Human time so bores me. Besides, surprises are a better way to assure you are helping instead of sabotaging me," said the woman who — let's take a wild leap here and call this sex bomb, Aphrodite. Then she seemed to point directly at me as she spoke to the demons. "Get me the girl. The rest I want dead."

My mind reeled back into the car. Matthias was yelling.

"Then tell me how much time we have!"

"None!" I screamed and grabbed Logan's shoulder. "Stop! Turn aroun—"

Demons rammed the car.

Chapter Ninety-Nine

With a violent screech of metal, the vehicle took a vicious impact. The driver's front end suffered the brunt sending the back end careening right, wheels sliding on wet asphalt. My head flew left, ready to crack through the window. Blake crushed me to his chest, enveloping me like my personal air bag, a cocoon of safety.

We took another hit and gravity disappeared. The car flipped into the air, plummeting off the road. The world spun and blurred as we spiraled out of control, somehow both whiplash-fast and in slow motion. Glass twinkled. Shards pelted and sliced. The car crunched, cracked, squealed, groaned, and rocked to a stop on four wheels. Maybe three. Because the SUV wobbled like a table missing a leg then teetered and *thunked* on its side.

A warped silence. Muted sound. My pounding heartbeat echoed against the ringing in my ears. Muffled shouts. Hissing. Groaning. Screaming getting closer. Everything out of focus. I smelled gas, pine, oil, and…blood.

I blinked. Wiped dirt and chips of glass from my eyes. I saw Logan cut his seatbelt with a slice of compressed air and reach for a bloody Tristan. Red blossomed all over Ayden and Matthias as they shook Jayden who dangled limp.

"Blake?" I pushed at the big guy collapsed on top of me. Blood oozed from the back of his head.

Logan flung a hand and the roof of the car exploded off with a scream of air. It gave us literal breathing room, and a heck of a view. Demons swarmed down the hill and through the trees like an army of maniacal red ants.

I unbuckled and crunched onto shattered glass. Ignoring the pain riddled over my body, I tried to stand as the other conscious Hex Boys crawled out of the car. The world wobbled. I used the car for support and reached in for Blake.

But another vision hit. I stumbled sideways, slid along crumpled metal as my mind lurched out of my body, spearing through the forest in staccato jerks, like a film stuttering on its reel. Disorienting. I felt nauseous.

In one final jerk, I stopped in front of a tree. An ordinary tree. Not a demon. Maybe the crash had broken my powers.

The bark from the ordinary tree suddenly wasn't so ordinary. It stretched. It bulged. As if the tree was covered in a plastic membrane and something was stuck inside, trying to get out.

A twig burst from the surface, growing longer, thicker, then shaped into a slender, sinewy arm. On the end, fingers formed, then a thumb, a palm, until finally, an entire hand opened and flexed. It reached around to the front of the tree, grabbed the malleable membrane surface, and pulled.

A body stepped out.

Bark split and crackled off the human form and revealed smooth olive skin and a face filled with beautiful angles and a savage dignity. Dark tattoos lassoed across her body in ancient-looking tribal swirls, thickest around her arms. Judging from the crown of antlers atop her raven hair, I'd bet the tattered, barely-there dress that clung to her lean, muscled form was the hide of an actual deer. Her eyes glittered silver, like the full moon on a dark, cloudless night.

My vision stuttered again, started to reel back, but paused when the woman knelt and threw her hands into the ground. I mean *into* the ground. Buried up to her forearms like the hard, rock-filled mountain soil was putty. Around her, the earth crumbled as claws burst up through the surface, tearing and slashing until a pack of feral, wolfish dogs had wrenched themselves from the depths.

The almost-hellhounds circled the woman with deference, snarling, yipping, and snapping their excitement. Blood-tipped teeth gleamed. Silver eyes glowed. Antlers, honed sharp as blades, sprouted down their spine and covered their tails, one happy wag slicing a tree in half.

The woman extended one arm and a thick tattoo came to life, sliding down the length, slithering over her skin like a serpent. It reached her palm and uncoiled into the air to form a bow. Her other hand drew back the string as another tattoo slithered off her fingertip into an arrow. She raised the weapon and aimed.

Artemis. Had to be. The Goddess of the Hunt had arrived.

She whistled once. The dogs paused to look at her.

"Fetch," she said, and let the arrow fly.

My vision snapped back. Too fast. I gave into the dizziness and dropped. A shadow loomed over me. I looked up. Screamed. A puss-oozing, near skinless demon with bleeding eyes howled with rage and lifted the kind of sword that would take my head off in one swipe.

The demon swung. Metal glinted.

I dove sideways, pulling the taser from my pocket. Too close to shoot, I jammed it directly onto the monster's slimy leg. There was a wet sizzle. A horrible stench. The creature paused mid-swing. Go me! But after a brief moment where I was sprayed by a furious, head-shaking, spittle-flying growl, the blade continued its deadly arc aimed for my neck.

I scrambled for cover. Saw my backpack on the ground. Had a hand on it. Was going to use it to block the attack—because nylon was so robust against steel— when there was a sudden *pfft-thunk*, and the woman's arrow buried right between the demon's eyes.

The monster staggered for a moment, looking confused. Then its head exploded. Brain and bone splattered against the car before the hellion burst into a mist and tornadoed into the ground, its sword toppling harmlessly at my feet.

I leaned my back against a wheel. Was Artemis helping me?

Pfft-twang. An arrow sliced my bicep and buried into the wheel's hubcap. Ouch! Blood trickled from the thin, shallow gash.

Nope. She was hunting me.

The ground trembled. I looked down at my blood splashed on the dirt.

It boiled.

In the distance, seen through what had now become a light snow flurry, Aphrodite's demons thundered down the hill in a bloodthirsty wave of malevolence. Ayden screamed my name. The earth in front of the barbaric pack exploded like a spewing volcano as Fido burst from the ground. Dirt and rock showered down. Her fierce screech brought my hands to my ears and literally blasted a few demons to bits, as if a bomb had detonated in their bellies.

With merciless ferocity, she scooped mouthfuls of grotesque fiends and squashed them with one crunch, slicing others in two with her pinchers. Some jumped upon her, fangs tearing at fur, while others whizzed past and continued right for us.

A wall of flames erupted in front of the demon mass. Some vaporized when they hit it, but the rest halted and backed away with inhuman cries of fury. A break for us. Until winged beasts flew down from above.

Logan and Ayden began shooting. Matthias pulled an unconscious Tristan out of the car, yelled something and pointed back at the Suburban, then joined the fight, lashing his shadow whips at the airborne threats. A few demons made a break through the fire wall, running towards us in flames. The guys took them down, but there were more on the way. Too many.

And more closing in from both sides, unbeknownst to the boys, who hadn't seen Artemis's hellhounds yet. All converging here. All coming for me.

Still gripped in my hand, the backpack started rattling, moving like something was alive. I dropped it. Watched it buck and bounce.

"Oh!" I said as realization dawned. I unzipped the backpack. Flint's metal spikeballs flew out and hovered around me like alien spaceships. "Uh..." I pointed at the demons flying above. "Attack!"

I'd like to say they were obeying my command, but the little slashers were already on the move before I got out the second syllable. Their spikes poked out and *whirred* into chainsaw-level action. Flames lit up on the ends and the spinning spheres sailed into the air, shredding through demons with ease.

Helpful, yes. But not enough for this growing crowd of hellacious groupies.

I ran to the truck, shaking Blake. "Wake up!"

He moaned and blinked. Then mumbled, "Hey, babe, I need mouth to mouth." His lips puckered.

I kissed him. Short and sweet, because...I don't know!

"Babe!" He jolted awake. "Not cool. Fireboy would *not* approve!"

"Get moving. They need you!" I shouted.

Battle axes morphed into Blake's hands before his first foot hit the ground, and before the second foot hit, he'd thrown them. One into the skull of a demon on the other side of Ayden's fire wall, and the other blade slicing the head off something diving from the air toward Matthias. Blake waved his arms. More battles axes appeared in his hands, the earth split wide along the line of demons, trees uprooted, boulders flew, and…

That Hexy Knight was in full warrior mode. I turned toward Tristan as he staggered to his feet and pulled out Jayden who started to speak in big words I couldn't understand. So I knew he was all right.

I inhaled a strong smell of gasoline just as Tristan yelled, "Aydcn, it's gonna blow!"

Ayden turned and slashed his arms through the air just as the Suburban exploded in a bright, thundering *kaboom!*

I dove for cover, expecting heat and a wave of pressure, but neither came. Instead, the flames gathered in a massive fireball and careened up into the air, taking out a dozen demons flying above. As it dropped, Logan shot an arrow into it, and the orb brightened to sun-blazing levels. It hit the ground and rolled along the massive meadow, leveling demons in its path.

Coughing against the smoke, I ran to Matthias's side. He growled, "Get your power working!"

I opened and closed my hands. Nothing. "I can't. Yet."

"Typical." His whip snapped out and cut a demon in two. "Then stay out of the way!"

"I've got a plan!"

"Not interested." Both whips wrapped around a demon's neck and the head popped off.

"It puts me in mortal danger."

Matthias's eyes slid my way. "I'm listening."

CHAPTER ONE HUNDRED

I left the boys in the dust, jumping over fallen trees, ducking under pine branches. In full force, my Divinicus visions let me know that as soon as I took off, the two—count them, *two!*— demon armies had changed course from the boys and were now after me. Gaining steadily.

Like the howls and weapons hurtling past my head weren't clue enough.

But it would buy the boys the time they needed. It had to.

Running along a roaring river drowned out some of the blood thirsty calls from my psycho fans.

My vision flashed on a demon incoming from above. Another one hot on my tail on the ground. The coolest part was that it didn't make me dizzy, and I didn't completely wink out. I saw the demons, their positions, trajectories, and still saw where I was going. More like a second — and third — sight happening all a once. A little weird, but I could get used to it.

And I could use it.

I leapt over a fallen log, grabbed a jutting limb, swung sideways, and hit the ground rolling, into the mud, almost to the river's edge. The demon behind me jumped the log, and landed —

where I *would* have been — as the winged beast dropped from the sky and snatched him up instead of me.

I'm that good.

The tree above exploded as an arrow tore through. Splinters rained. I scrambled to my feet, ready to run.

And got slammed from the side by something big and smelly. It launched me into a death-roll, splashing into the shallow water of the river's edge. Thc cold wet soaked through my skin. When we finally stopped, I grabbed the throat of the hairy beast on top of me and stared into a horror show.

A face of fangs. No eyes, no nose, no ears, just a giant, gaping hole of rows upon rows of serrated teeth and two larger fangs reaching toward me. It looked like a tarantula, only massive and way more scary. Liquid drooled off a fang. I twisted my face away. It dripped onto my hair, sizzled. My nose wrinkled at the burn. Through the smoke, I saw a hairy spider leg rise up, ready to spear me with its spiked end.

Pressure, heat, and buckets of panic flooded my system and released in a white hot sonic boom. The tarantula demon blasted into the air, hovered amid snowflakes falling from above, then legs flailed as gravity carried it down. I reached a hand up.

Power. Sweet, glorious power that I felt down to my marrow, lightninged off my fingers and ripped through the monster's fat belly. Guts splattered and rained down, then swirled into a black vortex and disappeared before the gooey mess splashed over me. Whew.

I grinned at my glowing skin. "About time."

I slogged through the water, up onto the beach, and shot my hands toward the stampeding hoard. A searing, white energy took out the whole front line of the pack and blasted a hole a mile long through the center of the rest. What trees and shrubbery hadn't disappeared, were left blackened and smoldering.

The hellions' war cries faded as the entire militia staggered to a stop and gaped.

I heard crickets chirping.

Okay, not really, because the crickets were long gone, cowering in there holes, but you get the point. The demons were stunned into silence. Because of me.

"Yeah," I laughed. "I can do that. So stay the heck—"

A spike-covered almost-hellhound leapt from behind. I ducked, it sailed over, clipping my shoulder as I rolled to my knees and blasted it. Fun times. Until I yelped in pain. An arrow tore through my shirt and nicked the skin over my ribs. Not so fun.

Like someone hit the play button, the demon hoard suddenly seethed forward, battle cries at max roar.

"Oh, come on!" I ran hard and fast, throwing lightning blasts over my shoulders.

I wasn't that accurate, but didn't need to be when my energy tore through layers of demons. But more monsters filled any gaps, and worst yet, each blast seemed to be weaker than the last.

Did my explody power have limits? Need some sort of re-charge?

I'd ponder that frightening thought later, because I'd run out of forest. So had the river. It crashed over the cliffs and into the plummeting mass of towering water that was Gossamer Falls.

Lacking pesky obstructions like trees, the flying demons dropped from the sky like missiles. I zigzagged, swerved, stumbled, fought for footing in the increasingly slippery earth, and lurched ever forward, gaining speed, even as the ground shuddered and crumbled around me, until I finally reached the edge.

And in one great leap, I launched over the cliffs.

Chapter One Hundred One

My arms and legs flailed. Wind whistled, water roared, mist sprayed, and my gut hollowed with terror. I couldn't think.

Falling so fast, out of control. No leverage. Had to twist my body…was harder than I thought…struggled to…

Mid-fall I spun. Facing the sky, I shot a storm of light at the demons on the cliff, hitting some, but I'd taken too long. Others had already leapt into the air and nosedived after me.

One bit into my pant leg. I kicked, but it wouldn't let go. Fabric ripped. I grabbed its neck, shot light. Its growl turned high-pitched and the demon disintegrated in my hand. Two more beasties barreled down, wings tucked, jaws yawning wide. One latched its talons around my leg. The other's mouth closed almost delicately around my arm, and the two flapped vigorously, breaking my fall, starting to fly me up, up and away to my darkest doom, where my deepest fears would be realized.

From below, heat flashed in a jagged blaze of raging fire, and one demon drowned in flames. Water splashed out horizontally from the falls and elongated into a spear of ice, impaling the other demon through the gut. It barely had time to scream as it jerked to a flesh-tearing stop then disappeared in a black mist.

Released from both threats, I was once again plunging through the air, out of control, wind whipping hair across my eyes, but I could see more demons diving fast, gaining on me. I brought my hands up to ready a blast.

A black line shot out from the bottom of the waterfall and lassoed around my waist. I gripped it tight. The tumbling waters parted, and I swung through the opening into the cave behind the falls, iridescent green algae on the walls illuminating my way.

Matthias released the whip around my torso. I somersaulted onto the ground then popped to my feet and ran past Jayden to the opening he was maintaining in the waterfall. Matthias reached forward, pulling the dark shadows from the cave, and cast them out over the lake, weaving them into a tightly knit net.

Demons rained down from the cliff straight into Matthias's mesh of shadows. They stuck like bugs on flypaper. I grabbed one of the lines Matthias stretched taut and poured energy into it.

Drizzling blue-white sparks, light fed along the dark lines until the entire net lit up as if electrified. Hellions screamed in agony as their writhing bodies disappeared in thick, black mists scented with sulfur and the sweet stench of burning flesh. Ayden threw fire for good measure. Jayden flung what looked like glittering ninja stars made of ice.

I grinned. "Told you that would work."

"You didn't tell us anything!" Ayden snuffed out the flames on his arms. "You just disappeared. Then Matthias said—"

"I had a brilliant plan?"

"That we were all supposed to ride Fido through the demons to the caves while you ran off to get yourself killed!"

Matthias shrugged. "I was hoping."

"You're a jerk!" Ayden punched the Aussie's shoulder then crushed me to his chest. He was shaking.

"Careful," I muffled. "Your burns."

"Enough about the stupid burns! I don't care!" He grabbed my shirt in both hands, yanked our bodies together and kissed me.

It was hard and deep and desperate. And I loved every second of it. It gave me thrills and chills, tingles and zingles. I put my arms around his neck and kissed him back. Adrenaline pumped through me. It was good to be alive. Good to be in his arms.

Someone coughed and said, "Coital impulses might best be delayed since we presently have an assemblage of demons vying for the opportunity to kill us."

Someone else made vomiting noises and said, "If I have to watch any more of this, I'll bloody kill myself."

Ayden jostled as someone whacked his shoulder.

A moment later he released my mouth, but kept hold of my shirt and gave me a look of granite. "Don't scare me like that again. *Ever*."

"Fine, fine," Jayden said impatiently, "Is that the extent of the demon legion in pursuit?"

I laughed. "Not by a long sh—aack!"

I shoved Ayden into Matthias as an arrow sailed between us and the hounds broke through the waterfall's mist.

We ran. Ayden flung his arm in a circle. Flames spiraled around the walls of the cave, sizzling the wet algae, permeating an aroma of vegetable soup. Startled yelps slowed the beasts, but not enough.

We raced down the tunnels, banging on metal catwalks, and barreled into the portal cave. Fido looked up from licking Blake's wounds. Logan kneeled next to a groaning Tristan.

"Good girl." I patted her side. "Now go find cover."

Logan stood, drawing his bow. "We have company?"

"Let's hope so," I said and headed to the portal wall.

The hounds bounded into the cave. Crouching and shuffling, bumping into each other as more and more arrived and filled the space. Other demons of ugly proportions pushed in behind them.

Ayden lit his arms on fire. Blake, Logan, and Jayden started to gear up too.

"No!" I said, watching the hounds closely. "Let them in!"

"Phase two of your plan?" Ayden gave me a look over his shoulder, then his eyes widened. "Watch out!"

Behind me the portal began to shimmer and crack. Lava oozed. Ayden ran toward me.

I dove onto the hard ground, skidded toward the portal, twisting on my back as I bumped into stone. Above me, the rock stuttered in and out of existence, letting molten goo ooze through. I felt the heat as it slid a wobbly path toward my face.

"Aurora don't!" Matthias put up a hand. "This part didn't sound so good."

The frontline of the hounds leapt with vicious snarls. I slammed my hand on the double spiral below the portal.

The furies of hell converged upon us, and a beat later, the ground opened up.

Chapter One Hundred Two

We plummeted down the waterslide. Screams echoed. Ayden wrapped his arms around me, and we hit the water together then kicked for the surface. The rest of the Hex Boys splashed into the pool. Everyone grabbed the vines hanging from the ceiling and climbed up out of the water.

The hounds splashed in.

"Demon infiltration." Sally Security was right on cue.

The water swirled beneath us. Tentacles lashed out from the surface. While the monster wrapped its clutches around demons, we swung — awkwardly on my part — to shore. I dropped, stumbling on the rocky, rooted surface. Ayden steadied me with an arm around my waist and pulled me flush against him.

"Don't know what Matthias was worried about," he grinned. "I love your plans."

"Uh, guys?" Tristan pointed a shaky finger.

The whirlpool and tentacles took care of some demons, but several were making it to shore. A slimy, webbed hand burst from the water and clawed at my ankle. My feet danced, Ayden twirled me out of the way, then Matthias wrenched me from Ayden's arms and shoved me down the tunnel.

"Find the stone!"

I balked. "So that they can unleash a demon army bigger than the one we're dealing with?!"

"No, you twit. So we can use it to open the portal and shove the gods into hell!"

"And you think my plans are bad?"

Shaking my head, I raced down the eerie green tunnels and slipped Eros's ring on my finger. Power hummed along my arm, warmed my body. The stone lit up with the mini-universe. Beams of bright, speckled light cascaded over the space like a kaleidoscope flashlight.

When I felt the ring tug on my hand, gentle as when newborn Oron would grab my fingers, I let the force guide me forward, skidding under the half-closed gate and into the treasure room, a mess from our last violent visit, but the artifacts were powered down, unmoving.

"Careful." A panicky Tristan grabbed my arm, as he and Blake joined me. "We're probably safer facing the demons than this place again."

"Stop being a baby," Blake stepped into the room. "We're perfectly safe."

Something *clanked.* Blake yelped, lifted me in front of his chest, and peeked around for danger.

Logan ducked under the gate. "It's just me."

I glared at Blake. "Are you seriously using me as a human shield?"

"Sorry, babe. But this place likes you a lot better than it does me."

"Who's the baby now?" Tristan muttered.

"Demons incoming!" Ayden and Jayden slid under the gate.

"Blake, put her down!" Matthias yelled, helping the other guys pull the gate down. "Aurora, turn it on!"

I dashed across the room and wedged into the alley crevice between the tomb and wall. I slapped my hand on the double-spiral. Stone split revealing the lever and the two buttons. The red one was lit.

The gate banged as something heavy slammed into it. Slobbering growls saturated the air.

"Ready?" I shouted.

"Now!" Tristan shrilled.

I wrenched up the lever, light switched from red to green, and I skedaddled out. Someone—or something—grabbed me and shoved me behind the slab of marble.

"Wait," Ayden said.

A grotesquely large demon hefted the gate up so more of its kind could surge in. The rest of the Hex Boys, armed with shields and weapons, ran head on at them. Flint's attack machines stuttered to life. Arrows, spears, and various flying projectiles flew overhead. Most aimed at the demons. But some attacked the Hex Boys as well.

"This was a terrible idea," I whispered.

"Have a little faith. We've got this." Ayden dropped the knight's armored chest plate over my head and wiggled it over my torso. "You find the stone."

"Sure." Just let me just wander through the death trap all alone with no powers.

Some of the witty sarcasm in my head must have translated to my look because he gave me a look of his own and said, "Don't worry, I'm not about to let you run off on your own again. I've got a substitute bodyguard."

Ayden whistled and in the time it took for him to discombobulate me with a deep, intimate kiss, Fido rumbled from the back of the treasure room.

"Go!" Ayden shouted as he spun away, and with a fierce, almost insane smile, grabbed weapons to join in the fight.

Fido acted as an extra shield as I ran, ducked, weaved and bobbed, sprinting through the deadly security measures. My side ached from the arrow shot, and every twist of my torso stung from the crusted blood pulling at my skin. I coughed on dust and smoke, gagged on pungent smells of blood, sulfur, sweat, oil, burning flesh, searing metal. My ears rang with the deafening noises of the fight.

Although the beams had dimmed to a subtle glow, the stone on my finger swirled with glittering life. I struggled to focus on the physical draw of the ring and not the battle waged against the Hex Boys, following the beacon to the wall etched with the double spiral at the entrance to Lizzy's sanctuary.

Because it only made sense to keep a weapon of this magnitude in your bedroom.

I turned to Fido. "Go help the boys."

She scuttled away. I wriggled out of the chest plate, clanked it on the ground, then raised my hand over the symbol.

A lizard tail, thick as a telephone pole, whipped around my ankles and yanked my feet out from underneath me. As I went down, my head cracked on the wall. Blood smeared my vision as a Jurassic monstrosity, an overgrown cross between a komodo dragon and a raptor dragged me over the ground.

"No!" I kicked, twisted, rolled onto my back. Something hard jabbed my spine. I reached underneath and pulled out what could only be considered a Hail Mary move.

Aunt M's tranq gun. The last of my arsenal. I aimed and squeezed the trigger.

The dart buried into the scaly back. The demon screeched, but didn't go down.

Yeah, these things worked better on the Discovery Channel. On *non*-supernatural creatures.

The demon swung around, furious, mouth agape. Hot, putrid breath bathed my face. I tried to scuttle back, but the tail still had me.

I was considering the ridiculously madcap and ultimately suicidal option of pistol whipping it when…

The creature dropped. *Thud.* And didn't move.

I wiggled free. "No way." My incredulous gaze bounced from the gun to the fallen demon. "Aunt M you are…*awesome!*"

Should I kick the beast? Make sure it's down?

No, you idiot. Run. *Run* while it's down! I raced to the wall, slapped my hand over the spiral symbol, and after the rock disappeared and the mechanized puzzle-box of gears and levers unlatched the door—which seemed to take *forever*—I stumbled in.

Inside the sanctuary, the ring trembled with greater force, nearly pulling me off my feet as it hauled my hand forward, past the mountains of books to Lizzy's monolith of a bed. But no twinkling stone waited on a lacey platter.

I bit my lip and looked around. Come on. There had to be something. Some clue, a hint.

A rattle. Slight, but coming from—

"You idiot!" Tristan screamed as he entered the sanctuary via an awkward tumble through the air. Logan followed, but executed a graceful somersault before landing lightly on his feet.

He glanced back. "Nice throw."

Blake came sliding in, clutching the unhinged top of a treasure chest covered in darts. "Find it?"

"Not yet," I said. "Shhh!"

The rattle came again. From the headboard. I leapt on the bed, dust poofing in a musty mess into the air, and laid my ear to the glossy wood. Yep. Definitely a rattle. I studied the intricate carvings then traced my fingers over one symbol buried amongst it.

The double spiral.

I hovered a hand over it, cringing with anticipation of a disappearing floor, wall — or life. Deep breath and…I pressed my palm down.

Something clicked. A drawer slid out. Atop deep green velvet lay a glittering metal necklace, the center stone about the same size as my enormous ring. It quivered with power.

Guess I didn't have to buy jewelry for a while.

Something *banged.* Covered in axes, darts, and spears, an upside-down canoe with legs collided against the edges of the entry, then bounced and scraped its way along the sides and lurched into the room.

"We look ridiculous!" Matthias voice echoed from underneath the boat.

"If you could backflip worth a darn, we wouldn't be doing this, would we?" Ayden snapped.

"Oh shut up!" Matthias flung off the canoe. "You can't even do a push up with those burns."

"Blake!" Logan flattened his palms on the stone door and strained to close it, but his feet slipped back

Claws, paws, and jaws pushed through the opening with wet snarls and inhuman screeches. The door bucked hard and opened farther. A thick, leathery arm with two elbow joints reached through and latched its claws around Logan's throat. His shout cut to a strangled garble as the demon squeezed. Logan pawed at his neck but couldn't pry off the relentless grip. His face turned bright red.

With a roar worthy of a mama grizzly protecting her cub, Blake thundered over, gripped the demon at the wrist and one elbow, then wrenched with a brutal twist. There was a loud, crackling slurp, and the hellion's arm ripped in two. The pieces dripped with shattered bone and long, wet, strings of shredded tendon.

Or muscle. Or both. But all gross.

On the other side of the door, the beast wailed. Blake flung the severed parts aside. The fallen hand wiggled along the rocky soil toward Logan who rubbed his neck and danced out of the way, losing his hold on the door. Demons started to surge through.

Blake stomped on the hand that wouldn't die then slammed his full weight against the door and shoved. The stone closed, severing a few more demon body parts in the process, and locked into place.

"Ha," Blake grinned. "Let them deal with the possessed treasure."

"Aurora, did you secure the pinnacle of our pursuit?" Jayden asked.

I looked around then up and found him hanging from the ceiling.

"How did you—?" I shook my head. "Yeah. Let's go take down three demon gods with a sparkly rock."

Chapter One Hundred Three

We rode up Lizzy's elevator and rushed out into the tunnel, racing through the cave behind the falls. Jayden parted the water of the falls, and as we started to follow the stone pathway to the beach, we skidded to a halt. The demon armies had congregated all around, in the sky, above the lake or on the lake, converging on the entrance.

But there was something far worse than demons.

Matthias shoved me into the shadows, out of sight, and uttered a panicked, "Dad?!"

Sheriff Payne pumped a shotgun one-handed and blew three demons out of the sky. Then he lowered a steely gaze upon his son. "We are not having a 'friendly conversation' when we get home."

The sheriff wasn't alone. I remained hidden as Ayden smacked his brother.

"You called Mom and Dad?"

Jayden shook his head, equally horrified.

"No," Mrs. Ishida said calmly then ducked gracefully as Mr. Ishida unsheathed a sword, swung it over his wife, and sliced off the head of a hound prowling out of the water. "But you should have."

No one so much as flinched when a demon burst from the lake and pounced on Mrs. Ishida in a deadly bear hug.

I started to…to — I don't know, do *something*! — but silver spikes suddenly exploded *out* of Mrs. Ishida and skewered the demon.

Then with a high-pitched *whirrrr* of a blender—or chainsaw—the barbed spikes started to spin. Fast. Basically turning the monster's insides into a gore-a-licous smoothie. It barely had time to squeal in agony before it disappeared into a black mist.

The silver blades remained protruding from all over Mrs. Ishida's body. She sighed. They retracted. But her skintight, black outfit was slashed and torn.

"Darling." She reached out to her husband. "Be a love."

Mr. Ishida tossed his sword at Ayden who caught it easily, then took his wife's hand. In seconds the fabric mended back together, and…

Wow. Now, *she* knew how to rock a leather cat suit.

Why did I date the guy with assassin parents? Only explanation? Death wish.

With an unearthly screech, a giant, dragony-looking demon which literally breathed fire, tumbled down through the sky. Riding it like a bucking bronco was a petite brunette. As the beast dove toward us with its fang-filled jaws yawning wide, the woman stabbed her hand deep into the beast's neck, and in one vicious move…

Yanked out the spine.

My trips to the Waiting World were the only reason I wasn't vomiting.

The ground shuddered as the dragony demon splashed into the shallows of the beach. The woman who had brought it down jabbed a finger at the boys, the bloody vertebra she'd just wrenched free waggling in her grip, dripping…fluids and stuff.

Logan winced. "Grounded?"

His mom glared. "*So* grounded."

She front-flipped off the motionless demon and stalked toward us, smoothing her hair into the ballerina bun while behind her, the "spineless" beast — I couldn't help it — burst into black dust and disappeared.

I ducked lower as a flippin' *giant* lumbered out of the forest, an axe the size of a tractor tire casually resting on his shoulder.

"Uncle Reece?!" Blake cowered behind Logan.

When the elderly couple strolled out behind Uncle Reece, Tristan yelled, "You're alive!"

Mrs. Ishida muttered to no one, "Why does he think anything can kill them?"

Tristan ran forward for a body-slam of a group hug with his grandparents.

"Of course we're alive," said his grandpa. "It's the demon hoards that go down, not us. Grandma was at her finest. And we didn't forget your present. Show him, sugar."

Tristan grinned at his gift, pulling on the colorful beanie hat complete with earflaps, tassels, and pom-poms. "I love it!"

"It's yak wool," his grandma said. "And our Sherpa said he blessed it with a protection spell. Now, what's this we hear about some shenanigans you've been up to?"

"Sorry," Tristan said sheepishly. "I know I messed up."

"Are you kidding?" his grandma broke out a huge smile. "This is the first dangerous thing you've done!"

"We're so proud of you!" His grandpa clapped him on the back.

"What?" Logan's mom snapped.

Tristan's grandma shot her a look. "Don't question our parenting style."

Matthias waved a jerking hand over his dad's chest. "You have Jenny's vest?"

The sheriff had ditched his megawatt smile and actually looked menacing. The lethal aura was helped by the fact that he was covered in all kinds of weapons and using Jenny's arsenal of a vest.

"No. Jenny has *my* vest," he snapped. "It was my design! He stole it!"

"Merciful heaven." Rolling his eyes, Jenny emerged from the cave as he fired a shot over his shoulder and took down the hound that had snarled out after him. "You're still on about that?"

"You!" Matthias growled. Light flickered. "You dragged my dad into this?!"

Jenny snorted. "'Course."

Sadie, the Payne's demon dog, bolted from the forest carrying in her mouth the bloody, ripped remains of some hellion's clawed appendage, which she quickly dropped so she could leap at the sky and bark furiously. Not bothering to look up, Sheriff Payne casually cocked the double-barreled weapon and blasted several demons diving from above. His other hand pulled out some huge handgun and brought down a few more.

Smiling, he rubbed the top of Sadie's head and said, "That's my girl," with genuine affection. Tail wagging, she wandered off, nose to the ground, sniffing voraciously while the sheriff turned a scowl on Matthias. "Did you really think you could handle one Greek god, let alone three?"

Mrs. Ishida muttered, "Typical teenagers."

"Think they can take on the world," Mr. Ishida agreed.

"*We* did." Tristan's grandparents high fived. "And we won."

"You blew up the entire—"

"Mom, let it go." Logan shuffled his feet.

Blake's uncle laughed. "She's just still mad about—" He caught the pint-sized brunette's scathing look, "—the thing that I agreed to never talk about. Ever."

"The gods aren't at the portal yet." Jenny glanced back at me and winked.

"Good. Gives us time to set a trap," Logan's mom said.

Mr. Ishida snatched back his sword and flicked black goo off of it. "Boys, hold them off out here. We'll deal with the Olympians."

The Hex Boys started yelling, their parents yelling right back. There was a definite "Hell no!" vibe from both sides. They all knew the chances of survival were slim. Nonexistent, if you asked Tristan.

I eyed the dark tunnel at the back of the cave, wondering if maybe I should try tackling this alone. Definitely not a good idea, but I didn't like the thought of being responsible for a body count.

Jenny raised his hands. "I'm the expert here!"

The sheriff waved at him. "You tell 'em!"

Jenny nodded like an all-knowing sage. "The boys go against the Olympians."

"Ha!" Matthias jabbed a finger at his dad just before all the parents started yelling again.

Jenny fired three shots in the air to silence them, cutting down some demons too. "They already know more or less how to work with Aurora's power, and she's the best shot we've got at taking them down."

Tristan's grandma scrunched her face. "The scaredy-cat neighbor girl too terrified to leave the house?"

I slapped a hand over my face. So much for low-profile. But if I could just stay hidden…

"*Woof! Woof, woof! Woof!*" Happily wagging her tail like she'd just won a game of hide-and-seek, Sadie jumped in front of me and wouldn't shut up.

Dogs. I hated them.

"I'm not too scared to leave the house." I stepped out of the cave. "Okay, maybe sometimes, but can you blame me with all this?"

Mrs. Ishida smirked at the other parents. "Told you she could see demons."

Ayden gaped. "You knew?"

"Duh," Mr. Ishida snorted.

"Why does no one say anything?" I said.

"Plausible deniability," they all chorused.

"Oh."

Jenny thumped my back. "I just need to get Aurora here riled up enough to activate her powers so I can amplify them. I'll boost the boys' too, but the fastest way to get Aurora started is to put your boys in a near-death experience."

I gripped Ayden's hand. "That is a freaking failure of a plan if I ever heard one!"

Logan's mom folded her arms. "Makes perfect sense."

"Used something similar in Venice with that pack of haptogian mols," Uncle Reece nodded.

"It was Istanbul." Sheriff Payne changed the clip on his gun and slammed it into place.

Uncle Reece twirled the axe. "No, I'm pretty sure—"

"Either way," Mrs. Ishida cut in, "it worked like a charm."

Mr. Ishida said, "Have at it boys, and stay sharp. We'll take care of things out here." He turned to his wife. "Darling, you have a little..." He wiped some black gunk from her cheek.

"Make sure to bleed a lot."

"Grandma!" Tristan paled.

"What? I said bleed a *lot*, not bleed *out*."

Chapter One Hundred Four

The Hex Boys hustled me down the tunnels to the portal.

"Still not liking this plan," I grumbled.

"You'll be fine." Jenny was full of confidence. But what can you expect from a lunatic? "Once the gods show up, you do all you can to help them get the portal open using—" He paused. "Where's that bloody stone they want?"

"In my bra."

"Nice, babe."

"Interesting choice," Jenny shrugged. "Anyway, you stay close to the gods."

Ayden stopped me with a protective arm. "We didn't agree to that."

Oh sure, *now* he was on my side.

Matthias gave me a shove forward. "The less chance she survives, the better it sounds to me."

Jenny reloaded his guns. "When I boost her powers, the closer she is to the gods the better chance she has to help us blast them back through the open portal. Without more training, she's better at short range. It'll be easy."

"We have very different definitions of *easy*." I took a shaky breath. "And what about that demon army waiting for Aphrodite? You're sure the gate will hold them if any get through?"

"It's at full strength and ready to go," said Tristan, looking ridiculously adorable in his brightly colored yak wool hat, pom-poms bobbing as he tapped with concentration on his computer tablet. "I can control it all from right here. I'll lower the gate but hold it open the last few feet until we're all on this side. Safe."

"Trust me, lass, you can do this," Jenny said. "We're the best backup there is. With us all working together we'll take down this lot and—"

Jenny stopped. The blood drained from his face, guns slipping from his fingers and clattering to the earth.

Artemis stood before the portal, hounds crouched and slobbering around her. In her arms, she held a trembling little girl, maybe nine years old, with a shock of ruby red hair brighter than mine, and pale green eyes shining with tears and terror.

I flinched as the guys all powered up.

"Ah, ah, ah." Artemis's fingernails, long shards of black obsidian, curled around the little girl's throat.

"Jen?" Matthias's voice shook. "Is that…?"

"My girl?" Jenny could barely catch his breath. "Chloe?"

Artemis studied me with either a smile or a snarl. "I want to trade. One girl for another."

Definitely a snarl.

Jenny settled a hand on my shoulder. "I'm listening."

Ayden yanked me away from the power-sucking hunter's dark look. "We don't even know if it's really her."

Jenny blinked slowly, the Golem look fading from his eyes. "Too right."

He bent to pick up his guns.

Artemis tilted her head. "It is simple. Give Aurora and my stone to me, along with your vow to never hunt me again, and I'll give you your precious daughter."

Jenny shook his head and bit his lip so hard it bled. "I accept."

"What?!" I said.

The boys joined in a collective protest and generating of their powers.

But Jenny was ready.

He slammed a foot into Blake's chest, the big guy's fall taking down Tristan and Logan. Jayden hurtled an ice blade, but it lost its shape and splashed harmlessly onto Jenny's shoulder at the same time Ayden's flames snuffed out and Matthias's shadow whips faded to non-existence.

The Ishida twins froze when Jenny sighted them down the barrels of his two guns. "Easy, boys. You have no powers. I'm the only one with weapons."

"Jen." Matthias stepped toward the crazed man, but Jenny shot the ground at his feet and the Aussie jumped back. "They never found her body, but that doesn't mean Artemis kept Chloe alive all this time. You can't trust a god."

Jenny's lips curved in a cruel smile. "Even the lass said the demon goddess wouldn't kill a young girl."

"I didn't say that…exactly." Kinda did. Nice big mouth, Aurora. "And even if I am right, she won't just hand her over."

"Artemis!" Jenny said without taking his eyes off the boys. "Send Chloe. I'll send Aurora." Jenny waved the gun at me. "Get going. And give Artemis a hug. From me."

Hug? Sure, because that makes sense. I stared at him. Hard. Tried to read his face. Did he have some brilliant plan? But his expression gave away nothing.

I threw him a dirty look.

"Aurora, no." Ayden was furious. "Jenny, you can't!"

"You'd do the same, lad. Go on Aurora. Showtime."

"It'll be okay," I told Ayden. Didn't look like he believed me. That made two of us. But even if it wasn't Chloe, what choice did I have? A child was in trouble.

Once Artemis gave the girl a push, I glared at the goddess and walked forward. She pulled out her bow and kept it trained on Chloe. I clung to the terror building inside, trying to spark it into energy I could shoot. As I got closer, I realized the umbra stone must be working because the portal wall behind Artemis was shifting. Parts of it blurred. It was starting to open.

Something clicked deep in my chest and stole my breath as warmth burned. I glanced back at Jenny, his eyes already glowed yellow from dousing the boys powers, but he stared directly at me, and…nodded. I think. It was so slight.

Then energy coursed through me. A power surge. Had to be from him. I hung onto it, fanning the flames, feeling the force of it grow.

Chloe and I passed each other by the pool with the stalactites dropping a steady *drip-drip* onto to the bubbling surface. I gave the wide-eyed girl what I hoped was a reassuring smile. Didn't look like it worked. Her lip trembled, breath coming in clumps, tears streamed down her cheeks.

"Chloe, it's okay. You'll be safe." I reached out and squeezed her shaking hand. So small yet her fingers gripped hard with desperation. "I promise."

"Keep moving," Artemis ordered.

Heartless wench.

Anger flashed through me in a seething mass. The kid was petrified. I had to peel her hand off mine. She gave me a look of anguish, like I was abandoning her. The wrath I felt for the goddess fueled my power.

Heat. Pressure. Energy building within me. I wasn't glowing yet, but it was coming, and when it did, I'd bring Artemis down.

I wrenched my eyes from the little girl and forced myself to move away. That's when Chloe lunged. With a wretched whimper, her arms latched onto me from behind, face buried in my back, her little form shaking uncontrollably.

"Help me!" she cried in a ragged whisper, before her body wracked with harrowing sobs.

"Stop!" I screamed, meaning it on several levels. At myself and Jenny, so I didn't power up and burn the little girl. At Artemis who pointed an arrow at my chest. At the world to slow down so I could figure out what to do.

"Move her along!" Artemis commanded.

Chloe hugged tighter, blubbering, shaking her head *no.* Jenny was yelling something.

I pulled out the necklace and dangled it over the bubbling, steaming water of the pool. "Relax, or I'll drop it, and no one will have it."

"No!" Artemis cringed with fright and lowered the bow. "I cannot lose it again." The hounds backed off.

Okay, good. I hadn't been sure what reaction I would get, but this was working in my favor.

Eros *poofed* into existence beside Artemis and gasped at her, horrified. "You dare to double cross my double-cross? I told you I'd get you your precious stone. Once we rescue Psyche, Aphrodite is all yours."

Artemis had been staring hard at the stone, but as I watched, her initial fear faded into fury.

"And I knew I could not trust you, Eros," the huntress growled. "I should have known when you insisted on kidnapping a Hex Boy instead of letting me kill one. I thought perhaps you had simply gone soft, but now I see you played me for a fool. Biding time with your lies to lure me here under false pretenses."

"I did not," Eros said. "I negotiated in good faith."

"Hardly." Artemis pointed at the necklace I held. "Because that is not my stone." She raised the bow and arrow.

"No it is not," a beautiful voice whispered in my ear as the necklace was snatched from my hand. "It is mine."

Chapter One Hundred Five

I had enough time to note that Aphrodite smelled like all my favorite desserts rolled into one before I turned, grabbed her shoulders and slammed her with a headbutt.

She yelped and staggered back. I reached for Chloe. Artemis shot an arrow directly at Aphrodite's brain. It was inches from burying between the Goddess of Love's eyes when Aphrodite caught it one-handed and shoved it under my jaw, the point digging into soft skin.

I froze.

"Cease!" Aphrodite clamped a hand on Chloe's shoulder. "Or the child will lose her heart." Her fingernails elongated into sharp talons that curled down and pressed into the fabric over Chloe's chest. Small pricks of blood blossomed on the crisp, white blouse.

"Let her go," I said, the movement drawing a trickle of blood down my neck as the arrow pressed deeper. "Take me."

I stifled the desire to use my power, too afraid I'd catch Chloe in the crossfire.

"In time, my pet. Have no doubt." Aphrodite curved a calculating smile and rocketed the arrow at Artemis who disappeared in a puff of smoke, then the Goddess of Love shoved me aside and dragged Chloe toward the portal.

I glared at Aphrodite's back, my fingers twitching with power. I took several steps toward her. If I could just get a clear shot.

Aphrodite turned, jerking Chloe with a violent twist, making the kid whimper and causing her eyes to become huge and shining.

The goddess sneered with malice. "I feel the passion of your hatred, your desire to avenge, but know this. I will slay her if you try to thwart me. Stand down."

My nostrils flared. "Fine." I put up my hands and backed away.

"Watch her," Aphrodite told Eros, then turned to stand in front of the portal, reveling at her triumph. She lifted the necklace high and pointed it toward the portal, gazing delightedly at the enlarging sections of shimmering blur where the rock was thinning and letting through a faint glow of dark red.

A direct line to the Waiting World and her hoard of demon recruits.

My brain was wimping out. On the run, scrambling for a quiet place to shut down until all this was over, but I muscled a firm grip on its coattails and forced it to think. This could still work. The gods were all here, my power was geared up, ready to pounce, so once the portal opened I'd use it to shove them through.

Easy, just like Jenny said. Only one hitch. Couldn't let Chloe get caught in the crossfire.

"Aphrodite, you've got what you wanted." I kept backing off while looking for a way to double-back on the gods without being noticed, because Jenny was right. I was better at close range. "Let the girl go and take me. I'm much more valuable."

Aphrodite spat, "I will have you soon enough, pet. Dare you not rush my triumph." She lifted the necklace higher and spoke in a grand voice. "My army will soon arrive. My hour of glory is…is…" She paused.

Her arm holding the necklace lowered slowly. The portal, which moments ago was opening, now started solidifying again, almost back to hard rock.

"What is happening?" she practically screeched. "*Eros?* Why does it close? It must open. It must *stay* open so your pathetic lover can bring me my army!"

Eros snatched the necklace from his mother, studied it closely, then swallowed and closed his eyes for a long moment.

He spoke softly. "This isn't the Portal Stone." Then he looked at me with accusation and misery. "How could you?"

"How could I what?" I felt panic rising. This didn't make sense. "I used the other one to find it. Like you said. It has to be the stone!"

Aphrodite looked to Eros. "Are you certain it is not the stone we need?" She saw the confirmation on Eros's face, saw the portal almost completely closed. She turned to me, teeth bared. "The child will pay for your mistakes." She lifted Chloe who squirmed and wailed as Aphrodite's talons penetrated fabric and flesh.

More blood on white.

"I didn't know!" I ran forward. "I can find the right stone! Eros, you said we had two days so give me more time!" And just one clear shot at this obnoxious *witch!*

A gun fired. The blast echoed as the bullet chipped the stone wall behind Aphrodite's head.

Sighting down his weapon, Jenny yelled, "Don't!"

With a murderous look, Aphrodite slashed her arm through the air. Jenny's gun flung from his hand. He was already pulling another when a slash of the goddess's arm catapulted him backwards. He crashed into Tristan who spun sideways, the tassels on his hat twirling erratically. The computer tablet ripped from Tristan's hands and slammed against a boulder, shattered and broken.

Aphrodite cackled with triumph, then holding Chloe in front of her, she turned toward the rest of the Hex Boys. Her face lit up with maniacal glee. They scattered, taking cover behind rocks. Except for Ayden who dove into the bubbling pool.

As blood spread over her shirt, Chloe screamed in pain, then suddenly bit down on Aphrodite's hand. The goddess shrieked, her hold loosened, and I barreled into her, knocking them both to the ground. I *thudded* against the portal. It shuddered and squealed, and the stone wall started to thin and dissipate again. Scorching waves of heat rolled through.

"It's opening!" Aphrodite smiled with insanity, then narrowed her eyes at me. "What are you doing? Do you have the true stone?"

"Run!" I told Chloe.

The gutsy little girl tried, but Aphrodite grabbed her ankle. I jumped on top of the goddess and bashed her beautiful face with my fists. I was feeling pretty tough, until she thrust one hand to my chest, and I vaulted straight up, my back crashing into the ceiling, body staying pinned by an invisible force.

I heard a rumble and a cranking of gears. From the ceiling around me, rock crumbled down. I felt pressure on my lower back. The metal net had started to feed out from the stone and began lowering, pushing me down along with it.

With a deafening *boom* the water in the pool shot straight up in a jet of steam, shattering stalactites like toothpicks. Then Fido burst from the pool with Ayden clinging to her like a trainer in some freakazoid Supernatural Sea World extravaganza. Her ridiculously many feet skidded to a stop as a dozen of Artemis's rabid hounds grew from the ground like weeds. With a squeal of fury, my Blood Contract diva faced down the monstrous pack. They crouched, snarling, fangs bared and drooling. Then they attacked.

Fido didn't flinch. She scooped up two leaping hounds in her mouth, crunching them into oblivion. During a graceful backflip off her furry body, Ayden incinerated three more.

As the other boys joined in to battle the remaining hounds, Matthias shot a whip around Chloe's waist and tried to pull her from Aphrodite's grip. But the goddess spun the girl so the whip wrapped around her body, higher and higher until it encircled the little girl's throat and tightened like a noose. Chloe groped futilely at her neck, strangled noises blubbering through her lips.

Matthias uncurled the whip and shot two more at Aphrodite. She gestured her arm and several of the fallen stalactites lifted from the ground and rocketed like spears toward the Aussie. He dived for cover, but one clipped his shoulder. He went down behind rock and his shadow whips disappeared.

Between Aphrodite's force still holding me up, and the net pushing me down, I felt like I'd snap in two. Pain and fear overwhelmed me. I couldn't think.

Chloe screamed. More blood oozed on her shirt.

I dug through the panic and found a surge of power. Sparks burst from my fingers. Light beamed and shot down toward the psycho-pseudo goddess. Her eyes grew wide and she disappeared, teleporting in a puff of smoke. Released from her power, I *thudded* to the ground.

Energy raced down my arms. I rolled away, worried Chloe was still near and I'd zap her and anyone else into oblivion, but when I looked around, Chloe was nowhere in sight.

"Eros!" I pushed to my feet, slipping and splashing in shallow puddles of warm water, eyes raking over the cave. "Where's Chloe?"

But he didn't answer, too busy running along the shimmering portal, screaming, "Psyche!"

I coughed on thick, humid air coming through the portal. It smelled like burnt compost and tasted worse. I blinked, moved to wipe the grime from my sweaty face and saw my fingertips looked like Fourth of July sparklers. The light buzzing from the tips grew longer and spidered out in jagged lines of electricity, sizzling across the floor of the cave, pulsing with life.

The lines of power moved along the ground as if searching, and tore through one of Artemis's hounds like paper. Bloody, gut-shredded paper.

The force took hold, overpowered me, dragging my hands forward, raising them up. I couldn't pull away. The ends of the spidered light moved closer to the portal, quivering with bursts of light until…

With a gathering roar, my energy hit the wall, and the portal ripped open.

CHAPTER ONE HUNDRED SIX

Everything shook. Dirt rained down from the ceiling. Eros was thrown to the ground as streams of orange-red light burst through from the other side of the portal, connected with the light from my tingling fingers, and caused more pulsing webs of electricity to leap from my hands in bright bursts of unnatural colors.

The jagged lines of power seemed alive. Ravenous, on the hunt. Pins and needles overwhelmed my body. I jerked my hands, tried to pull them away, but they were stuck. The lightning streaks tethered them irrevocably to the portal and the horror of the world beyond.

The Waiting World.

And in this version? The land of fire and brimstone. Not that I ever figured out what brimstone was.

Rolling over the fiery landscape, lava flows curved in rushing torrents, the remnants of dead bodies tumbling within their thick, steaming current. In the distance, volcanoes erupted. Fire spontaneously burst from the burning ground. Hot wind blew in a tempest, searing my face.

This was just not my night.

Matthias ran at me. "We need to get out of here!" He pointed to the metal net behind us which was now more than halfway down.

"Tristan can't stop it. We need to get on the other side before it reaches the ground. Shut down your power!"

"I can't!" I yanked my hands back, but the tethers of lightning just got longer, like I was stuck in gum.

"I can." Jenny's scarred hands clamped onto my shoulders, his fingers on the verge of breaking my collar bone. But instead of dissipating, my energy surged with intensity.

Matthias yelled, "Jenny, turn off her bloody powers!"

"I'm trying! But she's—" Jenny's voice broke from the strain.

"She's *what?*" Ayden was frantic.

Jenny's hands remained gripped tight, sweat dripping off his chin. "She's pulling power from *me!*"

I fought the pull toward the portal. "I'm not trying to!"

Jenny struggled, his body slumped, teeth gritted, as step by grunting step, he lugged me backwards trying to get me behind the demon-catcher net before it lowered completely. But it was slow going. The lines of crackling energy kept lengthening, pulling against us, refusing to release my hold on the portal.

Ayden reached for me. "I'll help!"

I yelled, "No!" just as Jayden dragged his twin back to the security of Blake's arms.

"Find Chloe!" Jenny's voice quaked with effort and desperation.

Something splattered at my feet.

A skull.

Decomposing. An eyeball dangled out like infected snot.

Tristan screamed. I wanted to but couldn't, my lungs shutting down from the Herculean effort to get myself out of this horrific mess.

Another skull splattered.

A blurred figure stood just inside the portal. On the *other* side. Someone was in the Waiting World. Throwing body parts out.

"Impossible!" Eros scrambled to his feet, shocked, pawing at the portal. "Aurora, keep it open! Please, just long enough to get Psyche out! She's right here!"

"Eros!" Aphrodite appeared in front of the portal, facing it, her back to us. "Where is my army? Your simpering concubine was supposed to bring them. We had a deal!"

Another skull flew through the portal and *thunked* Aphrodite in the head.

"How dare she!" the goddess seethed, then snarled her venom at Eros. "Your betrayal will cost you everything!"

Eros kept clawing at the portal. "Get her out and I'll do whatever you ask!"

"Too late!" Aphrodite's cold voice echoed. "For all of you!"

In a violent rage, she turned to us, and dread sliced through my gut.

She had Chloe.

Aphrodite gripped the sobbing girl by the hair, using her as a shield. They were so close to the portal. Too close. Both her and Chloe's hair lifted up and backwards, and started to get sucked in.

Jenny finally heaved me behind the metal net's path. He looked up and saw his daughter. With a guttural wrench of pain, he ripped his hands off me and lurched toward the portal, but his legs gave out. He collapsed and choked a pathetic, "Chloe!" before his eyes fluttered closed, and he went still.

Aphrodite's beautiful, crazy eyes landed on me.

"Close the portal and come with me!" She had to shout to be heard over the roar of my energy and the rumbling grind of the gate on its steady descent. "Or I will destroy everyone you hold dear. Close it now!"

"Can't do that until you let Chloe go." I didn't know how to do that under *any* circumstances, but Aphrodite didn't need to know that. So I bluffed. Kind of. What other option did I have but to give her what she wanted. A kid's life was on the line. "Release her and

I'll come with you and do whatever you want. With my help you can rule the world." Until I find a way to destroy you.

"Come forth then," Aphrodite said with a satisfied glint in her beautiful eyes. "We shall seal the accord."

The hand in Chloe's hair dropped to the girl's shoulder. The other reached toward me in an all too elegant gesture for a bargain so vile. I gulped and took one step forward. Someone yelled, "No!"

A hand came out of the portal. On a surprising note — because everything else so far had been completely mundane — it wasn't decomposing. It grabbed a fistful of Aphrodite's hair and yanked.

Aphrodite fell backwards, her body sucked through the portal and into the hellacious Waiting World. Which would have been cause for celebration except…

She took Jenny's daughter with her.

The net was almost completely down, ready to shut us off from the portal. And Chloe on the other side.

My body reacted before my mind made the decision.

I quit fighting the energy and instead, fed more of it into my hands, letting the jagged light streams keep the portal open, increasing the connection. Then I ran forward and did my best homerun slide, down on my side and under the net. I had barely enough room to get through, the metal edges so close they tore through my shirt just before they *thudded* their way into the stone floor and buried themselves deep.

I was cut off.

Didn't have time to worry about that because I was back on my feet, using the pull of the crackling lightning tethers still shooting from my hands to help me gain speed as I raced directly at the portal.

And jumped through.

Chapter One Hundred Seven

The ground proved slippery in the Waiting World. Fortunately, the bones of the decaying bodies provided enough traction to skid to a stop with a belching *slurp*.

My stomach quivered. I picked up the hem of my gown—because, yes, I wore yet another one since the Waiting World apparently had some absurdly formal dress code. My eyes watered from the revolting stench of sulfur mixed with rotting meat on a slow roast. My pores streamed sweat like they were dumping buckets from a sinking boat. Couldn't decide whether the gushing perspiration was from fear or the freakin' gazillion degree lava pulsing all around.

A scream diverted my attention from the visions of burning alive that were suddenly flashing through my mind.

Whatever bravado I'd managed to muster up, shriveled as I stared at the demon.

Aphrodite seemed to age before my eyes. Skin sprouting liver spots, then wrinkling over itself in folds. Actually, she wasn't aging so much as deteriorating. Like Echo had. Only slower. Somehow making this whole Wicked Witch melting thing all the more horrifying.

One of the corpses picked itself up from the gory muck of landscape and tackled Aphrodite. They squelched onto the ground, screaming, punching, clawing. Flesh literally flying. So…yucky.

There was a shriek.

But not from me.

Chloe tried scrambling to her feet but slipped deeper into the quicksand of rotting flesh. I *squished* to her side — wearing rain boots up to my knees, finally! — and pulled her into my arms.

"It's okay. I'll get you out of here," I assured her and whirled toward the portal. "Come with— Crap!"

An odd rock formation blocked out path. I peeked around it, but there was just more hellacious Waiting World. No portal. No Hex Boys or whacked out Jenny, not even a sliver of white light where the portal should have been. No exit where I could send Chloe back through.

I raised a hand, wiggled my fingers, trying to conjure portal-opening beams of light to find us a way back home.

Nothing.

Okay, not great. But I still had Gloria. Somewhere. Right? She needed to do her angel thing, destroy Aphrodite and set all right with the world. As gross as this one was.

"Look out!" Chloe grabbed at me.

I didn't look fast enough.

An enormous wing smacked me into the rock formation where the portal should've been. Stupid, stupid Waiting World.

The appendage — only one — that had hit me sprouted from Aphrodite's back like a flopping, giant bat wing with maggots dripping from oozing wounds. The Goddess of Love was ever so sexy.

Chloe screamed loud enough to shatter ear drums. Couldn't blame her. My hand slimed through the…death-covered ground for a weapon, bone, anything, as Aphrodite stalked toward us.

The corpse that had been fighting Aphrodite lunged again, but this time the goddess caught it by the throat, lifting the living carcass off the ground, legs kicking.

Only…it wasn't a corpse.

Under the smears of gross and soot, the skin was a rich honeyed tan. Frizzed out ringlets the color of amber hung over robin's egg blue eyes that flashed with hatred. What very little remained of a tattered, burned white dress, draped off a voluptuous form that put Aphrodite's to shame.

Even in this horrid abode, she was dazzling. A bit worse for wear, especially covered in all the guck, but physically intact, and in this place, that was practically supermodel status.

Aphrodite snarled, "Psyche, I should've killed you the moment I laid eyes on you. Ugh!"

Psyche's kick plunged through Aphrodite's stomach and they both went down.

I found a safe island of non-molten rock for Chloe to stand.

"Stay here!" I told her, then ran and leapt onto Aphrodite's back, hooking my arm around her neck. Her rotting throat squished and oozed around my bicep. I gagged. The Goddess of Love smelled like roadkill.

Shrill howls filled the air.

In the distance, monstrous figures started to descend from the steep side of a raging volcano. Blue leathery skin stretched tight over skeletal bodies. I could see the gleam of their fangs from here.

Not really. My imagination was just working overtime to liquefy my guts through abject terror.

Aphrodite bucked, wing flapping, and flung me off. My back slapped to the ground. She loomed over me, seizing my face with her half-skeletal hand, and smashed my head into the terrain with a gurgling *plop*.

I would've preferred concrete.

Fighting nausea, I slammed a knee into Aphrodite's ribs. Heard a satisfying *crunch.* She yelped. I swung an elbow. Cracked her face. A piece of flesh ripped off and, sticky as wet cellophane, it wrapped around my arm, then slid down onto my chest.

I squealed so high, only dogs could hear.

Then I kicked my feet into the goddess's gut. Her arms pinwheeled, and she fell back into—

Oh, dear God.

With a savage *splat*, Aphrodite hit a bubbling pond of lava. Her screams pierced the air. In the distance, shrieking howls bellowed from the demonic Smurfs. I rolled away from the sight of Aphrodite sinking into the thick, simmering orange liquid, her last shrieks drowning into desperate, wet gurgles.

Something slimed on my chest. I looked down. And shrieked. Aphrodite's slice of cheek still clung to my skin. Panicked, I grabbed at it, but it kept slipping through my fingers, and—

Fingernails, crusted with blood, pierced the chunk and flung it away. The beauty attached to them offered a hand and a shockingly white-toothed smile.

"I am Psyche," she said with polite formality.

"Aurora." I cleaned my palms on my skirt before shaking her hand, weirded out by the social nicety in this wasteland. I glanced around with a wary eye. "What about that demon army you were supposed to bring?"

"I gathered them as ordered. I am a dutiful servant after all," Psyche said with a smug little bow. "Then I sent them through the wrong portal. Tipped off by Eros, Mandatum hunters were waiting. It was a feast of demon death."

"Hmmm." I had a thought. "That portal wouldn't happen to be in Nepal, would it?"

"I am uncertain." The white teeth flashed again. "Through the carnage of demon destruction, I was fortunate to glimpse snow covered mountain peaks of majestic proportions."

"Yep. Sounds about right. So why aren't you a flesh-dripping zombie like the rest of them around here?"

From behind me, a cheery voice answered. "Psyche doesn't belong here."

I turned, then shook my head with a laugh. Chloe huddled against Gloria who was dressed like Mary Poppins, complete with umbrella, carpet bag, and daisy-laden hat. Although, the hot pink hair tucked underneath was all Gloria-issue.

"That's why the Waiting World hasn't claimed her after all this time," Gloria said then squeezed Chloe's shoulders. "Nor does my dear little Chloe."

"Remember that whole part about being the *worst* guardian angel ever?" I jabbed a thumb over my shoulder. "This is what I'm talking about. I already took care of Aphrodite myself."

"And you were..." Gloria raised the umbrella above her head, swaying it back and forth as she sang the next series of syllables. "Super-cala-fragil-istic-expi-ali-doe-cious!" She twirled the umbrella back down, and wearing a brilliant smile, resettled an arm around Chloe. "Honestly, I don't know why you're complaining."

"H-hello?" Chloe was wearing a blindfold.

"Fear not, child." Gloria patted the girl's shoulder and whispered to me, "I thought it best she not see anymore."

"We'll all be safe soon, Chloe," I said. "And don't dump us in the lake, Gloria. By the way, is my body back home in a coma this time?"

"No, of course not," Gloria said. "You entered yourself into this realm *body* and soul."

Yeah, like that explained it all.

"Whatever," I said. "Come on, Psyche, we're all getting out of here. Gloria, let's go."

Gloria suddenly looked morose. "Oh, dear me."

I groaned. "I'm not going to like this, am I? Let me guess, more of your stupid limitations?"

Gloria chewed a finger. "I am *limited* to remove one human who doesn't belong. As your guardian angel, I must choose you. Unless you refuse. Free will and all."

"Ha. Ha-ha. *Not* funny. It doesn't even make sense." I shook my head and pulled Chloe from Gloria's arms and held her tight against me. "None of us belong here, and I'm not leaving either of them to get gobbled up by the blue piranhas which are going to be here any minute."

Chloe shuddered and clutched me tighter. Great, Aurora, terrify the child even more.

"Sorry." Gloria lifted her hands in a helpless gesture, her perkiness wilting like a dying rose. "The rules were created for a reason. If I do not comply, I'll lose my wings. Fall as Aphrodite did."

I blinked. "Aphrodite was a fallen angel?"

Psyche nodded. "As is Eros. It's why we had such difficulty catching them. We believed them to be demons. But their powers go far beyond."

I glared at Gloria. "Gee willikers, that would've been helpful knowledge a few days ago."

Gloria shrugged. Chloe trembled. Demonic Smurfs shrieked.

Before I could completely appreciate how suck-tastic my life was, Psyche lunged for Chloe.

"No!" I screamed, shoved Chloe into Gloria, and rammed a fist into Psyche's face. Ow. You'd think my knuckles would've toughened up by now.

Psyche yelped. "What in Hades was that for?"

"I'm not letting you use a kid to save yourself," I said. "If only one gets out, it's Chloe. Now *back-off*."

"I wasn't!" Psyche rubbed her jaw. "I feared *you* would sacrifice the innocent. She is here because of my misapplication of revenge. When I pulled Aphrodite in, I possessed not the knowledge that the vile creature held the child." Psyche dropped her head. "So we are agreed about what must be done."

I stared at the miserable landscape. My heart dropped into what felt like a vat of acid, but once again, what choice did I have? Tears brimmed and spilled onto my cheeks.

My lip quivered as I pushed Chloe into Gloria's arms. "Watch over my family. They'll need your help. And can you somehow tell the Hex Boys…tell Ayden that…" My throat closed. Words were no longer an option.

"Don't be silly." Gloria bopped me on the head with the umbrella.

"Ow!" Did I say *bop*? It was more of a whack.

"Tell them yourself." At my questioning look, she sighed and shook her head with exasperation. "*I* can only take out one, but you can remove any and as many as you see fit. You've gotten yourself out before. This time take Psyche with you."

"Whoa!" I waved my hands in the air. "I don't know how to get out. *You've* always gotten me out!"

"Have I?" Gloria gave me a cagy look. "Besides, you said it yourself. You don't need me anymore."

"When did I say that!"

"Believe in yourself, Aurora. Like I always have." Gloria's umbrella opened with a crisp snap. Colorful streamers trailed off the edges.

"Enough with the vague crap, Gloria. Give me straight answers."

"I've already told you, but…fine." She looked petulant. I flinched when her wings snapped open. Dazzling white with hot pink polka dots. Cool. She spoke in a lilting sing-song. "Always take the high ground and a net will appear, when you leap to your faith having cast aside fear."

Then she smiled.

"That's *it?*" I ground out. "Not helpful. At all. Give me something that makes sense."

"Weakness is your strength. Fear is your salvation."

"Gloria!" I waded through the flesh and bone to stand in front of her. "Stop talking in riddles and mixing metaphors and tell me how we get out of here!"

"I already did. But first, might I suggest…" She glanced over her shoulder. "…that you'd better start running."

Her wings pumped, the force gusting a hot wind that sent her and Chloe into the air. And me flattened to the ground. When I looked up, I saw the skeletal blue ghoulies.

Closing in.

CHAPTER ONE HUNDRED EIGHT

On the run with a centuries' old fallen angel's wife in a demonic dimension while a hoard of fang-filled monsters gave chase was not my idea of girl bonding.

"She said high ground, yes?" Psyche panted. "What does she wish us to do?"

"Who knows? She says a lot of stupid things." I jumped over a trickle of lava. "Just keep running!"

We were headed toward a single outcropping of a high rock formation and had a temporary lead on the ghoulies, but they were gaining. I'd only be comfortable when we were separated by different dimensions. And then, only kind of.

I'd never been so happy Tristan and I had jogged — no run — to the Ishida home all those mornings. Psyche and I made it to the cliff faces without collapsing. My knees quivered at the thought of climbing. Heights. I hated heights. I glanced back. Despite the vertigo already warping my vision, I could tell the demons were only minutes away. And that was a generous estimate.

"Let's go." I jammed my stupid boots into footholds, grasped a ledge, and pulled myself up.

We climbed in silence. Other than the occasional grunt or yelp. I tried not to focus on the fact that the demons were looking less like a hoard of tiny ants and more like rabid squirrels.

Gaining on us.

Climbing was slow at first. Searching for a hold, getting a good grip, pulling up. Searching, gripping—very repetitive, very tiring, and very not what I wanted to be doing. But as we climbed higher, bare branches and gnarled roots grew out from the rocks to speed our ascent. Sure, the branches had plenty of thorns thirsty for blood, but I tried to focus on the positive.

"We're almost to the top!" Psyche called down from several feet above.

"*You're* almost to the top," I muttered. "Show off."

"When you've been here as long as I have, climbing is a necessity."

I gulped down some hot air. "So was falling in love with Eros worth all this?"

"Of course. Love is worth any sacrifice." Psyche swung down a root for me to grasp.

"That's pretty much what Eros said."

She sighed. "He is a true romantic. Our torment wasn't his fault. He knew I was a hunter, which is why he never wanted me to see his face. When I broke our bargain, saw him for who he truly was, my love for him was so profound, I did not care."

"He didn't believe you?" I panted.

"He ran before I could assure him of the truth of my devotion."

Something clunked me on the head. "Ow!" The skull bounced off my shoulder and tumbled down. I nearly lost my grip.

Psyche cringed. "Apologies."

"Be careful!" We kept climbing. "So what happened?"

"Aphrodite convinced my true love I'd double-crossed him."

"The gods do love a good double-cross."

"Aphrodite said I was using his love to capture him and take him back to the Mandatum." She paused to make a long reach. "He fled, heartbroken. Desperate to find him, and not knowing Aphrodite's treachery, I sought her assistance. She told me he'd gone to the Underworld, and to save him I must enter through Hades' portal."

"She's helpful like that." A few grunts later, I reached the level where she sat on a small ledge. Skulls leered. Dusty skeletons slept. How they got up here, I had no idea. But I wasn't going to suffer the same fate.

Psyche had a wistful smile. "Love makes you…"

"Stupid. Crazy. Desperate. Got it." I collapsed in the little niche barely big enough for both of us.

My fingers trembled worse than my legs. I rested my forehead against the rough stone. A mistake because that left me looking down. The pride for making it this high smeared into vivid images of landing in a bloody splat.

The demons had almost caught up. Their claws speared into the rocks. Better than steroids for helping them scuttle up stone.

New plan.

I grabbed the surrounding skulls and bones — thankfully devoid of any flesh — and chucked them down. Psyche got the idea and tossed entire skeletons. The bones bounced and shattered off rocks as well as the demons. The hellions screamed in protest, tumbling off and taking out fellow ghoulies as they fell.

I reached for more bones, but we were out of ammo. I kicked off my boots and sent them flying, took out a few more monsters. The herd thinned. But there was still a freakin' herd.

"Let's go!" I swung onto a branch and clambered higher, Psyche hot on my heels.

"What's the plan?" she asked.

"Get to the top."

"And then?"

"Devise the rest of the plan."

I used a thick root to claw my way over the final edge and onto the flat, smooth stone. Horizontal ground was vastly underrated. I helped Psyche up, then we ripped out skulls embedded in the rock and threw them with gusto over the edge.

Despite our shots nailing plenty, sending several plummeting down into oblivion, the demons seemed to multiply. Time was a luxury we didn't own.

"There's a problem," Psyche said.

"Just one?" I stood. "Awesome."

But it was a doozy.

We'd reached the peak. A large, flat plateau. A floating island of barren rock a million miles above lava-laden ground. Nowhere to run or hide. No weapons. And a gaggle of ghoulies converging on us any second.

Snap evaluation?

Psyche had the nerve to say it out loud.

"We're dead."

Chapter One Hundred Nine

"Not so fast Miss Doom and Gloom," I said. "We just climb down the other side." I scrambled to the opposite edge. More demons howled just below us. I jumped back. "Or not."

"Why would she tell us to go up? We're trapped! She's just like Aphrodite!"

"No!" At least I hoped not. "She had a reason."

To my left talons scraped. A clawed hand slapped over the edge, followed by a lipless fang-filled smile. I kicked its oval head. The creature spiraled into open air, clawing at its many friends, trying to gain purchase.

"Eros." Psyche dropped her face in her hands. "Am I never to see him again?"

"A little faith would be nice." I paced. Rubbed my temples. "I *have* gotten out of here before."

"How?"

I jabbed a thumb at the sky. "Gloria flies me out."

"And?"

"And that's it. She doesn't even do a good job. She always—Aw, *no!* No, no, no, no, *no!*"

Psyche shook my shoulders. "Always what?"

"Drops me." I peered over the edge. "From way up high. Like this kind of high." My stomach lurched. "I can't believe she's making me do this." I stomped my foot. "Bunch of leap of faith crap."

Psyche looked over the edge. "You mean…?"

"Yep."

She gulped. "Oh no, no, no."

"Scc, that's what I said."

A sea of claws curled onto the edge of the plateau. We were out of time. Surrounded. Heavy pants whispered past the jagged array of teeth and fangs. Lidless black eyes lit up at the sight of us. The ghoulies practically drooled. A few seconds more and they'd have their entire grotesque selves onto level ground. With us.

Psyche shook her head and cried, "I can't!"

"Yeah, well, neither can I."

"No!"

"Yes! If you want to see Eros again. You said love is worth any sacrifice. Here's your chance to prove it. It's do or die time. You with me?"

I held out my hand.

She blew out a breath and grabbed it in her own. "I am with you." She blinked back tears. "My friend."

Holding each other for dear life, we ran toward the edge. With a mournful wail, a demon reached for me. I leapt over his head and off the ledge, gripping Psyche hard to make sure she joined me in this insanity.

We dropped.

Seeing the shiny crimson ground far, far below, I choked on my heart, which was chugging up my throat, and realized I should've thought this through.

Maybe Gloria meant there was a non-fatal way out. Or maybe I needed to put myself in danger so that Gloria's restrictions would lift and she could fly in and save us.

Yeah. I liked that one.

I liked it a lot less as the ground kept getting closer. Psyche screamed louder. Oh, not louder. That was me finally joining in.

Wind ripped through my ears, seemed to crush all around me. My skin burned. Lungs emptied a few stories back. Couldn't reinflate. I closed my eyes at the realization that…

Gloria wasn't coming.

CHAPTER ONE HUNDRED TEN

I hit, skidding and spinning on cold, hard ground. Pain beat a steady rhythm into my bones and sung a high pitch in my jaw. Not the oh-my-God-I'm-dying kind of pain. This was the that's-gonna-bruise kind of pain.

The *alive* kind.

A whimper spurred me into action. Not much action. Just because I was alive didn't mean I didn't hurt. Badly. But I moved through it to drag my body into motion and push off the ground, noticing an immediate plus. No dead bodies.

Beside me, Psyche was slowly uncurling herself from a ball, her mouth open in shock and pain.

"Are you alright?" I said.

"No." She shuddered a breath. "But I will be."

"Good." I wobbled onto my feet. "Because we've got a problem."

"You're dressed like a man?"

I looked down. My usual sneakers and jeans get-up was back, mud and moss from the Gossamer Falls cave clinging like glue, but no human ooze or an anklet made from intestines. Yay.

"That's not our problem."

Psyche rolled to her side, arms too shaky too push herself up. "Where are your friends? Where is Eros?"

"*That's* the problem." I put hands on hips. "I have no idea where we are."

We'd landed on a gray, polished concrete floor — no wonder my body was cursing me out. White walls with big artwork that looked like it should be in a museum. A set of shiny double doors. A big rectangular table lined with leather chairs. Like some corporate boardroom. From the ceiling florescent light flickered from white to pale bluish-pink. The room was empty save one very confused me and my new immortal sidekick.

She struggled for breath. "We are alive?"

"Unless heaven upgraded its pearly gates for steel doors, yes." I yanked her up.

"Oh!" Psyche brightened. "We're in a society base. We are safe!"

Society? Surely she didn't mean *that* society.

My stomach went into a freefall. Been doing that a lot lately. At least this time my feet were firmly on the ground.

I strangled down my screech to a hiss. "Why would you say that?"

Psyche pointed above the doors and also the center of the long conference table, as well on the backs of the leather chairs. The symbol was clear on each. Four locking circles with a huge letter M in the middle.

"I should've just stayed in the Waiting World," I muttered, standing smack dab in a base or compound or whatever you want to call it, of the villainous wants-to-put-me-in-manacles Mandatum.

Above us, lights flickered red. I looked up.

Oh, no.

It wasn't fluorescent lighting.

The ceiling had a huge, gaping hole. The view through the hole wasn't of blue sky, but of red. The Waiting World sky. I was staring up the cliff face from which we'd just jumped. Much taller than I'd thought. Between the height and the fact that the Waiting World was only a few feet away, my stomach settled — or unsettled — on extra queasy.

I tore my eyes back down to the more normal, earthly room, then I tip-toed across the floor, pushed open one of the doors, and peeked out.

Empty corridor. Walls of cut stone. A few closed doors. Down the hall was a Gothic mullioned window with three thin, arched panes divided by vertical stone pillars. All was quiet. Finally, things were going my way.

Except…I did a double-take. Out the window, under the cloudy sky, I saw a city. Pretty city. Dense city. Full of old architecture city. Water. Bridges. Almost like—

I gasped. "No freaking way."

Psyche peered over my shoulder. "What?"

"Getting home is going to take a while." I slapped a hand to my face hoping it'd stop my head from spinning.

"What is that tall metal edifice?" she asked.

"The, um, Eiffel Tower." It was hard to speak with my jaw on the floor. "We're in Paris, freakin' France."

Chapter One Hundred Eleven

I slammed the door shut and paced the empty room. The frantic stride helped me forget we'd landed on another *continent*.

Don't think about that. Think about how we were going to escape a high-tech Mandatum base. Easy. Of course. A silly laugh tickled my throat. The Ishidas had private jets. I could get a croissant while I waited. If Psyche would just—

"Shut up and help me figure a way out of here!"

Hurt fluttered into her eyes.

Okay. Little harsh. But I'd somehow landed across the Atlantic in the base camp of the people trying to kill me — such is my luck — while Psyche pelted me with a gazillion questions about the "strange land" called France and I just didn't have time for a geography lesson.

"Sorry." I leaned against the wall and wrapped my hands around my head. "I'll show you a map or something, once we're home. But we are not safe. These people, the Mandatum, if they get a hold of me, I'm dead."

She laid a finger my lips, eyes wide. I strained to hear what she heard. Nothing. Other than my pounding heart.

"Wha—?"

She pointed up. Inside the gap to the Waiting World, something kept popping over the edge of the portal only to disappear a second later. Rather nerve-wracking.

Psyche squinted at the portal. "What is that?"

"Let's not stick around and find out." I backed up, wanting it all to go away. But I'd somehow opened a portal that I didn't think should be here in the first place, and I had no idea how to close it.

The doors burst open.

I jumped in front of Psyche. The guy who entered froze at the sight of us. Then he staggered a step back.

"Nossa!" he muttered, black eyes registering shock. "*Fiamma?*"

He was stocky, wore a heavy coat, his long, wavy brown hair pulled back in a ponytail. The look, the accent, reminded me of a conquistador. Definitely Spanish. Spain kind of Spanish.

"Um…" That was the beginning of my clever line to get us out of this mess. As it turned out, it was also the end of it.

So I ran. Forward. And slammed the doors in Spain's face.

Almost.

He took a hit to the temple but jammed his foot so the door wouldn't close. I strained against it. He shouldered it open with a surge of strength, which slammed me into the wall. Air hissed from my lungs, and I slid onto my butt. Spain stumbled into the room, falling onto one knee, directly beneath the freshly opened portal.

Eyes glued on me, he looked ill. Stunned. Like he was staring at a ghost.

"*Imposible*." He stood slowly, stepped toward me.

I balled my fist.

A leathery blue arm reached down from the open portal. Talons ripped into Spain's coat and yanked him up.

"No!" I launched through the air, wrapped one arm around Spain's waist, and shot my other hand up.

Energy coursed down my arm. Spiders of light burst from my fingers. The portal flashed bright. I turned my head away, felt a jolt, like I'd slammed into a buffalo, then Spain and I dropped to the floor, his body *thudding* on top of mine.

Heavy. Couldn't breathe. Couldn't get him off. Then the weight was gone. I wheezed. Someone turned me over. Pushed hair off my face.

"How did you do that?"

Psyche came into focus. Helped me sit.

I looked up at a ceiling. It was solid concrete. The portal was closed. Much better than when I blew a hole through the building and it almost collapsed on top of us. I was getting better at this. Or just plain lucky.

"How?" I rubbed my eyes with the heels of my hands. "Not sure."

Spain was on the floor, next to the open door, unconscious or—

"Is he dead?"

"No," Psyche said. "The portal closed as the creature pulled him up. He hit the ceiling hard then you both fell. He merely lacks consciousness."

Something twitched on the other side of Spain.

"Yikes!" I scuttled back.

"Fear not." Psyche walked over, picked up the severed blue arm, and brought it over so we could take a closer look.

Although why she thought I wanted a closer look was beyond me. Blood the color of ink dripped from just above the elbow.

"It was severed when the portal closed, but poses no threat now."

The skin was mottled, almost scaled.

"I think it's a ghoulie." I reached out a finger.

The clawed hand spasmed closed.

"Yaaaglg!" I squealed and nearly fell on my butt.

Psyche squealed too, but in some other language, then she chucked the arm away. I almost expected it to dig its talons into the floor and start crawling toward us, but it didn't move again.

"Keep an eye on it," I told her as I double-checked Spain's condition.

No blood, no punctures. But he would need a new coat. I turned out his pockets hoping for a weapon, a cell phone, a clue. Any freakin' thing that might help me understand this colossal catastrophe. On second thought, I didn't care about *why*, just give me a *how* to get out of it.

"The other one is coming," Psyche said.

"What other one?!"

Psyche grabbed my hand and dragged us out of the room and down the hall. Footsteps fast approached. I looked around hoping for a neon exit sign, but saw nothing. Nowhere to hide. No escape.

Except…I paused, turned, glanced back into the room.

Psyche pushed me away. "I am *not* going back to the Waiting World!"

"Psyche, we got out once, we can do it again."

"No!" She pummeled a fist against the wall. "*Nothing* they can do to us here is worse! Trust me. Do you have any idea *how long* I've been trying to get out?!"

A few millenniums, but who's counting?

"But *I* can get us out." Probably. "And Gloria will help." Probably. But admittedly, she'd been acting weird.

"No! She may help you, but I could be abandoned. Here, I have a chance. I am Mandatum. They will not harm me. And it isn't *hell*."

She had a point. Several actually. But I felt a little different about the situation. I could go on my own, but…could I open the portal? Make it up another cliff before getting eaten? Would I even land in the same place? What if I ended up in that barren flatland like the first time? Not a cliff in sight? I couldn't run forever.

I swore under my breath, tears of frustration blurring my vision.

Running footsteps. They raced closer. Then Psyche gazed over my shoulder and said, "We surrender."

I whirled. "No we don't."

A female figure loomed in cargo pants and tank top. Early twenties. Dark olive skin. Black hair in a single braid down to her hips, with two serrated knives clinking together as they dangled off the end. Sexy, deadly, and way beyond my pay grade.

Surrendering sounded really good. I raised my hands up, palms out, trying not to let them shake. Fat chance.

La Femme Nikita stared at me, her expression morphing from menacing to mortally shocked. *"Fiamma?"*

I narrowed my eyes. Why did they keep calling me flame?

"Fiamma!" the voice of some new guy echoed, bouncing off walls so I couldn't tell how close he was. Great.

Over her shoulder Nikita said, "I've got her!"

Wind gusted against my back. Nikita's eyes widened and she launched into a back hand-spring. An arrow hissed past my cheek. It caught Nikita in the head and she went down.

"No!" I ran to the girl, glaring at Artemis who held an arrow poised to shoot at me. "You didn't have to kill her!"

Nikita whimpered then stilled, but her chest rose and lowered. She was alive, just pinned down by Artemis's arrow because before it buried into the floor, the goddess had shot it through the *braid* at the base of her skull, *not* through her skull. Big plus. Nikita was simply out cold from knocking her head on the ground.

Artemis flashed a wolfish smile. "You have my stone."

"Maybe?" I squeaked. I'd thought I had Aphrodite's stone and that hadn't ended well. I dug in my bra then produced the ring Eros had given me on the beach. "This it?"

She breathed deep, eyes shining with relief. “Yes. Give it to me.” The ring started to glow. Artemis doubled over, wincing. She held out her hand. “Hurry.”

There was more shouting from several hallways. I couldn’t see them, but people — Mandatum — were coming from all directions.

“No!” Psyche grabbed my arm. “She has touched this umbra stone, so it has become the Artemis Stone, and since you wield it, you become her master. Order her to do your will.”

“Silence!” Artemis readied to shoot an arrow into Psyche.

“Stop!” I said. And funny enough, Artemis did, hands shaking as she glared at my sidekick. “Is it true? You have to do what I say?”

“It is not that simple,” Artemis looked grim. “There is danger. Power brings consequences. There is always a price.”

“*Fiamma!*” The guy’s voice was closer. Doors banged open and closed.

I held up the ring. “Get us out of here, and you can have your stone.”

Psyche made a noise of protest, but I ignored her.

Artemis’s eyes narrowed, wary. “What trick is this?”

People were shouting, coming closer. I fought the urge to run. I had nowhere to go.

“No trick,” I said, heart pounding. “I’m terrified of being controlled by these jerks, I’m not about to do that to someone else. But here’s the deal.” I put the ring on. Beams shot out. Energy surged through me. Power. It felt good.

Artemis stiffened and winced. “Your price?”

“Be nice,” I said. “You want to be left alone? Fine. Don’t kill, maim, *kidnap*, or harm anyone as an overall general rule, or I’ll go all Divinicus Nex and hunt you down.”

“As if you could,” Artemis scoffed.

“I brought down Aphrodite.” I cocked my head. “Something you failed to do for centuries.”

Her wolfish smile was back. "Indeed." She bowed her head. "You have my solemn vow."

She reached out her hand. Before I could give her the ring, Psyche stopped me with a touch on my arm.

"And you owe Aurora one favor," Psyche said. "Anytime, anywhere, and for anything she desires."

I was about to say no because all I wanted was to get out of here, but almost immediately Artemis gave Psyche a shrewd look then nodded. "Agreed." She snatched the stone from my hand, held it to her chest, and sighed.

Then she *poofed* out of sight. Gone.

Psyche turned to me. "You must bargain with a greater show of force and strength. The gods only yield high esteem to those whom extract suitable recompense for the gifts and deeds bestowed upon them."

"Wow," I said. "That sounds really fancy and all, but a lot of good it does me because she just left us here high and dry, and any second, Mandatum hunters are going to turn the corner, and we're gonna be surrounded. So, way to go girl. *Super* negotiating skills."

"*Fiamma!*" Behind me, I heard the guy race into the hallway. He was breathless.

"Tag," I whispered, "I'm it."

Chapter One Hundred Twelve

Tears brimming, gut hollowed with despair, I started to raise my hands and turn around. Running was over. For now.

Then the world blurred, swirled, and I was surrounded by a rushing torrent of brown sludge. Muddy rapids scooted me along. Light slipped in and out. I was enveloped in the murky depths of musty pond water, churning with dirt, oil, and debris. The smell was putrid, but otherwise the experience was energizing. Endorphin fueling.

Moments later I felt a jolt, and I was on my feet, steadying my balance, but feeling pumped.

I was in a clearing surrounded by forest. Damp leaves and soil smooshed beneath my feet. Mists snaked. Birds tweeted. The air smelled wet and earthy from the recent rain and snow. Pine was pungent. The waterfall thundered in the distance. No Eiffel Tower in sight. Hallelujah.

Artemis leaned against a tree, pale, breathing heavily, her breath fogging in the cold. Psyche was on her hands and knees, shaking her head and moaning.

"What's wrong?" I said.

Psyche grimaced. "Teleporting. It never gets easier. That must have been a great distance we traveled."

"That was teleporting?" I bounced on my toes. "Awesome. I feel good. Energized and…tingling. What's wrong with you guys?"

They both looked at me like I was nuts.

I wagged a finger at Artemis. "Scared me back there. Thought you reneged on our deal."

With effort, the goddess pushed herself upright and gripped my shirt, pulling our faces close. "I keep my word, but make no mistake, you should always fear me."

Still on my teleporting high—or just being stupid—I winked. "Right back at ya, toots."

Her eyes narrowed, then she let go and stepped away, her bow and arrow snapping off her arm as she shot an arrow into the forest. Shouts picked up, then a tornado of leaves blew her into smoke, and she disappeared.

"Yeah," I said. "Good talk."

Amongst a stampede of running feet, the shouts became clearer.

"That arrow almost hit me. I thought the babelicious goddess was totally Team Blake."

"Nobody's Team Blake!"

"You're just jealous because babe kissed me. Not my fault, dude. It's my animal magnitude."

"She *what!* Liar. There is no way!"

"Perhaps Aurora desired experimentation in erotic diversity. It isn't uncommon with young females."

"She's *not* experimenting."

"Maybe not with you, Fireboy."

"Okay, that's it. I am going to burn another shirt. With you in it."

"Ow! Careful, you'll start a fire!"

"Shut up! We need to find our moron."

Psyche sagged against a tree. "Do we run?"

"Nah," I smiled. "Only one of them wants to kill me."

"You're a strange girl."

"You're one to talk. Guys!"

The stampeding paused then picked up again with a chorus of "Aurora!" and "Babe!" and even, "I knew we weren't lucky enough to be rid of her."

I was offering a hand to help Psyche up when I was tackled and swung into the air. Ayden crushed me against him. I hugged him back, burying my face in his shoulder.

Thick arms lifted us both off the ground in a bone crushing hug.

"Babe, if you jump into a portal again, I'm so breaking up with you." Blake kissed the top of my head.

"Not me." Ayden muffled into my neck. "I'm coming in after you."

I smiled. Then couldn't breathe. And my shoulder hurt. And my arm. And my side. "Blake, put us down."

"Sure." Blake set us on our feet, then hooked an arm around my waist. "But chickadee stays with me."

"Relinquish her." Jayden jammed his fingers against my throat. "I need to analyze her vitals."

"I'm good." Other than I couldn't pry off Blake's arm which was digging into the cut from the arrow.

"She was in hell." Logan grabbed Blake's hand, planted a foot against the giant's thigh and heaved back. "We need to make sure she's okay."

"Nah-uh." Blake shoved Logan off. "The record shows babe's only safe in my arms."

"Don't be preposterous."

"She's plenty safe in mine," Ayden said.

"You could burn her to ashes," Tristan pointed out.

Matthias smirked, "I wouldn't complain."

"Because you'd be crying," I said. "Completely lost without me."

"Oh, please."

"*I* would be!" Blake said.

“Let her go!” Logan hopped up behind Blake and got him in a headlock.

“Has anyone ever mentioned that you bicker like old women?” Eros asked.

“Sixty-seven times,” Jayden said.

Blake finally let me go. “Dude, we don’t care what a dork in a toga thinks.”

Eros lingered at the edge of the group. He wore a long, flowing, white robe which hung off one shoulder and showed off his impressive chest and well-muscled arms. Very Greek. Very god-like.

“Aurora, I understand you’ve been through a lot. But did you see—”

“Eros?” Psyche pushed off the tree.

Eros froze, like he couldn’t believe his eyes, then his smile lit up the night. “Psyche.”

They ran to each other like lovers in a cheesy romantic chick-flick.

Until Psyche disappeared in flames.

Chapter One Hundred Thirteen

Through the wall of fire that encircled Psyche, she was unharmed, but absolutely trapped and scared. She cringed back, holding her arms across her chest. "Eros!"

Eros turned his fury on Ayden. "Hunter, I will end you."

Ayden, arms afire, walked over to stand in front of Psyche's flaming prison. "No you won't. At least not before I end her."

His eyes glowed so bright I thought fire would shoot out of them too.

His voice was low, calm. And dangerous. "You promised us information about the traitor. Tell us so we can protect my *lady love*" Ayden sneered and gave a subtle twitch. The circle of fire shrunk in around Psyche. She screamed. Eros stiffened. "Or I'll destroy yours."

Eros looked Ayden up and down. "Hunter, I gave you one pass. Now, you push too far."

"Give it your best shot," Ayden said as his arms burst into flames. "This time I won't miss."

"And this time, he's not alone," Matthias said as the rest of the boys stepped up behind him.

"Eros, tell them!" Psyche yelled. "Unless you are the unscrupulous maggot the Mandatum warned me of. On my oath, if you have become a shadow of Aphrodite and lack the honor of the man I fell in love with, I, myself, will drag you to the High Council."

"Ouch," I said. "I think the big bad godman has just been served."

Eros's eyes glittered with violence. Then his shoulders relaxed a fraction. "Of course. I will honor my word. I had planned to tell you anyway."

"I'm losing patience." Ayden cocked his head.

Psyche screamed again.

"Paris!" Eros blurted. "Aphrodite had a contact in the Paris headquarters. That is why I came through that portal. Her contact weakened security measures. Aphrodite and Vermis, parted ways shortly after I arrived."

"Vermis is the name of the traitor?" Finally, we had something concrete.

"No," Eros shook his head. "Vermis is what Aphrodite called the traitor. I do not know their true name."

"Vermis is Latin for worm," Jayden said.

"Fitting," said Ayden. "Why did they part ways?"

"After using Aurora to find the stone, Aphrodite wanted her alive to help control the army. The traitor only desires Aurora dead. When they couldn't agree, Aphrodite sent Vermis's liaison back," Eros made a face, "in pieces."

"Instead of ripping up contracts, gods rip up people," I said. "Nice."

"That is my mother." Eros shrugged. "Aurora, the traitor lost you before you moved here. Echo was sent by Vermis to backup Fiskick, mother's double-agent. Both disappeared before revealing your location. Now the traitor sends demons with trackers to hunt the Divinicus."

"Like the volcano monkey?" I said.

"Yes," Eros smiled. "The night of our first date. Also, the traitor seeks knowledge from the girl."

I frowned. "What girl?"

"Your friend Heather," Eros said.

I reeled back. "She's not my friend. Anymore. What does she have to do with this?"

"Your survival, of course." Eros's tone made it clear he was tired of dealing with idiots. He spared a worried glance at Psyche, then pressed his palms together as if praying for patience. "Orchestrated by Vermis, the attack in the alley should have killed you. The traitor desires answers as to why it did not. In regards to that night, Heather's mind is in shambles from the Hallucinator's manipulation, she has little recollection, but of all the assailants, her mind is the least damaged. She's imprisoned at Novo."

"No way," Tristan said.

"So Vermis basically kidnapped her and forced her into Novo so the gurus that help with Hallucinator damage can unravel her memories of that night?" I think I was going to be sick.

"Exactly," Eros nodded. "She is getting the best of care. Although attempts to resurrect her memories have proven unsuccessful so far, Vermis firmly believes that with the right…assistance, the answers will be found."

"She's in the same place as my dad?" Tristan said, chewing on a tassel. "Is he in danger from this worm too?"

"Absolutely not," Eros said firmly. "Vermis understands not to risk the attention harming your father would bring. Rest assured he is well cared for. Now, you can use this information to find at least a link to the traitor, if not an identity. I believe I have been of enormous help to your endeavors."

"And you swear, on your honor, that's all you know?" Ayden asked.

"I have no reason be reticent. I only agreed to help my mother find Aurora because she promised to rescue Psyche. But I knew that even if she did, we could never be truly free, so I agreed to deliver her to Artemis. My loyalty does not favor Aphrodite. If you have her, I can assist with the interrogation." His expression turned ugly. "For all the years my love suffered, I would enjoy repaying Mother."

"Yeah." I thought of Aphrodite going under in the lava pit. "Not gonna happen anytime soon. She doth been smited." Pretty sure I got the reference right.

A cruel smile rippled over Eros's lovely mouth. "A fate she has long deserved. I owe you my gratitude."

"That's true," I said. "And I'll take it in a favor. Actually, since I rescued your wife *and* got rid of your psycho mama, I'll take two favors, because according to a super good friend of mine, gods yield high esteem to those who, what was it?" I tapped my finger to my chin in a thoughtful repose. "Oh, yes, those who extract suitable recompense for services rendered. Or something like that. So I want a solemn vow that you will fulfill two favors whenever I ask. Have we got a deal? Because otherwise, Ayden just might have to…"

The fire around Psyche blazed brighter. She screamed.

Eros's cruel smile sliced my way with such fury I thought he may try to smite *me*. Then I felt the rest of the boys move in a collective group behind me, and Eros backed down.

"You have my solemn vow." He jerked his head in a stiff bow. "As promised, you may have this as well." From somewhere in the white folds of his toga, he produced a square of cloth and unfolded it. The umbra stone necklace glittered brightly within. "It was not what we sought, but I have no use for such things."

"If it doesn't open the portal, what does this one do?" I said, careful to keep it wrapped as I put it in my pocket.

Eros lifted a shoulder in an elegant gesture. "Each stone is a mystery to be unraveled. I leave it in your worthy hands." He smoothed the fabric of his Grecian getup. "Now, I would like to get my wife and be off. We have many years to make up for."

Ayden and Eros faced each other, and for several moments tension built. Then the fire dispersed and Ayden moved aside. Psyche fell into Eros's arms.

After an ardent embrace, she turned to me with a sly smile. "Well done. Or is it, way to…go girl? Your negotiating skills have improved immensely. I will make sure he keeps his pledge. And then some, because I too owe you my life."

Eros glanced from Psyche to me and back. "I do not think I approve of this alliance."

"And yet there is naught you can do to thwart it, my love." She kissed his cheek and gave me a dazzling smile. "Be well, my friend. And thank you." She gestured toward a tree. "Now, Eros, might I rest before we teleport away. I do not wish to repeat the experience too soon."

As Eros led her off, I had a sudden stab of fear. "Where's Chloe? Is she okay? Is she really Jenny's daughter?"

"Looks that way," Matthias said, and I totally saw both dimples. "Not long after you vanished he got a call from a convent in Greece. Chloe was dropped off there eight years ago. When they couldn't find her parents, they raised her."

"But where is she now?"

"Back at the convent," Ayden said with a mischievous smile. "Funny story. She went missing today. The nuns were frantic. But then she just showed up. No memory of what happened except that some wacky nun in a purple habit found her wandering in the village and led her back. Gave her a big pink feather with a phone number stamped on it. Insisted it was her dad's and the nuns needed to call him. So they did. Jenny's on his way."

"He'll have to prove he's her dad," Matthias said. "But as long as it is Chloe, they'll be fine."

"It is her." Eros stood, holding Psyche's hand while she sat against a tree. "Artemis would never slaughter an innocent."

"Just kidnap one. And kill her mother. Yeah, she's a peach." I breathed deep. "Thank you, Gloria."

"How'd you know, babe?" Blake asked.

My brow wrinkled. "Know what?"

"The weird nun who found Chloe today and gave her Jenny's number. Her name was Sister Gloria."

I pointed at Ayden, a huge grin on my face. "I told you!"

"I know," Ayden laughed. "And I told them it had to be your guardian angel."

Matthias snorted.

"What!" Eros shrilled. "Your guardian angel is Gloria?" His voice cracked on the last word. He turned paler than Logan.

Psyche patted his hand. "She was lovely."

"Lovely? She's a monster!" Eros combed his hair over and over with his fingers. "And they say the gods are bad. She is…she is…"

I bit my lip, smiling. "You know, she didn't seem too thrilled that you were doing the dress up thing."

"You *told* her!" He yanked Psyche to her feet.

"Eros, not yet, I'm still—"

He swept her into his arms. "We are leaving *now!*"

A *poof* of pink smoke later, they were gone.

As Tristan whined about the destruction of his car, we all took a breather and relaxed, feeling pretty good. Until the assassins, covered in death and looking ready for more action, walked out of the forest.

CHAPTER ONE HUNDRED FOURTEEN

The boys raised their palms in surrender. I cowered behind Ayden. So brave.

Sheriff Payne stood in the middle of the group of parents, grandparents, and uncle. "Boys—"

Blake's voice boomed across the landscape, "Jayden was in the shower with Aurora!"

Mr. Ishida gasped, "Ayden, I'm very disappointed in you."

Ayden went red. "He said *Jayden!*"

Mrs. Ishida groaned. "Jayden, we've gone over the inappropriateness. And with a *girl?*"

"I have been apprised of my error!"

"Shut it!" Matthias told the guys then turned to the Hex parents. "We know we've got some explaining to do."

"Nope." Sheriff Payne shook his head. "We spoke to Jenny, and he's assured us that it's best we don't know any more details."

"What!" My eyes bugged. "Not that I'm complaining but…why are we off the hook?"

"Plausible deniability," they all answered at once.

Sheriff Payne looked especially threatening covered in the vest, which was also covered in demon…guck. "But, gentlemen, if you ever get in over your heads again and don't invite us to the party—"

"We know," Logan said. "Grounded."

His mom rolled up on the balls of her feet and jabbed a finger at us. "*So* grounded."

"Whew," Blake wiped his brow. "I thought we were gonna get grounded now."

"Oh, you're grounded now," Uncle Reece said as the rest of the parents nodded and muttered agreement.

Logan's mom jabbed that finger again. "*So* grounded."

"But details to follow," Mr. Ishida said smoothly. "Everyone head home. Except Aurora. Better come over and clean up before *you* go home. I can repair your clothes. But that hair." He lifted his hands in a helpless gesture.

"What?" I touched my hair. Oh.

"And furthermore, young lady…" Mrs. Ishida nailed me with a piercing look and a finger pointed at my chest. I cringed, terrified a long, shiny saber was about to shoot from it and skewer my heart. "You'll be coming over more often. *And* I'm supervising your martial arts training."

"I'll take weapons," Logan's mom said.

"I wanted weapons," Uncle Reece whined.

The friendly bickering continued as the adults wandered off.

"Leave them alone." It was Tristan's grandma. "You always want to smother them."

"That's not true."

"I've missed this."

"Me too."

"Maybe we should…"

Voices faded as they melded into the forest.

"I've got a very bad feeling about this," Tristan mumbled.

"You?" I said. "Why can't I just get dance lessons?" I sighed and turned to Ayden. "What was with diving in the pool?"

Jayden folded his arms. "Yes, tell her, Ayden."

"Fine." Ayden shot his brother a tired look. "Because Jayden was trying to show off how smart he is and blabbered *incessantly* about all the mechanical crap he was reading in the Flint manuals, it stuck into my brain whether I wanted it to or not, so I knew there was a secret lever hidden in the pool that I could use to lower the net manually."

Jayden pursed his lips. "That is hardly an accurate assessment of my contribution."

"Nice move," I nodded. "And Fido?"

Ayden laughed. "No clue. She just burst out from—"

"The filtration system at the bottom of the pool," Jayden said quickly.

"Then she broke the bloody net again," Matthias grumbled. "And jumped through the portal. We thought she was with you."

"Wish she had been," I said. "Could've used her to take out the ghoulies." Tristan gave me a frightened look. "Don't ask. Anyway. We're done, right? Mission accomplished?"

"Absolutely, babe. And I dub it Operation Demons of Deathology," Blake said.

"We're not naming missions!" Matthias scowled. Then a twitch of his lips threatened to unleash a dimple. "But if we were, mate, that one's not bad."

"Agreed." Ayden slapped a smiling Blake on the shoulder. "But we still have plenty to be concerned with. There's the traitor on the loose."

"And what do we do about the treasure?" Tristan said. "And that extra umbra stone."

Jayden added, "We have the sanctuary with its endless information to sort through."

"Why can babe open a portal?"

"And suck Jenny's power," Logan said, moving slightly away from me.

Matthias narrowed me a hostile look. "And we have to figure out how to write believable Mandatum reports while covering up most of the truth in order to save our hides and protect an idiot freak like you."

"Yeah, yeah, yeah," I said. "But our team survived a Code Olympus. Took out a hoard of demons." I bowed deeply. "You're welcome."

"*Welcome?*" Matthias sputtered. "You're the reason we're in this mess! And you're not part of this team."

Shucks. Thought I could slip that one past him. "If you hadn't been jealous of Ayden and thrown me in your car, Eros would never have had to come to my rescue which started this whole fiasco."

"Don't try to pin this on me!"

"The lonely lone wolf didn't deny he loved Aurora." Blake chuckled and dodged out of the Aussie's swack.

"Ugh." Ayden walked beside me and put a hand around my waist. "Now I have to compete for your affection with both Blake *and* Matthias."

I rolled a dramatic shrug. "I tried to put him down easy, but he's so infatuated. It's embarrassing. Even with all those other girls after him."

"I can't bloody stand you!"

Blake sighed. "Me thinks he doth confess too much."

Chapter One Hundred Fifteen

It was a heck of a luau.

The Ishida's backyard, lawn rolling into beach, beach rolling into lake, looked like an island paradise.

Tiki torches, a pig roasting underground, a band, guys with ukuleles, a dance floor, bright Hawaiian shirts, grass skirts, and of course tons of colorful food. There were fire dancers — Ayden's favorites. And hula girls — Blake favorites. And everyone was barefoot, drinking through straws from hollowed out pineapples and coconuts. The Ishidas even trucked in some palm trees.

Aunt M had jetted off to an "undisclosed location" with my uncle, but the rest of the Laheys, along with all the Hex Boys' families were here enjoying Sheriff Payne's big shindig. Once the lawman had found out about the birthday party lie — I told him— he made Matthias throw it — my suggestion.

The boys were shirtless, wearing fragrant flower leis around their necks and grass skirts over their swim trunks— couldn't get better than that. Ayden's burns were healing nicely and all was right with the world. At least for the last several days since the gods had disappeared, one way or another. It was a nice break from dire and disastrous.

From the second-floor balcony outside the game room, I watched Mom and Dad on the beach attempting the limbo—yeah, don't ask.

Ayden came up the steps with fresh coconut drinks and handed me one. "Having fun?"

I took a fruity sip, staring down at the merry scene. "Yeah. Especially because it's all so…normal and non-lethal." I smirked. "Which means it won't last. Let's face it, disaster follows my every move. Like a newborn duck imprinted on a tsunami."

"That…makes no sense," he said. "But sounds like you need a hug which, being your official boyfriend, I'm contractually obligated to provide." Ayden set down both our drinks on the railing and opened his arms with a dramatic sigh. "It's a cross. I bear it."

I balked. "No hug. It will hurt the wounds *I* inflicted."

"Oh, come on. I was even going to throw in a kiss because I'm such a giver. And regardless of my idiot brother's claims which attempt to emasculate me and besmirch my long-standing and well-deserved tough-guy reputation, I am not a big baby."

Then despite my protests, which were half-hearted at best, because I'm not so stupid as to turn down a chance to snuggle into Ayden's warm and naked— okay, half-naked—body, he pulled me close. My check settled on his chest which felt solid and comforting.

And naked.

I almost giggled. Get a grip, Aurora.

"Enjoy the win." His voice wrapped around me like a soothing lullaby. "Because with the treasure plus all we've learned and will learn, I think we've finally got a leg up on the competition. Not to mention you're using your powers like a pro now."

I snorted. "Little fast and loose on the use of the word 'pro,' but I'll take it." I leaned back to look at him, and those eyes that were so easy to melt into. "I should probably get to the sanctuary for more reading."

"We'll go together." He tucked a wisp of my hair behind my ear. "After the party. Just you and me. I could bring dessert. Something chocolate. And that sparkling cider you like."

"Hmm. Very romantic. Especially if we set up next to the skeleton."

"Sure, try to kill the mood. But it won't work." In a swift move, he spun me around and dipped me low. My breath caught and I grabbed his biceps, muscles steely under my palms. His eyes glinted warm and provocative. "I'm the master of romance." He lowered his mouth toward mine.

"I love it!" Selena cried.

Ayden started to let go then caught me. I squealed.

"Just kidding," he said with a devilish grin. "Because, rest assured, now that I've got you, I'm never letting go."

My little sister flung her arms around Matthias as the two entered the game room, then she raced past us and down to the beach clutching a book and trailing remnants of colorful wrapping paper in her wake. Seeing us she sang, "Making a b-a-b-b-y-n-g," which wasn't embarrassing at all. Even when Matthias made vomiting noises.

"To be continued," Ayden dropped a light kiss on my lips, then lifted me up and led me into the game room. "Which one did you give her?" he asked Matthias.

At the sight of me, Matthias shut down the indulgent smile that always surfaced around Selena. "*Pride and Prejudice.*"

"I love that one," Blake said. "Heathcliff and Elizabeth were made for each other."

"It's *Darcy*. Or Catherine depending on—" Logan shook his head. "Never mind."

I cast a wary eye at the Aussie. "You said the guys didn't know about your…*collection.*"

Matthias tried to look serious, then laughter rumbled from his throat. His dimples even showed up.

"You should've seen your face. Thought I was breaking down." He put the back of his hand to his forehead and spoke in a silly, high-pitched voice. "No, Aurora, *please* don't tell them."

His shoulders shook. With laughter. Which, now that I think about it, was probably why they were shaking before. When I found the books. When he—holy crap, the Aussie played a joke on me.

I squinted. "It wasn't funny."

Okay, it was a little funny.

"It was priceless." Matthias wiped at his eyes and pointed a mocking finger. "Thought you were keeping some *big* secret."

Ayden threw an irritated look at the Aussie. "Did you tell her the whole story?"

Matthias tried to contain his mirth. "Hey, she invaded my house, my room, talked to my dad, and wanted to discuss romance. I had to have some fun. You can tell her."

"Oh, no," Ayden shook his head. "You're not sucking me into that again. You tell her."

"Somebody tell me!"

Matthias rolled his eyes. "Fine. My mother was a librarian. Those books were her favorites." When Ayden gestured for Matthias to continue, the Aussie gritted his teeth, then spoke with his words clipped, every syllable honed with precision. "Mum read them to Bindi, but I refused to join in. Called them stupid. After they were both…gone I read every one. Now I keep the books safe. Just in case. There. Happy?"

Not exactly. I didn't know what to say. The story was sweet yet sad and warmed my heart in some odd, convoluted sort of way.

Then my brow creased. "In case of what?"

Something rippled under the surface of the Aussie's carefully neutral expression, but he buried it too quickly for me to read. "We're done here."

"Not until you give me credit for keeping your secret. That shows that I'm a part of the team."

Matthias scowled. "It wasn't a secret."

"I didn't know that."

"Keeping secrets is dangerous," Matthias said. "The fact that you're still willing to keep them shows that you don't get it, and you're *not* part of the team." He turned on his high-horse heel and headed for the door.

I stared at his back. I hated when he was right. I squared my shoulders.

Ayden grabbed my arm. "Aurora, don't."

I blurted, "I'm the Divinicus Nex."

CHAPTER ONE HUNDRED SIXTEEN

Matthias froze. It was dead quiet.

Then it wasn't.

"No! No! No!" Matthias wailed and put his hands over his ears. He scooted around the room. The rest of the guys were in various stages of distress, moaning and groaning.

"What's wrong?" I'd been so proud of fessing up. "You said secrets were dangerous. You wanted me to be honest if I was part of the team."

"That was your implication," Jayden told Matthias.

Matthias plopped on the couch, grabbed a pillow and buried his face in it, grumbling, "Don't make it seem like she's making sense. Like she's not an idiot."

So much for my atta-boy.

Matthias jumped up and paced the room. "I *already* knew you were the Divinicus, I just didn't *know*."

"Talk about secrets," I said. "Why doesn't anyone ever say anything?"

"Because I'm *not* an idiot." Matthias ground out. "Because as long as your identity remained technically just a theory, I had plausible deniability. Until it was confirmed. Just now. By you. Which means you're an idiot. Again. Thank you. My world is back to normal." His laugh was a touch maniacal. "Did you miss the part where I live with a human lie detector? Sure, he said he wouldn't ask questions, but that's what he does. Like a vulture picking at bones." Matthias's hand made the shape of a beak and stabbed it at the air. "Pick, pick, pick."

Tristan stuck his head out of the secret room. "Hate to interrupt your meltdown, Matthias, but we've got another crisis."

Of course we did.

In the secret room we huddled around the computer Tristan and Jayden had put together from spare parts.

"It looks like Frankenstein," Blake said.

"She may not be pretty," Tristan said with pride, "but she's only connected to Aunt M's computer, which means I can access anything and stay invisible. Even if I hack into the Mandatum."

"What'd you find, mate?"

"First, Eros was right. Heather is at Novo."

At my old friend's name, my gut stung like I'd swallowed an angry swarm of bees.

I gritted my teeth against the memories of the attack, and asked, "Is she alright?" I didn't have warm fuzzy feelings toward her, but I didn't want her suffering either. My emotions were utterly flummoxed. "Should we go…help her somehow?"

"I haven't been able to access her records yet." Tristan said. "But I've got her on security footage. Seems fine as far as I can tell. I'll go visit my dad soon so we can talk to her then and find out. Second, I uncovered who signed out the tracker that was in the gorilla demon chasing Aurora. The crisis comes in how the two situations are related."

"Which is?" Ayden asked.

"The person who signed out the tracker and the person who authorized Heather's entry into Novo and is footing the bill are one and the same." Tristan tapped a key and one of the screens lit up with the image of a woman.

"Oh. No," I breathed.

Ayden put his arm around me. My knees unhinged, and I leaned against him. I felt cold. Couldn't breathe. Because I knew the woman. We all did.

Waves of long brunette hair, dark, intelligent almond-shaped eyes, voluptuous figure, and great legs.

"Madame Sophina Cacciatori." My legs officially jellified. I had to sit. "The Mandatum hunter in charge of finding *and protecting* the Divinicus Nex is actually trying to kill me?"

"It's not proof," Tristan said. "But she's stationed at the Paris headquarters where Eros said he came out of the portal because it was the location of Aphrodite's contact. Plus, Cacciatori signs out a lot for personal business, and while I haven't tracked her movements yet, here's something interesting." A document came up on another screen, and Tristan pointed to a particular line. "Check out these dates she was off the grid."

I understood immediately and went cold. "She was out on personal business during the time when I was attacked in the alley. So…Cacciatori orchestrated it? She's Vermis?"

"It's not definitive." Jayden's tone was grave. "And we would need irrefutable corroboration of the facts. However, with this particular evidence and her apparent connection to Heather and Novo, it is what the vernacular would term a 'smoking gun.'"

Tristan nodded. "I'll keep checking for more."

"If it is Cacciatori, we don't want her looking at us any closer than she already is," Matthias said. "Everyone go over your mission reports one last time so I can send them out."

Ayden put a coconut drink in my hand and kissed my cheek. "Go to the party. Have fun. I'll be there soon." Then he and the rest of the guys moved away to concentrate on paperwork.

I felt numb. Wasn't ready to join the limbo crowd, so I sank into the nearest chair. The room was quiet but for keyboards clacking and the usual bubbling of Jayden's lab concoctions. Next to me, Blake nudged my shoulder.

"Don't worry, babe, your hexy knights will always protect their queen." He placed something round on my head and went back to his paperwork.

Everything went black. I'm not talking about computer screens going black, I'm talking I went blind. I blinked repeatedly, but still couldn't see a thing.

"Guys? Matthias? Hey, Mr. Prince of Darkness, this is not funny."

No response to my underwhelming wit. I was sure my clever title for the Aussie would at least get a chuckle from Blake.

Then the room brightened and came into focus.

Just one problem. I wasn't in Kansas anymore.

Chapter One Hundred Seventeen

I stood alone in the middle of a very modern, very unfamiliar office.

Cream tiled floor, white walls, skylights through which stars glittered in the night sky. The room was in shadows, only a small desk lamp illuminated, but I could see sleek shelves lining the walls holding books and minimal knickknacks. A white leather chair. A stainless steel desk, the surface neat, files and official documents stacked and orderly. A laptop sat open, but the screen was dark. A silver-framed photograph. Tall ficus tree in a corner. The decor was simplistic, functional, yet elegant.

"Uh, guys?" I turned around.

Cue gasp of astonishment.

The office didn't have four walls. Only three and a floor-to-ceiling expanse of glass that offered a view of a four-story N.A.S.A.-like command center below, housing hundreds of diligently working folk in front of advanced technological equipment.

"What the heck did I do?"

Unfortunately, elves didn't dance in with the answer. I grabbed a stack of files.

Scratch that. My hands passed *through* the folders and the desk. Like I was a ghost. Just to make sure my mind wasn't playing tricks on me, I tried again.

Nope. The files, desk, its drawers, the chair, the lamp. Couldn't touch a thing, couldn't feel a thing. Me and Casper. Only instead of friendly, I was freaked out.

Even more so when on the desk I saw the photo of a woman and a young boy. Oh dear Lord, if I wasn't dead I was about to be. I bolted for the door. My hand passed through the handle. Super.

Just as I realized my idiocy of not running through the door, it opened. I jumped back.

The intruder did a double-take, then froze, eyes turning wild around the edges and zeroing in on me. He stayed so still I started to wonder if he was a robot with his pause-button pressed. A really handsome robot ready for the runway. Did Armani make robots for that? Or maybe I really was a ghost and he couldn't see me.

Then he breathed one word. "*Fiamma.*"

Great. Not again. So much for my Casper theory.

"Sorry. Don't know her. I'm just…me." I cleared my throat. "Some faceless minion. Dropping off files. For Miss Madame Sophina Cacciatori. Whose office this is. That we are standing in." I was as smooth as they come. The office's owner was a guess, but I'd recognized the woman in the photo. Cacciatori.

Lion's den, here I come.

Careful to keep his eyes tracking me, Armani shut the door and twisted the lock. That couldn't be good. A not so subtle look around provided no other means of escape.

His deep voice had a subtle accent. "You are even more beautiful than I recall."

"Sure." Who did he think I was? I must have some doppelganger. My eyes raked the floor, but no sign of a trap door. I even checked for a double-spiral that might offer some secret escape hatch because, well, I was desperate. And scared out of my wits.

My attention snapped back to Armani to find him standing too close, a gentle smile on his lips. I reeled back. "Whoa!"

"I did not mean to frighten you." He reached for me and his hand passed through mine.

He froze again. I did too. Mirroring the crazy just seemed like the safest course of action.

"You're not here." His voice trembled as much as the hand he hovered over my cheek.

I flinched. "I'm the ghost of Christmas future here to tell you that locking girls in offices ends badly for you. Police, manhunt, prison time." I considered throwing some karate chops to scare him off, but in my current non-solid form, didn't see much point.

"You can't be dead. I haven't saved you yet."

I'd contemplate that sound logic at a later time. Then for a split second, I wondered if I was dead. But that didn't make sense. Not that much did at the moment.

"Save me from what?"

"Artemis. She took you. But how are you here?" Confusion melted off his face, replaced by a look of cold, calculating control. "You're using Holocom."

"I'm what?"

"Something on your head?" His fingers poked through my forehead.

My hands buried in my hair, but I couldn't feel the thing Blake had put there. The round metal thing. "Oh, crap."

Holocom. It was supposed to be broken.

"No, this is good." He ran around the desk, knocking the chair to the floor in his eagerness to get to the computer. "Where were you before you were here? You are using Mandatum technology. I can trace you."

And here I was thinking my worst case scenario couldn't possibly get worse. "Neverland. Second star to the right."

His face twisted with confusion. "Tell me your true name. Your location. Anything. Please, *Fiamma*."

Why did they think they knew me? I backed away.

His mouth flattened to a grim smile as his fingers flew across the keyboard. "At least I know you are American."

Crap! "What? I bloody am not…mate."

"That could be the worst Australian accent I have ever heard."

"That's because…I'm British. Jolly good. Pip, pip! Long live the queen!"

He flicked me an amused glance and kept tapping keys. "Not British either."

"Alright, fine, I'm a lass from Ireland. Top of the morning, boyo!"

"So you are not in Australia, England or Ireland. Thank you."

"You're welcome," I grumbled, then reached for the keyboard. "Stop!"

He didn't have to worry. I couldn't get a grip if my life depended on it. Which it did.

He leaned over the desk, a lock of hair falling over his forehead. When he looked up, his hard gaze shimmered with cunning determination.

"I do not know what they have told you, who is holding you." His eyes narrowed. "Or why you wish to elude me. But you cannot. Nothing will stop me. I am the only one who can protect you. Help me find you and I will make you understand. You can trust me." His hand reached out.

I cringed and backed away.

"No!" His eyes flashed with fury as he slammed his fist on the desk, rattling the contents. "I will not let you escape!" He started to move toward me then stopped. He breathed deep and came around the desk with deliberate slowness, palm raised. "I am sorry. I should not lose control."

His eyes glazed over, his body stilled. Maybe the freezing thing was a tick of some kind. Whatever it was passed quickly.

He blinked, then spoke, his words rushed together. "They are coming for you. Please. Where are you? I need your *name!*"

I grasped at my head. If I could just rip off the stupid headgear keeping me trapped in this nightmare.

"No, don't try to— Don't go! Not yet." His hands hovered over my arms. "Give me something. Anything. I can take you away. Forever."

That's what I was afraid of.

I shook my head. "Guys, get me out of here." I didn't think the Hex Boys could hear me, but I was running out of options.

"Men are holding you captive?" His face darkened into a lethal expression. "Who are they? I can kill them. I *will* kill them all. With pleasure." His voice rumbled with a savage, steely edge. "When I find you. Soon. That I promise."

The computer beeped. He looked down. His smile turned primal. "I have you. North America. Of course. Not east coast. Or mid-west. It is—"

The world went black. Pain cracked through my skull. Someone pulled my hair.

"It's off!"

"She's out!"

"They're tracing us!"

"Terminate it!"

"We're so screwed!"

"She's such a moron!"

The secret room. The Hex Boys. No wonder I was in pain.

Chapter One Hundred Eighteen

"Babe, I'm sorry. How could I know Tristan fixed the Holocom?"

"How close did they trace us?" Ayden demanded.

"Western United States." Tristan was on the floor, screwing something onto the computer. "*Maybe* California."

Logan made a squeaking noise.

Ayden gritted his teeth. "Why didn't you shut it down sooner?"

"I couldn't. Holocom wasn't connected to M's computer yet." Tristan shifted uncomfortably. "And *I* didn't shut down the trace. Someone else did."

Into the sudden tension-filled quiet, I said, "Who?"

"I don't know. But when I tried to track them, they bounced me out of the system." Tristan gave an irritated snort. "Like I was some kindergarten hacker. I don't like this."

Jayden came from behind the bar holding a mug. "That is uniquely similar to when I attempted to track who removed my request of Aurora's DNA analysis from the Mandatum system."

Matthias looked grim. "So in both cases, it's someone with stellar hacking and high-tech surveillance skills, and Madame Cacciatori's hunter ability just happens to be electronics. She's a computer whiz. But why do this? You're sure it was her office?"

"Yes." I gripped the warm cup of orange-cinnamon tea Jayden put into my shaking hands. "She was in the picture on the desk. Younger. Shorter hair. But definitely her. Hugging a little boy. On a boat."

"Describe the guy who thought he knew you." Ayden said. "Tristan can put it through facial recognition to identify him."

I sipped the tea, hoping the sweet spice would calm my twisting guts. "Okay. Tall. I think."

"You *think?*" Matthias snapped.

"I'm trying!"

The tea spilled. Ayden placed it on a table and held my hands. "Keep going."

I nodded. Breathed. "He was tall, well-built. Broad shoulders."

"Like me, babe?"

"Not that big."

"Yeah, didn't think so. No one ever is."

Logan whacked him. "Let her focus."

"Just sayin'."

I floated my hand over my chin. "He had a scruffy shadow. Like he hadn't shaved for a couple days. Sharp jawline." I heard Tristan typing. "Hair was…medium brown, but with lighter streaks. Thick. Not short, but not too long."

Matthias grumbled, "Could you be any less specific?"

"Shut up!" I glared then pressed my fists to my temples, trying to hold his image. "He had curls at the back of his neck. Or…more wavy than curly. And his eyes were…dark? But not brown. I don't think. The room was dark so I'm not sure."

Ayden frowned. "You're sure you've never seen him before?"

"No. But…he was familiar somehow." Something nagged my brain, then I snapped my fingers. "The voice! An accent! It was subtle but…Italian. Like Madam Cacciatori, but not as heavy as hers. That helps, right?"

"Sure." Matthias was his usual supportive and enthusiastic self. "We've narrowed it down to a few million brown-haired Italian guys. Bloody brilliant."

"I think we've done better than that." Blake dropped into a wheeled office chair and nudged Tristan aside to type on the Frankenstein computer's skeletal keyboard. "Was he sexy?"

My brow creased. "What does that have to do with anything?"

Blake shot me a glance, hazel eyes piercing, lacking any form of amusement and brooking no argument. "Just answer me. Was he sexy? Deep voice?"

I blew out air. "Yes. He was handsome."

"I asked if he was sexy."

"I guess. I was a little too freaked out to worry about swooning. And, yes, the voice was deep."

"Was he a few years older than us? Maybe twenty or so?"

"I suppose."

"With an aristocratic nose?"

I blinked. "I don't even know what that means."

"Doesn't matter." With dramatic flourish, Blake's index finger slammed down on a key. "That him?"

In quick succession, the bank of oversized computer screens lining the walls lit up. Each held the image of the guy I'd seen only moments ago. He wore a tux, his hair darker than I remembered and combed to perfection, his expression serious rather than savage.

I nodded. "That's him."

Matthias stepped forward for a better look. "Blake, who is he and how did you figure that out?"

"Dude's my hero." Blake leaned back, hands laced behind his head. "Don't you guys recognize him? At the last conference in Europe, he's the instructor who kicked me out of his Seduction course."

Tristan breathed, "Oh, no."

Logan flopped in a chair, deflated. Jayden's thumbs started popping in and out of joint. Matthias muttered, "Son of a..." and turned away, both hands raking through his hair. Ayden stared at the picture, silent and utterly still but for the muscles in his jaw rippling under bloodless skin.

I turned a slow circle, my eyes scanning across each screen. "Who is he?"

Blake looked to Ayden who studied the floor for a moment, then raised glittering amber eyes to me.

"His name is Cristiano." Ayden cleared his throat. "Cristiano Cacciatori."

Goosebumps washed over me. And not the good kind. My knees threatened to buckle.

"As in Sophina Cacciatori? The Mandatum hunter in charge of tracking me down? The one we think is the traitor trying to kill me? *That* Cacciatori?"

"Yes." Ayden held my gaze. "Cristiano is her son."

Then my knees did give out. Ayden caught me and helped me into a chair. I wheezed a breath. "He said he wanted to protect me, so maybe...he's not in on it?"

"The best assassins often lure their victims with false proclamations," Jayden said.

"Of course," I nodded.

Everyone knew that.

"He called you *Fiamma*, right?" Logan pushed Blake out of the way to use the computer. "Italian for flame. Like the hunters that almost—"

"Caught me in Paris," I confirmed.

Two computer screens blinked on new images showing the Spaniard and La Femme Nikita from my encounter in Paris.

"That's them," I said. "Who—" My voice choked out. Did I really want to know?

Logan said with near reverence, "They're members of Cristiano's team."

"But his team is…" Tristan swallowed.

"Is what?" I asked.

Ayden pulled in a deep breath and released one word on a bleak sigh. "Sicarius."

Nope, didn't really want to know.

"Which is the Mandatum's elite, most ruthless assassin squad," Jayden said.

I shuddered. "Yes, Jayden, I know."

He continued, "And this specific team possesses the most lethal and prolific reputation for tracking their prey, which for some reason now includes—"

"Me! Yeah, Jayden. Got that too. But why? How do they know me?"

No one had an answer. Least of all me. I dropped my face in my hands. Ayden pulled me into his arms, trying to comfort me. But it was hard to breath with this noose tightening around my neck.

A breeze drifted in off the balcony. I smelled barbeque, heard lively music, singing, and joyful laughter. Normal and non-lethal.

Yeah, I knew it wouldn't last.

The Mandatum was on the hunt. Closing in. With their best assassin squad.

Coming for me.

ENJOY A EXCERPT FROM THE FIRST DIVINCUS NEX CHRONICLES BOOK ***DEMONS AT DEADNIGHT***

CHAPTER ONE

Someone's car was totaled and it wasn't my fault.

But who's going to believe a teenager?

"The demon did it" excuse, while more creative than "the dog ate my homework," was still as unbelievable. And much more likely to get me sent to the psych ward. So when the fang-filled flying hellion barely missed me and dropped like a wrecking ball onto the SUV, exploding shattered bits of glass and vehicle parts in my direction, I ditched the scene pronto.

And didn't look back. The savage grunts and metallic squeals provided a hefty deterrent. Like I needed more nightmare material.

I shot from the trailhead's near-empty parking lot and booked it down the road. A log-rail fence lined the thick woods, and when the demon's furious screech closed in from behind, I cut right. One hand planted on the top rail, slick from a recent rain, I swung my legs sideways, up and over. Home free.

Until my bottom foot clipped the post, and I spun as if caught in a crocodile's death roll.

Good news? The spongy forest floor cushioned my fall.

Bad news? Momentum slammed my torso into a tree trunk. Couldn't breathe.

But good news again. I'd rolled under a fat, bushy pine, which, along with the fading twilight, concealed my position. I heard the beast fly overhead in pursuit, taking out a few treetops on its way by.

Yeah, that was my plan all along. Man, I'm good. Except my body. It hurt.

My pity-party lasted until I could suck in a breath, then I pushed to my feet and headed for home. Demons salivated over remote locations like this. I needed to move.

Side aching, breath choppy, I shuffled-limped-jogged into town, made it to my neighborhood, and relaxed. Civilization. Where the demon wouldn't follow and—

Talons clicked an ominous rhythm on pavement.

Wrong had become my default choice.

I ducked behind an oak, huddling, chilled in my fear-and-sweat soaked T-shirt.

A malicious laugh churned through the air.

"Hide and seek. My favorite. How thoughtful of you to commence a game." A touch of crazy tinged the demon's smooth voice. Panic twisted my heart. "Ironic, is it not, that the great Divinicus Nex cowers in fear from that which should be her fated prey? A decidedly diametric circumstance."

What? It's irritating when the monster hunting you has a better vocabulary than your own. Maybe it could do my eulogy? This was crazy. I'd seen demons before but they were small, ignored me, or ran away. But this one? Well, it was a different breed. A psycho on steroids, and it wanted me dead.

Its chances looked good.

With my Amazonian height and auburn curls highlighted bull's-eye-red, all I was missing was an "Eat Me" sign taped to my back.

"You've got it wrong. I'm Aurora. Just some girl you don't want kicking you back to your hellhole." My plan to go on the offensive stemmed from my defense amounting to less than diddly and squat combined. Dusk began to devour precious daylight. My eyes ached from the frantic attempt to penetrate the emerging shadows. "Think of the embarrassment. The other demons will laugh and point, make fun of you behind your back. Your self-esteem will suffer and I'm late for dinner, so for both our sakes, I'll let it go. Just walk away and I won't come after you."

I hoped I sounded confident but I think my voice cracked.

Diffused light flickered to life from the surrounding houses. The ornate streetlamps lining the empty streets of the quaint mountain town buzzed to life reflecting on the shimmering fog that slithered across the ground. A sporadic drizzle hummed against the leaves on the branches above.

"I believe you suffer confusion, Nex." The volume of its voice lowered. Had it backed off, thinking I had something up my sleeve? "I harbor no trepidation but that you remain alive. And my immutable predilection is to deliver your corpse in a profusion of pieces." Then that laugh.

I couldn't comprehend much of what it said, but overall, I wasn't getting a warm and fuzzy vibe.

I fought a hysterical burst of laughter. I had nothing, nothing, but long legs and adrenaline. The spattering of drops above changed harmony. Feathering down through the branches, a grey mist swirled into a vague form my eyes strained to focus on. Mesmerized by its grotesque and lethal beauty, I almost waited a second too long. I ducked. With a menacing crunch, bark chunks splintered as the demon's claws gouged into the tree where my head had been seconds before.

I launched into a graceful ninja-like front roll, then stood my ground to face the monstrous heathen, fearless in my determination to vanquish the deadly foe.

Nah, just kidding. I bolted, discretion being the better part of not getting dead.

I'd been seeing demons for a few years now. Yeah, those nasty creatures that should be in hell but instead are wreaking havoc on earth. If they were close by, sometimes I could even locate them using this weird second-sight that I wished would go Helen Keller. It was the crappiest superpower on the planet, but I'd dealt with my unfortunate situation in a mature and responsible manner. I ignored it. And so did the demons.

Until tonight when this one changed the rules and attacked while I was on my run. I'd tripped and stumbled over a rotting log which is why the SUV had taken the death blow meant for me. Wish I could say it was a deviously clever move, but the truth is I've got grace management issues.

A guttural hiss vibrated the leaves. Ancient wings slapped the air with fury. The scary monster noises threatened to paralyze me, so I ignored them and concentrated on running. Fast. Counting houses to keep the panic at bay.

Something darted out from my left, ground level. I swerved right, nearly falling, but kept going. I glanced back. A dog, one of those tiny, foo-foo things, scampered out on stubby legs, planted its feet, and started barking skyward. The demon diverted its sights from me and swooped down on the yappy mutt.

Dogs aren't my thing.

I hate dogs.

And if this one was dumb enough to sacrifice itself for me, hallelujah. I kept running.

After I reversed course.

Stupid dog.

I dived head first and scooped up the mongrel as I slid by, feeling a rush of air from the giant beast passing overhead. A reddish sheen covered my eyes. I'd cut it so close the demon's talon sliced through my ponytail elastic and released an onslaught of thick massive curls that cascaded over my face.

On foot again, I flung back my hair and continued my retreat, the squirming dog growling protests against my chest.

"Ungrateful mutt," I growled back.

I sensed a presence looming overhead and dodged into a driveway, happy to toss the annoying pup into a garage where it tumbled under a sedan. A blow from behind lurched my body forward. I would've gone down but instead found myself airborne. And gaining altitude.

Not good, because last I checked, I couldn't fly.

ACKNOWLEDGMENTS

Thank you, favored and cherished reader, for all your gifs, images, and hilariously supportive comments. The day we uncovered you're enthusiastic and giggle-inducing remarks was the day we realized we would give you the best dang sequel you deserved, no matter how long and hard we had to work!

Thank you to all the people who patiently explained to Alyssa why social media was more efficient than showing up randomly at people's house and doing face-to-face interactions to learn the latest 411. Also for making it clear that people don't use the term 411 anymore. Duly noted, homeslice. Wait, we can't use homeslice? Since when?!

Thank you also for attempting to keep a straight-face while Alyssa mispronounced Pinterest (it's not Pie-Tourist, Pine-Trist, or any other way she slaughtered it) and learned how to use *The* Facebook, *The* Twitter and that stupid thing with the little red notification number that links to that blinky flag thing that links to something else that finally gets Alyssa to where she was trying to get to in the first place. You know who you are oh patient ones.

HUGE thanks to Mark. Best husband and dad ever who smiled and supported all our weird hours, nightmare inducing happy dances when we made a writing breakthrough, who also reminded us to eat, usually cooked the meal, and definitely baked delicious cookies when we sprinted face-first into writer's block.

Thanks to Gregory and Jake, best and oddest sons/little bros who got us weight lifting so we could Chuck Norris karate chop the writer's block. And who also executed sneak attacks when least expected upon an innocent sister to keep her on her toes for when the ninjas attack. Or the zombies. But most likely ninjas.

Thanks to The Sage, a.k.a. our editor, who moonlights as a ninja. Which is why we don't need training to defend against ninjas because The Sage would ninja-eliminate all possible ninja threats. Obviously. The Sage is all powerful and is the embodiment of patience and wisdom, and the DIVINICUS NEX CHRONICLES' awesomeness is due so much in part to him. Thank you so very, very much. And we're not just saying all that so you, The Sage, ninja-dispatch any potential ninja threats.

Thanks to our fantastic interior designer, Cheryl Perez, at You're Published, whose ninjistic skills make the inside of our book look amazing, and way more designer than the inside of our house.

And finally to our cover artist, Elena Dudina, our favorite lady from Spain, who takes our crude drawings for cover ideas and uses supernatural skills to make our fantasies come true. No, not *those* fantasies. The ones about how our covers should look. Jeez, people.

And for those who are wondering why we're so obsessed with ninjas, the answer is...we have no idea. Not that anyone is asking, because, honestly, who reads these acknowledgements anyway? Oh, wait. You do.

Wow. Thanks. You must be a ninja.

About the Authors

This mother-daughter duo were in and out of inter-dimensional paranormal prisons until they finally quit making up cover stories for secret societies and started writing novels. The Supernatural Continuum Warlords of the Supernatural Continuum Warlordian High Command had pity upon them, and instead of having them slaughtered by the slow, tortuous flesh eating underwater, earthworm squid, they transported them into a habitationally friendly dimension called OOARCHTOHUTHLAMADILFRUMP, also known as 21st Century Earth. Due to a demon infestation in their sleepy mountain California town, and a lack of sexy Hex Boys to stop them, Alyssa and Eileen were forced to relocate to Los Angeles.

The Amazon best seller, DEMONS AT DEADNIGHT, is book one in the DIVINICUS NEX CHRONICLES series, and the first of their exclusive re-creations of supernatural society secrets. You can uncover more paranormal, inter-dimensional classified information at **AEKIRK.com** and **Facebook.com/AandEKirk**. Citizens of Earth, you are welcome.

Made in the USA
Las Vegas, NV
01 October 2021